WHAT CHILD IS THIS

KURTIS ANTON

ARCHWAY
PUBLISHING

Archway Publishing books may be ordered through booksellers or by contacting:

Archway Publishing
1663 Liberty Drive
Bloomington, IN 47403
www.archwaypublishing.com
844-669-3957

Because of the dynamic nature of the Internet, any web addresses or links contained in
this book may have changed since publication and may no longer be valid. The views
expressed in this work are solely those of the author and do not necessarily reflect the
views of the publisher, and the publisher hereby disclaims any responsibility for them.

Scriptures taken from the Holy Bible, New International Version®, NIV®. Copyright
© 1973, 1978, 1984, 2011 by Biblica, Inc.™ Used by permission of Zondervan.

ISBN: 978-1-6657-2893-5 (sc)
ISBN: 978-1-6657-2891-1 (hc)
ISBN: 978-1-6657-2892-8 (e)

Library of Congress Control Number: 2022915662

Print information available on the last page.

Archway Publishing rev. date: 10/07/2022

DEDICATION

To my dearest and most beautiful wife, Holly - I love you now and forevermore. Nothing in my life would have been possible without your unconditional and abounding love!!

To my dearly beloved children, Timothy and Ambrielle. I love you two so very much and long to be a better dad. Forgive me for my past and grace me eternal binding with you.

Don't be overcome by evil, but overcome evil with good
—*Romans 12:21*

1

Late Fall 1871

The blizzard whipped up the huge, glacial-carved valley, propelled by nature's unyielding power. Blowing from the southwest in restless fury, early winter spread a blasting snowflake curtain, enveloping the surrounding trees and mountainous landscape into a white and gray, oblivious abyss. Whether it was dawn or dusk was impossible to discern in such a storm.

Suddenly a figure emerged through a thick wall of blowing snow into a treeless clearing, fully exposed to the elements. Shrouded in a thick buffalo frock, he strenuously placed one foot in front of the other, moving slowly yet with concentrated determination. A wide-brimmed hat shielded his face from the blast of incoming snow. He might have been the only human for dozens of miles—or so it seemed to him, being so alone and isolated by the snow.

The stranger worked his way across the remote Minaret Vista, high up in the Sierra Nevada Mountains, teetering on what looked to be the edge of the world. Pausing for a moment to adjust his grip on something heavy he was dragging behind him, he caught his breath while gazing out across a deep, fog-filled canyon meadow to his right

1

a thousand feet below. The gap revealed an unobstructed view of the devil-toothed mountain range, miles across on the other side of the vast, storm-filled valley.

Peering over the ledge, he tugged and pulled his cargo along the deep, crusty snow. In that instant a gust boiled up from a thousand feet below, just as a stone fell, stirring the fog into a swirling vortex while the powerful force rose and blasted ice particles, peppering his face at the same moment. Shielding his face and quickly looking upward, he observed the jagged mountain range as it quickly faded into the mist of the storm.

A dark and theatrical backdrop loomed high over the mountain saddle he was struggling upon. This bridge perched between two mountain ranges, their peaks standing firm like castle towers in the distance, funneled the wind and elements right through this lower pass where the man labored and then blasted him like there was never going to be a tomorrow.

The steep hardness of the far-off mountains made the tips look less like a range and more like the smooth sheet metal of a giant timber saw turned upside down, the vertical rock pinnacles rising thousands of feet into the sky resembling the teeth of a devil, with the devil's mouth being the bottom of the dark and foggy valley below.

The man removed his focus from the conditions and continued to trudge his way through the elements. With both arms behind him he awkwardly lugged the heavy, bulky object. Under labored breath he slowly made his way toward a mound of dirt and snow, piled up ahead of him. The air was so cold and thin that with every deep heave of breath he drew in his lungs would petrify, and a broad haze left his lips when breathing out.

The stranger released his death grip on the dark object behind him. It was so frozen that the thud echoed through the unstoppable winds. After pausing for a moment to breathe again he reached out, grasping a shovel stuck in the pile of dirt-and-snow-mixed spoils. As the stormy wind's gust drove ice particles into his cheeks yet again, he cowered for cover for a brief respite behind his arm, heavily sheathed by his buffalo frock.

Leaning onto the shovel as if it were a cane the man shifted his gaze to the object he had dragged through the snowy wilderness. Crouching down, he restrained his hat from the fierce snowstorm and then grasped the frozen object, rolled it over and revealed the body of a very dead white male.

The dead man's eyes were frozen wide open, his petrified stare fixated on the snowy sky. His face was completely frozen, with the blood once pumping through his veins having stopped in its tracks, making the face a deep purple and black. Though lifeless, his eyes still showed traces of both shock and terror. In the right temple was a deep crimson hole and dried blood, exhibiting the violence that had befallen this very unfortunate man.

Scanning the corpse before him, the stranger knelt down and began rummaging through the pockets, careful not to recast his gaze on the dead, frozen face as he continued his task. He peeled back layers of clothing—once finely woven textures that had since transformed into a stiff, cardboard-like texture—snapping a coating of ice that had taken its own shape in a frozen state of moisture and blood.

As he opened the outer garment, he peered over a second deadly wound in the chest. From a pocket of the inner garment the stranger retrieved a piece of yellow, folded parchment that appeared to have a bullet hole through the center.

Struggling against the elements and forceful gusts of the relentless wind, he rose and slowly unfolded the document, transforming the one bullet hole into four bullet holes, surrounded by dried, frozen blood and black powder. He could still make out the writing on the paper which read:

WANTED

DEAD or ALIVE

$5000 REWARD

Below the text was a face staring back at him, a sketch almost entirely obscured by the frozen blood, powder burn, and wet, falling snow. He could, however, still see the eyes. They looked as cold and endless as the winter storm that angrily swirled about him. The wind groaned yet again, ripping the paper from his hands and carrying it into the gust as if it were a snowflake.

As the stranger kept looking for more, digging deeper through the dead man's clothing, he withdrew three large brass keys on a single ring buried deep in the inner pocket of the jacket, an ineffective attempt to remain hidden from prying eyes and hungry fingers. From his crouched position on his knees the stranger raised the keys, taking a focused image in his mind as if they held some kind of potential value.

Cold as it was, he quickly pocketed the keys and unsuccessfully tried to close the dead man's frozen eyes. Then with a firm and forceful shove he rolled and pushed the corpse over into a shallow pit as it filled with blowing snow. With a muffled thud, the fully frozen body landed faceup in the bottom of the pit.

Grasping the shovel again as if it were a cane, the grave digger slowly rose to his feet in the blazing storm. He then scooped up a considerable amount of dirt and snow, heaving a pile directly into the grave upon the dead man's face and open eyes which peered up to the heavens for the very last time.

2

War was heavy in the air. Jacob tugged nervously at the new navy sailor Dixie Cup cap clenched in his hand. His grandfather Emil, a tall, still-strong, wide-shouldered yet thin man, walked a couple of steps ahead of him, ascending a steep hill toward the headstones of the Bennington National Cemetery in San Diego, California.

Rows upon rows of white crosses sat on an immaculately-trimmed lawn as if to remind Jacob that he might never come back. A small tractor pulling a draw reel mower was moving along between endless straight lines of parallel stone crosses that ran down the slope, away from him and across the rolling terrain. It seemed as though the rows of never-ending, white grave-marking crosses went on for as far as the eye could see.

Jacob had just received his new uniform two days prior, a week after that dreaded letter of his impending deployment had arrived. The conflict he was heading for changed everything he had known of peace and a very happy youth. He had set in his mind to remain strong, so as to not reveal his fear to anyone which was potentially the reason he hadn't slept the past three nights.

He questioned himself, *why did I volunteer for this? Is it because it's the manly thing to do? Is it because all my friends have done it?* The biggest question on his mind was however, why he felt so afraid. *Can I even be courageous enough?*

During the past week the young man had found himself afraid to share his true feelings with anyone. His family had grown so proud of him for leaving the comfort of home to serve his country in America's Second World War. It had only been twenty-four years since the first great war ended, and Jacob couldn't understand why the world had sought war after war after war. But he acted strong around his family, and they had no idea he thought these things. They had become proud of the strong will he grew to exhibit, that which his family knew, and in fact, that which his Grandfather Emil who walked with him now, knew. Yet Jacob found himself filled with fear as he followed his pappy up the hill.

Jacob hated cemeteries. Until then he had lived a full life. He loved life. He loved the limbs he straddled and had run his pony so fast upon since he was a child. His granddad had seen it all. *Is Grandpa proud of me? Is he afraid for me?* he wondered.

Jacob couldn't help but ponder his lost side of thoughts while he was going up that hill, yet he didn't mind the scenery at all. In fact, the sapphire-blue Pacific Ocean made for a lovely backdrop behind the national military graveyard. It was a beautiful day, and for a brief moment Jacob felt a deep stillness as he listened to the seagulls crying overhead and the waves crashing against the rocks far below them. With precision pelicans flew in a line just above the surface of the water, their wingtips inches above the cresting, curling waves.

From the top of the hill where the cemetery was located, the San Diego naval base and shipyard was visible in the southeast distance, taking shelter in a large harbor between an opposing sandy, flat peninsula, home of the naval air base and the beachy, urban suburb of Coronado. The view was amazing. A gardener raked up leaves around a grand oak tree standing sentry among the headstones, while on the other side of the cemetery a worker hand-watered the green, stone peppered landscape.

It seemed ironic that his grandfather would take him to a graveyard, particularly on a day like this. Deep inside he knew that very soon he would be surrounded by more than enough death, the kind of death that never finds refuge and peace in the mind. As Jacob's thoughts wandered, his grandfather found the grave he was looking for and stopped.

Jacob knew that his grandfather, Emil, had an unyielding story he had never heard, a section of life never spoken of. His grandfather carried a certain dedication to legacy, so Jacob trusted in the fact that Grandpa had a reason for bringing him to see his great grandfather's grave. Jacob couldn't quite tell if he appreciated his grandpappy's presence or if he just needed a moment alone. It was such a beautiful day, and he innately knew it might be the last time he saw the vast Pacific Ocean, secluded in such a peaceful stillness and glory, alongside his grandfather.

The two men stared in silence at the gravestone. It read:

COLTON JAMINSON

Son - Father - Hero

1849–1925

As Jacob looked away and stared blankly into the horizon, he felt a comforting hand greet the light padding of his uniformed shoulder. He looked up toward his grandfather, making an effort to blink away the moisture that rimmed his eyelids.

"Jacob," his grandfather said, "I hope you know why I brought you here today."

"I think so, Grandpa." Jacob just wanted to hold on to the stillness, preferring the company of life on that day in lieu of looming death.

"I wanted to give you something special." His grandfather paused shortly. "Something I cherished myself when I was headed off to war that protected me, something that reminded me of who I was and where I came from."

He reached into his left pocket, withdrawing a beautiful silver pocket watch. Jacob concluded the piece must be quite old, as it looked quite ornate and heavy, with a beautiful silver chain. Despite its seeming age the silver shone brightly, twinkling in the sun. Clearly the watch had been well-maintained. Jacob tucked his white navy sailor cap in between his arm and his side, freeing up a hand to take the watch from his grandfather's outstretched hand.

"Grandfather, I … uh … I," Jacob muttered, while sudden visions of being blown up by the Germans in the ocean started flooding his brain. In a momentary daze, he saw the pocket watch sinking down toward the deepest part of crimson waters off his landing craft, disappearing into a bloody, bottomless grave for all eternity. "Are you sure this is a good idea?"

"Let me finish, Jacob," his grandfather said in a voice lined with both kindness and firmness. "My dear grandson, this was from your great-grandmama to the man who loved her fiercely. He gave it to me when I was your age. This man I speak of is your great-grandfather, my father, Colton Jaminson." He gestured toward the gravestone.

"My father was a great and honorable man who fought many battles in the American migration West. He fought with justice and integrity. He saved lives in these battles at great risk to himself. But most of all, he held a deep love in his heart for God, this country, and your great-grandmama, Wyola Everest."

"What was she like?" Jacob asked with curiosity, wondering why her grave wasn't next to Colton's.

He pondered, *shouldn't she accompany him in death, as she seemed to have done in life?*

His grandfather continued sadly, "For her, my father fought the hardest battle of all, a battle of good and evil, of right and wrong, a battle for supreme, unadulterated justice, a battle within his own soul. That conflict, the most difficult in his life became an endeavor of impartiality over revenge, fierce and steadfast anger over compassionate and forgiving virtue, and the prospect of he himself committing murderous, rampaging revenge." Emil paused and took a deep breath.

"These emotions burned heavily within himself, tearing him from his own love of Wyola and the others who were unjustly murdered, placating reconciliation for his own life, a life ripped apart and left in tatters. Yet even in his darkest hour he found the courage to choose honor, doing what is right and continuing in the ways his father had taught him. This kind of fortitude is the reason that you and I are even standing here today."

Jacob didn't understand what kind of battle his grandfather was talking about. He turned the watch over in his right hand and was filled with a newfound appreciation for it, the gravestone, and especially the great-grandfather he had never met. He opened the watch to find a picture of his great-grandparents inside.

Colton had dark eyes and wore a stern expression on his face, yet there was a curiosity and a kindness that somehow beamed through the whites of his eyes and the softness of his brows. Next to him was Wyola, a stunningly beautiful woman with smooth skin and eyes that seemed to radiate tender-heartedness and warmth.

"Grandpa, thank you," Jacob said, feeling a certain gallantry in his voice that he didn't have before.

Far away, emitting from the distant shipyard a powerful horn sounded two long blasts, signaling it would soon be time for Jacob to join the sailors on the departing ship. As it blew with incredible volume, startled birds flew off from a nearby tree. It was then that Jacob could not hold back the tears any longer, as the knowledge that he might never return to this place and his life started seeping into his consciousness, yet again.

"There's one more thing." His grandfather reached back into his pocket, pulling out a ribbon with a medal attached.

"What's that?" Jacob asked, wishing he and his grandfather could spend the day reminiscing rather than facing a future that remained murky and uncertain.

"Take this medal. It was mine for what I did right here a long time ago. I could not have earned this medal without the grace so freely endowed to me by my father, your great-grandfather, this great man buried here before us."

"What did you do?" Jacob asked, somewhat fearfully.

"Never mind that! You just come home! I *will* tell you then. Keep that watch with you to remind you of your great-grandfather and his courage. Keep this medal with you to remember what we all endured and our walk here today. This is who you are to be. This is where you come from. This is your legacy. Today, Jacob my boy, you are officially a man. Right now we need to get you going. Let's walk and I will tell you the story of how my life started as told by this man right here, my father."

3

Late Fall 1871

"I reckon we should check this out." Bart Runion pointed to a distant mountaintop log cabin that had just revealed itself through the blizzard.

His partner, Earl Perryman, nodded his head in agreement. He was relieved at the suggestion, even just to step out of the cold momentarily. He welcomed a hut, a warming place, somewhere to get out of this freezing hell he found himself in.

It was a bitter and cold morning, high up in the Sierra Nevada Mountains as the wind whipped icy crystals into their faces and around their heads. The sun was not yet high enough in the sky to deflect the coldness that swirled around them. They made their way to the summit of Vista Grande atop their horses, huddled and bent over from the cold. A dog creeped behind following in their tracks, cowering his head with squinted eyes in an effort to protect himself from the howling wind, strolling as close to the horses as he could get without getting himself kicked.

Bart stopped his horse and took a brief moment to absorb an otherwise beautiful scene. The dog ran toward him as if to seek shelter. Bart shushed him away with a kick of snow. Although it was snowy, a small sliver of sun was beginning to help illuminate the mountains, looming in the backdrop about twenty miles away. Beneath them Bart could see the snowy tree tops of Long Valley, separating them from the mountains. The dog scurried his way to Earl's mount while growling at Bart.

They had been riding for many days without finding so much as a trace of the criminal they sought. Sure, as a bounty hunter Bart was looking forward to the reward money for finding the wanted man, but the money was more serendipity than anything else. Justice was the real goal. This formerly peaceful mining town, where the townsfolk had pooled their money together in the pursuit of truth and had hired them, had morphed into a lawless hellhole marked by the tragic and early deaths of far too many good people the year earlier. Bart wanted to do his part in bringing a final end to the tragedy. But gosh darn, it was going to be a cold and a deep snow year, judging by the harsh conditions they were already encountering in late fall, high up in the mountains.

His partner, Earl, was a former U.S. Marshal and Texas Ranger who would have never returned to the business of wrangling outlaws or being a bounty hunter, had it not been for Bart pleading for him to come. Two years earlier, Earl had retired and moved to become a deep wilderness woodsman, a Jeremiah Johnson of sorts, a real mountain man, a one-man commune who lived and hunted alone. But that didn't matter to Earl now, for this was bad. This issue of innocents having been murdered had to be cured.

Bart knew that Earl's primary motivation to ever do anything like a bond retrieval usually would be for reward money. This time, however, it was different. This was a hunt for evildoers, something way bigger than money and something of great value for Earl to fight in his mountains for. Bart appreciated and trusted this rare type of partner implicitly.

As they were getting closer to the cabin in their careful approach, Bart noticed a small stream of smoke rising from the chimney. The cabin itself was small, with two windows, one on the east wall facing them and another window on the opposite side of the cabin. There was one door facing south and the Sierras. It didn't look like it could comfortably fit more than a few people at once.

Bart whispered as he calmed his horse. "That there be smoke."

Earl nodded in concurrence.

"Woah ... horses," Bart whispered, as he motioned to the door side of the cabin where two horses were tied up to a hitching post.

He thought, *have we just stumbled upon something of nothing, possibly another person who can point us in the right direction? Or could this be just the gent we've been looking for?*

Bart and Earl looked at each other, nodding in unison without saying another word. The two men slowly and cautiously dismounted their horses while scoping out the scene unfolding before them. They were taking great care to make as little noise as possible and to keep the horses calm, all the while positioning their ponies between themselves and the structure.

The men crept in silent retreat toward some trees, down a small hill about thirty yards to the northwest of the hut. They carefully made sure to remain out of sight of the cabin as they were on their way, maintaining as low a profile as possible. They tied their horses to some pine branches, and Earl nodded to his dog, commanding the hound to stay with the horses.

Turning to head back up and toward the dwelling, Bart whispered to Earl, "Keep down!"

The two men continued toward a berm near their hidden retreat, remaining about twenty yards away from the small log cabin. They took cover behind a fallen tree covered in snow, creating a blind for them to hide behind.

"What do you think we've got here, Bart? Who's in there?" Earl wondered, through a whisper.

"It could be anyone. But there shouldn't be anyone up here this time of year," Bart responded softly, as if not to speak at all.

He found himself preparing for the worst. He had seen a lot in his day. He saw what gold, or the lack of it, could do to a man, ripping out his soul with false promises. He saw the extremes man would go through in the name of self-preservation. Bart had seen it all in his career as a war veteran and gunman. The human condition in all of its ugliness he had witnessed up close and personally. And yes, that same human condition was responsible for Bart amassing a small fortune as a highly sought-after U.S. bounty hunter. However something about this situation, intuitively, felt different.

"Should I go on up, maybe give it a look? Sorta check things out? Closer maybe? What do ya think?" Earl asked.

Regardless of his hesitation under the circumstances, his Texas Ranger past background and training had taught him to zero in on the source of the danger suddenly, quickly, and quietly.

"Hold on up here for a short spell. Let's just sit tight. See what we might find. Whoever is here may be about wandering around," Bart replied, much preferring stealth and reconnaissance to immediate action.

The two men quickly scanned their surroundings. Everything seemed very quiet to Bart. After a few moments of stillness he started shivering. "It's mighty cold," he said quietly, huddled behind the berm while scoping out the cabin.

"Ok, let's meander on up around to the left. You head out first. I'll cover ya."

Bart pulled out his 1865 Spencer carbine, gripping it tightly. "Just head on over to the left of the hut." He pointed ahead of them, directing, "There. To the right of the snowbank. Actually, over there." Bart redirected his plan and his weapon. "In the heat-well, the wind scour formed around that side of the cabin."

Earl raised an eyebrow and frowned slightly, acknowledging, "Don't look like no one's here, outside I mean. Anyone here is inside. No tracks. Just sayin'. Looks like the snow done covered any up."

"Let's get down in that gap between the building and the snow," Bart replied. "Keep keen eyes, Earl. Whoever is here, it seems they are right inside. Now let's git goin'!" Bart was eager, knowing his reward, justice, or at least a clue could be on the other side.

Earl silently worked his way up to the rear of the cabin from their position, crouching below the window frame. Bart inched slowly behind about five yards while keeping his rifle low and ready, providing cover for Earl.

Then it was showtime. They nodded to one another to move toward the cabin. Earl was right. Whoever was here had not been outside since the new snow began or was still outside for an extended period of time, allowing the snow to cover any signs of recent movement.

Earl opened his frock coat, revealing two 1851 Colt Navy revolvers with brown wooden grips over his sheepskin chaps. A long bayonet, contained by its sheath, caught a ray of sunlight and glinted by his side.

As they neared the cabin, Earl retrieved one of his revolvers and then jumped down the snowbank at the rear of the structure, calmly sliding into the wind scour gap between the building and the snow as Bart had directed. He immediately snapped upright, gluing himself to the exterior wall of the small log structure, low and tight, slowly and with caution cocking his firearm amidst the motion of his movements.

Bart slid down just behind him. The two men took one last look from where they came. The dog, barely visible over the berm about thirty yards away, was watching them with his ears up as if standing guard of the horses. Thinking they should move fast now that they were at the cabin, Bart signaled for Earl to cover him and then moved quickly around to the front of the hut. Both men made sure they were not visible from the frosted east window, as they crawled under it, to make their way along the wall toward the front door.

When he reached the front side of the cabin, Bart spotted a patch of dark-crimson snow tight up against the front door. His experienced eyes knew immediately that it was blood. The snow had begun to fall with more ferocity, continuing to hide details of the horror that might have occurred at the remote hut. As he looked closer he could make out what looked like blood in the hoof marks the horses were pressing into the snow as they shuffled and kicked about, exposing it.

Bart moved up to and proceeded to calm the horses tied up next to the front door, wedging himself between them. They barely moved in the frigid cold. Earl walked up to the door until he was just inches away, motioning for Bart to keep cover. Holstering his weapon, Earl placed both hands on the door's old, wooden handle. Bart signaled: three, two, one. And *crunch-woosh*! Earl pulled the heavy door handle through the snow with full-body force as Bart lunged in across the threshold, rifle at the ready.

Bart quickly scanned the room for a sign of movement or weapons, peering down his gun sight. *Nothing*, he told himself. His weapon still poised, he noticed a small cast-iron stove. The stove was still hot. Aware of Earl backing into the room quickly from behind him, Bart observed two saddles set neatly on the floor. A rifle in a scabbard was attached to one of the saddles. He also noticed an empty gun scabbard on the other saddle, indicating that one gun was possibly missing, potentially outside with someone who could be roaming around.

With no one being in the room he understood there was no immediate threat. Lowering his weapon, he took inventory of the finer details. An old shirt served as a makeshift curtain to cover up the west-facing window. Although it was shuttered the glass was broken, and the wind and blowing snow were leaking through.

Bart moved toward it and slowly drew back the shirt to peer outside to the west through the cracks of the shutter. There he could see the saw-toothed minarets of the mountain range. Turning around he saw freshly chopped wood laid by the stove, with splinters strewn about, and a seat made of a stump, set as a stool, obvious for chopping wood upon as well.

The aroma of coffee permeated the air with a pot having been recently percolated on the woodburning stove. In the center of the room he noticed a small ax and a bowie knife, stuck upright into the round telegraph wire cable spool that was being used as a table, a sign of the recent installation of the telegraph throughout the region. Above that was some fresh deer meat, hanging by a crude wire from the ceiling with a small pool of deer blood underneath, alongside a gun coiled in a gun belt. A rat scurried off the table, jumping to the floor away from Bart and toward the corner of the room where a saddlebag was hanging from the wall.

Who has been here? Bart asked himself. *Obviously, they are still nearby.*

Suddenly Bart noticed another crimson puddle, just feet away from his right boot. He silently motioned his rifle as if directing Earl. Earl's eyes moved to the rear of the cabin toward a cot in the back corner of the hut. Buffalo skin was bundled at the foot of the bed, and beside the cot stood a single boot, fit for a very large man.

"What's this?" Earl asked, noticing the boot, while he was moving in for a closer look. With his back turned toward Bart, he peered down into the boot before grunting inquisitively. He motioned for Bart to take a look inside.

"Looks like snakeskin. Pull it outta there," Bart said.

"A what?" Earl asked.

"Just pull the damn thing outta there, Earl!"

Bart, still positioned at the west window, drew the shirt curtain back again and took a second peek outside through the cracks of the shutter. Earl holstered his Colt and reached down for the boot. He pulled the snakeskin out with two gloved fingers, clearly intent on touching as little of the boot or its contents as possible. The long, skinny sac opened and a white, liquid substance leaked onto the floor. Bart turned his attention back to the room.

Earl scrunched his nose in disgust and crouched down. He took a hearty sniff of the spilled liquid and dipping an exposed finger into it, took a quick taste.

"What the … sour milk?" Earl exclaimed to himself.

"I knew it," Bart said. "That boy can't be too far off now!"

"You knew what?" Earl mumbled under his breath.

"A Paiute showed me once!" Bart was excited. They were finally getting somewhere.

"Showed you?" Earl asked. A look of disgust and confusion painted his face.

"How to make a liquid vessel," Bart said. "A canteen of sorts, when you ain't got one! That there is rattlesnake skin. Not from around these parts. Lower elevation. And these ain't no Indians been in here."

Bart stopped talking suddenly and took another more hurried look around the interior of the cabin. Doing a 270-degree turn with his weapon as if to be confused just for a moment, Bart had a feeling there was something else to find in the cabin, he could feel it. There were two horses tied up outside, two saddles and dressage inside, so he knew there had to be other clues which would tell them where the occupants had gone.

He questioned himself, *why is there so much blood everywhere? These had to be the men the general was looking for. Where are they now if not in here?* It was unbearable outside. *Why would they be out there? Are they dead somewhere out there? Can this be the man we are specifically looking for? Did he have someone join him along the way? Where are they now, doubling down? Why is the armory left inside on the table for anyone to find? What is the blood we saw leading away from the door?*

Looking back and forth between the rest of the cabin and the door, Bart redirected his weapon and pointed toward the door. He reached out a hand to grab a buffalo skin bunched up at the foot of the bed and lifted it, tossing it aside. What he saw made his stomach lurch.

"Weez in hell!" Bart yelled, nearly jumping back. "Something's not right!"

Bart and Earl looked in shock at a small, white baby boy lying on the cot who had evidently been startled by the two men. His face filled with pink, and he screamed at the top of his lungs. The befuddled men exchanged surprised looks at each other and Bart leaned back down, situating the buffalo skin gingerly to re-cover the child.

Unsure if he heard movement or was still spooked Bart snapped upright, dazed and confused, staring at the child while steadying his gun toward the door. Quickly recovering from the distraction by his training he made his way back to the west window, while Earl moved toward the child with his back to the front door. The infant was screaming to high heaven!

Some time had passed as Earl and Bart turned at the same moment to stare at each other as if to question what to do. In an instant, the door screeched open with the rushed swing of power, revealing a wind-driven field of blowing snow and the silhouette of a man casting a shadow into the cabin space.

Bart, just as he was distracted by the instant while in a slow-motion turn from the window, heard Earl's gunfire and a bullet impact into the front wall of the cabin, missing the man. The man fired back at Earl with a pistol in his right hand while maintaining sight with a rifle in his left trained straight on Bart's face. In that split-second of realization of what just happened, Bart heard a loud thud as Earl's weapon fell to the ground.

"My hand!" Earl groaned. He had clearly been hit.

There was a brief pause as Bart looked toward Earl. He felt the situation was quickly turning out of their favor, and he glanced back at the stranger who remained in the doorway with a Henry lever action trained to his face, but Bart couldn't make that out. He couldn't make out this man's face either due to the immense amount of light reflecting off the dusty, blowing snow.

It was like a ray of blue and white light burst into the cabin's darkness, the sunrays creating beaming shadows and casting silhouettes of the man in the doorway. Bart was in such a bad perspective to see anything. He could, however, make out the shape of not one, but two weapons pointed directly toward himself and Earl, one in each hand of the stranger.

He heard Earl grunting, attempting to reach for his other pistol with just one hand, and it wasn't his shooting hand. The stranger cocked his pistol, and Earl stopped suddenly. For a moment there was complete silence. The baby continued wailing in the background.

4

A Year Earlier, Fall 1870

Ardie Perseval had been riding for almost two weeks to cover the nearly three-hundred-mile difference between the eastern central Sierras and the city of Los Angeles. It was his first official assignment as a newly appointed mail courier rider for the federal government, and he wanted to make a good impression on his boss to prove he would be one of their most reliable and quickest delivery riders. He had been doing the route before, helping out Stan Walter, but Stan had recently gotten sick to the point where he had to give up his route, following two years of developing the team.

Ardie was proud of his new position. He liked the freedom and the variety of traveling through constantly changing scenery, with the wind blowing in his face. To Ardie, it was he alone and the elements, he and his horse. And most of all he wanted his wife, Rachel, to be proud of him. They had only been married for six months. She was pregnant with a child. He wanted a son. They didn't like the fact they'd be separated for weeks on end each time he was on assignment, but they both recognized the source of income couldn't be changed. In his thoughts, it would make his homecoming only sweeter.

It was early in the morning at Vasquez Rocks near the Agua Dulce outpost, where he had set up camp for the night. The sun was just rising in the cloudless sky, and the morning was crisp and clear. The night had been quite cold, and there remained a lingering chill as he warmed his hands at the fire. He poured himself one last cup of coffee, took a sip and set it on a rock as he started to break camp and gather all his things to stow them in his saddlebag and onto a horse. Two wranglers approached him with an unsaddled horse in tow as Ardie turned to greet them. This would be the last pony exchange of the trip, with a two-day ride left ahead of him.

"Good morning, Ardie," one of the wranglers said, tipping his hat.

"Good mornin', guys." Ardie nodded and greeted the two men while cinching the strap of his saddlebag. "Think I've been makin' good time so far. Ten days I made it to here, I did, all the way from Benton. I should be in Los Angeles sooner than I thought I would be, the day after tomorrow. Midday, I reckon!"

"Here is your new horse," the older-looking man said, as the other wrangler dismounted his horse and untied the fresh mare. "All fed, watered, and rested."

Ardie lifted up his mail saddle and hoisted it onto the new pony. "Thanks much, guys. I'll see you on my way back. Gotta get going' now." Ardie mounted the new horse while a wrangler grabbed the reins of his old horse.

"See ya! Be safe!" the two wranglers voiced as they trotted away with Ardie's tired horse in tow.

Two days later Ardie reached the furthest outskirts of the hustle and bustle of a great growing city below. From the hill he was riding over he could see tall brick buildings lining the sides of the road in the central district in the distance. The "Bay of Smokes," as it was known at the time, was about ten miles off in the distance. Smog and commerce of ships and wagons were stirring a cloud of brown, smoldering plume up and into the air, making obvious how the

Portuguese explorer Cabrillo had named the great bay in 1542. Near the sea a long and smoky train was approaching the central hub of commerce from the east.

Ardie gave his pony a break and then slowly galloped down toward the heart of the metropolis it had grown to become. Known as the City of Angels, three hundred miles and twelve days later, whew, he was there! The hustle, the bustle, the smoke of life! It was the symbol of a new industrial age, and it excited him.

But it was also midmorning, the rush time of the day, and Ardie had to scramble his way among carriages, wagons, and people, moving livestock across the wide valley, with hundreds of crisscrossing streets becoming visible the closer he got to his destination. It was like nothing he even ever imagined, how much it had changed since his last time in the city, when he first took the ride from Benton to Los Angeles, on a trial run for the job a while earlier. That time he had also done the ride in twelve days, unloaded. No one had themselves done that as a single, continuous ride, and Ardie was the first to do it and very proud of that accomplishment. Mail and goods over the past five decades had been transported by mule freighter, a trip that took nearly two months. Now was the time for a new generation of young pony riders, who were excellent horsemen and survivalists, who could cut that time in half or more, at one tenth of the cost.

There were people everywhere, and Ardie couldn't help but feel a lot smaller than he felt in the less traveled lands he came from, the Owens Valley. Here, he seemed so insignificant while in the wilderness he was, in the least, noticeable. He certainly could not picture himself and Rachel living here, although he knew it's what she wanted. In his opinion, Benton was so much nicer than this city, a place where one could breathe and raise their children. Rachel, on the other hand, loved the prospect and opportunity of the big city. Ardie's thoughts quickly shifted as he reached the Farmers and Merchants Bank office, which was the tallest building down the boulevard he rode, at the corner of the street.

Ardie dismounted his horse, just as a freighter wagon with eight horses quickly galloped by him. Following a pause of caution, he led his pony toward a watering trough. He stood in wonder as he observed the area, the hundreds of people, while watering his horse. That five minutes was something. Ardie tugged his pony toward the front rail of the bank and tied it up to the hitching post by the main entrance.

He quickly dusted himself off and unharnessed the U.S. Mail saddle from his pony. He hoisted the heavy load as he stepped away, backward from his horse. A small child ran by, crossing in front of him and the horse, causing him to stagger a bit. The child's mother voiced an apology, and Ardie nodded back and then turned around, carrying his saddle quickly up onto the boardwalk and toward making an entry into the bank.

The two men at the door reached out and opened the double door for Ardie, greeting him as he made his way inside. It took him a split second to get used to the diffused, dusty light gleaming through the windows, in order to refocus on the numerous activities happening inside the building. One thing was for sure, it was dirty and dusty in the city. There was dust in the air everywhere you looked, it was impossible to get a breath of air without it, and it was certainly all over everything. Ardie pondered how the dust probably collected faster on the counter surfaces than the lady he observed wiping them could keep it off.

The bank's interior was bustling with energy and commerce that morning. Tellers were working behind counters with iron bars at one side of the big room, and loan officers, sitting at desks, were discussing business matters with patrons. Ardie made his way to the rear of the bank's interior, to a separate barred area that was guarded by several security guards, with rifles and sidearms at the ready. They greeted Ardie, as he passed them, while opening the iron bar gate for him to enter.

"Ardie!" one of the security guards said. "Why, it's been some time! How's life treating you, my friend?"

Ardie nodded. "Good, good. How's it going', guys?"

The bank manager, Tom Lundsford, a tall and impressive man, was sitting at a large desk and quickly finished scribbling a note when he noticed Ardie approaching him. He placed his quill into the holder and quickly rose from his seat, straightening his jacket.

"Ardie, come on in. So good to see ya." He walked around his desk as Ardie put down the saddle in front of him. "You have some mail documents and papers from Morgan ready for processing for me? I received a wire from Morgan two days ago."

"Not quite sure." Ardie opened the mailbag and handed Tom a folder containing a stack of documents, which he quickly scanned, moving his eyes back and forth, and set down on his desk.

"Have a seat." Tom gestured to a chair in front of his desk.

As both men sat down, Tom grabbed some documents from the opposite side of his desk and slid them across the desktop toward Ardie. Then Tom extracted a key from his vest pocket to open a drawer. He reached inside and pulled out a bag.

"Here, Ardie. You get this bag back to Morgan along with the certification of purity right here and these other mining certificates. I know he has been waiting for these for some time."

"Will do." Ardie nodded and took hold of the items. He leaned over and proceeded to place them securely into the mail saddle.

"Morgan's gonna be pleased with our determination of equity he now holds in the mines up there," Tom continued, "Especially that new north vein."

Both men stood up, and after bidding each other farewell, Tom resumed his work as Ardie exited the bank to start his journey back to the Sierras and home to his beautiful Rachel.

5

Colton Jaminson didn't mind his job, working at the Morgan mine. For one thing, it was a job that paid real money. For another, the gold mine was one of the largest revenue generating businesses in Benton and the surrounding areas. While the work was hard, his position was well respected among the other members of the town. But most of all, Colton liked his job because of his freedom. It was still *his* job. And he could walk away any time, not that he'd ever wanted to. The pay was fair, Randall Morgan was an honorable man, and even the more laborious work was offset by the presence of his cousin and friend, Cyrus. They were both freed slaves, who had come together from Georgia after the Civil War had ended five years earlier. They loved the Sierra Nevada Mountains in California, especially since the climate provided for seasonal opportunities a lot better than back in Georgia, where it was always humid and uncomfortable in the summer months, yet still freezing in the winter.

Cyrus was generally lazy but an endearing man, who didn't take life too seriously. Considering everything they had been through, Colton loved being around Cyrus's personality. The two frequently complained, jokingly, about their job, knowing full well that they would never trade it for the alternative of being back in Georgia, picking cotton. Their hands were marred with the scars of picking the white fluff from thorny bushes. Too many of the dark memories of the years they spent there hindered their souls. Regardless of this, Cyrus and Colton both still complained once they moved out West, especially how often and how little they ate.

"Wish we had some real food," Colton said.

It was Friday, and he was tired after a long workweek. It was the end of the season for mining, and they had just endured seven months of the roughest of it, busting down a new north vein. He had been in the middle of going through some boxes, searching for blasting caps, near the mine's stock house as an enticing aroma pierced the stiff mountain air.

"I dunno about you," he grunted toward Cyrus. "But I am more than ready to head home."

"Ya, I am hearing you," Cyrus said, letting out a big yawn and pausing for a stretch.

Cyrus was a stocky man with caramel-colored skin. Though he was shorter in stature, his broad shoulders were considerably large from all the years of hard labor. He was always joking around, and a mischievous sparkle usually glinted from the whites of his eyes.

"We ought to be heading into town any day now, wouldn't you think?"

They had been working deep in the mines for several weeks, survived an accident where a young immigrant died, and were due to be given leave to return to Benton in the coming days.

"I surely do," Colton replied. "Boy, am I ready to see my girl. I can't remember the last time I spoke to Wyola. I can't even remember the last time I saw a pretty face. You're not that pretty, Cyrus."

Wyola was a gorgeous woman of mixed African American and Cherokee Native American blood. She and her sister Lola worked on the other side of Long Valley, down the grade into the northern end of the Owens Valley, near a place called Chalfant, on the property of Judge Kensington, a wealthy landowner with plenty of influence over Benton. Colton had taken a liking to her from the moment he laid eyes on her striking beauty. She was kind with a strong attitude and a commanding presence. The boys went into town every so often, to stock up on supplies and mail, and Colton always made a point to head to Chalfant to visit Wyola.

"Well, all I can say is that at least we are free now, Colton," Cyrus said, distracted by the delicious smell of food that once again wafted through the air.

"Depending on what freedom sings, that's for sure." Colton laughed.

"What I want to know," Cyrus said, as he carefully began stacking the boxes of dynamite and detonating fuses, "Is that girl of yours gonna set me right, by setting me up formally for dinner with her sister Lola?"

"Hmm." Colton smiled to himself.

"I do love her. That is the truth," Cyrus said. "But Lola is not aware of me. Just not payin' attention at all. I would like the enlistment of Wyola's help on this now, Colton."

"Well," Colton responded. "Since you be feelin' so free about yourself, so distracted in love 'n all, why don't you carry my stones for the day?"

Cyrus frowned, evidently shaken out of his fantasy. "There's gotta be a better way than this, Colton. Whatcha think? Can you get her to do that for me, Colton?"

He often spoke about a *better way*. While Colton liked to daydream about a better situation, about owning his own property, starting a family and raising a son of his own, he knew that this kind of talk could get dangerous. He'd seen men so focused on the better way, that they'd forgotten about the blessings of the current way. He'd seen men so focused, that they made big mistakes.

"Oh, there is a better way! Patience, cousin. Now get back to work," Colton heaved.

"Ain't that for sure," Cyrus responded.

Colton and Cyrus exchanged sighs. Colton knew deep down that they wouldn't have to lug heavy stones around the mine forever. *Patience*, he told himself. *Patience*. One day, he dreamed of having a property of his own, with Wyola and Cyrus, along with some horses, and maybe a dog too. He would get there, he knew it. Maybe, after a couple of seasons in the mine, he could find a piece of land, buy it, and build a home and life for him and Wyola. The mine was doing well after all. Colton often daydreamed of this prospect, while distracting himself with the thoughts he had, as he was working himself into the ground.

"What are you two niggas up to now?" an all-too-familiar loud and deep voice called out. "Are you gonna keep spitting your tongues or getting back to work?"

The harsh voice cut across the cold air, startling Colton out of his reverie. He quickly bent down over the boxes, putting his hands around a heavy one, marked: "Peligroso—Danger—Explosives—Dynamite."

"We were just about to be getting something to eat, boss man," Cyrus quickly responded.

Reese Clybourne strode up toward the men. At six foot and six inches, he towered over Colton, Cyrus, and pretty much everybody else in the whole region. Colton thought Reese had something major to prove around the mine. Or he still hadn't let go of the war and had something against black folks being on equal terms with their rights. As right-hand man to Randall Morgan, Reese followed his boss around like a puppy. Yet, whenever Randall wasn't around, Reese acted like he ran the whole mine.

Reese clapped his two giant hands together, as if in a hurried reprimand, sarcastically commenting, "I ain't heard no chow bell! You, Colton?"

"Nothin' yet, sir, but we smell—" Colton said defensively.

"Never be mindin' what you be smellin'! Get yer dumb black asses back on up to the mine. I ain't called no break! Certainly, ain't heard no bell. Watch yourselves with that dynamite now, dummy, at least when me or anyone else is standing round. Just what we need, another accident around here!"

Colton saw flecks of anger peppering Cyrus's otherwise bright and mischievous eyes. He noticed Cyrus paused slightly before speaking. Colton found himself pausing quite often around Reese. He had to conscientiously hold himself back and think before he spoke. That was how people survived up here.

"Well, boss," Cyrus said, his voice sounding carefully measured, "We haven't eaten anything all day. We were smellin' the grub while up here, collecting blasting caps and cords, to do just what you're asking. We were just hopin' to be doin' it after the evening break, boss man! You just now come up on us. We'ze be working hard all day, Reese. Dinner gonna be—"

"Never mind dinner!" Reese cut off Cyrus, his taunting tone turning to anger. "You ain't done gettin' stones. I need two more carts of ore for today. Now get on up there, before I gotta beat them carts outta you! I'll have Jordon bring blastin' caps. Uh, no I won't! You go and pick-ax all them ore pieces outta there the rest of today, one at a time," Reese finished with a split-face grin.

Cyrus looked as if he was going to burst. His caramel skin turned dark and hot, despite the cold that nipped the thin mountain air. Just as he was about to respond, a voice in the distance interrupted them.

"Reese! You will be sure to check the locks after dinner. When the pack gets in about an hour, best be done! No more strays wandering around in the morning wastin' time rounding them back up!" It was the firm, but welcoming voice of Randall Morgan, the owner of the mine.

Reese jerked his head toward the distant voice and, in an obedient tone, answered, "Yes, sir! Got it, sir!"

Like the quick switch of a train track, Reese turned on Colton once more. "Now git on up. Plenty of daylight left! Besides, in there, certainly don't matter what time it is now, does it, nigga' boys, as long as it's done and no assistance there from the explosives?"

"Two more carts at this late hour?" Cyrus cut in, his voice as cold as the low clouds hanging in the sky.

"You want me to beat them outta ya, boy?" Reese taunted.

"Ya, we got it, Reese," Colton interjected. "We goin' now. Cryus, let's go!"

Reese turned and marched toward the mine without another word.

"Let's get along now, Cyrus!" Colton whispered. "Gather your things up. We certainly don't need any more trouble cuzza your mouth."

The pair slowly made their way toward the mine entrance, stopping briefly at the separator trough. Colton dipped his hat in the ice-cold water and felt his hands crack in the cold, dry air. He splashed some water on his face, which was covered in dirt and dust.

"Listen," Colton said in between winces, "I can't keep saving your ass, Cyrus. No more. Now let's do what he asks. The last time was the last time! I need to be leavin' in the morning." He thought of Wyola. He thought of her hazel eyes and the way her warm skin would feel against him, in this autumn chill. He wouldn't let Cyrus's stupid mouth get in the way of his visit with Wyola.

"Doesn't he know the war is over? For five years now!? We are free, Colton," Cyrus argued, throwing his hat into the water with a frustrated move.

"Never mind that now. Let's go and get finished, so we can eat!" Colton picked up the hat and handed it back to Cyrus.

"You know he lost his family a couple years back in the great quake down in Independence, Cyrus. He's alone now and a lot angrier because of it. It's how he came to work here, don't you remember? We shouldn't be judgin' the likes of men. Remember, what we will be learning on Sundays now, Cyrus!" Colton stated in a manner of human doubt himself.

They finished washing and walked toward the mine shaft as the sun dropped beyond the mountains. Cyrus said nothing. Colton figured, Cyrus must be in deep thought, as a look of furrowed concentration painted Cyrus' face. War or no war, freedom or not, Reese's loss and anger, nothing mattered to Cyrus at this point. Cyrus himself pondered, how Colton would be seeing Wyola the next day, how Colton had something to live for, and how unfair life had been to him by comparison. Cyrus could get trapped in his own consuming and bitter thoughts.

The two trudged forward in continued silence as they entered the mine shaft, a dark cave about ten feet high. With a great heave, Colton and Cyrus began pushing a steel ore cart, on its tracks leading into the mine. They passed Sun Xing, a stern Chinese immigrant, who never smiled, as he led a group of workers out of the mine.

Colton suddenly remembered that he had something to say to him. "Sun Xing, Randall is requestin' the mail from the workers, the mail ya want to be sent to your families. So sorry about your friend dying!"

Sun Xing had lost a miner the week before due to the tragic accident in the new north vein. "Yes," he responded humbly. "Let's go, people." He went on ignoring the acknowledgment of loss Colton stated, yet still bowed courteously to him as he left.

Colton and Cyrus gathered a couple of oil wick cap lamps near the mine's entrance, along with a shovel, two pickaxes, and a digging bar, clanging the tools together into the ore cart. The last wisps of daylight faded behind them as they headed deeper inside the mine shaft, surrounded by the rhythmic drops of water dripping from the ceiling.

6

Reese thought the world had been transformed into a huge pile of horse manure ever since the war ended, the loss of his brother and a cousin of his own in the great Civil War weighing heavily on him. He believed that the way things used to be was the way things ought to be. He reckoned there just wasn't enough paid work to go around, and boy, oh boy, business had suffered because of it. The end of slavery meant one thing: more competition in the workforce. Reese didn't understand why more people didn't see it that way. After all he had worked his way up from the bottom, leveraged only by his ambition and social nimbleness to get to where he was. A leveling of the playing field, a tolerance so to speak felt like a personal injustice if you asked him.

Reese saw this new working mindset as one that guaranteed everybody a fair shot and a fair wage, except for him. It didn't matter if they were fresh off a boat or a plantation. And nobody in town embodied this mindset more than Randall Morgan, his boss. Reese thought a middle-aged businessman like Randall might value tradition. He had assumed wrong.

Randall Morgan, a well-respected man in his late fifties, owned and operated the Morgan mine. His square face was deeply etched with lines from years of manual labor, mountain frost and dust from the mine. As the largest employer, supplementing the largest payrolls in the whole valley, Randall enjoyed the respect and gratitude afforded to him by all the townspeople. Reese didn't quite understand the obsession with Randall, but he enjoyed working for the mine nonetheless. The work and position he had distracted him into believing he held a sort of power over other men, concealing his own anguish of loss. He had some of his own ideas about the way things should be run around there, but decided patience was the way to go. One of these days, he'd have property and a business of his own too. He might even be open to nefarious deeds in order to accomplish it. No matter, Reese had no doubt he would one day accomplish his dreams as well, regardless of other men's more sincere and selfless good deeds.

As dusk settled, Reese and Randall strode downstream toward the mining separator. It was getting late, and Reese was glad he had already made his rounds to make sure Colton and Cyrus weren't lazing around.

"One moment," Randall said, holding up his hand as they passed by the central meeting house of the mining camp.

The place was filled with Chinese immigrants milling about, organizing equipment and laundering clothes. Reese didn't like coming around there. The Chinese talked quickly under their breath, and their English was terrible. Sun Xing, their leader of sorts, made his way toward Randall. He was a short man with sun-browned Asian skin.

As Randall and Sun Xing discussed the matter of mail, Reese exited the camp to make sure everything else was in order. Randall had a tendency to talk, and frankly, endless conversations about the mail bored Reese. He figured while Randall ran his mouth, double- and triple-checking the mail and the laundering, Reese would see to the important matters around the camp.

He walked past four *vaqueros*, Mexican cowboys, whose heads were obscured by their black hats as they finished tending to their horses. Reese shot them a look of mistrust before strolling by a couple of nearby wranglers, who were gathering horses to corral for the evening.

"Hey, Pete!" Reese yelled toward a pale and gangly wrangler. "Morgan wants those locks fixed on the corrals tonight. Just sayin'!"

"Yea, I was 'bout to get to that. I know. Certainly don't need no wandering ponies in the mornin' again," Pete replied, looking exasperated.

Reese teetered on the balls of his feet for a few more minutes as the *vaqueros* and wranglers packed up for the evening. Nobody spoke, as everybody was generally tired so late in the day.

"Reese, why don't ya get on over here? Need to speak with you," Randall Morgan said.

Reese turned around to see his boss, Randall, making his way toward him from the entrance of the meeting house. "Ya boss, just lining up those lock repairs with Pete. What do you need, boss?"

"Could you please tell the laborers to get that laundry stowed away for the morning? And be sure there's no water on the screws of the mine jacks. Get 'em inside."

"Yes, sir," Reese said.

"Last time we had water on the mine jack screws, they froze up and busted," Randall said, while removing his chocolate-colored hat and running a dirty hand through a full head of graying, brown hair.

"Sure, boss."

Serves him right for hiring these no-good immigrants, Reese thought.

Randall looked up toward the sky. "Saw a ring around the sun again today. I feel it's gonna be freezin' again tonight. Rain in three days, maybe even some snow." He paused and then continued, "Well, I best be gettin' on up to the swell house. Gotta get a telegraph off to Benton. Ardie's in next week, I suppose. He'll have the mining certs and reports. Got the new deed coming from the bank for the mine reconveyance from Judge Kensington," Morgan said.

"Oh yeah?" Reese responded, his interest now far more piqued by the inner business dealings of the Morgan mine than those boring, frozen mine jacks. He had his reasons.

"Sure thing," Randall said, "things are lookin' good for next year, I'm suspecting."

"Hey boss, whaddya think about—" Reese was interrupted by Sun Xing and two of his men walking by.

Randall again reminded Sun Xing about making sure the laundry was getting done, and that the mail would be gathered that evening. Sun Xing bowed.

"I want you to get the men to bring any letters they want delivered to the housing outpost near my ranch," Randall said as he redirected his attention to Reese. "Give their letters to Colton. I'm gonna have him stop by there on the way to Benton in the morning. I need a note sent on over to Barbara myself."

"He ain't gonna be too happy about that now, boss," Reese said, feeling a strange sense of glee. "He thinks he is gonna get one day off from riding to spend with that black girl of his over at the judge's ranch."

"Yeah, well, give him an extra five dollars this week in his pay and an extra day off. He's been doin' a fine job. Gonna make a fine family someday," Randall responded, seemingly lost in thought over Colton's future.

"Why, boss, he's fine!" Reese interjected, fuming.

Randall frowned, shooting Reese a reproachful look. "Ok, Reese. You take it easy on him," he snapped, a sternness cutting through his otherwise genial tone. "I've been watchin' closely what goes on around here Reese, and I'm not rightly likin' yer attitude toward the colored folks or the immigrants, for that matter. You're a right fine worker, Reese, but they ain't doing nothin' wrong. In fact, they're serving us well. We should be grateful to have them here, Reese!"

Reese thought of the miner's death the week before. He thought of Colton and Cyrus slacking off at the prospect of food. It seemed like the only person serving the mine well was him.

"Boss, now, come on," Reese said imploringly. "I'm real nice to them boys. Now how do you think so much is gettin' done around here? I gotta push 'em or they might just start slackin' now, sir. We have a lot to do before the mine closes for the winter, and we are behind now."

"Well, you keep that up, Reese." Randall often looked into the distance as though he had a lot on his mind. "And get those ore samples onto two mules for Colton and Cyrus to be takin' in the morning. I need a verification on the quantities of gold per ton for the investors."

"I will, boss," Reese responded, thinking how much better the numbers could be if he didn't have to spend half his day teaching the chinks basic English. It was impossible for them to understand even the simplest instructions. To Reese, every foreigner or slave had a title, and Chinese were chinks to him, like Cyrus and Colton were a lower breed of human than even the Chinese workers. Cyrus and Colton to Reese were, simply put, just niggers, period!

"Right, well, I got to get on up to the swell house and get a telegraph down to Morrison. As everyone knows around here, a young man died last week, and I be the one deliverin' the sad news to his family and our investors." Randall looked worried and concerned at the thought of the pain such a letter would deliver to people, with their own kind of dreams, in this new land being settled.

Reese fumed once more and said defensively, "Now that wasn't my fault, boss! That was a terrible accident! The shoring gave way, and there was nothin' no one could do for that boy. Hell, I almost got trapped myself."

"Now, I'm not sayin' it was your fault, Reese," Randall said thoughtfully. "Just wanna be sure, it is worth all the trouble that's been happenin' there in the north vein. Can't have any more risk to you or any of my men. That boy was from China. I have no idea how to alert his family now to his passing. They're way off in San Francisco somewhere," Randall continued, trailing off into thought.

"Sun Xing oughta know, boss," Reese said.

"Sure, sure." Randal waved with his hand and placed his thumbs through his belt loops. "Well, I need to get to those letters. As I said, Ardie is bringin' in the last estimates and some certified specimens with his delivery this week, all graded and appraised." Then under his breath, he muttered, "I'm gonna make some fine jewelry for Barbara and the girls with those specimens."

He began walking toward the swell house, still muttering to himself about laundry, specimens, and letter writing. Reese wondered about the mine's profits. Randall Morgan was a hard worker, but a stupid businessman, since he was yapping his mouth about numbers all over the place.

Reese followed slowly behind him, smiling. "I'll be up in a bit. Randall, I'm headin' down the mountain in the mornin'. I think, everyone but you is clearing out of here for the three-day leave. Most of the livestock is coming as well."

"Sure, sure," Randall said with another wave. He turned his back and strode up the hill, just as the setting sun cast a brilliant purple-orange glow across the valley from over the mountains.

7

The sun rose early Saturday morning at the mining outpost, across the Long Valley and beyond, unaccompanied by a single cloud. A sharp chill cut through the mountaintops, blowing what was left of the burnt-yellow leaves down toward the valley below. Nestled between the mountains, the valley retained moist insulation. Yet there was no doubt that the nights were getting shorter.

Despite the early hour the Morgan girls, along with the other miner wives, had already begun their morning chores, eager to take advantage of the bright morning. The outpost was just about a day's ride south, downrange of the Morgan mine. It was a simple resident camp, where in the midst there was a crafty architecture for the main residence. There was a large wooden barn with a separate stable area that housed the horses of visitors and residents alike. Huge areas of corrals were adjacent to the barn on three sides. Other typical Western wood structures and tents were scattered around the ranch, where native Paiutes and travelers pitched their space of rest. The Morgans were very hospitable and kind to most everyone, but stood firm as to right and wrong.

The biggest property at the outpost, adjacent to the barn, was Randall's ranch. The Morgans had erected the barn to assist the westbound settlers in the area to get on their feet. They had also used the structure and corrals every spring as a stockhouse waypoint along the cattle drive trail from Los Angeles to Reno, Nevada. The beef to be harvested for the Long Valley and Upper Owens River region would be traded and sold there. The Morgan ranch supplied the whole Eastern Sierras with black Angus beef. Livestock was Barbara Morgan's passion, and that of her daughters and the ladies of the outpost, too, together mastering the craft of cattle ranching, while their men worked up at the Morgan mine. There had been a thousand head of cattle corralled just the day before, ready to be driven south for the winter. Barbara assisted in forming bonds between amazing horsemen of international, diverse cultures, European immigrants, the Paiutes, *vaqueros* and local young wranglers, all joining to drive the cattle south and then back north for the season and eventual sale.

Although wealthy, the Morgan house was humbly built and not extravagant by any means. It was beautiful, but had no grandeur to its construction. The Morgans always felt that the beauty of the mountains and valleys which surrounded the outpost were magnificent and glorious enough, and no man's attempt could stand against it. They were a practical and compassionate clan who cared for so many.

Randall and Barbara's two daughters, Harriet and Marcia, tended to the horses when their mother approached the young women.

"Woah! Charlie, woah!" Barbara Morgan coaxed as she entered the barn, greeted by a loud neighing of her favorite horse. She was a tall woman with a stern face, prominent cheekbones and long, rusty-blonde hair. As head of the Morgan ranch outpost she was well-respected by the other ladies in the valley. Her demeanor was hardened by years of frigid winters and hard work, but she had a big heart for her daughters, as well as the other ladies and residents in the camp and across the Long Valley.

Marcia, Harriet's older sister, looked up from brushing the horse as her mother made her way toward them. Harriet watched her graceful older sister soothe the horse with a loving pet.

"I love you, Charlie," Marcia whispered. "Your spirit excites me," she said with a smile, stroking the horse's nose with a long, thin finger. Marcia had bright-green eyes, fair skin and dirty-blond hair. She was slim and tall like her mother, her face delicate.

Harriet admired her older sister, who always had a magic type of effect on people and animals. Maybe it was the way she flashed her teeth as she spoke. Or perhaps it was the way her eyes sparkled. As Harriet set down a wooden pail, she looked at her own dirty hands, which were calloused from the afternoons she spent riding. She cared less about combing her hair and more about discovering different sections of the valley on horseback. She had just turned sixteen, and as a present her family had gifted her with her very own horse.

"Mother," Marcia said, "I wonder if Rudy is gonna be home tonight with the others. He's really been drinking a lot. I'm really gettin' tired of it!" She sighed and looked back at the horse.

"Have you let him know, Marcia?" Barbara asked, her deep voice stern, as she made no attempt to hide her disdain for the young man. She raised her eyebrows and turned her dark-blue eyes in Marcia's direction. "Best let a man know when he ain't treating you right. For the life of me, I find no understanding in him, to not coming to see you and to keep breakin' your heart. No remorse or repentance for his wrongdoin' ways. Don't say I didn't warn you 'bout him last year."

Harriet's mother continued to stare at Marcia, who looked down quickly. It was true. Rudy had been the subject of many arguments between the women. Harriet didn't like to see either of them upset like that, especially Marcia, who didn't deserve either Barbara's scorn or Rudy's insolence.

Over the past year, Rudy had become the town drunk, who had a better reputation than he deserved because of his family's past good fortunes and money. Harriet knew that her mother didn't like the family's hardworking image being soiled by Rudy's most recent behavior.

Rudy hadn't always been a drunk, certainly not when he first started seeing Marcia. He didn't become a louse until a couple months later, when his family's home burned to the ground, his mother died from tuberculosis, and his father gave up trying, becoming incognizant and a drunk himself. Soon thereafter Rudy started working for Judge Kensington and began revealing a more sinister method to achieve for himself in life. He started gambling heavily and losing. In fact, he lost everything to the gambling disease in a very short time. He took many trips up to Virginia City, saying he was going to work but would return broke, dirty and drunk. His true colors came out and were exposed over that year. His lack of commitment toward Marcia showed too often, and Barbara was very upset about this. She had tried to warn Marcia often not to waste her feelings on Rudy, for somehow, intuitively in her gut, she knew Rudy would turn bad soon after she first met him. But she wanted Marcia to be happy, and Marcia had pleaded to her mom some year and a half ago that Rudy was a good and sincere man deep down. Marcia still loved that man and held hope, he could be one day again the man she fell in love with, and that they would get married too. The West had hardened many men, Rudy more so than most.

Marcia continued to look down at the ground in embarrassment. "I know, Mama. I am sorry I let my desires take in a man, especially that one. I'm feelin' foolish. I'm about done with him and all his drinking and mistreatin' all the folk the way he does."

"I'll believe that when I see it," Barbara muttered and walked away.

Marcia hurried after her, explaining that she really was fed up with Rudy.

Harriet quickly ran toward the last stable on the left side of the barn where she said hello to her new horse, Magic, a beautiful, all-white Spanish mustang with light eyes. Harriet named her Magic because of the eyes. She had never seen a horse so magical.

"You'll love these carrots I have for you," she said as she led Magic toward the corral. "Oh, Magic, I love you. You know, you are the sweetest horse, and I want you to take care of my mommy today, ok? Don't let no critters or badness come upon her."

Harriet flung her arms around Magic's neck as Barbara rode toward them, mounted in Charlie's saddle. In the meantime, Marcia had made her way back up to the house. Barbara was clearly in a better mood when she arrived. Perhaps she had moved on from letting Marcia have it about Rudy. She smirked as she dismounted.

"Harriet, dear," Barbara said, a huge smile painting her otherwise hardened face, "I want you to come with me today, honey. I want to ride downstream to meet with Thocmetony today."

Harriet was ecstatic. She was normally forced to stay at home and tend to the chores as her mother and sister went to visit the Native American tribe. "Really, Mama! Can I?"

"Yes, my dear. We are gonna have ourselves a fine time. Angel has a basket for you, I believe. Now go and grab your little pistol, and don't forget yer frock. I'll be waitin' here! Now hurry!"

She was suddenly impatient. After sprinting into the house and back, Harriet was prepared and ready to go. Marcia returned shortly after carrying a light-brown pommel bag and a shotgun. Harriet noticed that she seemed to be in better spirits, humming quietly to herself as she gracefully fastened the rifle into the mounted scabbard.

"I take it yer wanting Harriet to tag along with you, today, Mama? She has too big of a smile on her face, for you to be bringin' me along," Marcia said, flashing her white teeth down at Harriet, who was much shorter than the other two women, sitting high upon their horses.

"Thinkin' she'll wanna be seeing Wyola today, and Angel made a basket, I'm told. I'm sure she's dying to get it to her."

Marcia asked her mother about dinner later that evening as there would be a large group of men joining them from the mine. She eagerly shuffled through the possibilities of different kinds of stew and cornbread.

"Bye, Marcia. I love you, Sis!" Harriet beamed, interrupting the talk of dinner. She was practically bouncing into Magic's saddle.

"You watch Mama close. Don't get lost now in your daydreamin'," Marcia said, waving. She stuck her tongue out at Harriet, jokingly, acting jealous that she had not been invited. But Harriet knew that Marcia preferred to stay at home, preparing for Daddy and the rest of the men. The wranglers would be leaving that next day south to catch up with the herd. There was a lot to do, and Harriet was quite glad she didn't have to help today!

Finally the two Morgan ladies were off, trotting east toward the Paiute encampment. They made their way to a lower elevation, the trail leading alongside a rocky stream, deep into a canyon with high walls, leading to the top of steep mountains on either side. Off in the distance, across the Long Valley, the White Mountains glistened in the morning sun from an early season snow capping their peaks. The river rushed with added gusto, as the sun melted the early snow on the mountains above them. It was a cloudless day, and the sun illuminated the valley. Steam from the melting frost on the weeds ahead of them reminded them of the season that was coming.

Harriet wrapped her frock close around herself as the wind nipped her rosy face. "Oh, Mama!" she said, delighted. Things had been getting better for her ever since her birthday. "I love this, you and I are off for a little adventure. I can't wait to see Wyola."

"What about Henry, honey?" her mother asked with a mischievous grin.

"Mama!" Harriet blushed, unable to hide her suddenly larger smile, as she thought of the handsome young boy. "I know, Mama. Isn't he just the wonder of the world? So kind and gentle and good to me." She looked longingly toward the east and the White Mountains.

"A hard worker and handsome, too, I suppose," Barbara added.

Henry was young, but he quickly rose in the Benton community as one of the most respected young gentlemen. Harriet reckoned she had fallen in love with him from the moment she saw him. He was tall and lean, with broad shoulders and a long face. Harriet admired the way he rode his horse fast and gracefully, like a dance, as though the man and the animal were made for each other. She wanted Henry to teach her how to ride just like that. Harriet wondered if he would have time for her or even notice her, with all the work and schooling he had going on in his life, as he lived in town. After all, Henry was brother to Harriet's favorite person, Sarah Devine, who was engaged to Henry's boss, JR Morrison. It could all turn out to be such a family affair!

About an hour later, Harriet and Barbara arrived at the Paiute Native American encampment along El Diablo Creek. There were about a dozen wickiups, small huts made of tulle reeds covered in brushwood and grass. They were insulated with mud that lined the base of a short hill near the creek. At the center of it all was a large wickiup, about three times the size of the others. Harriet supposed it was for something special, such as ceremonies or gatherings. She looked around and smiled. The encampment was bursting with activity and life. Two teenage boys skinned a doe nearby with scrunched faces and then gutted the dead animal. Several children shrieked with laughter, as a black dog chased them in circles. Two young women sat huddled near what was left of the night's fire, knitting baskets between their knees. Harriet inhaled a deep breath of crisp air, catching a whiff of something delicious. Near another outdoor fire, four women sat preparing food stocks from a pile of what looked like acorns. Some of the activity ceased, as more took notice of Harriet and Barbara's arrival. The children, with a dog following behind, darted toward Harriet with excitement as she and her mother headed toward the center of the camp.

"Hi, Harriet!" Angel yelled, the leader of the pack of children. She was a cute eight-year-old girl with wide brass eyes. "I have a basket for you!" The Paiute people were known for their basketry, and Harriet loved the ones with colors and unique tribal symbols.

"I brought you all some candies!" Harriet beamed, reaching into her frock coat pocket to hand the children some candy as she rode slowly by the group of them.

They pounced on the candy, overjoyed, and continued hopping, following the horses. Barbara continued riding until she reached the hut of Thocmetony, a woman also nicknamed Sarah by the settlers, and as known by all in the region. Thocmetony was a proud woman and a strong advocate for the Paiute people. She was also the sister of Chief Natchez and the great Paiute War Chief, Numaga. Thocmetony was skeptical of the settlers, but Harriet did notice that she had a soft spot for Barbara's family.

"Oh, Sarah, how great to see you!" Barbara nodded toward the woman as she dismounted her horse.

"Dearest Barbara! I was wondering if we would see you today," Thocmetony said, bowing her head toward Barbara. She was small and sturdy, with bold, dark eyes and waist-length black hair, braided tightly behind her back. She wore a fringed deerskin dress with leggings underneath. Harriet noticed an elk tooth necklace, laying on top of her protruding collarbones.

"Well, I can't compare our burden to yours," Barbara said as she walked toward Thocmetony, taking her hand between her gloved fingers. "It has been a much more terrible time for the Paiutes, and I can't help but wonder sometimes, where God is in the world today."

"We will be fine," Thocmetony replied, dignified. She raised her forehead to the sky, and the sunlight bounced off her high cheekbones. "Our God is clearly seen all around us, every day in His creation. Come with me."

Harriet followed her mother and Thocmetony toward a wickiup, accompanied by a group of young children. The small wickiup was lined with a deerskin rug and several tribal tapestries. It smelled of pine and bark.

"Barbara," Thocmetony said, offering Harriet and her mother small pieces of dried elk meat.

Barbara obliged and reached into her pockets, extracting a handful of thick, short candles, and a box of wooden matches.

Then Thocmetony suddenly looked serious. "We haven't seen Wyola for three weeks now. She is usually here, as you know, at least every couple weeks, and knowing you and the men are coming through this week, we really expected to see her today. I'm not too worried, but I'm growing more and more concerned at each sunrise."

"She's not here?" Barbara asked, taken aback.

"Last we spoke, she was very distraught about the judge and his torment of her labors at the ranch," Thocmetony stated cautiously.

"Why so?" Harriet shuddered.

Harriet had only met the judge a couple of times and had never considered him a decent man. Judge Kensington was known for his hardness and pre-war ideals, so Harriet could only wonder what kind of experience it would be to work on his ranch. She knew that Wyola and her slightly older sister were orphaned children of indentured servants who had owed the judge money. The judge treated them more like slaves. Here, in Long Valley, it was no different to him than back in Savannah, Georgia, prior to the Civil War.

People in the valley knew the story of how young Wyola had gotten very sick on the trip West, and during that time, while she was asleep in the back of a wagon with her sister Lola, her parents were found dead the following morning by other parishioners of the wagon train, who had recovered their badly beaten bodies. There was no explanation as to what had happened. Wyola's mother had been stripped of her clothing and brutally assaulted, and her father was found with a fatal stab wound to his chest. Everyone in the valley assumed the judge knew how they had died, just because of the way he intimidated people. But he played the role very well of an arrogant, uninformed bastard child, claiming it had to have been the Indians. But then, why was he or any of the others in the traveling wagon party not killed? People wondered how Wyola and Lola would not have been awakened by a murderous rampage of a war party of Indians.

The judge had relocated West, taking over land that didn't belong to him in some kind of a homestead power grab claim. He fenced off hundreds of acres of Native American hunting grounds that weren't even his or part of any deed. And the government did nothing. There were a lot of other evil rumors surrounding the judge, and although he had retained great wealth which he acquired back in the South before the war, he seemed very bitter to the fact that his ideals were lost in the conflict's defeat, and also that he had to go West to start a new life. Why should he have to move all the way across the country into the wild frontier? However gold and greed seemed to quelch that misnomer for the judge, making him ok with it. Such an opportunity was right up his alley.

Thocemetony had especially missed Barbara, but this commentary of the judge, the ranch, and Wyola was leaving a lot of open questions for everyone. "Well, I'm not one to condemn a man, but from what she said, he has been very tough on her and the other ladies working at his spread. I felt she was holding something back, you know," Thocmetony continued, seemingly implying something. Harriet wondered what she meant.

Barbara nodded. Thocmetony continued to emphasize that there was a deeper secret Wyola had yet to reveal.

"Well, the men are expected home from the mine today. I do wonder what poor Colton will say. I was gonna prepare a nice meal and celebration this evening for tomorrow. Was hopin' you all would join us up at the ranch house." Barbara gave Thocmetony an encouraging look. "We can all make plans for some better shelter for you all for the winter, so you can stick around. We really hope you all will consider comin' up to the outpost this winter, instead of migrating up north to the Great Basin Reservation."

"Well, that may be possible." Thocmetony nodded. "I'll have to see when brother Natchez returns from the north. Brother Numaga is not doing so well, Barbara. He has contracted the white man disease."

"No!" Harriet cried out, thinking of poor Thocmetony and her brother Natchez having to take care of sick Numaga, the leader of the whole tribe.

"Yes, I'm afraid so." Thocmetony shook her head solemnly. "Natchez is concerned. Since the last treaty, we've all been starving more and more each winter. The children are suffering the most, and there's even talk of war again up north!"

Harriet didn't like the thought of war. She had only known peace in her community. She couldn't imagine her people fighting Thocmetony and her tribe.

"What can we do?" Barbara asked desperately. "There must be somethin' that can be done. I know my husband won't tolerate any suffering! As we have done all winters, there will be plenty of beef and provisions for you this season."

Thocmetony shook her head. "Your husband's a good man. Just wish there were more of them amongst the whites. You are not the keepers of all the land. There is not enough from you alone for all the suffering, Barbara."

Barbara continued pleading with Thocmetony, offering more invitations to stay at the ranch and outpost. "Oh, how could I forget!" Barbara exclaimed. "I brought you something!" She searched around, looking for something that wasn't there. "Harriet dear, can you please grab the pommel bag off Magic and bring it in?"

Harriet nodded obediently and ran out of the wickiup, where Angel and the other children continued to play. When she returned to the hut, the two older women seemed to be in better spirits.

"I'm sorry for involving you in these adult matters," Thocmetony said.

"I want to know!" Harriet insisted. "I want to help!"

"Oh dear, now smile! You are far too pretty and young to be troubled now with these things. I was speaking to your mother, Harriet," Thocmetony said with a smile on her face and a small shake of her head.

"I'm sixteen now. I'm practically a woman."

"Of course, you are. How's your sister, Marcia?"

"Oh," Harriet said, sounding uncertain. "She's—"

"She's fine," her mother interrupted as she opened the bag, removing a small white pouch. "Now this is for you, Sarah. I've been saving a piece every time I see Randall. I want you to have it and use it for your children."

Thocmetony took the pouch and untied the string. "Barbara, thank you, but you have already brought me great joy with the candles and matches."

Harriet peeked over to see what was inside. It was gold, no doubt from her father's mine. Harriet felt her eyes well up with tears as she observed Thocmetony and her eyes filling.

"Oh my, Barbara!" Thocmetony said, a single tear dripping down her stoic face. "This is too—"

"Stop! Say no more! You are like my own, young sister. You have done so much for us, with nothing. You have shown nothing but kindness to my family. It's the least we could do."

The two women embraced. Shrieks of excitement coming from outside the hut interrupted them.

"Colton!" the children yelled. "Colton's here!"

8

Colton beamed with excitement as he and Cyrus entered the Paiute encampment on their horses, with two mules in tow, loaded with large bundles of ore specimens draped across their backs. It was midmorning, and the sun finally started to warm the air. Twenty yards ahead, a small hoard of Indian children was running toward them at top speed. Seeing the children shriek with glee put a wide smile on Colton's face.

"You know, I can't wait to see another face that's not yours," Cyrus said.

"I hear you, brother." Colton laughed. "Or Reese's for that matter." He couldn't wait to see Wyola and the other ladies as they prodded their ponies to trot ahead.

They slowed down at the center of the encampment, pulled their reins and stopped next to a fallen tree with a protruding, broken branch they used to tie their horses. Angel and the other children watched them eagerly as Cyrus grabbed a canteen from the side of his horse and took a large swig, then dismounted.

"May I have some?" Angel asked, batting her long eyelashes at Cyrus.

He handed the canteen to Angel who quickly took a drink and ran over to a nearby well to refill it.

Firechild, a teenage boy, watched Angel as she raced toward the well and turned to Colton. "Can I fill your canteen for you, too, Colton?"

"Sure, thank you, Firechild. Why don't you go on ahead and take the horses and the mules over to give 'em some fresh water, too? They're, no doubt, more thirsty than I."

Colton looked up to see Harriet, Barbara and Thocmetony meandering toward them. He hadn't seen a woman's face for longer than he liked to admit. He noticed that Harriet was growing up to be awfully beautiful. She was shorter than her mother and older sister, with amber hair instead of blonde. Though not as graceful as her older sister, she moved with spirited determination and youthfully innocent grace.

"Hello, ladies!" Colton smiled exuberantly. He had never seen three women look so beautiful, except for Wyola, of course. "Good to see you all here and together!"

Harriet leaped toward him and gave him a massive hug. She was stronger than she looked. Colton noticed Barbara, shooting her daughter with a reproachful look.

"Hello, Barbara," Cyrus said.

Thocmetony greeted the men with a slight bowing of her head. "Gentlemen, glad to see you."

"Cyrus, Colton, how's things? What are ya doin' up here, and why so early?" Barbara asked.

Colton liked Barbara. Even though she wasn't as friendly as Randall, she had just as big of a heart. He wanted to have a relationship like the Morgans, the family he constantly dreamed of, one day too. He admired the way they loved each other and supported the people they cared about. The Morgans lived so humbly for their great fortune. One would never recognize such wealth in these good folks, while sitting in a humble abode.

"Mr. Morgan sent us over here on our way to Benton Crossing, to get you a message and drop some letters for the others. I'm so sorry to say, he won't be makin' it this trip. We had an accident at—"

"What happened?" Barbara interrupted, the smile wiped from her face.

"The mine," Colton continued. "Well, one of the immigrant workers was crushed in the mine, the new north vein. After a small tremor some timber failed, and we had a horrible collapse."

Barbara nodded. "We felt that here at the outpost!"

Colton watched the ladies shudder and shake their heads. He hated having to deliver bad news, especially when he was so excited to see everyone.

"Mr. Morgan thought it proper he stuck around and delivered that terrible news himself to the family, ya know. See to the boy's tendin'."

Thocmetony slowly shook her head. "Colton, I'm so sorry."

"Ya, we are too. Mr. Morgan felt best if he stayed behind and tried to get word to the boy's parents over in San Francisco. Although they don't speak any words of English, he felt he is responsible for takin' care of the boy's body, in returning him to his family this weekend somehow, or burying him properly up in the meadow near the mine. At least get word to them 'n all, you see!" Colton continued explaining the situation Randall was caught up in as boss of the mine.

"Why, that is terrible news," Barbara said sadly.

"Well, I came here to deliver you this note from Mr. Morgan. I gotta get down to Benton and get on over to Colby's office come Monday morning, to get the ore appraised." Colton nodded toward the packed mules. "We're really just droppin' by."

Cyrus smiled in silent acknowledgment.

Thocmetony insisted that Colton and Cyrus stay for at least an hour to eat and relax. Colton, hungry from the ride, obliged without hesitating. He walked with the women toward a smoldering fire surrounded by four large logs, cut and shaped for sitting, as Cyrus followed.

Colton sighed heavily as he sat down. Thocmetony passed him some dried elk meat, which she had brought from the central wickiup. Colton separated some, handing it to Cyrus. He then took a big grip and bit off a large chunk. Chewing the jerky, Colton reckoned he hadn't tasted anything so flavorful and delicious in quite a while. The food up at the mine was bland and mushy. *Boy, do these Indians know how to make jerky,* he thought.

"Colton," Thocmetony said softly, "I'm afraid we haven't seen anything of Wyola for three weeks or more."

Colton choked on a mouth full of the meat and coughed. "What are you sayin'?" he replied, his face suddenly looking worried.

"I'm feeling slightly concerned," Thocmetony went on. "She's been having a tough time over at the judge's ranch, last we spoke. She could very much use seeing you."

Colton's stomach turned at the thought of Wyola having difficulties. A million scenarios raced through his head of what Thocmetony could mean by "a tough time." He was so disappointed Wyola wasn't there. "Of course, Sarah. As soon as I drop this ore I'll head on over there and try to pay her a visit, first thing tomorrow mornin'."

"Well, you just have to be careful!" Barbara said. "You take good care of that girl. What about you, Cyrus?"

Cyrus was busy chowing down on the elk meat jerky with a mouth so full, he was only able to creep out a murmur. Colton wasn't sure if he had heard a single word of their conversation.

"Well," Cyrus said, swallowing partially the mouthful of meat. "While he'll be all 'bout carrying on with Wyola, I'm gonna have me a nice, warm bath."

Everybody laughed. Cyrus never missed a moment to work some laughs out of a crowd, especially in light of the sad news they had delivered earlier in the conversation.

"Hey, Harriet," Cyrus said, looking in her direction.

Harriet had been nibbling on the end of a piece of meat. She looked up, surprised, and pushed a lock of amber hair behind her ear. "Yes, Cyrus?"

"You're gettin' prettier and prettier every time we see ya! Why don't you get yourself a man already?"

Harriet blushed.

"Now hush up, Cyrus!" Barbara said with a stern expression, elbowing Cyrus in the side. "That is my child!"

Colton made eye contact with Harriet and rolled his eyes. She smiled.

"Just kiddin', ma'am," Cyrus said, chuckling and tipping his hat at Barbara and Harriet.

Barbara waved the comment aside. After Colton finished the last bites of his jerky he grabbed his canteen and his hat. Barbara insisted on them coming to the outpost for dinner, but Colton declined. They had to get moving along to Benton if they wanted to make it there by nighttime, and now he was doubly anxious to find Wyola. Food suddenly became secondary to him.

9

It was nearing sundown by the time Colton and Cyrus rode into the town of Benton to deliver the ore. When they reached the assayer's office, the lights were off. They were exhausted from a long day's ride, and Colton did not want to wait until morning to make their delivery.

"You think he's asleep?" Cyrus whispered as he dismounted his horse and grabbed the reins.

"We're about to find out," Colton said as he walked up the two steps to the front entrance of the small office. There was a thinly curtained window next to the wooden door. To the right of the door, Colton noticed a plaque that read:

COLBY FLOWERS
BENTON TOWN ASSAYER
OFFICE

Colton peeked through a hole in the curtain, catching a glimpse of a cot in the right-hand side of the office and a dimly lit lantern burning inside. He saw Colby lying comfortably on the small cot.

He tapped lightly on the glass. "Colby," he whispered. "You awake?"

"One moment," croaked a voice from inside. "One moment. Let me throw on my pants."

Colton stepped away from the window, and a moment later a slightly overweight balding man in his mid-thirties opened the door. He never missed an opportunity to chat a subject to death, but he meant well and was a very friendly man.

"Colton," he said, yawning and rubbing his eyes. "Is that you?" He was in the process of drawing a pair of brown suspenders over his shoulder.

Colton apologized for being late.

"Ya, I got the telegraph from JR earlier today, sayin' you'll be coming in late this evening. That's why I'm here and not at home with Penelope. Well, I hear it'll be a good find based on Randall's note. He seemed mighty excited 'bout that new north vein. Sorry a boy had to die though, digging it outta there." Colby shook his head. "Terrible news. No gold is worth the price of a life. Let's see what you got for me to test, boys."

"Got two mules," Colton said, gesturing toward the mules around back. "About four-hundred-and-forty pounds of ore."

The two men walked around the office to find Cyrus leaning against one of the horses, his eyes heavy with exhaustion.

"Let's get 'em unloaded." Colby seemed to get more energetic and eager at the sight of the large bags hanging on each mule.

"So how are you doing, Colby? How's the missus?" Cyrus asked, rolling up his sleeves.

"Oh, she's fine. Everyone be fine. Let's get these mules unloaded, Cyrus," Colby said, evidently more eager to see the ore than to chat at that moment. "Get a couple of those wood pails over there. Fill 'em with some of that ore and then bring 'em on back inside. Come morning I'll get to the extractin'. Tell Morgan, when you see him, I'll send the ore specimens with the weekly freighter down to Fort Independence. He knows the routine. It would be great if you boys remind me in the mornin' to get you back some small extractions with a preliminary certificate of purity."

Colton nodded, tipping his hat. "Will do, Colby. Word has it, be good specimens from that new north vein."

"I'm trustin' Morgan knows. It's an instinct!" Colby said.

Colton apologized once again for the late hour and bid Colby goodnight.

"I would say, it's time to get some shut-eye." Colton rubbed both his eyes and yawned. Seeing Colby reminded him just how exhausted he felt after such a long week.

"Speak for yourself," Cyrus replied. "I'm gettin' me a drink!" He gestured down the road, toward the direction of the Benton Saloon.

"I guess I could join you for one, but only one!" Colton said as they were leaving Colby's.

—⁓—

The Benton Saloon was a rowdy and raucous joint filled with smoke and laughter. That evening most of the saloon's small tables were occupied by men playing cards and ladies preening about in their fancy dresses. Everyone was oblivious, for the most part, as to who was coming and going, thanks to plenty of alcohol. There were a lot of men in town due to the weekend off from the mines which were scattered throughout the whole Eastern Sierra area, and for most of them it was their last evening off on leave, before they all headed home for the off season. It was a last hurrah, so to speak.

Madam Candice Mackannel, the cheerful saloon owner, was a middle-aged, strong and well-shaped woman with rosy cheeks and curly red hair that she tied up as she ran around the saloon, serving her drunk patrons. Despite her hardened attitude toward overly drunken men there was still a kind-heartedness about her.

The room was abuzz with chatter, but one particularly loud voice penetrated the noise, which belonged to an obviously very drunk Rudy Schaefer, who was slumped against the bar. Rudy was now the top town drunkard who nobody respected any longer, but everybody endured because of his family's loss. What Rudy lacked in height, he made up for in bravado and exaggeration. He was carrying on about a recent hunt, in which he killed "The largest damn mountain lion you sorry bastards have ever seen," when one of his hands suddenly knocked over his beer. Froth and liquid spilled all over the counter.

Madam Mackannel, who was cleaning behind the bar, jumped back. "Rudy!" she yelled. "I do declare, I'm gonna be nice to you and have you thrown on outta here! Givin' ya till tomorrow, when you come in, hungover, to pay up your tab. I don't know why we keep lettin' you run a tab in here. You disrespectful son of a bitch!" She shot him an exasperated glare, fuming over his antics.

"Oh, pipe down, Candice," Rudy slurred, steadying himself against the bar. "It'll all pan out!" He pointed a drunken, unfocused finger at Candice. "Half my tab is your own doing, Candice, cuzza your ladies carryin' on with me. I see you pushin' them on me. Yer obviously makin' money off me! There would be no excitement 'round this here saloon if it weren't for me." He burped loudly and picked up his empty mug, shoving it toward the madam for a refill.

"Don't you wish, Rudy!" Madam Candice yelled. "I doubt it's your money at all! You best be leavin' now. I don't believe I have the patience in me to say it again." She walked toward him, short arms outstretched, shooing Rudy out of her sight.

He stumbled slowly toward the door. "Oh, go clean yerself, ya whore!"

"Best stop at your trustee judges for some money, before you come on in here tomorrow mornin', you drunken fool! No more tabs for you!" she yelled.

Everyone in the town knew that Rudy was tight with Judge Kensington. The judge was intimidatingly powerful and well connected, a volatile combination in these parts, and yet another reason why Rudy was untouchable. Back in Georgia he had also been a federally appointed judge as part of the South's reconciliation with the North, although everyone knew, money was how that appointment was made. The judge liked to think he followed the letter of the law, which he did for everyone else. It just didn't apply to him.

Rudy, barely able to walk, stumbled toward the double saloon door. He looked back toward Candice and gave a smart-ass laugh out loud, while pointing his finger, resembling a pistol, over to the card table, where Candice's backup man, the bartender Payton, was sitting. Right as he turned around to walk forward to exit the establishment, finger still somewhat outstretched, with his body twisted and contorted and facing Candice, Colton came bursting through the saloon door into the club, with Cyrus right behind, not seeing him exiting on the other side, and knocking drunken Rudy to the floor.

"Ouch!" Rudy squelched.

"Sorry, Rudy," Colton said, looking down. "Didn't see ya."

Rudy held up his left hand in pain. "You broke my damn trigger finger, you damn fool, nigger!"

Colton looked down as he stepped past him, to see a pathetic Rudy sitting like a child on the ground, too drunk to get up, while the saloon folks burst out into loud laughter. Rudy reached with his non-injured hand toward his empty holster.

Suddenly Payton stood up, holding an upside-down pistol in his two fingers. "You lookin' for something, Rudy?" Payton had a smile stretched across his face.

The rest of the saloon, again, erupted in laughter as Rudy staggered up and stumbled out of the door. Colton looked at Cyrus who also burst out laughing.

"Man, what's up with this Rudy? He never knows when to stop!" Cyrus shook his head. "Did ya see his finger? Looked bent ninety degrees sideways. Oh, I bet that hurt! I'm sure he's gonna be feeling it even more so in the mornin'!"

With Rudy gone, the evening carried on with a renewed calm. Colton and Cyrus had a couple of beers before the exhaustion from the day overcame them and they trudged upstairs toward their vacant room.

Colton woke up early Sunday morning, unable to sleep any longer. He awoke, restless over the news he had received from Thocmetony the day before. Consuming thoughts of Wyola danced in and out of his mind all night long as he tossed about, like a fish out of water, the moment his head had hit the pillow. He did get enough rest, though, by the time he awoke, enough to hit the road on his search. Judging by the dimness outside, Colton reckoned, it was still too early for anybody else to be awake. He glanced at Cyrus, who was still fast asleep and snoring lightly.

Colton reached for the ceiling and flexed his sore muscles in a deep stretch as he yawned one final time. He arose and gazed out the window. Outside, he saw Rudy stumbling out of a barn across the street and down the road. Colton smiled. *Is he still drunk?*

Colton loved the brief stillness of dawn before anyone got up. The animals were first to awake. The birds, roosters, and livestock were the sound of the early morning, before man's disturbing noises could disrupt nature. It reminded him of his days on the plantation, when he woke up before anybody else, just to get a few brief moments of peace alone in nature. He would enjoy this special time, prior to an arduous day of work, long before the scorching sun beat down upon his back, and before anybody could tell him what to do. It was in those moments, when Colton found his first glimpses of freedom. The animals were the definition to him of what it meant to be free. He wondered if Wyola also awoke before the rest of the house. *Is she sleeping right now? She must look so peaceful. But no, where is she?* he thought.

Colton was interrupted by Cyrus stirring. "Why you up so early? Geez! Get some rest, Colton," he blurted.

"Go ahead and sleep. I'm gonna head over and see if I can't find Wyola over at the judge's. Wait for me here. Don't leave or get drunk. I'll be back."

"Ya, ya." Cyrus yawned, rolling over in his cot to go back to sleep.

"Best lock the door after me." Colton smiled. "I saw Rudy walking around, lookin' quite grumpy."

Colton retrieved his pistol from under his pillow to clean and load it before leaving. He holstered it and grabbed his rifle, which was leaning against the table, before heading out the door. As he went downstairs and into the saloon, Candice was just wrapping things up from the night before. He acknowledged her with a head nod which she unknowingly ignored.

He exited the saloon, glancing down to each end of the avenue. Then he proceeded sluggishly toward the Colby barn, retrieved his horse, cinched his saddle, mounted, and galloped quickly to the east as he left Benton, heading toward Chalfant and the judge's ranch.

His head was so distracted by thoughts of Wyola that he barely noticed the picturesque scenery blurring past him. The steep mountains loomed in the distance on either side of him, cutting diagonal lines in the gray sky. The wind whipped his face as he pushed forward, the horse's hooves kicking up dust in their trail.

With the town of Benton far behind him, Colton eventually passed a junction in the road. He decided to ride to the right, a new path, but one he was quite certain would lead him to the judge's homestead faster. As he rode along a land bridge and crossed the Owens River, he noticed thick, dark clouds moving into the distant Sierra Mountains to his west. It was still early, but the lack of sunlight made Colton feel like he was riding at dusk. The fall season air felt cold and saturated, with dust particles wafting in each breath. In the distance, he noticed a dust cloud stirring.

Finally his mouth was so dry from breathing in dust and crisp mountain air that Colton decided to stop for a drink before leaving the river. He maneuvered his horse and dismounted. Perhaps it was the weather or the impending visit, but as he led his horse toward the small creek he suddenly felt exposed. In those parts of the valley, there was no telling of who or what somebody could run into, especially when they were alone. Colton retrieved a looking glass from his saddlebag to scan the area. About two miles in the distance, he observed three men on horseback riding away from his position toward the Sierras. *They must be coming from the judge's*, he pondered. They must have created the dust cloud he had seen. He quickly filled his canteen, repackaged his looking glass into his saddlebag, then mounted and spurred his pony toward the direction from which the men had come.

Judge Kensington's ranch did not belong in the Sierras. It was hard to miss, even from far away. No less than eight white columns supported the two-story plantation-style house that sat at the top of a small circle drive on a raised, low plateau, in the Chalfant Valley. The enormous property was still somehow dwarfed by the seemingly endless amount of land that surrounded it and was protected by a massive wooden fence. Even the enormous fields surrounding the estate were a shade of green that was otherwise unseen in the Sierras, especially during the winter. *Who built this place?* Colton thought. He wondered if it had been transported, brick by brick, column by column, from the deep South. The scene, reminiscent of older, less free times, sent shivers up and down Colton's spine.

There were no less than two dozen people working on the property. The estate was partially obscured by a horse stable and corral on the right-hand side that led into a separate fenced area. Several *vaqueros*, all dressed the same and looking like real cowboy horsemen, led some of the largest stallions that Colton had ever seen into the fenced area. One of the *vaqueros* looked up, noticed Colton, and nudged his companion.

Colton rode through the large, open, wrought-iron gate at the entry onto the ranch that bore a large encircled "K" in the center. He saw several women, all dressed in long dresses and bonnets, scrubbing the steps of the estate, while others refilled the horse's water troughs. With such business the entire estate seemed oddly quiet. Everybody was busy, yet no one said a word.

He strained his neck, looking for Wyola. His heart beat faster. Everybody moved about their daily chores, however, Colton couldn't help but sense a darkness that hung in the air. For one, nobody talked or looked at one another. Colton knew Wyola had to be there somewhere. He strained his eyes but could not see her. Perhaps she was in the house, tending to the children or preparing food. He sped up his horse's trot. It was breakfast time after all. Colton noticed that one of the women scrubbing the porch by the front-entry French doors of the huge house was Wyola's sister, Lola Everest.

Seeing him riding up quickly, she rose and stood upright, holding a brush dripping water, with a pail near her feet. Colton stopped quickly and waved. Lola nodded and began walking toward him as Colton dismounted his horse and greeted her, still holding his reins.

Before Colton could say hello, he was interrupted by two cowboys riding toward him, coming from the left. He recognized one as Zachary Morris, a pompous teenager who talked out of his nose. Although he held no real power or fortune, he fashioned himself to be a mini version of the judge, never hesitating to speak on his behalf. Colton didn't recognize the other stumpy kid, who must have been a friend of Zachary's. They galloped fast and stopped quickly in front of Colton, kicking up a rather threatening cloud of dust.

"Get back to work, Lola," Zachary snapped, accenting Lola's name, who quickly stopped in her tracks. "What are you doin' here?" He puffed out his adolescent chest from on top of his horse at Colton.

Colton was used to white folk making that move. They always talked with more confidence when they were physically higher than Colton, who was standing on the ground. It reminded him of the evil southern cavalry who intimidated, murdered and raped during the Civil War. They didn't sound as sure when they got down to his level. Colton was broader and taller than the average man in the mountains. He reckoned that was the reason why they liked to do most of their talking down to him while mounted atop a bigger and more powerful animal. That was everyone except Reese of course, who, a giant of a man at six foot and six inches, was the only other man who towered over Colton.

"I—" Colton only got the first character out.

"She ain't here!" Zachary cut him off, as if he could read Colton's mind. "And that's all I'm gonna tell ya. And the judge doesn't want no one around, so you best be on your way. Ain't gonna tell you again, Colton. Now be gone!" Zachary's right hand rested on his pistol, suddenly revealed in his holster belt.

"Now why you drawin' your pistol? You afraid of something?" Colton said confidently and rather irritated. He was certain he could yank Zachary off his horse before the boy could so much as cock his pistol. He caught Lola's eye behind Zachary.

She nodded her head and mouthed the words, "Yes, it's true," as he stoically looked at her while comprehending the message.

Colton quickly jumped back on his horse without another word. "I'll be returning." He directed his gaze toward Zachary, delivering the same stoic stare at another two men now riding up to back up Zachary, stomping in behind the young man's horse in a threatening way.

"Oh, no, ya won't, if you know what's good for you. Git on. The judge never liked you around here anyway. Git goin'!" the brawnier one of the men stated.

As Colton turned away, picking up speed, he heard Zachary's voice yelling at Lola in the background, "What did you tell him, woman?"

10

It was only midmorning on Monday, but JR Morrison felt as though he had been working all day. That's usually how things were around his business, the Benton Town Mercantile. JR didn't mind a hard day's work. In fact, he embraced it every chance he got. That's what made him a self-made man, and JR knew he had to carry on that way until he died.

JR was originally from Pennsylvania, which in his opinion gave him those educated, gentlemanly heartland values and a manner of speaking that one just couldn't find in the West or the Sierras amongst all the transient adversity. He didn't mind it though. It certainly gave him favor and prestige with the rest of the town and valley.

JR had struck gold, literally, in California and used his newfound fortune to settle down and create the mercantile, almost by accident. Due to his financial background, he, somehow without election, found himself as the regional Farmers and Merchants Bank agent and remote outpost banker soon after the place was first opened. He was a trusted man to handle some of the largest fortunes in those parts of Long Valley and the Eastern Sierras.

The mercantile which was nothing more than a wooden built general store and stagecoach drop-off point originally, by its own nature, afforded a satellite operation for Farmers and Merchants Bank headquartered in LA. They saw they could position a manager of sorts halfway up the state, on the east side of the Sierras, nestled in the California central high desert commune of Benton Crossing.

Benton had become the central stop for folks traveling the Eastern Sierra byway to spread out along the Long Valley area from there, but it was a primary midway point for the long haulers, traveling from Los Angeles to Reno, who didn't desire to make their stop in Bodie, which was not too far away.

Bodie was raucous, with saloons and whore houses on every corner and even in between. JR relished in the idea that the local, sole mercantile he had built with his own two hands became that more secure satellite stop compared to Bodie because of a certain destiny bestowed upon him by the local citizens of the valley, who deeply trusted him. It was the Eastern Sierra central main telegraph station as well, appointed to his establishment by the federal government, officially installed as a hub in that newly crafted technology network of line wire and infrastructure maintenance along the byway. But it was also a stopping and gathering space, a mail house, and a valued resource of commerce in their small and tightly knit community.

JR believed there were four kinds of people in the world. Those who knew what they wanted and worked hard for it with steadfast determination and persistence, standing in contrast to those who did not, but instead worked aimlessly. Then there were those who didn't work at all, or worse, the ones who gained their income by way of thievery and greed. Accordingly, these four types of people were the types of men Morrison had grown to segregate in all his business dealings and ventures. He was leery of them as well in his new founded role as the "watcher" of the village.

JR knew what he wanted. As the owner of the most successful business in Benton, second-most in the whole valley following behind that of the Morgan mine, he had his "watcher" sights set on politics. The reason was partly because of those first types of folks, but also because of the threat of the other three types of folks, potentially growing to become a cancer of sorts along the Eastern Sierra byway. The West demanded a strong and honest leader. In his opinion there was much opportunity because the way he put it, "The area lacked polish or protocol, and there were simply too many vagrants and no good drunks lingering about." He wanted to influence the raucous Bodie types to 'stay clear of his Benton.' Soon signs were becoming prominent in and around the town, painted with the bold words: "Keep out all vagrants and criminals!" It was almost as if he wanted to attract such men there to root them out of the valley. But JR wasn't at all a violent man. He solved all the problems he encountered with a steady, cool, and even-tempered head upon his shoulders. His motto was: "All a man has control of are his actions and his attitude". JR was very logical and discerning, yet stern and forthwith. He strolled about the streets of Benton with honor and integrity and was friendly to most all folks of the Long Valley region.

JR also had his sights set on other goals, namely the stunning and elegant Sarah Devine, one of the most beautiful women in all of California that he had ever laid his virgin eyes upon. Her heart was as beautiful as her face, and JR knew she would be the one with whom he wanted to continue building a life with. Sarah was also from the East but had followed her younger brother Henry out West to seek more opportunity and a fresh start, following the dreams of her education. Some days JR felt like the luckiest man west of the Mississippi. Many in the area envied him and truly believed he was. Having Sarah in his life brought with her a certain kind of dignity and respect for JR.

Most days were busy days for JR, and he was content with that. It was hard not to be distracted, being surrounded by myths of much gold and precious fortune. However he had seen the underbelly of the never-ending quest for fortune and fame. He was careful not to be drawn back into that, instead holding steadfast to toe the line at the mercantile.

JR was accompanied that brisk fall Monday morning by his young apprentice, Henry Devine, Sarah's younger brother. He was a squirrely, yet eager teenager and a very reliable and trustworthy helper in the mercantile. Henry looked up to JR, thinking of him as his long-lost older brother he never had. The two sat outside the store, taking a much-needed break, when two familiar figures slowly rode toward them.

"Hello, Colton, Cyrus," JR said, nodding, as the two men dismounted their horses.

They had just come from the assayer's office, picking up the certificate of purity Colby had written out for Morgan, meant to accompany the gold extractions from the ore samples they had dropped off.

Before JR could properly welcome the men, a stagecoach rolled in fast from the north, stopping in front of the building, kicking up a large cloud of dust. One driver quickly jumped down the side steps to the ground and opened the door, assisting two well-dressed, middle-aged ladies down from the carriage. One wore a lilac dress, and both women had feathers in their hats. They didn't look like they were from Benton or the West. If they were from anywhere, it was the East, or possibly even the other side of the Atlantic, Henry Devine thought.

"Why, hello, ladies!" the young lad said in confidence, full of eagerness. "Welcome to Benton Crossing!"

"*Guten Tag,*" the younger woman wearing lilac said, reflecting a heavy German accent.

"*Dankeschoen, junger Mann,*" the other one said as Henry hurried toward the coach.

Befuddled by his misunderstanding of what they were saying to him, Henry smiled with a bit of curiosity and quickly moved on to help the women with their bags, while they continued across the street, making their way to the only hotel in town located above the saloon.

From the roof of the stagecoach the second driver shuffled and lowered dusty baggage down to Henry on the ground. He swiftly brushed them with a mohair hand brush made of wood and flung them quickly onto a small cart. Henry then awkwardly struggled to pull the heavy cart behind him, while focusing on the ladies now off in the distance, entering the saloon.

JR pondered what was the reason for Germans visiting Benton from so far away. He was used to Germans in Pennsylvania, but he hadn't met any Deutsch women yet this far west, especially up in the high desert, at least not beautiful, educated women. Oh well, it didn't matter. The bounty of his incoming freight was on the back of the stage in a heavy steel chest. He moved on to the business thoughts at hand, removing himself from such curious distractions.

After handing the mail bag to JR, the two heavily armed stagemen moved to the rear of the stagecoach and proceeded to unlock a heavy chain and two very robust padlocks. They hoisted the heavy, vault-like container off the back of the coach and struggled to carry it from the road, up across the boardwalk and then straight through the front door. Taking a brief couple-second break, the men resituated their hands for a better grip and moved onward to a rear, separate area of the mercantile, moving behind the counter and through the doorway of an adjacent wall into the back.

The women had disappeared inside the saloon, so JR turned toward the mercantile boardwalk, grasped both Colton's and Cyrus's shoulders and led them into the building. He looked at Colton's stoic, yet handsome features. He always looked serious, even when he smiled. But that day JR noticed Colton looking particularly disturbed. Not wanting to stick his nose in another man's business he waved the men further inside.

"Go ahead and get what you men need. I have a list in the back, wired in from Morgan yesterday for supplies." He followed the men deeper into the mercantile, a large and dusty warehouse full of supplies, farm equipment, grains, homely merchandise, and other relics for sale.

"Hey, Colton, check this out!" Cyrus gestured toward an object JR could not see.

"Put that back down," Colton hissed.

JR was used to Colton snapping at Cyrus in jest, but that day he appeared stern and distracted.

"Who is that?" Cyrus asked, holding what JR could see as a photo frame.

"Mind yer own business and quit worryin' yerself," Colton said.

JR caught up with the two men and smiled, when he saw Cyrus holding the framed photo of Sarah. "That be my fiancée, boys! The most beautiful gal in all of the world, Sarah Devine. She also is young Henry Devine's here, his older sister. The family is from Pennsylvania, too, like me no less!"

JR stared down into Sarah's striking face, imagining her vibrant green eyes, high cheekbones, and thick, curly, light-brown hair in the black-and-white image. Cyrus had never seen a beauty quite like Sarah. Even enduring years of dust and frigid winters out West had made her no less delicate.

"She's a looker," Cyrus blurted out as he placed the photo frame back down on the counter.

Colton, who had disappeared a moment before, returned with a list. "Get these things for Morgan," he stated curtly to Cyrus. Then turning to JR, Colton said softly, "Hey, JR, has Sarah seen Wyola? Have you seen her?"

"No, Colton, I haven't," JR responded, slightly taken aback.

Colton's hushed tone caused JR to wonder if he shouldn't be more concerned.

"I'll ask Sarah when I see her this afternoon. If I do hear anything, I'll send you a telegraph on up to the mine," he promised Colton, hoping he would be able to deliver good news.

JR finished helping the men gather the supplies and instructed Henry Devine who was already breathing heavily, having just returned from the saloon, to scramble over to Colby Flowers to retrieve an open wagon for Colton and Cyrus. As Henry left the store, sweating profusely, JR turned the "Come On In" sign to "Closed." He looked outside the windows to ensure the German ladies and their stagecoach drivers weren't hanging around. He wanted to make sure nobody was watching, a precaution he usually took when handling other people's gold.

JR reached into his vest and produced a key from his pocket as he walked toward the back room of the store to inspect the steel-wrapped, wooden chest the stagecoach had just delivered. Colton and Cyrus were still perusing the aisles. He opened the chest, which contained dozens of small bags marked *Farmers and Merchants Bank*, each one locked with a small lock. He checked one of the bags and opened it to confirm it was filled with U.S. Gold Mint coins, before closing the chest and locking it again, just as Colton and Cyrus walked toward him.

JR straightened up. "You boys seem to have everything loaded."

The men nodded.

"Why don't you take this on out now and put it right behind the carriage bench in the middle?" JR said, gesturing toward the chest.

He liked that Colton and Cyrus didn't ask too many questions. One could never be too careful with a chest full of gold. The men struggled to heave the chest and maneuver it toward the back door, where hard working and hustling Henry was already arriving back with Colby Flower's horses and wagon.

"Here," JR said, holding a canvas and a chain he had brought from inside the shop. "Cover up the chest with this canvas." JR, with his long reaching arms, stretched over the side behind the buckboard to make sure the chest was securely in place and that the padlock was fastened tightly. "Now weave this chain through the lock and then through the buckboard springs." Colton and Cyrus looked at each other, and then at JR, and finally nodded. "Morgan's orders," JR clarified, seeing their confused expressions. "Here, now slap this other lock over the chain. Lock it tight. Drape the canvas over everything and tie it with that rope you got there, nice and tight. Yes, just like that. Great, now cover everything up with this last one." Colton and Cyrus double-checked that the locks were fastened tightly, draped the canvas over the back of the wagon, double layered, and then secured it tightly with the rope.

When the two men completed tying things down, JR exited the mercantile and approached them. "Ok, I want you boys to have Morgan be sure to send me a telegraph straight away, when you get on up to the mine. I'm gonna run in and check for any mail heading that way," JR said as he turned to re-enter the store. A moment later he turned back around. "I forgot, I had something for you boys."

JR went to the store's back office, shuffled around briefly inside and came back while sorting through a stack of mail inside a mail bag. He turned to Colton and then passed two individual letters to each of them, marked 'Colton Jaminson' and 'Cyrus David', respectively, which he had retrieved from the bag.

11

Reese could not shake a feeling of nervous excitement that bright autumn day. He knew big things were on the horizon, and he was excited to be a part of it all. Reese was on his way, on the two-day ride between the judge's ranch in Chalfant and Morgan's mine, accompanied by Judge Kensington and Rudy. They had left early Sunday morning from Kensington's ranch and rode alongside the road near Mineral Creek.

The main concern of the task was to keep a low profile, so they took the narrow road that was less traveled, in order to not be seen. They had camped out the night on the way and had made good time thus far. Eventually, the narrow road converged with the wide Benton Road into one road, leading up toward the Morgan mine operation near the Sherwin Meadows.

Reese was not due back at the mine until evening the following day, and he did not want word getting to Randall that he was making his way back up there earlier than expected. Reese was looking forward to the day's events. The judge was on a mission to go up to Morgan's mine, in order to claim what he believed was rightfully his.

After learning the news of Randall's potential for vast, growing profits, soon to be extracted from the new north vein, Reese had consulted with the judge, who had been a joint owner in the start-up days of the mine, before getting bought out by Morgan. The judge was a keen, yet shrewd businessman, and he was clearly about to miss an opportunity to see the mine for what it was growing to be worth, following this new discovery. Reese had appealed to the judge, all innocent, to see what he had to say about it.

"Judge," Reese had said over a quiet, midday drink at the saloon. "I reckon, Morgan's makin' a killin' up there soon. I got word that the new north vein will be bringin' in unexpected profits."

"Hmm, new north vein? You don't say," the judge murmured, leaning back into his chair.

"Yessir," Reese replied. "But it sure is becomin' a slippery slope with that Chinese worker's death. Morgan probably don't want nobody takin' a closer look as far as that's concerned. You know, an investigation could alert some unscrupulous fellows, such as ourselves, that there be gold in that there mine," Reese snickered.

"Some of that mine's profits are legally mine," the judge had told Reese. "If I don't sort it all out now Morgan will be the most powerful man in the county, and that ain't gonna happen. Some of that is stolen money, stolen from me. We never discussed any new north vein."

Reese, who had begun to consider the judge not necessarily a close friend, but more an exploitable mentor, was happy to oblige. He wasn't crazy about Rudy, but like many others he tolerated him nonetheless like a pathetic protege. Rudy was a lonely guy, and the way Reese figured, every one needed someone, sometime. But that's about as compassionate as Reese could be.

Reese, having now told the judge about eavesdropping on the mine and the profits expected that quarter, realized if there was a time to make his break, it was now, and it was with the judge. He also was a lazy giant, so he preferred Rudy's accompaniment as his gopher or laborer in crime. Labor was beneath Reese. He was a foreman in his mind, and anything other than that was a regression. Even if the position was by way of a fateful destiny, he was chosen by Randall for that position at the mine.

Now with that immigrant death business, things were threatening to get out of hand. The boy would probably still be alive, hadn't Reese, as Randall's foreman, cut corners in the construction of the tunnel's shoring. Plus, Reese in no way wanted Randall to conduct his own investigation of the events that went down up there, lest he discover his shoddy foremanship and terminate his job forever. In all reality, he had grown quite tired of Randall parading around so nicely with such humility, everyone admiring him for ethical "qualities as a man". Reese took it off its face, like he owned the whole valley. Maybe the judge's reinvolvement in the matter could clean up some of the worker's deteriorating attitudes toward Reese. Moreover, the judge promised him a hefty share of any profits from any venture they might enter into together. Good or bad, Reese could assist to tether the judge's way back into whatever agreement the two men had, back in the first founding days of the mine operations.

"I reckon Morgan doesn't pay you what's rightfully yours anyhow," the judge had said to Reese. "Greedy son of a bitch, if you ask me. If it were me in charge of those profits, I'd be sure you got more than your fair share. It's only right. You are the one keeping those heathen niggers and chinks all in line, earning Morgan those there profits."

"No sir, he doesn't," Reese mumbled in agreement as they were sealing their pact.

Back to his current mental thoughts, Reese refocused on the day at hand. As the three men were on their way riding, he expected they'd make it up to the mine by sundown. According to Rudy, the rest of the mining crew was down in Benton, or a day's ride from there over in Paradise or beyond that, down in Round Valley, Mill Creek and Rovana. Reese knew that Randall would be all alone at the mine that evening. It was the perfect time for a business pep talk to help Randall see reason. It was a crisp, sunny day, and the men had been riding for hours by now. Thus far they had remained low-key and out of sight of anyone along the way.

Just about the time they reached the point of the two main roads converging they observed two Indian riders on horseback, about a half-mile to their northeast, nearing the same intersection. They were coming from the wide Benton Crossing Road out of the north and heading for the fork in the road, an intersection with the road they were on, which led up the steep canyon to the Morgan mine. The judge and his accomplices quickly moved off the dirt road and down an embankment to the riverbank before they could be seen, remaining on their horses. They maneuvered to take a brief respite at the bottom of the hillside in a condensed grove of smaller aspen trees. This obscured their party from the dirt road, now adjacent and above them. There was a creek in the drainage they were hiding, named Morgan Creek. That irritated the hell out of the judge. "I can't believe I'm on my horse, hiding in a creek the town folk named after Morgan. What a farce!" the judge clamored under his very disturbed breath.

"Are you sure about this, Judge?" Rudy asked hesitantly, while looking at the judge. Realizing his foolish question, he retrieved a small flask from the inside breast pocket of his jacket and took a large swig.

The judge didn't answer. After knowing him for many years, Reese had concluded that the judge didn't like to speak, unless it was necessary. When he did talk he spoke slowly, emphasizing every syllable with his deep Southern drawl. Or he spoke in a complaint, as he had just done regarding the name of the creek. He had black, beady eyes and a round, plump face that had been whipped red by many years of riding in the wind, rimmed by a bushy white beard. The judge removed his hat temporarily to wipe his brow, revealing his balding and thinning white hair and shiny dome of a head.

"Rudy, shut up," Reese snapped as Rudy forced the cork back in his flask.

What a stupid thing to ask, Reese thought, uncertain as to why Rudy was with them in the first place. Rudy was half-drunk more than half the time. If anything, he was a wandering liability rather than an asset to any cohesive plan. The judge looked at Reese and then at Rudy, but suddenly his eyes shot quickly to the hillside.

Looking serious, he placed a fat finger in front of his lip. The hair on the back of Reese's neck stood up as he heard a twig snap, accompanied by heavy breathing that sounded like it was coming from a horse making its way down the same hill they just did, toward the creek. Reese looked toward the direction of the noise and saw a small, round face peeking at them through the grove of small, yet very thick aspen trees.

"You there," Reese yelled toward the figure. "Show yerself! I mean it! We're armed."

Reese breathed a sigh of relief, as a young man emerged from between the trees, now dismounted, and holding his hands up as a gesture of an uncomfortable greeting. Reese recognized him as Ardie Perseval, the local contracted mail courier rider for the Eastern Sierra route. He was well-connected to the town of Benton, particularly with Randall Morgan, JR Morrison and the mercantile, where mail was sorted and handed out for the area. Reese was certain he was making his way to the Morgan mine with a delivery, as the mine was where the road above them ended.

Why else would he be out here, so far from anything? Reese wondered. There were no other towns or outposts in that direction, so he knew there was a delivery with this rider destined for Randall in the carrier's mailbags.

"I know him," Reese whispered over his shoulder. "He's the local federal courier rider. He's married to Rachel Perseval and lives in Benton proper. We need to have a look into his bags. The only place he could be headin' from here is up to see Morgan, Judge."

Ardie, sneering, did not put his hands down. "Judge Kensington, it's me, Ardie Perseval. Yes, I'm delivering documents up to Morgan at the mine. I was just taking a break and watering my horse down here in the creek. You remember me? And yes," he said, turning to Reese, "I am Rachel's husband. We aren't in Benton any longer though. We are actually living over at the outpost at Lake El Diablo, you know, Randall's ranch. I mean, I'm away from home now for weeks at a time, making runs south, so it was best for Rach—"

"Ya, well, that's too bad now, Ardie. Was that your name?" the judge interrupted, speaking, as he shuffled his horse closer toward Reese's pony with Rudy following close behind. The judge's mouth was scrunched to the right as though preparing for the next, perfect response.

"Yes, that must be your name cuz you said it, ha! What am I saying?" The judge chuckled out as he elaborated toward Ardie. "Unfortunately …," he paused, "You're in the wrong place at the wrong time, young man."

The judge removed his pistol from his belt. Waving it in the air, he motioned for Ardie to come toward him. He then dismounted his horse. Reese wondered what the judge would do next. He didn't quite see the point in making a big deal of the encounter. There was nothing wrong with three men traversing through the wilderness after all. They weren't hurting anybody. Reese was certain he'd be able to talk his way out of this and they'd be on their way. Reese and Rudy dismounted their ponies and moved in alongside the judge.

Ardie released his reins. As his horse ducked in for a drink from the river, he moved closer to the three men. "Look, all I need is to be goin' on my way now, up to the Morgan mine. Randall's been waiting for these important documents I have, and I need to get on up there as soon as possible. If you don't let me go on right now, you know, you'll be obstructing a federal government mail officer, and I'm sure ya don't wanna do that. So please let me be on my way now, Judge Kensington." Ardie stood up straight and pulled on his horse's reins to move on.

Then in a manner of swiftness Reese had never observed executed by the judge in the past, the judge raised his pistol and struck Ardie in the side of his head with all his might. Ardie fell to his knees on the ground right in front of them, grabbing the side of his head, as blood raced between and through his fingers, running down the back of his hand to his forearm.

"What the—" Reese asked incredulously of the situation.

He had barely registered the first incident, but what happened next passed in front of his eyes before he could consciously process it. Ardie, still on his knees, looking down in a static daze at the dirt in front of him, his face twisted in disorientated pain, murmured, "Why?"

The judge, in surprisingly rapid, fluid movements, grabbed a larger, brick-sized rock with two hands. He raised his hands once more and brought it cracking down on Ardie's head, splitting the young man's head wide open. Reese looked at Rudy and then looked at the judge, who once again said nothing.

Rudy removed his flask once more and took a longer drink this time, pointing at Ardie, lying on the ground, and giggling slightly. "Look at you now, you dumb-ass mailman."

Rudy walked toward Ardie who was clearly unresponsive, positioned in a tripoint stance, knees and head. Blood dampened the dirt around him as it spilled from his skull. *Certainly a death blow*, Rudy wondered.

Reese, who considered himself to be a very logical man, was still trying to make sense of the series of events that led to the young, well-known boy lying dead before him. Reese couldn't make sense of what had just happened. *So much for keeping a low profile*, he pondered. He was beginning to second-guess his accomplices and this mission.

He scratched his head and turned to the judge. "What's up, Judge? Why'd you kill him?" Reese would've certainly handled the encounter differently, not because he particularly cared about Ardie, but he could sense that things were getting really messy. Reese took off his gloves and reached down, checking Ardie's pulse. "He's still pumping blood, Judge. He's still alive, sir!"

"He won't be for long. Now let's get going," the judge responded.

"I can't risk any knowledge of what we may be about to undertake here today," the judge said, returning to his steady drawl. "We don't need anyone knowin' that I am aware of this new north vein. I owe Morgan a reconveyance and a signature to a deed of trust I never gave him. Morgan, I know, was seeking a remedy, a solution that could be right here, in these here postal bags. If it's not, I'm sorry, Ardie … If it is, well, like I said, he was in the wrong place at the wrong time. I certainly do not need any witnesses to what may happen later on, today, up at that mine or any wisdom of who may have been up there when I force Morgan's hand."

Reese chewed his lip and looked up at the sun gleaming its way over the mountains. There was no changing the incidents of the past ten minutes. *Best to be proactive about the future*, he thought as he tucked his gloves into his gun beltline. At least there wouldn't be anything that could tie them to Ardie's mishap. This area was vast and dangerous anyhow.

"Where are those Indians headed?" he asked, changing the subject. "This road only heads up to the Morgan mine and beyond to Duck Pass. I can't imagine they'd be headin' to the mine. Maybe they were cutting the Sierra route through Duck Pass and the Deer Lakes Basin?" he uttered, as if talking to himself.

"We're about to go and find out," the judge said, flashing a smile. His gold back tooth caught the late afternoon sunlight, glimmering a beam of sun into Reese's eyes.

The men decided they should get going and moved in on Ardie's horse to get into the *mochila* placed over the saddle of the rider's pony, a type of bag the horsemen used when the pony express riders roamed the valley a decade earlier. The job was still a need in the region, but the dichotomy of the job description had morphed into a new type of rider and work requirement, a freelance sub-contractor of the federal government of sorts and federal mail courier. Rudy unharnessed the *mochila* from Ardie's saddle, dropping it at the judge's and Reese's feet. The pony began to stir, bucking up its front legs and stomping to break free.

"Woah," Rudy said, trying to calm the horse.

As Reese and the judge began rifling through the pouches of the mailbag, they suddenly heard a loud gunshot blasting from right behind them. The blast echoed its way up the soundless valley, over the running sounds of the river and breezes of wind slightly rustling the trees. Reese snapped his neck up only to see the pony drop instantly, half into the river, half-wedged into the aspen grove, with Rudy holding his pistol and looking stupid yet again.

"What the—" the judge yelled. "You stupid dumb ass. What the hell was that? Ya, let's let everyone within two miles know we are here!"

Rudy looked like a child who had been scolded by his parents. "Well, he was carrying on like it was the end of the world or somethin'. Thought he was gonna rear up and jump on yer head or somethin', Judge."

"So you kill a perfectly good pony?" Reese shouted, wondering again why they had brought this idiot along for such a delicate business task that had quickly turned ugly.

Rudy holstered his weapon and took another gulp from his flask. The judge looked at Reese, shook his head and redirected his attention to the *mochila* mailbag. Everything went silent once more. Birds chirped high in the sky as they quickly shuffled through the letters until they heard the soft click of a hammer cock. Reese turned right around.

It was Ardie, hunched over in pain, with a gun aimed in their direction. Reese jumped up, followed by Rudy and the judge. They attempted to draw their weapons but were too slow.

"Hold on, man," Ardie chuffed in desperation. "I'll shoot you dead." His voice strained, as though every syllable caused his throat to constrict. The left side of his youthful face was covered in blood, as a gaping, bloody hole was showing at the top of his head.

How is this man still alive? Reese thought.

"You can't shoot all three of us at once," the judge said, as though he was giving a Sunday sermon.

"No," Ardie gasped. "But I can shoot you first." He pointed his gun at the judge.

"Judge?" Reese looked at the judge for direction.

The judge smiled. "Now hold on, boys. This guy is tougher than I imagined. His brains are about to leak out of his head. Look at him! He still has gumption!"

"Why the hell did you try to kill me and shoot my horse dead, and why are you digging through them bags?" Ardie gasped in agony before he continued. "That there is U.S. government property, property I've sworn to defend with my life!"

"Well, I'd say yer doing a terrible job of that," Rudy smarted off.

Ardie slowly tried to get up, his breathing labored. He immediately fell back down, his pistol now wandering side to side. He moved the gun from the judge to Reese and then to Rudy, while having a difficult time holding his arm steady. Reese looked at the judge who took note and drew his weapon. Bam! Ardie fired first, missing the judge. The bullet ricocheted off a rock. Ardie's shot was followed a split second later by the judge firing a single bullet that hit Ardie directly in the right side of his throat. He fell back down, sideways this time, landing in the shallow part of the river beside him face down. Now he was surely dead or drowning.

Reese looked to his right to see Rudy on the ground. *Oh my!*

"He shot me!" Rudy yelled, curled into a fetal position, one hand covering a wound on his right thigh, while holding up his other hand with the bandaged finger he had injured at the saloon, two nights before.

"It's just a scratch. Man up," the judge said, delivering Rudy a scathing look, combined with a palm slap to the back of his head.

Reese, who was closer to Rudy, leaned over and took a look at the wound. It was just a graze on the right side of his leg.

"Get on up. It's nothin', you lady," Reese said, turning to the judge. "Judge, we got a big mess to clean up here. We need to head up to the mine."

The judge cackled. *Has he lost it?* Reese thought. He had never seen him anything but slow, cold and calculating. The judge refocused on the contents of the mail bag and pouches.

The wind started blowing mail all around when suddenly the judge blurted out, "Aha! This be it, a God-given miracle!"

Reese asked, bewildered, "Be what? Whatchya lookin' for, Judge?"

The judge dismissively waved his hand. "Never mind. Yer too dumb to know what I'd be talking about anyways, no offense! I already explained and apparently you weren't even listening! Let's get on up to that mine. I'll give you a proper education later. Grab the kid's rifle off that dead horse! And grab his pistol and gun belt too."

Rudy was still busy tending to his wound, while Reese asked, "We just gonna leave everything like this?"

"Why not? We got a plan," the judge snapped back at Reese.

"I'm not clear on your plan, but thinking we should be rid of this stuff," Reese insisted.

"Now what do you think you're gonna do with that horse, Reese? You guys continually amaze me with dereliction that is dumber than a doorknob sometimes. Rudy, get up and grab your damn flask. And since you scared away our horses and killed the other one we had here, why don't *you* go fetch our horses, so we can get the hell outta here?"

------- m -------

Colton and Cyrus had been on their way for most of the day, after leaving the mercantile in Benton, and were coming up Benton Road toward the fork of the two roads converging. From here it was the home stretch up to the Morgan mine.

"Woah. Woah!" Colton pulled the reins of the horse and slowed down the wagon, noticing something was shimmering off the side of the road, down the bank in the water of the river. It was nearly dusk and visibility was decreasing, driving his curiosity even further.

"Why are we stoppin'?" Cyrus questioned in a most disturbed way.

Colton raised his hand, hoping Cyrus would shut up. "I think I saw somethin' shimmerin' in the water just behind us. I'm going to take a leak and get a quick check on it," he whispered back, just as sarcastically.

"You gotta pee. Why didn't you just say so? Ha, sure there's a shimmering!" Cyrus complained, indicating they should get to the mine as quickly as possible.

Colton was in no mood to hear any of Cyrus's lazy excuses and stared him down with a sarcastic grin, pulling the wagon to a stop. "No, let's check this out. Saw somethin' down there, behind us, down by the creek. And I gotta piss anyway. Just go back to sleep!"

Colton dismounted the wagon, walked to the rear and then down the embankment to the water's edge, squinting his eyes to make up for the lack of visibility from the sun's rays reflecting off the water. *Is it just the water? No!* Looking closer through the glare, it was larger than it appeared from the road. *How in the world?* Colton wondered. Goose bumps developed as fear and adrenaline flushed over him, sending his hand immediately to grab a hold of his pistol handle as the object came closer into focus. It was a reined, dead horse with the brand of three painted hands on its hindquarter.

Colton looked around, pistol now out, to make sure that nobody was waiting to ambush him. Taking a look at the front of the horse, Colton noticed both of its front legs were broken, the shoulder bones protruding through the skin of its back. There was also a gaping hole in the top of its head, and the jaw was completely ripped off, dangling sideways by some skin and tissue. There were also two bullet holes in the side. It became obvious it was an Indian horse, since there was no saddle or branding on it other than the paint derived from the blood of a deer making the hand prints, with only a leather rein and a buckle around its neck. Colton surveyed the whole area as he unbuttoned his pants and took a pee. There wasn't a body anywhere.

While refreshing himself, he concluded in his mind it was a tragedy of some sort. He didn't see anyone and quickly scurried back up the bankside toward Cyrus, much faster than when he left. *Who would shoot a perfectly good horse?* Colton thought. *Was it sick? Why are its legs and face nearly ripped apart?*

"Well," Cyrus said, yawning, "What was it?"

"A dead horse," Colton said. "Actually, a shot-dead-and-ripped-apart horse, an Indian horse!" He climbed back onto the wagon and readied the reins. "Let's get out of here." It was an eerie sight, and Colton would rather put some distance between himself and that horse.

Seemingly unperturbed by the news, Cyrus said, "Hold on, man. Let's take a break. I'm tired." He rubbed his eyes with his dirty hands.

"What happened to getting up there as soon as possible?" Colton responded queerly.

Cyrus insisted he only needed ten minutes to rest a little and get refreshed. Colton agreed, as long as they could get at least a quarter mile away from the dead horse. They pulled up to a grassy knoll and stopped the wagon. Colton pulled out his canteen and remembered the letter JR had given him earlier, addressed to him. He opened it and within the fading daylight that was left, which created early evening shadows, the concerned man read the letter in his hands.

> *Colton,*
>
> *Wyola has been making her way back to the north. She is with the Toi Ticutta in the Washoe encampment now. My brother and our heroic chief, Numaga, contracted the white man's disease. There has been talk of rebellion from the people. Numaga is to ride out the winter on the Great Basin reservation to help their brothers near Toi Ticutta organize and then work to free their brothers down south at Ft. Tejon.*
>
> *Sincerely,*
> *Natchez Winnemucca*

Colton folded up the letter, feeling a strange mix of relief and anguish. He finally knew Wyola's whereabouts. He knew she was safe and would be in good hands with Peace Chief Numaga at the reservation. *But why has she gone without telling me first? And so suddenly?* Colton had to see her and find out what was going on. He would find a way. He was certain Randall Morgan would understand and let him leave the mine to go and see her.

Suddenly Colton jumped up, realizing he had to get to the mine before Randall turned in for the evening. He knew what to do. He would see Randall, deliver the chest and take off before sunrise.

"Cyrus," he said as Cyrus fell in and out of sleep, "Let's go. We gotta go now."

"All right, all right." Cyrus yawned, and soon the two men were on their way again, greeted by the rising moon and a purple sky.

12

Rudy had ceased complaining about his wound, no doubt thanks to the empty flask that dangled from his horse's neck. Reese retrieved a worn leather jacket from his saddlebag and put it on over his shirt. He watched the sun setting behind the mountain crest in front of their path and looked up to the sky. It was shaping up to be a dark night due to a large blanket of clouds, obstructing an otherwise starry sky, and it looked like it was going to rain sometime soon. The three men finally were close to arriving at Morgan's mine.

Reese, again felt in control of his surroundings, smiling in anticipation. The confrontation with Ardie had shaken him slightly, sideways. In Reese's opinion, anything that was off plan required a nimble form of adaptation, which he was uncertain someone like Rudy possessed. Quite frankly, he was still getting a feel for the judge. A lifetime of adaptation had taught Reese not to trust many others. He did trust the judge somewhat, unless money came between them. Yet Reese resented feeling subservient to men like him and Randall. If he were in charge, he had no doubt that things would be a lot better for him personally and run a lot smoother around town and the mine. Reese thought of himself in a warped sense and believing in his own narcissistic way that he remained a good and uncorrupted man. Maybe he had a little prejudice, harboring some superiority and control issues, but he considered himself relatively a good man who meant well and certainly meant well for himself, so to speak.

"Woah," Reese suddenly shouted, slowing down his horse.

He was quickly shaken out of his wandering thoughts as the threesome rounded a corner, finding themselves just two hundred feet away from two Paiute Indians riding their horses straight toward them. The two Paiutes were talking between themselves and hadn't noticed the three murderers approaching them. Reese immediately recognized one of the riders as Tahn-Se, Chief Natchez's right-hand warrior. They were no doubt returning from Morgan's mine. If that was the case, they apparently had not ridden on through to Duck Pass or Deer Lakes Basin, possibly for hunting deer, as the men believed earlier, when they saw the two near the crossing just before killing Ardie.

Reese continued riding at the front of the gang. He looked briefly behind him and made eye contact with Rudy, who seemed more nervous than drunk. He looked at the judge who gazed forward, a blank expression in his eyes. Reaching down, Reese put his hand on the handle of his pistol, just in case.

They strode closer to the Paiute Indian warriors, just a foot away from passing them completely. *Yes*, Reese thought, *the one on the left is definitely Tahn-Se.* He didn't recognize the other one. The two Indians looked directly at Reese, their backs arched in confidence. Their chins were raised high and their eyes scrunched in stern skepticism. Both wore long-sleeved deerskin ponchos and pants. His hand was still on his pistol as the groups finally passed one another. Reese's face remained fixed forward, but his eyes darted around, waiting for something or nothing to happen, as if the opposing cultures had crossed some strange point of no return, as the two groups of completely different backgrounds and heritage passed by each other on their horses.

Immediately after they had cleared the Indians the three men stopped, almost in unison. As if they were executing the physical orders of one shared brain they paused, looked at each other, and then looked behind them once more. The judge drew his gun and then Reese and finally Rudy. In a moment that flashed as quickly as a bolt of lightning across the mountain sky, they turned their horses and charged, full speed, toward the Indians. The three men rounded the bend in the road once more. The Indians turned around, looking startled. Reese felt the wind whip his face. He saw the Indians reach for their rifles, but before they could grab a hold of their weapons all three men had fired.

Bam! Bam! Bam! The gunshots rippled through the mountain air. Reese could not see where the bullets landed, but a moment later, both Indians had fallen from their horses and were on the ground. He looked at the judge, who in a blur of movement jumped off his horse and emptied his weapon into Tahn-Se, who was muttering something incoherent toward the sky.

"Throw 'em in the river. Get rid of them horses!" the judge yelled, moving with surprising speed once more.

They moved swiftly and silently, as though they were still separate limbs to a singular brain.

"Judge," Reese said, interrupting the flow, "What about Ardie?" One body on their hands was one thing, but with two dead Indians, people would wonder what had happened up here.

"Hold on, Reese. I was getting to that." The judge paused, thinking. "Get the quivers with the arrows. Wait! No! Just grab the arrows. Yes, yes. And we'll drape the bodies over their ponies, herd 'em over to the edge, and drive 'em right over the cliff, down into the river. If the ponies don't cooperate, shoot 'em, too. After we leave Morgan's, we're gonna put them arrows in Ardie and his horse on our way back south."

"Ha, I like it, Judge," Reese said, impressed.

The judge nodded. The momentum of the plan guided its ingenuity. "If anyone asks, we chased down the Injuns who killed the rider. We shot 'em and chased 'em over the edge, with their horses into the river."

The three of them gathered the two Indian horses and proceeded to execute the judge's orders. They heaved the two dead bodies by the arms and legs, draping them over the horses' backs. The men tied them loosely with pieces of unthreaded rope strands, just strong enough to hold human to animal until everything hit the water and rocks below. Once they steadied the bodies, the men ushered the horses toward the cliff and fired their guns. At the sound of the blast, with Rudy and the judge's horses blocking any possible escape, the Indians' horses were startled and ran just up to the edge of the high cliff.

Trying to turn and maneuver away, while being forced by the push of Rudy and the judge's ponies, the two horses errantly stepped backward in fear. Attempting to rear up on the hind legs in a last-ditch effort for survival caused them to lose their footing. Their rear hooves crumbled the edge of the loose, shaley soil at the top of the cliff, and they tumbled backward over the mountainous cliff to their deaths, thirty feet below. Their landing was only a few yards upriver from a huge waterfall, and a few seconds after impacting the water the horses washed over the fifty-yard-high fall, followed by the Indians' corpses.

It was almost dark by the time the Morgan mine became visible in the distance. The last half hour of the journey had passed silently, and Reese was feeling back on track. Killing those damn Indians wasn't so bad after all. Reese could justify things to himself. He was once a soldier from the South. He knew war. He knew of the many Indian wars. He could justify almost anything to himself by thinking back to all the injustice he witnessed, on both sides of the good and evil lines in the sand. Indians had done plenty of evil. That was his calming justification, better to have no witnesses than to leave anybody around who could start running their mouth off around the valley with rumors and innuendos. He felt satisfied, even proud of their cover story. All loose ends had been tied up. Plus, once they finished their plan he would be a rich man, a wealth he deserved in his heart of stone. Maybe he'd be so rich that he wouldn't need to be taking orders from the judge any longer, or anyone else, especially a mine owner with a lot of blessings and grace on his side, for that matter. Oh, how those words coming from Randall's mouth annoyed Reese beyond simple irritation!

At the swell house, Randall Morgan was getting ready to tend to some paperwork after a long and busy day. He had an arduous letter to write, and he couldn't quite clear his mind. Tahn-Se and his Indian friend had left about an hour before after riding up to the mine to speak to Colton and inform him of Wyola's whereabouts. Randall had explained to them that Colton was gone, but he would give him the message when he'd get back that night.

Randall sat down at the table, rubbing his tired eyes, as he started to write a letter to the family of the Chinese worker who had died in the mine collapse. It started hailing, and the wind began to blow, creaking the door to the swell house. He could hear the sound of millions of hail balls clacking against the wooden deck outside and the tin roof, random pieces hitting the glass window.

Crr-crack! A very close round of thunder, right with a flash of lightning, struck like it was directly over his shelter. Suddenly he heard the neigh and winney of horses and hooves approaching. *Colton can't already be back, can he?* Randall thought.

He grabbed his shotgun and walked to the door to see who was coming, hail pounding down with heavy rain all around him. The ground turned white in the sudden flurry of sleet and rain.

When the judge, Reese and Rudy reached the mine, they did nothing to obscure the incoming sound of their horses' hooves as they strode toward the swell house, getting drenched in the sudden rain.

Rudy yelled out to the judge, "I saw everyone in town this weekend, and as far as I could tell, Morgan is alone up here, Judge."

Sure enough, as they approached a light turned on from inside the house. The door opened as the three men remained mounted on the horses, completely oblivious to the rain and sleet, focusing on Randall coming out as their objective. Rain was pouring off all their hats and running down their pommel slickers. It was as evil-looking as it could get.

Randall looked solemn and confused when he opened the door, ice balls bouncing off the wooden planks in front of him. He was dressed in pony pants, hanging suspenders and undergarments. Exhaustion lined his sunbaked face, the thick diffusion from the elements falling from the sky obscuring his once-handsome features. A suntan line circled his forehead from his hat he wasn't wearing. As if he did hear them coming, he held a rifle, wearing a mixed expression of familiarity toward the sudden arriving men and confusion at their untimely presence. It was clear he hadn't been expecting any guests. It was obvious who it was, and Randall could imagine what they were packing under that rain gear.

The three men all threw their slicker and under frock to the side, affirming to Randall, they were carrying arms. They abruptly approached the front door, mounted atop their steeds, a dark and imposing sight to Randall as they rode themselves right up onto the deck and under the roof of the porch. The horses' hooves splashed the pooling water, trampling muddy waters flowing down the slope across the deck in front of Randall's door, with an intimidating threat of harm.

Morgan, standing at his door that was now fully open, cocked his weapon and addressed the men, as if he knew there was no good thing they could have possibly been there for. To not show counter hostility, he set the butt stock end of his rifle to the floor while holding the barrel, inquiring, "Judge, you're more than welcome to come up onto the deck with your horse and get on outta the rain."

"Reese, what are you doing here?" He turned to Reese, whom he knew best, and then toward Rudy and the judge. "And why are you with them? You're not due back 'til tomorrow."

"Never mind now, Randall," the judge interrupted, his hands crossed, holding reins, and resting forearms on his saddle horn, while restraining a Spencer rifle laying across his saddle, tucked tight against his belly. "I'm here to be discussing some business with ya, Randall."

The judge was considerably shorter than Randall but nevertheless seemed like a giant upon his horse in this crappy weather, crowding in under the roof of the porch. Randall's typically genial facial expression turned cold. His tired eyes narrowed. He straightened up, remembering his height. He glared at the water pouring off the judge's hat.

"Now what business would I possibly have to be discussin' with you now, Kensington?" Randall's voice turned cold as he turned to Reese again, evidently hoping his right-hand man would have some answers for him. "Reese, what are you doin' here?"

Randall turned to stare down Rudy while talking to Reese. "Why did you bring this drunkard of a man 'round my place for? Now I'm not goin' to ask you again. Whatchyu' with these men for?" Randall tightened his one-handed grip around the barrel of his rifle, raised the butt from the floor and secured the gun in both hands.

"Why, that's mighty disrespectful there, mine owner Morgan," Rudy spouted sarcastically, taking off his hat and bowing his head at Morgan, reacting to the move Randall had made with the rifle, while acknowledging his previous statement in the same breath.

The judge kicked the side of his pony and stepped the horse up further onto the wooden deck, making himself even bigger to Randall. His horse stomped a hoof, which got the judge smiling. "What are you gettin' all worked up for now, Randall? I've come here friendly-like. You know, we've had some unfinished business for years, and I think it's about time we settle it up."

Randall seemed genuinely trapped in a memory. He looked at Reese who averted eye contact. Then he beamed his eyes back at the judge. He was looking for an answer, since nobody would explain. "The only unfinished business we have, is that you never gave me my reconveyance for the deed to my mine, years ago, when you were too lazy to work it any further, wanted no more of it!"

"Now wait a second," the judge said, still smiling. "Why you gettin' all hostile for now, Randall?"

"Well, the way I remember it, I bought your half, at your request, Judge. You wanted out for a thousand dollars. Did I not give you a thousand dollars?" Randall, now highly aggravated, questioned.

"Well, that's actually why I came on up here, Randall. I wanted to sit down and talk about that very subject, Randall." The judge continued, "Ya see, that's not exactly the way I remember it. I remember loaning you a thousand dollars, and I'm here to collect that money. From what Reese has been sharing with me, you seem to have stumbled upon quite a find up there, in our shared mine claim. The new north vein, ring any bells? I'm just here to see my half and how it's become profitable it seems. Seems you might now be owing me a lot more than a thousand dollars now, Randall." The judge leaned in, and water poured from his hat all over Randall's feet, splashing it into his house.

"Now wait a second!" Randall exclaimed.

"Boss man," Reese interrupted in his deep, long-drawn-out drawl, hoping to negotiate some sense into the argument. "I'd hear him out now. You should let him finish."

"Well, if I sold him anything as he is claiming, I certainly don't remember any conversations about any north vein." The judge further motioned.

Randall fixed his glare at Reese, trying to figure out what was going on at such a late hour, and then crescendoing with every word, "Why are you here, Reese? For this? Is this yer doin'? You put him up to this?"

"Now Randall, that's no way to talk to our workers now, is it now, boys?" the judge remarked arrogantly, backing his horse off the deck and looking at the two men in the process. In his eyes, these were *his* men.

"Wait a second. I see now," Randall extended. "Reese done told you there was some kinda thing up here. And you, being so lazy, didn't wanna stick around here and work this mine. You took a thousand dollars from me for your half and walked away. You think yer just gonna waltz right back on up here, on your own merit, and take that claim back?"

Randall pointed his finger at the judge in anger. "I ain't ever gonna have a change of heart on that, Judge. You walked away! Took a thousand dollars from me to do so, and any court will see you ain't put a nickel of blood, sweat or money into this here mine or into the wages of these here men. Now, workin' here or not workin' here. North vein or no north vein." Looking at Reese and the judge, he continued, "Any worker over the past year who worked here, is gonna attest, you ain't … you ain't never even been up here in a year!"

"I wouldn't be too sure of that now, Morgan, boss," Reese poignantly bounced back at him, while cleaning his fingernails with a seven-inch-long bowie knife he had taken out of his saddlebag.

It was finally his chance to say things the way he'd seen them. The judge was right after all. They went into the mine business as partners, and the north vein had never been discussed in their original settlement. Reese had nothing to concern himself with about right or wrong. Randall should have never allowed this day to happen. *Ya, it is his fault. His own doing*, Reese arrogantly pondered.

"Well, I'm done with this conversation," Randall yelled, exasperated at the judge. "I have documents that say I own this mine now, regardless of you reneging on our agreement and never givin' me my reconveyance. I got me plenty of witnesses to that fact. I got a government man on his way here as we speak, deliverin' me them very judgment papers!"

The tension was growing. Rudy had no more liquid in his flask and instead occupied himself by nodding at the judge's every word and saying "yea" or "very true, Judge." He practically giggled with mirth. It was dark outside, except for a small lantern hanging in the doorway to the swell house, but Reese could still see a flash of white as Rudy smiled at the judge's nod in his direction and brandished a folded stack of papers from within his breast pocket.

"He must be meanin' these here papers, judge?"

Randall's eyes widened, as he, in a confused state of mind, saw the thick brown file of folded papers in Rudy's hand.

The judge nodded. "Yup. Those be them papers. And the way I see it, he's gonna be signing 'em over to me and gettin' back to our agreement, working this here mine, if he be wantin' no trouble for his workers, Indians, or women for that matter, down at that god-awful outpost he calls a ranch. Now I'm done talking about it! Let's get this paper signed here, Randall."

The judge's eyes narrowed. "I don't think you really know what I'm capable of doin'. I am the county seat. You ain't gonna have any say in my court, and this thing will be over before it even gets started. Now, I recommend that you sign this certificate and deed of trust, or I'll be forced to implement my laws, right here, right now!" He took another step forward up onto the deck with his spirited horse, puffing his chest out once more and straightening his hat with his left hand, sweeping the water from the brim with his flattened, left hand. His right hand rested on the stock of his cross-saddled rifle.

Randall clasped his rifle as his palms slid closer to the trigger. He teetered toward Rudy, craning his neck for a closer look at the papers. Reese had never seen him look so terrified, and he didn't want this to get much more heated. *That would not be good for me*, he figured.

"Where," Randall said slowly, as though the realization rolled over him like clouds across the Sierras. "Where's Ardie? How'd you get those papers? Rudy, come on now. How'd you get them papers?" His head swiveled around, looking back and forth between all three of the now villainous and evil, murderous men. "What did you men do?"

"Don't be a fool, Morgan. Do as the judge says!" Rudy arrogantly mocked.

"Where's Ardie, Judge? What did you do? Give me them papers! Now, Rudy!" Randall lifted his rifle and aimed it at the judge, screaming, "Give me them papers! Give me them papers now!" The corners of his mouth quivered in fear, yet wrangled with anger.

Reese wasn't sure. The judge jumped back, yelling, "Woah, woah, woah. What do you think yer—"

BA-BANG! was the sudden sound of a percussion cap, igniting a simultaneous instant gun cylinder powder blast.

The cold, wet, and late fall night was instantly interrupted by the loud gunshot blast that reverberated and echoed throughout the vacant camp and surrounding mountains before bouncing back, to be heard again and again, over and over, in what seemed like an eternity.

At that instant Long Valley changed forever.

The only sound to be heard was the fading echo as the rain, running off the roof and pounding on the ground, diluted the reverberation into history, as the horses' hooves cracking the wooden deck became amplified. It was as if these tones were the only sounds left in the world.

Randall dropped like a bag of beans to his knees, slumping over onto his forehead, the rain turning red all across the wooden deck and out onto the mud, under the dancing hooves of the evil men's ponies. Reese spun around while Rudy let out a cowardly half yelp.

"I tried to tell him!" Rudy exclaimed, still holding his pistol. At the speed at which Rudy could think half-drunk, he suddenly changed from coward to a hero in his tone and held back his grin from going ear to ear.

Randall was on his knees and forehead like a surveyor's tripod, in almost the identical position as Ardie was left. Then just as suddenly as he had been shot, he let out a low, liquid-sounding growl and flexed straight forward, causing his torso to plane out, as if extending in some kind of spasm, facedown. Now protruding half on and half off the deck, resting flat on his face in the mud and pouring rain, between the judge and Reese's horses, it was not a poised ending for such a graceful and very loved man. Blood washed down the road below the horses' torsos, like small tributary rivers being diluted in the still-falling rain.

For being such a drunkard Rudy sure had a quick draw. Reese fumed, feeling the anger rise to the top of his head. *Who does Rudy think he is, shooting Randall without orders from the judge or I?* He lunged at Rudy, grabbing him by the shoulder until Rudy turned around to face him. Reese, standing nearly a foot taller than Rudy, looked deep into his blank, dark eyes.

"What the hell did you do, Rudy? You hot-headed trigger finger!" Reese did not let go of Rudy, whose stupid, drunken smile turned into a little, scared-boy frown.

For Reese, he couldn't believe it. The day's surprises had thrown him for a loop, turn after turn, certainly, but he did not expect the confrontation with Randall to end in yet another death.

The town would be upset about the death of Ardie, and not too many whites would miss the Indians, but Randall was the town hero, the biggest employer in all of Benton and Long Valley. Reese, who had just worked his way to the top of Randall's organization, suddenly found worry in himself. He was standing on the precipice of losing it all. He'd have to live on the run now, for sure. He would clean up at the mine and leave, go south to Mexico maybe, or just do something different than this.

If only I could get my share of the judge's mine claim money first, he thought. *But how am I going to do that?* He had no paper and no title. He had nothing but rocky ore in a mine shaft that he had to dig out to get. Maybe a couple pieces laying around the swell house here and there, but nothing worth killing a man over. He had to remind himself, a man he didn't kill, but who Rudy had killed. *Ya, that's it. The fact will always be that Rudy killed him*, Reese thought, *not me!*

Rudy stammered, wincing at the pain from Reese, still squeezing his left shoulder, pleading, "He was gonna shoot ya, Judge, and, and … I'm skittish as hell after all the killing we done today. I panicked. I pulled the trigger. He's dead now. Ain't nothin' he's gonna do now, Judge?"

The judge didn't move. He continued to stare at Randall's lifeless body. The judge's left hand rested on the back of his neck, his right still holding the bridge of his cross-saddled rifle. Reese waited for him to scream at Rudy, or better yet, to shoot Rudy. It was the judge's moment after all, and Rudy had completely spoiled it. And then it dawned on him. With Randall being dead, the judge was now the undisputed owner of his share of the mine. *Morgan is dead. Who is going to dispute the judge making that claim now? We must destroy all evidence of murder*, he calculated.

The judge, perturbed himself, said in his measured tone, "Rudy, you are about as dumb as a box of nails, I do declare. It wasn't his time yet!" Then suddenly changing tone and course, he continued. "Well, it ain't no horse now or an Indian—that's for sure—or a Mexican horseman who looks like he's from Saudi Arabia," the judge clamored, referring to Ardie's appearance.

"Get on down there and see if he's still alive." The judge looked at Rudy who dismounted, walked around to the front of his horse, bent over and grabbed the brown hair on Randall's head. He lifted the head, arching Morgan's prone and extended body backward, to see if he was completely dead.

"Oh, he be dead. Shot him in the face, I reckon. Can't believe I aimed such a good shot with a broken finger and all! Right in the eye!"

The rain partially rinsed Randall's face of mud and blood, while Reese calmly added, "I'll say Rudy, you're one crazy son of a bitch!"

Rudy dropped Randall's head with a splash back down into the mud.

"Right, Reese, we all know that," the judge concurred and dismounted his horse, seemingly unfazed by such an abrupt and deadly end to his and Randall's conversation or past relationship. He gestured the two others toward the swell house. "Let's get him inside. We're gonna have to burn this place to the ground now."

Reese, already at the door, saw the judge smile slightly, evidently pleased with the new plan that introduced a little more confidence into Reese's mindset. The judge entered the structure, moved to a side wall and opened the door, stepping into a small hallway that led to Randall's study. The judge turned around and gestured at Randall's body outside, signaling that Rudy and Reese should pick up the corpse. With another awkward heave the two men followed, careful not to get blood on their boots or clothing. After all, it was draining out of Randall, spilling everywhere, with all the water and blood soaking his body.

Reese was surprised to see the judge acting so casually. *It only takes a man with slightly more brains than Rudy to put these pieces together,* he thought. Trusting, not just hoping the judge had some genius way of getting them all out of this situation, created the thought in him that it would be a plan that made him richer than he'd ever anticipated becoming in his life. Anything good coming out of this day was going to have to be a devil's miracle, which would definitely be fruitfully worth all the grief he had just been put through, by none of his doing.

Randall's office was a small, cozy room with a wooden desk, a chair and a small fireplace in the corner. The judge shuffled about with added zest, rifling through the papers lying on the desk. Reese and Rudy finally set Randall's body down in the center of the room on the hearth rug next to the fire.

"Rudy, be sure you put a lot of wood over his body. Move the table over him. We need to cook that corpse like a side of beef, burnt to the bone!" The judge picked up the papers from Randall's desk. "Here," he said, holding them in his outstretched hand. "Throw these papers down there. Throw this rifle down there too. We can make this look like a suicide."

"How Judge?" Reese asked.

"He couldn't take it anymore," the judge said, while continuing to rummage through Randall's things. "A kid dying and such in his mine, and it being his fault. The guilt. The paperwork. I had the papers to his mine. That's what it was. It was simply too much guilt. So he shot himself with his own rifle and burned his own house. That's the problem with a soft heart, the way I see it. Too much guilt," the judge laughed, pausing. "Or maybe it was them Indians. They came up here and robbed Morgan and we saved the day! No, ya, that's what it was." the judge spewed out of his contorted and evil mandible.

He picked up the last letter Randall had been drafting and started reading a short bit of it. "Well, I'll be stupefied. We will just leave a mystery for the world to solve. Ya see, right here, he couldn't deliver this. It was far too much for him? Let's get some water on this one. Umm. Wait! We'll leave this one with the quill out in the barn. Ya. Hang a noose over a beam like he was gonna hang himself, but he was such a coward that he thought the gun was a faster way. How are they ever gonna prove that didn't happen?"

Rudy pulled out yet another item from his breast coat pocket, a box of matches. "All right, boys," he said. "Let's torch the place!"

The judge exited the room through the front door, grabbing the lantern off the front porch as he readied to throw it into the building. An evil pride of his own dominance came over him as he observed, with the devil's eyes and heart, his own two accomplices preparing the body and room for total destruction. Blinded by their own greed and a cold-blooded obedience to his command, they performed the evil task, just as they were instructed by him to do. This was evil of the most impure kind.

13

Colton heard the unmistakable sound of a gunshot send rippling, subsequent echoes, racing through the thin, cold night air. It had started to rain heavily. Cyrus, who had been slumped over in the wagon, sleeping from a long day's journey, slowly awakened as the raindrops hit his face. He bolted upright like lightning, in an instant, at the sound of the gunshot.

"What, huh? Little late for target practice, don't you think, Colton? What could that be … or who?"

Colton nodded, giving rein to the horses. The noise had startled him, too, recognizing its volume sounded close. Without hesitation, he whipped the reins. "I concur. Let's get on up there and check it out. Sounds like it came from up near the mine camp! Hyaaa!" He pressed into the buckboard, driving forward. "Maybe someone was just shootin' a coyote, or something," Cyrus clamored.

They neared the last stretch of the road leading up to the Morgan mine, a steep, narrow path, surrounded by tall, red fir trees, looming like dark-shadowed giants, closing in all around them. Colton spurred the horses on to push through the final ten minutes of the journey. They weren't used to pulling such a heavy wagon up a muddy, uphill slope at this speed.

Finally the thick tree coverage cleared, and the swell house broke
into their view about two hundred yards ahead. Oil lamps were radiating
a pulsating light, illuminating a figure exiting the front door who
was holding a long rifle in their right hand. Colton, remembering the
dead horse and the rest of the day's strange events sensed immediately
something didn't feel quite right. For one, from what little he could see,
the figure looked considerably shorter than Randall and walked with a
slight limp. In the pitch-black darkness, he pushed forward to within
one hundred yards, needing to get a closer look to be sure, but without
drawing any attention to themselves. He elbowed Cyrus to make sure
he was awake, glancing over to notice he did have his rifle nearby in
the scabbard and was now wide awake and attentive.

They neared the swell house as the dirt path evened into a flat,
open area. To their right were a small barn structure and a fence that
usually kept the horses penned up. It was mostly empty. Only a few
of Randall's horses remained, as they should have been that "off of
work" day, Colton pondered. Then he saw the figure walk into the area
covered by the light once more.

"It looks like Rudy," he blurted out under his restrained breath,
now elbowing Cyrus to come to attention.

As if to reach for his rifle first, then moving into a sub conscious
self debate, Cyrus decided to instead unholster and check his pistol's
chamber first to see if it was ready to go as well, but unfortunately
it wasn't. Due to the rain, the men hadn't loaded their cap and ball
revolvers yet. Cyrus reholstered his pistol, then reached for his Henry
Yellowboy rifle from the scabbard, which was fastened to the side of
the wagon and was fully loaded.

Now closer, they both acknowledged each other, mirroring each
other's grin, confirming the awkward swagger of the town drunkard.
The two men had seen him two days earlier waddling around Benton
with his broken finger, following their encounter at the saloon.

Colton did have his pistol, although unloaded, which he was
wearing under his slicker and concealed from the rain.

Due to the humidity, this type of pre-centerfire cartridge weapon could have gotten moisture in it, causing the cylinder cartridge gunpowder to misfire. Colton knew this, but he also knew it was the only six-shot weapon he had.

Rudy held his rifle low in his right hand, stepping back into the swell house with a labored walk, as though his leg had also been injured at some point over the past couple days. Colton wondered, *what is he doing at Randall's? And how did he get up here?*

With great care, slowly rolling forward in their wagon and keen to remain sheltered by the darkness, Colton stopped the horses, pulling the wagon brake softly, realizing the light at the cabin would make it difficult for Rudy to see outward.

He immediately withdrew his pistol and started to load it, pouring powder into the individual chambers, careful to not get the handgun wet. He then loaded lead balls into each cylinder cartridge by cartridge and made his weapon ready to fire.

Uncertain if Rudy had noticed them through the darkness, he saw three horses at the front porch of the swell house. He knew Randall didn't allow any horses tied there. Randall hated horse manure in front of his residence.

Colton said, "I have a weird feeling 'bout all of this. Let's put the wagon and the horses behind the barn and go inside, around and through the back, to spy what's goin' on. It doesn't appear he saw us, and I certainly hope he's not up here for some sort of revenge on me for what happened at the saloon, but why would he ride nearly a full-day ride from Benton," he questioned, "All the way up here and be coming and goin' out of Randall's house? That shouldn't be."

Both men knew Randall very much disliked Rudy, especially when he fell into the bottle, after he started courting his daughter Marcia.

"Something no good is up, Cyrus," Colton said, now handing the reins over to Cyrus. He turned around and retrieved his own, single shot Kentucky Rifle from behind the wagon's bench and gently released the brake. He then gestured with his hand for Cyrus to roll forward as he loaded the single shot firearm with a single round. As the wagon creeped ever so slowly forward, Colton signaled to turn right, between where the barn was attached to the barbed wire fence.

"Quickly, Cyrus," he whispered.

The two men quietly jumped down from the wagon while remaining in the shadows of the barn. They silently fastened the horses to a post, so they would remain secure and out of sight. There were no lights near the barn, but thankfully some of the clouds had cleared after the rain stopped, and a bright moon allowed Colton to see the path in front of him. He looked at Cyrus, whose eyes once heavy from exhaustion, remained widened in a militant alertness.

"Colton," Cyrus whispered, "I don't know if I like this. What business does Rudy have up here? Randall said nothin' about that."

"I know," Colton agreed. "Let's head around the back." He knew Rudy to be a volatile drunkard. It was better to take him by surprise than announce their arrival.

They moved away from the barn and were once again in clear sight of the swell house. Colton took a step and heard a twig snap beneath his boot. It was otherwise completely silent. Even the horses had gone quiet. Colton's eyes fixed upon the swell house's front door entrance, searching for any additional signs of movement. The mud was mucking to their boots with the squishy, sticky sounds of wet clay.

Suddenly there was a gunshot blast coming from inside the building. Colton crouched immediately and quickly steadied his weapon. The front door swung open so violently that it collided with the wooden panels on the side of the porch. Three figures jumped out in unison. Before Colton could identify their faces, he felt his conscious brain leave and his body take over as he felt himself drop to the ground, just as a sudden, cacophonous burst of more gunfire erupted toward them.

Everything happened so fast, yet Colton somehow felt like he was watching it all in slow motion. The figures ahead became shrouded in moonlight, lantern flickers and gun smoke. Colton felt a deep pain in his right leg. *Have I been hit?* He heard Cyrus yell in shock or pain and drop to the ground next to him. *Has he been hit too?*

The clouds had moved over the moon once again, and Colton could barely see a thing, but the gunfire continued. Rounds were striking the mud all around them. He thought he saw Cyrus crawling to his right. *He must be heading to the barn, toward the horses.* Before he knew what he was doing, Colton, still on the ground, dragged himself to his left. He was close to a patch of trees and bushes that covered a small cliff to the left of the swell house. The gunfire continued. Colton thought, rather hoped, that he was out of their line of fire. The pain in his right leg was intense, and he could instinctively tell the wound was deep.

Have they moved? Where is Cyrus? The gunfire ceased. Colton strained his eyes in the silence and darkness of the night, seeking Cyrus.

"Cyrus," he whispered loudly, once, and then again, in the direction he saw him scramble for cover. There was no reply.

Colton dragged himself through the dirt, the clumps of melting hail balls, and muddy sloth toward the barn, and there Cyrus was, laying on his back in the mud. It started to rain again, and the rain was hitting his face, but his eyes were wide open. Colton checked his pulse. Cyrus was dead. Colton, now desperate, turned to crawl away, his leg still on fire with pain. He dragged himself toward the river, bumping and crawling through seedling pines as he went. If he couldn't run, he could at least try to walk. He fought fatigue and exhaustion, finally rolling down a small hill that he knew eventually dropped off toward the river and the falls below. Colton pulled off his belt and in the near-pitch darkness began to press gently on his leg to identify the location of the bullet wound. Wincing, he tied the belt around the hole in his leg, which applied pressure to help stem the flow of the blood leaking from his body. It was a good stream. Fear came over him as he realized the gravity of his wound. Colton searched for his long gun but couldn't see it anywhere. He must have dropped it when he got hit. He pulled out his pistol, saw it was drenched in mud and water and would be of no use now.

"Colton," a crisp, clear voice rang so loud that it sounded as though a megaphone was directed toward his ear.

Colton winced. He had heard that voice before. *But where?* He felt dizzy.

"Col-ton," the singsong voice called once more.

Then it dawned on him. It was the judge, the man who paraded around in a free state acting like a slave owner. He didn't know how he remembered, but somehow he did. Colton's vision went blurry. He could not pinpoint where the voice was coming from in his delusional state of consciousness, other than it was close and above him as he was clinging to the steep bank just above the river.

"Yer buddy Cyrus is lyin' up here, nearly dead in the road. Now what do you think you're gonna be able to do, Colton, to help your cousin from dying over here? I'm pretty positive I hitchya. I know I hit him. I'm staring at him, Colton, and he's gurgling his own blood and all."

The judge rambled further, "Look, we've got you surrounded. Give yourself up. We won't hurt you! In fact Colton, I'll actually tend to any wounds you might have and help ya get back to town, young man. Your cousin here, looks like he ain't gonna make it. You really should get over here and help him. I mean, he is yer cousin and all."

Colton said nothing but remained frozen and still, lying vertically against the slope. He then slowly slid down carefully, to the edge of the river, then into it. His legs grew numb in the ice-cold water as he pressed his body against the side of the embankment of the Morgan creek, flowing through the camp. He knew his cousin Cyrus was already dead, and the judge was lying in order to get him to blow his cover.

"If you think I'm lying," the judge continued, as though he had read Colton's mind, "I'm not. Reese, Rudy, bring that fool's body here."

Reese? Reese is there too? Colton heard a shuffle, a heave, and what sounded like a heavy object being dragged through the mud and then dropped.

"Let's see, he's wearing a tan hat and, uh, a green shirt underneath his frock coat. And what's this? Hmmm, looks to be a letter in his pocket that's addressed 'Cyrus David.' Looks like it's a letter here from lovely Lola Everest. Would ya look at that? Ya know, Colton, that's my girl. What does this here nigger think he's gonna do with one of my working girls now, Jaminson? That is your last name? Haha! Colton Jaminson! Now, where on God's good earth did you acquire such a ridiculous name like that? That certainly ain't no nigger name, Zimbabwe." The judge attempted to anger Colton more and lure him out of hiding, but to no avail.

Oh my God! Colton wanted to scream and kill this man right then and there, but the sound did not leave his throat. His mind was playing tricks now. *No, it can't be.* Cyrus was dead, and he wouldn't be convinced by the lying judge that he was still alive, no matter how much he wanted to believe it. What he really wanted to do was grab anything he could, charge the judge and beat his brains out. But he had nothing, no rifle or a functioning leg. He felt anger, hatred, confusion, and fear, all simultaneously swelling up inside of his heart and soul as though he had swallowed a hot coal.

Soon Colton had no idea where anybody was, nor how much time had passed. He'd lost a lot of blood. *Am I going to die right here, right now?* he pondered. *Have I fallen asleep? Did I just wake up?* Time was an illusion. He was now freezing cold. He hung somewhere between alertness and unconsciousness as the bullet hole in his right leg began to throb even more. He slowly began releasing his grip on the branches at the riverbank's edge, his torso now sliding further down the embankment deeper into the water. In a desperate move for survival, he released himself from the edge and got captured by the stream's current, rushing at a high rate from all the rain, as he let himself sink fully into the cold, frigid water. He didn't want to die, so he reached out again for the branches along the creek, stopping himself slightly downstream to observe. Soon thereafter, using lanterns, the judge,

Reese and Rudy were combing the riverbanks as they searched up and down the embankments in the darkness, with no success.

"Judge, I think he got away, and we gotta find him, don't we?!" Rudy questioned, more of himself than of the judge.

Fanning his rifle, he shot continuous rounds into the river until the weapon was empty, a couple bullets striking the water very close to where Colton was clinging to the embankment. Click, click, click, with the firearm empty, a fanatic Rudy threw down the rifle, reached under his slicker and whipped out his pistol. He began pulling the trigger, randomly aiming and emptying the remaining rounds from the handgun into the river to the sound of click, click, click, yet again.

Rudy had no more bullets and no more guns. He moved to grab the judge's weapon. "We can't let him get away, Judge. He saw me, Judge."

"Cease fire, Rudy," the judge irritatingly responded, pushing his hand away. "He ain't gettin' too far. With this much rain, he is done for. The falls will get him downstream, if we didn't already. Reese, gather our horses, in case anyone else shows up unannounced. Let's get this place burned to the ground and get the hell outta here."

"Sure, boss," Reese acknowledged as Colton heard him stomp off. Just then it started to rain, hail, sleet, and snow again, this time harder, as thunder and lightning roared, echoing thru the canyon.

Colton clung to the side of the embankment until he couldn't hold on anymore. The stream turned into a river torrent, and he was far too weak to hang on any longer. His right leg had gone completely numb from the loss of so much blood and the freezing-cold water. His teeth began to chatter violently. He felt his eyes grow heavy as he closed his eyelids momentarily. Everything started to feel like a dream, and he was also absolutely exhausted. For a brief moment, Colton wondered if he was back at the saloon, waking up before the crack of dawn, full of anticipation to see Wyola once again. He felt himself drifting away, literally, down what was now a river. The thought of letting everything go to sleep was too tempting.

Wyola. Colton smiled at the thought of her as he was bobbing and floating along. He felt like he was late for something important. He had somewhere to be. But where? He didn't know. Exhaustion hit him like a rolling wave as the tide seemed to pull him firmly away and closer to the edge of the falls. He batted a blurry eye toward the dark sky and felt tears slide down his cheeks. Colton let himself go, and everything went black.

—〰—

The rain was torrential and became stronger as the judge, Reese and Rudy walked back to the swell house, soaking wet themselves.

"What should we do with this body?" Rudy inquired, gesturing toward Cyrus lying in the mud.

The judge knelt down and picked up Cyrus's guns.

As he did so, Rudy was exasperated. "Looks like they have a wagon tied up over there, between the barn and the fence," further pointing out a potential problem. He walked over to the wagon and pulled the tarp aside, muttering to himself, "Now, what do we have here?" He exposed the chest, chained securely to the wagon. "Judge, Reese! Check this out!" Rudy yelled out over the thunderous downpour.

The judge paused and walked over, followed by Reese. Both their faces lit up at the sight of the chest. Reese drew his weapon and jumped onto the wagon as Rudy and the judge stepped back. Following three shots from Reese's rifle, the lock of the chain finally broke. They heaved the chest off the wagon and carried it into the house.

The men set the chest down onto the floor, near Randall's dead body and the heavy table in the middle of the room. The judge walked in with a giant sledgehammer and a wedge he had found in the storehouse. They placed the wedge between the lock housing and the breech, and Reese hit it as hard as he could until it broke open. Rudy opened the chest and revealed its valuable content.

"Throw one of these bags on the table here," the judge demanded.

"Yup." Rudy's eyes sparkled, understanding where the judge was going with it. He picked up a bag and handed it over to Reese, who set it on the table. After yet another strong swing with the sledgehammer the small lock of the bag was broken, and the gold coins flew out, spilling their bounty onto the floor.

"Ok," the judge said, "We see what we got. Certainly it looks good, but let's get outta here, or it ain't gonna be worth anything to us very soon!" He scratched the back of his neck with his right hand, his mind swiftly revising his plan. "Rudy, ride that wagon over to the storehouse and put it all up inside. Bring those saddlebags from the wagon bench on inside here. And hurry it up!"

Rudy nodded. "Yup! What about their horses?"

Reese couldn't help it and snarled, "Why don't ya just shoot 'em? Seems yer good at that!"

"Reese," the judge snapped. "Get that Cyrus inside here. Shoot him a couple times with Randall's gun. One in the head." He lifted the pistol he had taken from Cyrus's body. "Take this pistol, load it, and shoot a couple into Randall. Put it in Cyrus's hands over there, by the door. We are really gonna confuse the townsfolk as to what went on up here."

Turning to Rudy, the judge continued, "Pull the saddles from them two ponies. Bring 'em inside. We'll char up that as evidence too! And scare them horses off. Spook 'em good." He then added, "Let's set this chest over there too, and put the hammer over there near Cyrus."

Reese was amazed at the judge's ingenuity. It seemed like just when everything had gone wrong, the judge came up with a plan for everything. He knew he'd better not ever get on his bad side.

The judge then moved to the table, overturning it, as if it were a screen of protection from gunfire for Randall. Then he scattered Randall's papers about the room, as though someone had been randomly digging through them.

While Reese and Rudy were following through with his orders, the judge exited the swell house through the screen door and returned a short while later with two of the arrows, taken from the Indians.

He pushed one of them deep into Randall's side, and the other one he tapped with the sledgehammer into the tabletop, turned on its side.

After they had stowed away the twenty bags of gold into the saddlebags of their horses, Reese lit a kerosene lantern at the front door and threw it into the house, where it smashed against the overturned table and quickly turned the swell house into a raging inferno.

The three men quickly rode away from the now fully engulfed building, the spooked horses at the corral frantically running in circles, trying to escape.

The night was pitch-black as the rainfall continued its intensity. Rudy, on his way returning from the mine, kneeled down by the river embankment and stuck one arrow into the eye and two more into the trunk of Ardie's stiff body, while the judge and Reese waited for him up by the road.

It had been one hell of a day.

14

Chief Natchez was sick and tired of brokering peace between his people and the white men. When he assumed the position of Paiute Peace Chief, he had not expected things to be so difficult. At times he wasn't sure if the conflicts were a reflection of mankind or if he had simply failed his oath to maintain peace. Since the white man had arrived and brutalized his people, herding and scattering them like goats, he had come to know only death, betrayal, starvation and sickness. While things had been relatively calm for some time, he could now sense looming turbulence, like the black-gray clouds that rolled in before a monstrous storm. The Modoc wars were gearing up, and things were just not well between the U.S. Army, the settlers and immigrants moving westward, and the Northern Paiutes.

His brother, War Chief Numaga, was sick with the white man disease and wanted war, as though triumph over the white man would be one of the last achievements he could accomplish. Tensions continued to rise with their brothers in the Great Basin. *When will it end?* Natchez knew they were in for yet another long winter ahead, and he wondered sadly how many more of his people, both old and child, would have to die before there was lasting peace and enough food to go around.

Natchez shook himself out of this daydream to take in the scenery. He remembered a time when he was young, and he could be entirely focused on the sounds of the stream, the green of the trees, and movements of his horse beneath him. These days, his mind wandered more often than he would have liked, and he knew that such indulgences made him vulnerable to his surroundings.

Natchez and two of his warriors were riding halfway between the Lake El Diablo encampment and the Morgan mining camp. Having left before dusk, in the wee hours of the morning from Rush Creek, further north near Silver Lake, they had made substantial progress in this last leg of their journey south, considering the sun had just begun to rise over the valley.

The day before, Natchez had sent his right-hand man, Tahn-Se, with another warrior to relay an important message to Colton. However, Tahn-Se and Wanu had not returned from their mission to locate him. So as a matter of seriousness, Natchez was making the trip in full war dress along with his two top tribal council men to investigate the delay.

The three men rode in silence. Paiutes, when riding, typically did not converse, to be more aware of their surroundings and any potential danger. Natchez listened to the rushing of the nearby river in an attempt to resist another daydream. *It will be freezing soon*, as he noted there was ice formed along the creek banks, with frozen frost among the riverside weeds.

Tavibo, Tsanomo and Natchez rounded a corner, which followed a curve in the river to their left. Before he saw anything, Natchez could sense that something was off about the place. He paused on his horse to scan his surroundings and noticed something strange in the river. *No*, he thought, *not something, someone.*

Natchez accelerated the pace of his horse to trot the last one hundred feet towards the body as Tavibo and Tsanomo stopped and then followed suit. What he saw before his eyes made his heart sink. Before he consciously processed what was going on, he rushed toward what appeared to be the body of an Indian man in the river.

"No!" he yelled, wishing more than anything that he was back in his daydream.

It was Tahn-Se, his Paiute brother in arms, lying face down in the river. Natchez knew immediately that it was him. He had grown up with Tahn-Se and knew his long, black, braid very well. He leaped off his horse before it came to a complete stop and jumped into the water. The river was calm but muddy from the storm the night before. The icy water sent what felt like lightning bolts into his skin.

"God! No! Why?" he cried.

He grabbed the man's shoulders with both hands to turn the body around. Natchez stared into Tahn-Se's face, still painted with fear. He held the young warrior in his arms, now waist-deep in the water, and walked to the bank, howling with grief. His brother, his advisor, had been murdered in cold blood. Natchez felt sick and disoriented as he looked up to the sky, begging God to tell him it wasn't so.

His two companions had joined him in the river, to help bring Tahn-Se back to dry ground.

"There's someone else," the warrior Tavibo yelled as he dove underneath the surface.

Tsanomo helped steady Tavibo as they pulled another body out of the water. Natchez recognized the face as Tahn-Se's young apprentice, Wanu. The three men worked in silence to heave the two bodies out of the water and onto the banks at the side of the river. With the gentle care of a mother, Natchez laid Tahn-Se on his back and pulled up his deerskin shirt to find several gunshot wounds and broken bones protruding his lacerated flesh.

"He's been murdered," Natchez cried, feeling the anger rise up inside of him. "Murdered. Shot in the back! Only a white man would shoot a man in the back." Natchez had seen wounds like these too many times in his life.

When will the suffering and murder of my people end? he thought.

"Both of our valiant warriors shot in the back," Tavibo said, wiping a tear from his eye and shaking his head. "By more than one white man!"

"Look," Natchez pointed out a series of broken bones on Tahn-Se's lifeless body. His arm was almost completely severed from his body, and his foot was twisted backward, both legs were broken, and the back of his skull had sustained a severe injury.

"They were thrown from the high cliff down into the river and washed over the great falls," Tsanomo said, pointing upstream toward a cliff about three hundred yards further, beyond a massive waterfall that was about two hundred yards from where they stood, wrestling with the dead bodies. The cliff rose straight up at least fifty feet above the water, and was above the one hundred-and-fifty-foot waterfall.

The seriousness of the situation dawned on Natchez. *I must act immediately.* Blinking away tears in his anger, Natchez stroked Tahn-Se's face once more. His Indian brother was gone forever, murdered ruthlessly by white men. *And for what? What caused such a brutal and unjustified death?* The anger swelled in his gut. Peace be damned. Natchez would seek justice and revenge for his warrior brother's death.

"We must get them home," Natchez said, trying to make his voice sound stronger than he felt. "We must see what Numaga wishes to do. This is not our place. Numaga must decide what should be done."

"What should we do with the bodies?" Tavibo asked, nodding his head in approval.

"We cannot carry them home ourselves," Natchez responded. "Let us bless this space and hide them in the brush. We will return."

The three moved in silence once again to cover the bodies in some nearby brush, so they could remain safely out of sight until Natchez returned with a war party. After Tsanomo blessed the space, the men prepared their horses for the ride back to Lake El Diablo. There they would gather Thocmetony and the rest of the clan for their winter migration to Toi Ticutta.

"Natchez!" Tsanomo yelled, startling Natchez into an upright position. "What is that? In the river, over there?"

Natchez spun around and loaded a bow in his arrow in one fluid movement. Slightly up the river, he saw the carcass of a dead horse that had been washed up on the bank. The horse was entangled in debris from the river, lying in a shallow pool of water, but there was something or someone on top of it, partly obscured by some low-hanging branches beside the river.

"It's a man," Tavibo yelled, who was closer and could see a person lying on top of the horse that was halfway immersed in the water. "Natchez! Come quickly. Is that Colton?"

Natchez threw his bow to the ground and sprinted toward the shallow pool, just yards away from where they had found the other two men, wondering, *has Colton been there the whole time?*

"He's alive!" Tavibo said. "Get him! Get him out! Colton!"

Natchez darted toward Tavibo who stood in the knee-deep water and was beginning to pull Colton off the dead horse. It seemed like he had pulled himself up on top of it to get out of the cold water. Colton appeared just barely alive. Tavibo immediately wrapped a bear skin around him to bring warmth to his body. Colton blinked, confused, before coughing heavily and starting to shiver violently.

"Oh, my friend, Colton. What has happened?" Natchez yelled, searching his body for injuries, noticing the belt wrapped around his leg that covered a bullet wound.

The men carried Colton up the riverbank into the morning sunlight, while Tsanomo quickly started a fire. Colton's eyes widened as he tried to sit up, as if to help, but with one last groan he collapsed back to the ground and passed out cold.

The plan to migrate the Paiutes at Camp El Diablo would now have to change, the three men realized. Natchez instructed Tavibo to head back to El Diablo alone and gather the Paiutes for the winter migration to Toi Ticutta, while he and Tsanomo would hurriedly get Colton to care, taking a shorter route, ahead of Tavibo and the migrating Paiutes. On their way north, Tavibo and the others were to gather up the bodies of Tahn-Se and Wanu by the river. If all went well, they'd all arrive at the north reservation shortly after them, where Numaga would be waiting.

15

On Tuesday morning, Harriet Morgan accompanied her mother into Benton Crossing to pick up some supplies from the mercantile. They didn't get out much, nor away from the ranch too often, so they usually liked to make a day of it. Harriet loved seeing the other women in town. She loved Sarah Devine and Penelope Flowers, the wife of Colby, the assayer. Every time she visited, there was usually some news for them to discuss.

Barbara Morgan wanted to have a discussion with the local saloon owner, Candice Mackannel, to get to the bottom of Rudy's shenanigans on behalf of her daughter Marcia. As Harriet found the whole subject quite annoying, she convinced her mother to let her walk the short distance from the saloon over to the Flowers' residence, where she knew she would find her friend, Sarah Devine.

"Hi, Mrs. Flowers," she said to Penelope, a hospitable woman of Mexican descent. "Is Sarah home?"

"She's out back, sweetie. How are you?" Penelope smiled. She had no children of her own but still acted very motherly toward the younger women in the town. Penelope owned the property where Sarah rented a room.

"I'm good," Harriet said, feeling excited to tell Sarah about her new horse. "How's your filly? Did she have her pony yet? I'd love to see if she has."

They were interrupted by the elegant Sarah Devine, who fluttered into the room, her green eyes radiating warmth and excitement. "Harriet, my angel, how are you?" Sarah was always cheerful and seemed very animated.

"Hi, Sarah, so good to see you!" Harriet hugged her friend. No matter how many times she'd seen Sarah, she was always somehow surprised by her beauty. "I was just telling Mrs. Flowers how Daddy couldn't come home this week, so Mama and I fed the men who did come home. We've been on our own little adventure, visiting with the Indians at El Diablo. We saw Thocmetony."

"Well, what are you doing all the way down here?" Sarah asked, grabbing Harriet's hand. "Come on in. Let's go see the new colt."

"I should wait for Mama. She's in the saloon talking to Madam Candice. That Rudy's been so bad to my sister and makin' my mama so sad."

"Aww now, come in!" Sarah said, tugging Harriet's arm into hers. "Your mama will meet us here, and we'll all have some tea and fresh bread. Let's prepare it together."

—m—

Across the street at the saloon, Candice Mackannel was cleaning glasses at the bar counter and setting them onto the shelf behind the bar. Barbara Morgan stood across from her, sipping some coffee.

"Where are you headed today, Barb?" Candice asked, inspecting a glass after she was done, wiping it clean as they were finishing up their conversation.

"We gotta pick up some things from the mercantile and get back to the ranch today. Thank you, Candice." Barbara set down the empty coffee mug.

"No problem, dear lady friend. He's a jerk. Nothin' can be done about that!" Candice rinsed the mug and then placed it on a tray.

Barbara continued, "My daughter is a faithful, hopeful child with some naivety still in her heart. Rudy never was that bad when they met, for the whole first year, as a matter of fact."

"Well, he's gotten into owin' some people money 'round here, especially that Judge Kensington, whom I truly dislike. Too much drinking is catchin' up to that Rudy, as it does most men 'round these parts. He is not that man she is hoping for anymore!" Candice said sarcastically, shaking her head. "Alcohol and loss of a definitive path to fortune will do strange things to a man."

Barbara gathered her pouch and headed for the door. "Thank you, Candice. We will talk again soon. Come up to the ranch sometime!"

Candice laughed. "Oh, honey, I can't leave this place! It'll probably burn down if I leave for a moment!" She laughed and then leaned over and grabbed a broom from the wall.

Harriet and Sarah were still outside the house when Barbara left the saloon across the street and strode toward the Flowers' residence, shaking her head. Harriet wondered if her talk with Madam Candice had made her feel better or worse about Rudy's behavior.

"Hi, Sarah, Harriet," Barbara said, breathless, standing at the entrance to the porch. Her cheeks were red, and she did not smile. "Harriet, I'm heading to the mercantile." She turned to Sarah and smiled. "Sarah, would you like me to say anything to Robert while I'm there?"

Sarah's face went flush as she tried to conceal a smile. Her pale features turned into a rosy glow, and her eyes seemed brighter than ever. Harriet was beginning to understand that giddy, excited feeling Sarah felt whenever someone mentioned JR or, as her mother called him, Robert.

"Tell me, Sarah," Harriet said.

"Oh, you never mind now," Sarah answered, still smiling. "You wanna go see the pony?"

"Not until you tell me. I want to hear everything about you and JR. Please, you know." She giggled and then continued, "I have to confess somethin' to you. I think I'm in love with your brother Henry, and it gets all these warm feelings goin' inside of me," Harriet said, looking down and blushing once again.

She couldn't help but feel jealous about the fact that Sarah lived so close to the man she loved. Sarah wasn't much older than Harriet, just a couple years or so, and she was hopefully soon to be married. Harriet wondered if it would ever work out with her and Henry. He was so handsome, valiant and tall, and he was such a hard worker. Everyone in town admired his youthful ambition. Plus, he loved horses just as much as she did. She often dreamed of them going on long rides together beyond the local township, maybe embarking on an adventure together someday. They were from two different worlds, but perhaps one day, they, too, could create a world of their own.

"Harriet," Sarah said, moving toward the entrance of the house. "Hold on. I'm gonna get my cape. We can go to the store. I wanna see him too!"

This was suddenly nerve-wracking for Harriet. *Now? Right now? Oh my, I must clean myself, brush my hair and put on some perfume,* she thought.

"Can I come quickly and have a look at myself in the mirror, before we go?"

"Come on now, Harriet. You look absolutely beautiful. Henry won't notice any difference. He's not so vain, honey."

"Are you sure, Sarah?" Harriet implored.

"Yes, sunshine. Let's go!" Sarah quickly grabbed her cape as they left the house.

Without further ado, the two beautiful young women ran out the door and down the main road toward the mercantile, giggling and laughing all the way. Harriet loved the mercantile, a big, dusty shop that always stocked the most interesting kinds of objects, and everything one could possibly need. Maybe Harriet would find something for Magic, or perhaps she could even find something for Henry. The problem was that he had no idea of her crush on him.

When they arrived a few minutes later, they found Barbara and JR in the middle of the store, both looking stern. JR nodded at the girls when they came in, but shot them a look that instructed Harriet and Sarah to wait until they'd finished speaking.

"Like I said, ma'am ..." JR reached for some boxes on top of a tall shelf. "I've been trying to reach your husband."

"Do tell," Barbara said, looking intently at JR.

"Well, it's just that," he continued, still assembling the boxes. "Colton was supposed to message me last night when he got on up to the mine, and I haven't heard anything yet."

"Should I be worried?" Barbara asked, putting her left hand over her collarbones, which she often did when she was anxious or deep in thought.

"Not to worry," JR said, flashing his usual boyish smile. "I mean, the telegraph line up there is problematic, always having to repair that thing, especially with some of these winter winds and the thunderstorms we get around here. We had thunder and lightning last night, which could have definitely been the cause. I'll get some supplies together and head on up the line to see if I can't locate the problem."

When JR turned to Harriet and Sarah again, his expression changed. He smiled. Harriet had never seen such an important man look so shy.

"Hi, my love," Sarah beamed, walking toward JR. The two embraced as though they hadn't seen one another in months.

Harriet's heart melted. They looked so happy together. She giggled, unable to control herself.

"You're working too hard in here today," Sarah continued, running her hand teasingly through JR's messy brown hair. "I love you so much, honey. You know that. Yer so sweet of a man and cute when you're working!"

JR rubbed the back of his neck with his hand and said playfully, "Oh, come on now. Don't be talking like that 'round here. Someone might just hear that and think I'm made of some kinda fruit or something."

Barbara and Harriet laughed in unison.

"Oh, don't worry," Harriet teased. "We all think you're cute, JR, and a real peach."

All the women laughed as JR blushed bright red. Interrupting the ladies' laughter, he mentioned something quite incoherent about getting a box from the back room and disappeared back there. Harriet and Sarah wandered about the shop, looking at hats and bonnets, as Barbara gathered the supplies she needed to bring home. Harriet loved the random assortment of things at the mercantile. She wanted to buy a new pair of riding boots to wear when she rode Magic. She really wanted Henry to notice she wasn't a dainty girl, but a strong woman he could count on as a mate, someone who could tend to his needs as a hardworking girl and beautiful wife. Oh, what a fantastic dream she lived within every time she thought of such things.

Harriet heard the front doorbell jingle as Colby Flowers entered the shop. He looked tired, as always, but he smiled when he saw the women.

"Hey, Sarah." He nodded. He was somewhat out of breath as though the walk had tired him. "Where's your man? Your brother Henry told me that JR was lookin' for me."

Sarah turned to get JR from the back room.

"This better be good, for you to interrupt my afternoon nap. What can I do for you, JR?" Colby asked.

JR walked toward Colby carrying a pile of tools and placing them in a box. "I need you to ride with me up the telegraph line. I think it's down again. Henry can stay behind and tend to the store. Can you break away for the day today?"

"Yeah, sure." Colby shrugged. "Why not? Just playin' with ore specimens here, nothing that can't wait."

Harriet exchanged a look with Sarah. It seemed like their fun was over, now that the men were talking business. She was hoping to hang around the mercantile for longer, perhaps run into Henry.

"Great, meet me in ten minutes out by the back of the store. Gonna take some line wire, insulators, some hardware, tools and timber. Colton's got the wagon, so we'll have to take the carriage. The boys never telegraphed last night, so I figured the lines may be down. Barbara's now showing deep concern, so you and I best be going to see what we can find. It's not like Colton to ignore important instructions, so best we go quickly, Colby, straight away to investigate."

"Well, we can take Sheriff Hightower's wagon here," Colby said. "He owes me a favor anyhow. Can you just send a telegraph note on up to Sweetwater, lettin' him know we took it, to check the lines?"

"Sure, can do. I'll have young Henry take care of that. See you in a few."

Colby exited the shop as JR began to rifle through some more boxes. He gathered wires and a couple of insulators. Then he stood up, wiping the sweat from his brow and looking longingly at Sarah.

"Honey, I have to go see to this telegraph line leading up to the mine. Henry will be here in a bit. Can you please direct him to send this note to Sheriff Hightower, telling him where we've gone? I love you." He kissed Sarah on the cheek, and she blushed. The two embraced once more before JR brought the gear to the back of the shop.

Harriet, Barbara and Sarah walked back to the Flowers' residence, carrying two canvas bags of rope and other supplies for the barn. As they passed the saloon, Harriet noticed a very tall man, smoking a cigar, sitting in a rocking chair outside of the shop.

Her mother stopped. "It's Reese!" Barbara said, exasperated. "Come here, ladies. I want to get a word in with him."

They walked toward Reese, who looked slightly disheveled and held a long cigar between two giant fingers. As the women approached, he stood up and tipped his hat, his tall frame towering over the women.

"Ladies," he said with a small bow. "To what do I owe this distinct pleasure?"

"Well, Reese," Barbara said, standing up straight, although Reese's stature dwarfed her. "I know you're friends with Rudy, and when you see him, you tell him I want a word with him about his mannerisms with my daughter."

"Can do, ma'am." Reese nodded, twisting the upper-right corner of his mouth into a smile.

"Anyway," Barbara said. "How's my husband?"

"Oh," Reese said, absentmindedly taking a particularly long puff on the cigar. "He will be fine. Hardworking man. We should have things closed down up there soon, by the end of the month."

Barbara looked relieved. "Oh good. Say, you didn't see any lines down, did ya? JR was trying to reach him this morning. He hasn't telegraphed back. Did you see Colton?"

"No, ma'am, I have not. I haven't seen Colton since Saturday morning."

Harriet watched her mother rub her collarbones beneath her frock coat. "Well, thank you, Reese. Tell my husband I'll be venturing on up too." She paused, thinking. "Actually no, don't tell him anything. I think the girls and I will go up tomorrow and surprise him or maybe Thursday morning."

"Sure, Barbara," Reese said, smiling and returning to his rocking chair. "Won't say a word. You ladies take care now. I gotta get up there myself tonight."

Barbara strode away from Reese. Harriet and Sarah exchanged looks and followed behind.

"Now, Harriet," Barbara snapped. "We should get goin' before dark."

"But, Mama," Harriet objected. She didn't want to leave yet. She hadn't even seen the newborn colt and wanted to stay with Sarah. "Can't we wait for word on Daddy? Sarah, we can stay, ya?"

"No," Barbara said. "Let's get goin'."

Sarah smiled. "Barbara, it's fine. She wants some words on her daddy. Why don't you gals stay one more day? We can make a nice breakfast. Penelope would be absolutely thrilled!"

"No," Barbara responded stubbornly. "It's quite alright. I'm sure everything's just fine. It's gettin' late, and we best be getting on home before it gets dark now."

They reached the Flowers' residence, and Penelope opened the door. "Now what are you ladies gossipin' about me now?" She laughed as she let the women in.

Barbara dismissively waved her hand. "Oh, nothin', Penelope."

Sarah said, "We were just planning—"

"We were gonna spend the night and ..." Harriet attempted to complete the sentence.

"Harriet wishes to stay and get word on her father," Barbara said.

Penelope reached out and took Harriet's hands into her own. "Why sure, of course!"

Sarah nodded toward Harriet. "See. I told ya not to worry, honey!"

Harriet beamed all over at the prospect of spending the night with her friend.

"Thank you, Pennie," Barbara said. "We can do some extra work for you with the animals, maybe, since you are so nice to take us in."

"No worries," Penelope said, smiling at Barbara. "You women are always welcome here."

16

Natchez had not said a word since he had mounted his horse and began the ride continuing north together with Tsanomo. His horse, carrying both him and Colton, led the way toward Toi Ticutta, but Natchez's heart felt like it was left at the river with Tahn-Se, looking into his stricken face and broken body. He knew this would mean war. Natchez felt hopeless. *If I couldn't keep my best friend from being a victim of cold-blooded murder, how can I save my people? Why did I send Tahn-Se up there in the first place?* He retraced his thought process. *If I only hadn't sent him into danger, he'd still be alive. What will Numaga say?* He needed to tell Numaga what had happened, before anybody else got word of it.

Natchez checked on Colton frequently throughout the ride to make sure he was still alive. He groaned and coughed frequently, hovering somewhere between life and death. Whenever they stopped, Natchez cleaned Colton's leg wound and applied a layer of new poultice he had made from herbs, but things didn't look good. Colton drifted in and out of consciousness. His body felt like it was on fire. He had not much time left. The tissue around his leg wound was turning black. It took them way longer than expected to reach Toi Ticutta, since they had to slow down and take long breaks in between riding due to Colton's serious condition.

When Natchez and Tsanomo finally arrived at the entrance to the north reservation at Toi Ticutta, Thocmetony, Tavibo and some of the children ran up to meet them. Their smiles turned to sadness as they noticed the body on the back of Natchez's horse. He looked around, unable to focus properly on the beauty before him. The Toi Ticutta reservation included a massive expanse of wickiups, an encampment at least fifty times the size of the southern camp at El Diablo. It was nestled in a huge green valley, crossed by the Walker River, surrounded by elm trees and shrubbery. Behind the encampment sat a picturesque backdrop of some of the valley's tallest mountains. Towering over the greenery and life below, they perched as valiant protectors.

But after all that had just happened, Natchez was unable to give thanks to his protectors. Instead, he stared at the solemn faces of his people, who greeted him as he rode into the encampment. The others looked like they had recently arrived and were waiting patiently for Natchez to speak with Numaga.

"Natchez," his sister Thocmetony cried out. Her typically angular face was puffy and her eyes moist. "How is Colton?" She stared wide-eyed and concerned at Colton.

"Get the Ghost Dancer healer, Wovoka," Natchez instructed, nodding at Tavibo and Thocmetony. He could no longer lament the tragedy of what had happened. The time to act was upon them.

Thocmetony and young Angel quickly moved toward a wickiup, while Natchez and Tavibo staggered to carry Colton inside. The tribe's chief healer, Wovoka, looked incredibly stern as he sat cross-legged on a bear skin rug in the center of the wickiup. Natchez's people were extremely suspicious of outsiders, especially when it came to healing.

"He's been shot," Natchez said, putting force behind his voice, so he did not have to hear any protest. "By a white man, not a Paiute. We found him in the river and didn't know how long he was there. Please ..." he said, pausing, "Help him."

Wovoka looked at Natchez and then at Colton and finally nodded. Natchez gave him a small bow and turned on his heel to leave the wickiup. The others followed behind him.

—m—

Colton awoke from what felt like the longest dream he had ever experienced, but in reality, he had been in a coma, beginning to come out of it. In the dream, he had fallen down a waterfall. Every time he hit the bottom and crashed into the river, he found himself back on the top of the edge. *Am I still on the edge?* He struggled to find consciousness and open his eyes. His leg throbbed a dull pain. *No,* he thought, knowing what it meant. He began having memories come back as he was waking. Cyrus was dead. Randall was dead. *Maybe even I'm dead.* He inhaled deeply and opened his eyes to see willow twigs making a thatched roof above him. He had only seen such a structure once before, in the southern Lake El Diablo encampment. *Where am I?*

"Colton, my love," a familiar voice whispered in his ear.

Slowly, he turned his head to his right and focused on the most beautiful face he had ever seen, his Wyola. She was kneeling beside him, tears running down her face, as she was wiping his feverish forehead with a cold, damp cloth.

"I'm so glad you are alive," she sobbed. "I could not have bore to lose you." She bent down to kiss his forehead.

Colton resolved he must still be dreaming. Yet he felt so awake. *Am I dead? Is Wyola a ghost, and we are in heaven together?* A sense of peaceful sadness washed over him until a dull, throbbing pain emerged. *With pain like this I must be alive,* Colton thought.

Even though his pain felt excruciating, Colton managed to smile and lifted his hand to touch her face. "I would never ever leave you! You are my everything. You keep me alive," he whispered.

Wyola was just as beautiful as Colton remembered. Her skin was the color of cinnamon. She had warm, buttery-hazel eyes with long, black, curly hair falling off her shoulders. Colton loved her shoulders, slim, and narrow, but strong from years of hard work. She was wearing a long, light-green dress and a tattered brown frock coat.

"You've got to rest now, my love." Wyola stroked his cheek. "You have to get well soon."

Colton still smiled as he fell back into an exhausted sleep.

It felt as if he had slept for days when he woke up again, completely alone, and was afraid that seeing Wyola had just been a dream. He slowly sat up and gasped. A sharp pain seared through his right side. He must have broken some ribs. Colton looked around the small hut. It smelled of cedar and smoke. Woven tapestries covered the walls. As he scanned the room, he noticed a familiar figure sitting by the entrance, staring back at him. It was Thocmetony. She smiled with her mouth, but her eyes did not follow.

She was worried. "Colton," she said, striding toward him, her long, sleek braids swaying at her side. "How are you?"

"I'm alive." He grimaced. "That's gotta count for something, don't it? Where is Wyola? What happened?"

"Wyola is getting some water for you." Thocmetony then explained how he had been found unconscious and had been asleep for three days, since his arrival at the camp. Her eyes welled up with tears as she explained how Natchez and his warriors had seen the bodies of their Paiute brothers floating in the river. "They were on their way up to Morgan's mine when they found them." She proceeded to explain to Colton that he was also found in the river, on top of the dead horse, and barely alive with a bullet in his leg, broken ribs and a lot of severe bruises.

"I must have fallen," Colton said, remembering his dream. "The last I remember was being on a ledge by the river, trying to climb down, up behind Morgan's swell house. Did your brother make it up all the way up to the mine?"

"No," Thocmetony said, looking confused. "Why do you ask?"

Colton relayed the horrible night at the Morgan mine. He told her how he lost Cyrus and he was pretty sure Randall also was dead. "It was the judge," Colton said, feeling the anger rise inside of him, when he thought of Cyrus lying on the ground. "They talked about burnin' down the place, probably to destroy any trace of their misdeeds. I imagine they killed your people too. Reese was there, and so was Rudy. I thought he was Randall's friend." He felt hot tears of anger streaming down his face.

Thocmetony looked stunned. Her thin eyebrows rose as her eyes widened. "We knew it was a white man responsible. No Paiute would do such a thing, especially to that white man, who has been so compassionate to our people, but we didn't know who. I have to tell my brothers. Numaga must hear this. I can't let a criminal deed by a couple of bad men foster a new war after thirteen years of ceaseless and senseless suffering, because the Paiutes have been betrayed so many times by the whites." She got up, as if about to leave the hut. "They cannot continue to starve us and treat us as slaves anymore. The men are angry. This will trigger an uprising, leading to an expanded war with the whites."

"Wait," Colton said. "Numaga is here?" He remembered the letter.

"Yes," she said. "Colton, I must go."

"Are we at El Diablo?" His letter had said that Numaga was moving north and Wyola was with them.

Thocmetony shook her head. "We are in Toi Ticutta." She got up and left the hut while Colton took some time to rest. His leg and his right side were still hurting badly. After what felt like an eternity, Colton heard the sound of footsteps approaching the wickiup. Chief Natchez entered, followed by Thocmetony. Both looked grave. Natchez sat on the end of Colton's small cot and asked Colton to repeat his story. The chief did not interrupt him but simply nodded and occasionally inhaled deeply, acknowledging his every word.

"This is worse than I thought," Natchez said.

"Cyrus is dead. Randall is dead. Your people are dead. And I don't even know why," Colton aimlessly chanted.

Natchez nodded again. He looked as though his mind was still back on the mountain. He rose up and left the wickiup, followed by Thocmetony. A short while later, Wyola entered the hut with a jug of water. Colton smiled. He felt like there was no sense left in the world, except for her. He loved the feeling of peace and utter bliss he felt in her presence. Her calmness was intoxicating. Slowly Colton sat up and took in her inner beauty as she smiled and poured some of the water into a mug, which she handed to him.

"Colton." She stroked his hair as he emptied the mug. He took her hand and kissed it, holding it tight. "My love, I will never leave you, ever again!" She threw her arms around him and squeezed him tight. He winced, feeling the sharp pain in his side from her weight.

With pain and difficulty Colton held her as hard as he could, burying his face in her hair hanging over her bosom. Before he could even attempt to stop himself, he felt the tears flood his eyes as he swallowed a giant sob.

"I had to run," Wyola said slowly. "The judge. I couldn't be there one more day!" Tears streamed down her face as she shook her head. "How can a person be so wicked? He was going to kill me for carrying inside my belly the truth!" Her body was heavy with sobs. She had a secret to share, but she couldn't reveal it, not now and not here. As the strong woman she was, she bore the grief within her spirit, looking forward to a day that she could reveal this darkness to the man of her life. His rejection of her was her constant fear. *I am no longer pure for him. What will he do? What will he think of me? Can he still love me?* She held back.

"My love," Colton said. "You will never ever have to be afraid again! I will make sure of that!" His body stiffened with resolve, and he felt his strength returning with force, wondering, *What does she mean by carrying the truth inside her belly? Is she pregnant?* She didn't appear pregnant.

Because Wyola was so distraught, Colton let it go, figuring the truth would be told by her when she was ready. Regardless, as the words sank deep, one fact emerged: If she was pregnant, it certainly wasn't his child.

17

"What the hell happened here?" Colby wondered in disbelief.

"Man, I wish I knew," JR shakingly uttered, equally dumbfounded, as he and Colby surveyed what was left of the swell house at Morgan's mine.

They had arrived at the mine in the evening to discover the aftermath of a very large fire. JR could not believe his eyes as he found the havoc of a crumpled mass of wreckage. He was not expecting to find such devastation. He simply thought there was a telegraph line down, not an entire mining establishment effectively razed. The swell house and the surrounding buildings appeared as though they had been absolutely and chaotically set ablaze. Smoldering sections of multiple structures were extensively destroyed, charred and smokey. Some of the floor architecture to some assets had remained intact due to the dampness of the ground below, although all were covered by twisted piles of fallen timber and roofing debris, with signs of equipment contorted and charred within, with pieces sticking out here and there.

JR spent a considerable amount of time walking around, looking for clues as to what had happened. He most accurately deduced this must have been a huge and tragic fire, yet the place was not all turned completely to ash. He reckoned there had been a heavy rain or snow to prevent the fire from completely destroying the place.

"JR," Colby screamed. Even though it was a chilly day, his shirt was stained in sweat and marred with charcoal, as he moved a charred wooden log aside. "JR," he continued in despair, "There's a body under here."

JR swallowed and inhaled deeply, bracing himself. Even amid all the rubble, he assumed that anybody who was at the mine would have fled when the fire started. *Is it possible that someone has been trapped inside?* His mind immediately drifted into thoughts of Harriet and Barbara, whom he had just seen this very same day in the morning, before they left. Young Harriet was eager to see her dad return for the week. *Will I be the one to tell the Morgan girls that their father has been burned alive?*

"You sure?" JR called over, scared he was about to see the dead body of a man he knew well and highly respected. He hustled quickly through the debris toward Colby, to see a human foot with a burned boot and trouser leg sticking out from beneath a pile of charred wood. The skin was badly burned. JR noticed something shiny beside the foot.

"What's that?" Colby asked as he lifted more wood from the pile of rubble.

"Looks like a coin," JR said, dusting it off and flipping it over in his hand. "From the mint we shipped Monday with Colton and Cyrus."

"What in God's green ..." Colby said, trailing off, as though he were putting together the pieces of an extremely complicated puzzle.

"Let's get the rubble off, and quickly," JR said.

The two worked in silence for a few minutes, heaving pieces of burned wreckage and ruin off the pile. The body below had been crushed and the skin charred. What was left of the body was lying face down. Beneath the burnt clothing, JR perceived the figure might have had dark skin.

"JR," Colby said solemnly, "I recognize the frame. I think it might be Cyrus. There are only two blacks working here, aren't there? He's too short to be Colton."

JR wiped the sweat off his forehead with the back of his hand as he shook his head. He ran through every possible reason why it shouldn't be Cyrus and why it couldn't be Cyrus. *But then again*, he thought, *it does make sense.* He had sent Colton and Cyrus up to the mine. If there had been an accident over the past few days, then the two men would have been on site.

JR's heart dropped. "Let's get this body on to the wagon and keep looking. If Cyrus died up here, Colton might be near. Same with Randall. Let's comb through everything."

Colby walked several feet away to a spot, where half a chimney remained. "This would've been Randall's study. And there's what looks like his table, broken here." Colby kicked aside some more wood. "JR, we got another body here."

Colby maneuvered the pieces of the table away from the body. As he exposed the remains, he bent over to pull out two objects stuck in the back. "Arrows," he muttered under his breath. "JR, come take a look at this. And there's more gold over here too."

"Was this some kind of robbery?" JR wondered, thinking out loud.

He then thought to himself, *did somebody else know about the delivery? Have Colton and Cyrus been intercepted by Indians? Did the Paiute do this? Impossible!*

"JR," Colby said gravely. "Do you think this is Randall?"

"I have a bad feeling it is Colby, unless by some miracle he's back in town and somehow escaped. But judging by this scene up here, I don't know if we're going to get that kind of grace today."

Together, JR and Colby picked up the second body and carefully brought it over to the wagon. JR tried not to breathe in the horrid stench of burnt flesh and ash. He was not a soft man, but he still wrapped a spare cloth around his hands to protect himself from any open wounds. Once the two bodies were lined up on the wagon, JR took a closer look at the second body's burnt face. There appeared to be a hole just above his right eye socket. Wrapping the cloth over his finger, JR poked inside of a hollow wound.

"Hmm," he said, removing his finger. "This ain't no Indian weapon wound. That's the hole of a large caliber, maybe .44 Henry or .56 Spencer, from close range, perhaps five feet at the furthest."

They combed through the scene once more, this time looking for weapons, hoping to be able to put together a better scenario of what went on.

"You look where the second body was, I'll look around where we found the first."

As JR suspected, the men found weapons in both places.

"Lookin' to be a Spencer carbine rifle," Colby said, finding only the metal remains of the weapon under a collapsed chair in the study.

"And over here too," JR said. "Looks like we got a Dragoon pistol."

As time passed, the two men discovered Colby's wagon, buried under collapsed debris from the barn. The lock was shot off, they determined, meaning this was definitely some kind of a robbery. Realizing that neither Colton nor Cyrus had a key didn't prove that they or an Indian shot the lock. Wandering around, they found shell casings all around the front door, Henry .44 caliber as well as a few .56 caliber inside. They knew Morgan owned both a .46 and a .44 because JR sold him the ammo from the mercantile regularly. He also knew that Colton and Cyrus were carrying cap and ball weapons as well as a Henry Yellowboy. Unfortunately, the casings proved nothing.

An hour later, the men were back on their way to Benton. JR shuddered at the thought of the townsfolk and how they would react to the news. He figured Barbara should know first. *Or should I alert the authorities, so they can begin their search for the culprit?* He replayed the hypothetical tragedy at the mine, and either way he sliced it, it simply made no sense to him. He thought of Colton and Cyrus, ambushed at their arrival to the mine by some rogue Indians. That didn't seem right. After all, where was Colton? And plus, JR had never known Indians around the Central Sierras to act in such a way, at least not since the Williams Station Massacre, some ten or so years earlier.

Could this have been a reprisal for white man deeds? Did Colton get greedy and turn on his friend and employer, along with his cousin Cyrus, for that matter, while staging the incident to make it look like an Indian sneak attack? Did Cyrus and Colton act together, and Cyrus lost his life in the struggle? That didn't fit right either. None of the possible scenarios matched up with the men and local Indians he knew. Morgan's mine was one of the most well-respected establishments in Benton. *Who would have it out for Randall?*

The ride down the hill was bumpy, as their wagon was laden with more weight than usual. They rode along the road, where the river was running parallel, just below. After encountering a particularly sharp turn in the road, JR heard something heavy and metallic fall off the wagon and collide with the ground.

Colby halted the horses at the sound. "Think it's the insulator," he said. "I'll go have a look."

He dismounted and walked to the edge of the road, along the creek, to relieve himself, before picking up the loose insulator. Colby looked around at the aspen trees as the night sky was getting darker but was crystal clear. It may have been a beautiful fall season day, had it not been for what they had encountered earlier.

"JR?" Colby asked, breaking the silence.

"Ya?" JR responded, absentmindedly.

"Check this out. You better come here," Colby said, sounding uncertain.

Uh-oh, JR thought, *did something break?* He walked around the front of the horses to find Colby still standing at the edge of the creek.

"What is it?" JR asked impatiently. They didn't have time to stop and take a look at the scenery.

"We got another body and a dead horse," Colby replied.

JR craned his neck to make sure he heard Colby right. *No, not another body. How?* He picked up his pace to get a closer look at the asymmetrical mass slightly upstream. Much of the creek was shadowed by thick aspen growing around the banks. JR saw wet paper sagging over a thin, low-hanging branch of aspen. On another branch, he noticed what looked like a tangled saddle. Two feet away, and partially obstructed by the tree, was a dead horse.

"Oh my …" JR said, trailing off.

As he got closer, his heart sank. He could see a body toward the middle of the creek, half wrapped around a dead tree. He looked young. He looked … *Wait a minute!*

"That's Ardie!" JR cried out.

Sure enough, he quickly recognized the athletic frame of Ardie Perseval, the contract mail rider, a young man whom JR had grown quite close to. He couldn't believe he was seeing Ardie like this. Judging by the looks of it, he must have been dead for a day or two in the water. Ardie's body also had three arrows sticking out of his back, just like the other body up at the Morgan mine. It made JR dizzy to the point where he thought he might be sick. Ardie's body and the tree acted as a kind of dam, where dirt and other debris had accumulated, pressing the body tight between numerous seedling aspens. The smell was nauseating.

Unable to believe his eyes, JR wondered what Ardie could possibly have to do with all of this. *What violence took place along this stretch between here and the mine, and why?* He knew why. *The gold is gone. Men are dead. It's a robbery gone bad, but why this young man?*

"Colby, we've gotta get him out of there." JR sadly removed his hat, wishing it were possible for him not to feel anything at all. "Do we have anything we can cut these trees with?"

JR braced himself for the hypothermic waters of the creek. He and Colby struggled to separate the corpse from the tight configuration of the trees, intertwined with all the debris.

Colby went back to the wagon, retrieving a shovel and a digging bar. "We'll try this." He returned to the river, while JR worked away to free the body. Wedging the shovel and bar between the seedlings, they pried apart the four to six inch diameter aspen trunks and wriggled Ardie free. Together they pulled him to the embankment, along with the small accumulation of random debris, wood and what looked like some clothing.

Once they were safely out of the water, JR began inspecting the contents of the clothing, searching for any signs. He looked at Ardie, and then back at the river, to try to understand where or how Ardie had first fallen in. Looking back at the river, JR noticed a dark-brown leather object caught in the vegetation. Still crouching on the banks, he reached his arm out to grab the shovel laying nearby, using it to retrieve the item.

"What's that?" Colby asked.

"A glove," JR said. He held up the glove with his left hand and raised his right palm at Colby to show the difference in size. The glove was huge. "This is a big glove, for a big man," he said, eyeing Colby shrewdly. He only knew one man whose hands would fit in a glove so big, Reese Clybourne, the tallest and biggest man in the valley.

"What," Colby said, a look of realization lighting up his dark, beady eyes. "What would Reese be doin' here?"

"What indeed," JR nodded. "Well, it ain't been out here too long. And there's what looks to be blood on it," he said, pointing toward the dark crimson swipes on the palm.

Colby's puzzled look mirrored the confusion JR felt inside.

"Pretty damning evidence," Colby said, looking at Ardie's body.

"But why Ardie? What did he ever do to anyone? We are gonna hang Reese for this," JR responded in anger and quick judgment. "There's too much death here for one man to conduct all this by himself. He had to have help. But let's get back and figure it out in consultation with Sheriff Hightower, what action should and can be taken on something like this. There will need to be further investigation. We may need the militia's help."

"But what do you make of the Indian arrows everywhere, in everyone?" Colby questioned.

"I wish I had the answers," JR quickly followed, as though he was pleading with some invisible force to understand what exactly had happened. "It may not be what Ardie did, but what he was carrying in them mail bags. There were a few gold nuggets around Randall's body, and I know Ardie was delivering nuggets, along with valuation bank assessments, back to Morgan. Randall was looking to get a loan, to break deep into the new north vein. Let's gather the gear."

JR knew that Reese wasn't the friendliest of men. In fact, he thought Reese certainly had a hidden agenda, half of the time, like he was trying to outsmart the rest. But JR also knew that he wasn't as shrewd as he thought he was. JR tried to recall when he last saw Reese. He remembered seeing him that morning down in Benton before they left, but the day before, he wasn't sure. Either way, if Reese wasn't dead, he'd better have some pretty good answers for them. As to what they had seen and discovered here near Ardie's place of demise, Reese had to have been there, unless there was another giant of a man in the valley. *Well, I've never seen one!*

"Hmm ..." Colby said as the two men wrapped Ardie's body in cloth and placed it in the wagon with the others. "Maybe he didn't find what he was lookin' for on Ardie, or maybe he stumbled across the scene while we were up at the mine finding Morgan's dead body. Reese could possibly have an explanation. But then, we would have crossed paths on the way here. No, that can't be the case," Colby analytically stated to JR.

"Maybe that's not what he was looking for! I'm figuring, it wouldn't have been left on the floor near Morgan, if it were something intentionally gone after, premeditated," JR commented in a type of self-questioning cross examination.

After they had put Ardie on the wagon, they drove it a mile further down the hill until it was almost too dark to see. They found a protected area by the side of the road and set up camp for the night. Because they had to travel slowly with human cargo in a wagon, they didn't make it back to Benton Crossing until the next evening.

—ᶰᶰ—

At dusk, the saloon was filled with people as two young fiddlers played out front on the boardwalk of Benton's main street. Harriet and Sarah sat with a group of friends, listening and singing to the music, while clapping their hands. Harriet was happy they had stayed another day and that had stretched now into another night, even though in the back of her mind she was worried about her dad, wondering why they hadn't heard from him, and why Colby and JR had not yet returned. The fiddler's tunes were a welcome distraction from her thoughts.

Suddenly a wagon came rolling into town in a cloud of dust, passing right by them. Harriet nudged Sarah as she looked up, observing Colby and JR, who hurriedly went past them. Her heart dropped. Something seemed very wrong. She saw the canvas covering something quite large in the back of the wagon, not realizing there were three dead men piled atop each other under it.

The fiddlers stopped playing, and the people who were gathered on the street started to follow the wagon to see what was happening. Alarmed, Harriet and Sarah started running. The wagon came to a screeching halt in front of the mercantile, and JR quickly jumped off the cart and ran inside.

Just before he entered, he turned around and yelled at Colby, "Stay with the wagon! Keep the townsfolk back 'til I get out."

Colby was holding a Spencer rifle across his knees, his face grim. Harriet's heart sank as she looked at him. He dropped his gaze and looked at her sadly, shaking his head. The back of the wagon was covered, but it became obvious there were human bodies under the canvas. Then Harriet started to scream as she had never screamed before. Everything went black as she hit the ground beneath her feet, fainting.

18

It seemed like all the townsfolk had gathered in the Benton courthouse the next evening. The Morgan sisters and their mother clutched each other close and sobbed. Marcia held Harriet's hand as they were trying to comfort each other, their faces puffy and swollen from crying. Barbara buried her bloodless face in her hands, letting out small, concealed sobs under her breath. Rachel Perseval sat stoically in her chair, in utter shock, gawking straight ahead in a trance-filled daze, while stroking her growing belly. Sarah sat next to her, embracing her in a futile attempt to ease her suffering. The baby would never know who its father was.

The news about JR and Colby returning from the destroyed, burned-out mining operation had spread like a brush fire around the whole town. JR and Colby had agreed they would share only general information with the town. They would hold the specific, gory details for the authorities.

"Who did this? JR, tell us what you saw!"

He was overcome with demands from the crowd for information or even just his opinion. JR merely shook his head. He had one shot, and one shot only, to get real justice for his friends. He wasn't about to let a loose tongue start wagging. There was no way he was going to let any evidence trickle out early. He knew this would just enable the culprits to concoct some alibi. Wildfires paled in comparison to the speed by which rumors traveled around Benton and the sparsely populated Eastern Sierras.

Judge Kensington, along with the town's attorney, Jack Russell, and Sheriff Hightower, had been summoned to review the case. This was not a formal trial, yet all the people congregated in the small room. After all, there were no witnesses or concrete suspects. JR made direct eye contact with the audience as he painstakingly relayed every single detail of what he and Colby had encountered at the mine and in the creek. He was, no doubt, a more gifted speaker than Colby, yet Colby piped up every now and then, amateurishly corroborating JR's retelling of events.

JR caught sight of a large clock on the wall. *It's only six o'clock? This will be a day that never comes to an end*, he thought defeatedly. He told his tale, mustering up focus, precision, and calm. He'd be damned if anyone doubted his account because he was emotional or lacked precision. It was difficult to describe where and how they found Randall's body. His wife and daughters absorbed and hung on his every word, openly choking back sobs and tears as he spoke. It wasn't any easier to talk of Cyrus and Ardie, both loved by the townspeople. Sounds in the courtroom were muffled cries and sobs, as the occupants grasped the full horror of what had transpired that week.

"So, we left the mine the way we found it, except for a few pieces of evidence," JR testified, still maintaining steady eye contact with the floor while rubbing the back of his neck. He felt stiff and hot, maybe because he literally felt as if he were on the hot seat, as information provider, tale teller, evidence finder and discoverer of the dearly beloved men's dead bodies. The room had become quite stuffy from all the people and emotions circulating in the air. The lack of fresh air made him feel as if he were suffocating.

The judge listened intently to every single word. In JR's mind, however, he felt the concern on the judge's face seemed somehow inauthentic and hollow. Something wasn't ringing true to him. He just couldn't put his thumb on it. He knew the judge to be a hardened man with a fervent obsession for the nitty-gritty details. While JR had never attended a court proceeding before, he was taken aback by the judge's seeming lack of emotion. *Does he not sense the heaviness of the situation, and the effect it has on the townspeople? Is he so disconnected from the people who have supposedly voted him into office?* The vote remained in dispute still to this day. Half the valley said, it was routed by corruption for him to ever be elected. There was no way to know. *Is the judge not perturbed by the Morgan women, who seem to shrink as the meeting progresses?* There was a mess of quivers, sobs, sniffles and hungry grabs for each other. He wondered why the judge wasn't seeing that. Or maybe he did see and just didn't care.

Judge Kensington leaned forward in his seat, his elbows resting on his desk, as he pressed his chin against his two forefingers. He wore a dark-purple velvet vest over a white shirt, his wide-brimmed black hat resting on the desk beside him. The dim light illuminated his red face and white beard and shined a glare from his balding head.

"And the hole in the head of that nigga Cyrus was the size of, you say, a Spencer, .56 caliber?" he asked curtly, with what seemed to be a juvenile fascination in his pitched Southern accent.

"Judge, I object!" Jack Russell stood up. He was a young but accomplished attorney, who had been a close friend of Randall Morgan.

Jack's forehead creased, and he appeared visibly upset that the judge was not handling such a sensitive and horrific situation with more grace and professionalism. He was a judge, and yet he seemed to completely lack any stature, calling a respected young black man by such terminology.

The judge waved aside Jack's comment. JR looked down at the floor, unwilling to see the look on the Morgan girls' faces.

"Well," the judge continued in his slow and measured pitch. "It sounds to me that Randall shot Cyrus, and that Jaminson fellow shot Morgan after that and then ran off with the gold. You found no trace of Colton, am I right? And the gold, where it be?"

"That's right," Colby said, piping up beside JR. He couldn't conceal his shaking hands as he was tightly holding on to his hat. "We found neither, but Judge—"

"It seems to me," the judge said, drowning out Colby, "You may just find Mr. Colton on the rezzie with a couple of them Injuns. It appears from what I'm seeing, he teamed up with, you know, those Paiute, you folk love so much. I don't know how much you love 'em now that they've gone around killing all our townsfolk and stealin' our gold. This all has the same earmarks, you ask me, of them killings back in 1860 by that tribe of acorn eaters, up near Washoe County."

JR cleared his throat. "Well, I wouldn't jump so fast, Judge."

He'd always considered the judge to be an intelligent man who gathered all the facts before reaching a verdict. However, his assumptions about the judge now clearly seemed baseless. *What business would Colton have on the reservation?* There was simply no way Colton was capable of turning against Morgan. It wasn't in his nature. JR knew this beyond any doubt. Colton was a kind and loyal man. Some things he just knew about people.

The judge raised an eyebrow and opened his mouth to respond. Before he could get a word out, attorney Jack Russell fumed. "Your *Honor*," he said sarcastically. "We," he placed great emphasis on the word as he looked around the room. "We don't quite see it that way. What if ..."

"What if what?" the judge taunted as he leaned back in his chair. "What if Colton is some kind of hero? I doubt you'll be seeing that nigga boy ever so soon. He's either dead or hidin' out somewhere. Like I said, I'd start looking on the rezzy."

"And why would you say that?" Jack asked, exchanging an exasperated look with Colby and JR.

"Have you seen him?" the judge asked casually. "If he were so innocent, don't you think we'd be see'n him? Like I've said already, and you all know how I do not appreciate having to repeat myself, he's either guilty as hell or dead. We can't know the impact of Colton Jaminson in all of this, without him here to speak for himself, so I say we go find him first and hear what he has to say!"

JR waited for the judge to finish. He glanced at Colby, who looked back at him and nodded slightly. They had agreed, they would not reveal the rather large evidentiary detail about the glove until the very end of the hearing.

Marcia stepped forward toward the center of the small circle, until she was standing in front of the judge. Like her mother, she was tall and statuesque. She towered over the short, plump judge, who didn't attempt to rise from his chair or offer any condolences of any kind.

Her eyes were puffy and red from tears. "What about your man, Reese Clybourne?" she asked, pointing a finger at the judge. "How do you know he didn't have somethin' to do with this? He worked up there." She looked back at her sister and mother and then over to Reese. "How do we know that you didn't have something to do with this, Reese Clyborne!!?"

Reese had been sitting at the back of the room, his large frame leaned against the wooden wall by the door. He looked tired and bored until Marcia mentioned his name. He suddenly awakened to attention, of the nervous kind. Many of the townspeople snapped their heads in Reese's direction. He raised his eyebrows and pouted his lip, feigning surprise. His reaction quickly turned into an unconcerned smile, and despite his outward demeanor, he was ruffled internally.

"Oh, Marcia," he said, shaking his head slightly, trying to hide his anger on the inside.

The judge shook his head slightly and cackled. "Well, darlin', I'm about to get to that."

"Let's hear it now, Judge," Barbara said with a firmness that was surprising to hear, given her state of mind. She focused her eyes on Kensington with a hateful, almost deadly glare.

"Yeah, let's hear it now, Judge," Marcia said. "Your *opinion*!" She wiped back tears with her sleeve.

JR stood up and walked toward Marcia. "It will be ok," he said, putting a hand on her shoulder, wishing beyond anything that his words could be true. He tried to believe what he was telling the poor girl with worthless words of encouragement, so they seemed. JR made eye contact with Sarah, who stepped forward to comfort Marcia. The tension in the air briefly subsided as their grief was clearly on display.

"Ok, everyone," JR said, looking at the Morgan girls, the judge, and Jack Russell. "Before we go around making accusations, I think it would be prudent to remember the details of this case. Remember, we found blood at Morgan's swell house down the embankment, and it led into the river. So more happened up there than we know. Someone did slip away into the water, but who, that is the question."

"I wanna know who killed my daddy," Harriet burst out as she turned to her mother in tears. "And Ardie and Cyrus, Mama. And where is Colton then, Judge?"

Barbara hushed her daughter and drew her close as she gingerly wiped away tears from her cheeks.

"Well," the judge continued. "Like I said, young lady, he is either dead or on the run. I'm issuing a warrant for the arrest of Colton Jaminson. He worked with Cyrus, whom we can all agree was shot by Randall. He was Colton's sidekick, so there is no doubt they were workin' together on something. We just need to find out what that something was. Since we have multiple murders here, the court will set his bounty at five thousand dollars. Order the printer to set up for the print of a hundred wanted posters. Hightower, if I can have you deliver some up to Aurora as well as Bridgeport and Bodie, so we can get this young man behind bars and wrap this case up. In the meantime—"

The judge then continued. "And let's get word immediately up to Ft Mcdermot and alert the cavalry to go inspect that Indian camp in Toi Ticutta as well as that other destitute encampment over near Mt. Diablo. He might just be hidin' there, as good as anywhere. We'll get the words outta them Injuns, or die tryin.'"

"Now, hold on, Judge," JR interrupted. "I agree we should talk to Colton. But there's something you should know." He looked at Colby, who reached his hand inside of his canvas bag and pulled out a large, wet glove. Everybody in the courtroom, including the judge, craned their heads to get a closer look at the contents of the bag.

"We found this glove near Ardie's body, stuck to an aspen branch in the river," JR said, holding it up and walking toward Reese. "Does this look familiar, Clybourne?" Then turning to the judge, he redirected his question. "I don't know anybody in town with hands like these, do you agree, Judge Kensington? Plus, I've seen Reese wear gloves that look just like this, before, into the mercantile. Anybody else?"

Marcia gasped as Harriet burst into tears.

"I knew it!" Marcia yelled. "George, uh Sheriff, Jack," she yelled out, looking at Sheriff George Hightower and attorney Jack Russell.

"Ah," the judge said, leaning back in his chair once again. "Hmm, what do we have here? Reese Clybourne, do you have anything you'd like to say for yourself?"

Reese's false bravado evaporated. He sat up straight in his chair, his eyes fixed on the judge. "Why, no, Judge," he said with a thick tension behind every syllable. His voice was quivering, and he suddenly felt very hot. "I … I have never seen that glove," he swallowed. "B-before in my life! You know, Natchez the Paiute is big. So is his brother, Numaga. Could be one of them's glove."

Reese looked like he wanted to say something else, but he seemed to tense up and stopped speaking. Instead, he made fleeting eye contact with the judge, waiting expectantly for him to reply.

"Let me see that again, JR," the judge pressed further.

"Look," JR said, looking back and forth between the judge and the attorney. "I don't like this any more than you do. These people are upset and need answers. I agree, we need to find Colton and talk to him. But there is no denying that Reese was at the scene. Why else would his glove be next to Ardie's body?" He held the glove up again for the judge and everyone to see.

Jack Russell nodded in agreement, looking indignant. He looked at Judge Kensington.

"Well, well, well," the judge said. "JR has a point here. Evidence such as this does not lie, Reese. Those Injuns you mentioned, well, they're not as big as you, son. Why don't you come on up here and try on the glove?"

Reese made his way toward the front of the hall, stopping in front of the judge, as JR Morrison met him there with the glove.

"My thoughts, exactly," Colby added, nodding his head toward the judge. The room was filled with chatter of all types. Most people were very curious to see the results of the fitting.

Sheriff Hightower picked up his rifle, leaning against the wall by his seat, stood up and walked slowly toward Reese.

The judge looked at the sheriff and nodded. "Try on the glove, son."

Reese was handed the glove by JR, when Sheriff Hightower interjected. "May I see that first?"

Reese chucked the glove over to the sheriff, who inspected it and then tossed it back to Reese. He proceeded to try on the glove. It easily slipped over his hand, shocking the audience immediately to a roar and high-volume chatter. Bang! Bang! Bang! The gavel pounded, stricken by the judge.

"Sheriff," the judge said, making a solid attempt to be serious. "We need to hold Mr. Clybourne in custody until we can get more answers. We can't have him fleeing if he's involved, so no bail. After all, Reese and Colton have worked together in the past. They could have planned this together."

JR fixated on Reese, who shifted in his stance, not absorbing what was happening to him so suddenly. Appearing visibly uncomfortable and mystified, as his face reddened and pearls of sweat appeared on his forehead, he gazed at the judge in disbelief. The sheriff approached Reese, who for being such a big and imposing man, suddenly looked downright puny. Reese looked, as though he wanted to blurt something out. Instead, he clamped his lips together.

"Let's do this, Reese," Sheriff Hightower muttered, removing a pair of iron shackles from his waist while gesturing at the judge.

JR was expecting Reese to defend himself, to lie, to say something, anything. It seemed too easy. A shrewd man like Reese ought to have an explanation or an excuse. *Is the evidence too damning?* JR looked at Colby, who shrugged back at him with wide eyes. JR felt more confused than he had before, especially at Reese's silence. He didn't even attempt to defend himself. *Why?*

"In the meantime," the judge snarled and leaned back in his chair. "I want Colton back here, dead or alive! I will repeat: I'm issuing a warrant for his immediate arrest, five thousand dollars, and anyone harboring him, knowingly or unwittingly, either way, we are takin' them in as criminal accomplices as well, including any Injuns."

Barbara stepped forward once again. "Well, that's not what I think happened." She looked around the room expectantly, as though anticipating the townspeople to join her in agreement. "I've known Colton for years." She gestured to the room, no doubt suggesting that the others knew Colton as well. "And," she said, looking back at the judge. "We still have a missing beautiful young girl, Judge, who worked on your ranch!"

The judge raised his eyebrows, visibly taken aback. "Wait, wait, wait. What are you implying? No, now, Barbara, you quiet yourself. Let's stick to the facts here. I know you're upset about the young woman, but lady, you are out of line. We are goin' after Colton, as I said, dead or alive! As far as that Wyola, she's just a tramp runaway! She's probably with that Colton as we speak, if either one of them is even still alive somewhere."

19

Reese sat fuming in a small, rusty cell. The Benton town jailhouse wasn't a jailhouse at all. It was a boarded-up, old adobe *vaquero* bunking house the locals had converted to a vagrant shelter. It had some barred rooms for property storage. These were the makeshift cells. There were only three holding cells for petty criminals and drunkards, but this was the only one occupied. It was late in the evening, yet Reese remained alert. He tried to wait patiently, to get a clearer picture on his next steps, yet nobody had said so much as a word to him since he got arrested at the hearing. *What a manure show! That was an ignoramus failure and a dismal flopping fiasco, far beyond a dog and pony show,* he thought furiously as he mumbled the complex jargon, rambling around in his brain. *How can they convict me of murder just by finding the damn glove. I could have dropped it anytime goin' to work on the way to the mine. The judge better have a pretty damn good plan for getting me out of this impossible disaster.* He figured the judge had some master plan that would clear his name as soon as they found Colton. They'd probably bring him in dead, if they were smart, as he hoped, so he couldn't make a defense or blame any of them. In fact, he had a million confused thoughts flinging around in his destabilizing brain, as he jargoned more synonymical acronyms of twisted nothings.

Henry Devine, the local errand boy, sat at the front of the holding house in Sheriff George Hightower's stead. Sheriff Hightower had his main place of enforcement in Aurora, a two-day ride from Benton. Hightower was rarely in Benton, as there had never been multiple murders committed there before. It seemed like the people of the valley had lived in harmony for eleven years until the judge arrived five years earlier. Reese wondered where everybody was. *Will I really have to sleep in a dingy cell before I am allowed an explanation?* Reese heard the door to the sheriff's office open, but he could not see who entered.

"Evening, Judge," Henry Devine said in veiled respect.

Reese stood up. *This better be good.*

"Henry, how are you doin', boy?" the judge articulated, friendly-like and undisturbed. "Why don't you run outside, Henry, and let me have some words in private with the prisoner?"

"I don't know, Judge," Henry answered hesitantly.

Don't be stupid, boy, Reese thought.

"Sure, you do, boy. Now go get on and don't you be arguin' with the judge now, young whipper snapper."

Reese heard a chair scoot across the wooden floor. It sounded like Henry was getting up. *That was easy*, Reese thought.

"Git on, boy," the judge said again. "I only need a minute."

"Five minutes, Judge. That's it. Five minutes. I'll be right outside!"

"Oh, young Henry, now don't you be eavesdropping. This is a private and privileged discussion we are about to have. Under the law, Henry. Now, you get to skedaddling. Reese Clybourne, he has himself no representation but a lot of explaining to do, nonetheless. So, move along and stay away from the door. I need to speak with him in privacy. To hear a bit of what he has to say 'bout all these happenings now, boy!"

"I'll be back." the young man asserted.

Reese heard the door open and close, followed by footsteps heading toward the cells. The judge appeared in the hallway, his typical cheeky grin wiped clean from his face. He was still wearing his purple velvet vest and black hat he bore at the hearing. As he approached, shaking his head slowly, he clamored, "Reese, Reese, Reese."

This was it. Reese was sure the judge would tell him the next steps. *Maybe he snagged a key from Henry Devine and will sneak me out into the dead of night.*

"Judge," Reese said desperately, grabbing the bars with both of his hands. "You gotta get me outta here, Kensington. Why are you letting 'em do this to me? Why now?" He wanted the judge to get straight to the point.

The judge looked back at Reese, his beady brown eyes casting a beam directly into the cell. "Because you dropped your glove, ya creton muttonhead! And pipe down." His voice changed to a whisper. "Once we get Colton, if he is even still alive as they are claimin', we is gonna—"

Reese interrupted. He couldn't stand the idea of being stuck in this small, dirty jail cell any longer. "He went over a waterfall, Judge, wounded. He ain't still alive! My goose is cooked, Judge!" Reese felt the desperation rise in his own voice. He didn't like feeling so out of control and being at the mercy of the townspeople, looking to hang someone, most certainly, for all these killings, in addition to the town being put at great risk for an attack from the Paiutes for the murder of their two warriors. The people of Benton wanted someone quick, if even just to show the Indians they weren't going to rest until justice was served.

"Now look here," the judge said, making a stern attempt at calming him down. "You ain't cooked. You know, I always got a plan. I'm the judge." He began to talk faster and quieter. "And if you want yer share of the money, then you'll wait patiently in Carson City while I see to it that your monies are making a good investment. We'll get Colton. He looks more guilty than you do right now. And if he's dead, even better cuz' dead men tell no tales, Reese. You know that!"

"I dunno, Judge. Carson City? Carson City, Judge?" Reese quietly cried out.

"This is a federal matter, Reese. There's a federally contracted mail carrier who's been murdered. You know that!"

"Judge, but you killed him!" Reese pushed back and then forcefully whispered, "The townsfolk love that nigga, includin' the Morgan family and their lawyer! They've always been wary of me." It angered him that the white folk in Benton were so quick to turn on one of their own. *No-good traitors*, he thought. To Reese, they were all cowards for letting the judge intimidate and take advantage of the whole town and valley, the way he had done since he got there, years earlier.

"Remember what I said," the judge pointed out. "Dead or alive. So, I'm shootin' him the first chance I get. Then I'll worry about why, after I do. He'll be dead, you'll be free, and we can all live happily ever after." The judge continued, "You can't say anything. If you do, the town gets the gold, and you get nothin'. If you only tell 'em of me, well, yer glove places you there. You'll just hang with me. You don't have a choice, Reese, but to hang out and earn your gold. Look at it like that. You don't have to even work, like up at that miserable mine. You're going away to a new job, away from the mine for a short spell, but this time yer actually gonna make a lot of money, like double or triple a life of wages. Just hang tight and keep your mouth shut!"

"Oh, them Morgans are never gonna leave me alone," Reese mumbled. He didn't like the judge's plan and wondered if he had really thought the whole thing through.

The judge waved his hand through the air. "Oh, they'll be moving along, I suspect, after some time goes on by. Silly women. You are just gonna have to watch yer back until they do. I have my own plans now for them."

"She ain't just gonna leave and give ya the mine," Reese said, seeing the holes starting to form in their original plan.

How did it once seem so clean, so simple? he thought.

"No, but she ain't gonna want to be partners with me either, and I ain't sellin', so she's gonna have to take a payment from me and move along. Plus," the judge said, seemingly impressed with his own artistry,

"She won't want to live with the reminder of where and how her dear husband died every day. She's got them beautiful young daughters to see out of this mess, so they can go off to start a normal life, maybe even get an education, wouldn't ya know." His voice trailed off as he looked aside. "Anyway," he snapped back at Reese. "I gotta run now. We don't need no suspecting goin' on with our relationship and all. You just keep yer mouth shut and play along, and I'll have you out in no time." The judge tipped his hat at Reese, almost cheerfully.

Reese felt strange about the whole thing. In his opinion, not a single step of their plan had gone right. "You watch that Rudy," he said, remembering their third partner. "I don't trust that boy 'round my money."

The judge shook his head. "You certainly don't need to be worryin' yourself about that drunken vagrant Rudy."

Reese heard the front door open once again. Henry Devine was back.

"Anyway, boy," the judge said loudly so Henry could hear, "we'll try to have a lawyer for you in the coming days, but in the meantime, the sheriff has decided to send you to Carson City federal prison. You'll be moved tomorrow. Try not to cause any more trouble than you already have. I need to get you outta this town anyway fer yer own good."

The judge turned, and as he left, Reese slumped down on the hard, wooden bench, still in disbelief of the sudden change of events that seemingly vastly extended the whole ordeal, he was going to have to go through, to even get out of this mess.

20

August 1871

Spring and a long, hot summer had passed. The mornings were slowly beginning to get cooler with dew forming. Wyola stood on the hillside overlooking a huge lake and took a deep breath as she let her gaze rest on the beautiful scenery in front of her. Taking in the majestic mountains and the broad, green valley below, which was home to a large encampment of wickiups surrounding the lake, she was amazed at the beauty and the people.

Her face was glowing in the morning sun as the soft, early fall breeze blew strands of her long, black hair into her face. She got a hold of some wayward strands and tucked them behind her ear as she looked down and rubbed her ever-larger, growing belly with her other hand. She smiled as she felt the baby move. Instinctively, she knew she would be giving birth to her child in a matter of weeks.

Colton walked up behind Wyola as she smiled, turned, and leaned into his embrace. She looked up into his eyes and saw they were filled with so much love for her. As he grabbed her hand, to pull her closer toward him, the sun made its first reveal with a beaming explosion as it rose over the southeastern mountains. Colton was still limping ever so slightly but had otherwise fully recovered from his injuries. The months of healing had passed. Wyola and Colton had spent the happiest time of their lives here together, and even through the drought and famine of the day, they found a joyous peace in each other's embrace and companionship. Colton had adapted to her pregnancy, in spite of the circumstances. He never made her feel blame or guilt that any of this was her fault, as she had secretly worried and feared might happen.

Wyola turned around to face Colton and reached into the pocket of her dress. She pulled out a heavy, shiny silver watch, dangling from a chain, and smiled at him.

"What's this?" Colton asked as she placed it in his hand.

"It belonged to my father. He gave it to me before he died. My mother had it made for him when we lived in the East. Open it," she said while looking expectantly at him.

When Colton opened it, there was a picture of the two of them inside.

"I had planned to give it to you before, ya know, before all these terrible things happened. It's the only thing I took with me when I ran away from the judge," she said as her fingers trembled. Wyola, embarrassingly, looked down to a view obscured now by a huge belly.

"It's very nice," Colton said in a reassuring voice, kissing her forehead. "The most beautiful gift I have ever gotten from the most beautiful woman, inside and out, that I have ever seen or known," he passionately added.

Meanwhile, down at the large encampment, the Paiute Indians were busy tending to their morning activities and getting ready for the day. Some of the women cooked rice grass millet, other women were working with deer meat or on the mortar and pestle, grinding grain and corn. Young children were running around, chasing animals and each other, laughing in joy.

Peace Chief Natchez entered the largest wickiup in the Toi Ticutta encampment to meet with his honorable brother, Supreme War Chief Numaga, who appeared incredibly sicker than just a few months ago at his arrival. His square face had sunken in, and his once deep-brown skin looked pale, almost ashen. The fire that Natchez used to see in his brother's eyes had been replaced by a yellowish glow. His thin, gray hair, which once was braided in two long, tight braids, hung loosely over his shoulders. Thocmetony was taking care of him mostly and preparing medicine in the corner of the hut.

Peace Chief Natchez was surprised to see a white man sitting beside his brother. It was General Edward Canby, the army officer who oversaw the Paiute settlement and was in charge of the western quadrant of Washington, Oregon, Idaho, Montana, Wyoming, Nevada, Arizona, and California. General Canby wore a dark-blue uniform with a lot of golden buttons and dressage, a sign of his many years and valiant service to the nation. He had tall, black, army-issue boots with silver spurs and a long cavalry sword in a solid silver sheath attached at the hip. He tended to talk out of the side of his mouth. Still, he was an honest man who wanted peace among the immigrants, local settlers, and Chief Numaga's people. Supreme War Chief Numaga had a great amount of respect for the general, therefore his younger brother, Natchez, the Peace Chief, did as well. They were just ending a conversation about the provision that was allotted by the government for the tribe. Numaga had pointed out it wasn't enough.

General Canby put a large, white hand on Numaga's shoulder. He did not show his concern, but Natchez could sense it. "Thank you, Great Chief."

Numaga nodded. "Although our hunting lands are dwindling, we remain hopeful. We will appreciate the provision."

"Chief," General Canby spoke as he rose from his seat. "We gotta take Colton with us."

Natchez gazed at his brother and looked, as if to say, *Brother, no.* His brother nodded ever-so-slightly in return.

With great difficulty, Chief Numaga spoke. His hoarse voice rasped in his throat, as if every syllable took great energy from him. He turned to the general. "We only have honor in our ways and justice. Colton has shown the Paiute people both honor and justice."

"We are not Colton's keeper!" Natchez burst out, unable to control himself. He would not let them take him. Colton could make that decision for himself. This was all their land after all, given to them by the Great Spirit.

"Now, gentleman," Canby said in a measured tone. "I respect one man's doing or undoin', but if the world says his undoin' must be looked at by the others, it must be undertaken." Canby then continued to explain that Colton was wanted for questioning, and he would be needing to take him to Benton, regardless of guilt or innocence. It was up to a jury of his peers, and that due process was still finding its way in what remained as a country, suffering from the growing pains of several wars, wars fought both abroad and here, in the great land of the United States of America. In fact, it survived and was somewhat united again, following that calamitous Civil War with its death and destruction. It was time to let the people of Benton and the others in the region, who had been impacted so devastatingly by this tragedy, be able to find a resolute conclusion to the crimes in question, of what had been an incredible year since.

Numaga coughed. "If one man takes from another man, this man I will send. But if one man has never taken from any man, this man I cannot send."

Canby stood up straight. "I want justice as much as you do, Chief, which is why I need to do my job." He looked at Natchez as he strode toward the exit of the hut. "I will be back for Colton in the coming days. I have no choice. You have no choice, if you wish for them to bring the winter provision." With one last nod at Natchez and his brother

Numaga, the general left the wickiup, accompanied by Thocmetony, the sister of the two great chiefs, a rising, advocating activist.

Several days later, Colton was startled early in the morning to a sudden, loud groan from Wyola. He woke up beside her, feeling damp hides beneath them, knowing what it meant. Water had drenched the furs. Her water had broken. It was time now, he knew it, and the baby was coming. Colton jumped up instinctively, unable to process his own tornado of feelings and emotions. Questions swarmed into his brain as he donned a frock coat and hurried outside to find Thocmetony. *Can I really love this child as my own?* He wondered to himself in silence.

"Thocmetony! Sarah!" he yelled outside of the wickiup, the cold morning sending a shiver through his bones. "It's time. The baby is coming!"

Wyola slowly sat up, visibly in great discomfort, pierced with a stab of pain deep in her abdomen. It was enough to jolt her into the awareness that the baby was coming. She let herself sink back on her mat and tried to be calm. The Paiute women were experienced when it came to childbirth, and she was relieved to be in such good hands.

Colton nervously waited as Thocmetony made preparations to come to Wyola's help. Women dying during childbirth was common. *Will she survive? Will the child survive?* He shuddered at the unknown future for the woman he so desperately loved. He felt like he had just been given a glimpse of a life with Wyola over the past months. *Please, God, don't take her away from me,* he pleaded.

Ten minutes later, several women joined Wyola and Thocmetony in their wickiup while Colton waited outside, nervously pacing back and forth. Everybody worked in silence to set up the space, nobody spoke, and no sounds were heard except for Wyola's moans, which grew increasingly louder by the minute. Two teenage Paiute girls helped her lay on top of a cloth, propped up by several folded blankets. The women had brought herbs, and a girl ran to fetch a bucket of water as another woman rekindled the fire.

Thocmetony sat beside Wyola on the ground, holding her hand. This time, she was smiling, and her eyes matched her smile. "Wyola," she said, "We are with you. You will be fine. The baby is positioned well and will come out easily."

Wyola nodded silently. Beads of sweat dotted her forehead, and she winced every minute or two. She looked up, her light eyes wide and expressive. She wore an expression of elegant calm, even though she was in excruciating pain. There was stress in her eyes and around her mouth, but still, her beauty remained unmarked. The discomfort became a subtle accent, enhancing her appearance rather than detracting from it. She was incredibly strong. Thocmetony felt it in the way she gripped her palm.

Colton couldn't wait for the birth to be over. His eyes moistened, and he quivered at the thought of what Wyola had been through, while he was pacing back and forth in front of the hut.

The next several hours whirled before Wyola like snowflakes in a winter storm. The Paiute women talked in their native tongue. It seemed as though half the time they were instructing one another, and the other half, they were muttering prayers or blessings under their breath. When Wyola went into the harder part of her labor, one of the women massaged her stomach lightly. Thocmetony coached her on her breathing.

Wyola's moans morphed into screams, shrieks that hurt Colton's ears outside the wickiup. It hurt him to know she was in such agony, but it was even worse to think about the suffering she had endured before this all happened.

As her screams reverberated throughout the small hut, Thocmetony looked into her eyes. "Breathe," she said gently. "You are strong. You are strong," she whispered repeatedly.

With a final scream, surely loud enough to cause an avalanche, Wyola pushed her body with what seemed to be the last bit of energy left inside of her. Suddenly everything changed, and she felt the presence of a new life. She could smell it, feel it, and hear it. New life filled the room like the sun's warming rays after the passing of a cold, heavy cloud.

"Thocmetony," Colton called from outside the hut, unable to stand it any longer. "Tell me she's goin' to be alright."

Thocmetony came out of the wickiup and held her finger up to her mouth, gesturing for him to be silent. Moments later, the shrieking sounds of a baby's cries pierced the hut. Colton froze as he heard the baby wailing.

"It's a boy," Thocmetony said, a huge smile stretched across her typically stern face, as she led Colton into the wickiup. The women were wrapping the baby. Wyola looked exhausted but happy. Colton was captivated by the tiny human being. He had never in his life seen a newborn baby before. *How strange-looking.* The baby was so small and fragile.

Wyola burst into tears. "Colton," she pleaded. "What about the baby. Is he ok?"

"Yes, love," he whispered. "Yes, *he* is."

She crumpled into exhaustion, until one of the women handed Wyola her newborn child. Colton looked at the baby, never having held anything like it. The child's light skin looked almost white. His face was pure innocence as Wyola brought him to her chest. Colton couldn't help but notice how helpless the child appeared as he sucked from Wyola's breast. *How can the child, with no understanding of his situation, be so trusting, so willing? Doesn't he know how he came into this world?* This mother, to whom he was so greedily clinging, this mother, who bore so much anguish and humiliation, the price of his entry into this world. Colton laid down, to comfort and hold a sleepy Wyola and the baby she just bore, as the women cleaned up the hut.

"What will I call you?" Wyola cooed, petting the baby. Looking up, she asked, "Colton, what should we call him?"

"Well, my love, what do you want to call him?" Colton asked.

"We should both decide. I like the name Emil. I think he looks like a little Emil."

"I think that's a perfect name," Colton concurred as he kissed her on her forehead and tasted the salty sweat on his lips.

As Colton gazed into the baby's peaceful face, he heard a noise that made him look up. Natchez's tall frame stooped low to enter the wickiup.

"Colton," he said with a smile that did not match the serious look in his eyes. "May I have a word with you?" Natchez didn't look at the mother or child.

Colton nodded and got up, hoping no bad news would befall them on such a beautiful day. Judging by Natchez's tone and facial expression, he knew it wouldn't be a pleasant conversation. Colton wondered how many more surprises he could take.

"Colton," Natchez said again as the two stood outside of the wickiup, "You must go."

"What?" Colton was genuinely confused. "Go where?"

"Off the reservation," Natchez said curtly.

"Why?" Colton asked in defiance. He caught himself and softened his expression, so as not to insult the great chief. "Why now?"

Natchez remained calm but unflinching. "Things are getting worse out there, Colton, for our people. You are a wanted man. General Canby wants us to hand you over to them for questioning."

"But I didn't do—" Colton protested, unable to fathom what would happen to Wyola and the baby if he had to leave. "You know what happened, Natchez." He was pleading more than he would have liked.

Colton felt desperate. So much had been taken away from him when he lost Cyrus and Morgan. He wanted justice eventually, but now was not the time for it. The two lovers had just started to build back the possibility of a new life, a better life. He figured, once they settled somewhere, when things were safer and Wyola was strong enough, then they would go together to seek justice, although justice for him grew to be secondary to protecting his family.

"I know, Colton. I know. But Canby is threatening the provisions owed to us, and this winter is going to be worse than the last. I cannot jeopardize the well-being of my people. They have suffered enough." Natchez looked concerned, but his face remained stern.

Colton looked at him and wondered if he did not understand what had just taken place inside the small hut. *Does he not understand that there is a woman and new child laying inside, who need me to help and protect them?* He had learned where and how this child came to be in the prior months they had spent together, and that reality warranted a divine intervention. He couldn't fathom what he would do in the name of serving out that justice.

"Two days," Colton said, almost pleading, as if Natchez were his master. "Please, just give me two more days with her until she is stronger. Please." He shamelessly begged the chief for more time.

"Colton, blessed are you with a child, my friend," Natchez said, trying again to smile. "General Canby swore he would be back with troops and provisions. We must all be here to receive our rations for the winter. They will starve our people, if we are not all here for the counting of heads and disbursement of provisions. They will take you when they come. We cannot protect you anymore, Colton, any of you." He gestured toward the many, many wickiups, as he added, "We need to eat."

Natchez's long, handsome face was stricken with grief and exhaustion. Colton looked around at the encampment. He couldn't deny that his people were thin, some even emaciated. Colton understood. He would do anything to protect Wyola, and he would do anything for his Paiute friends. Natchez felt the same way about all his people. Colton had more questions than answers, but he knew, with one look at Natchez's face, that staying was no longer an option.

Colton stood up straight and nodded. He knew what had to be done. "I am ready. I am healed. And I am grateful. We will go and seek justice." He thought of the judge. "Justice for all, including this child. Wyola will be ready. She is strong. She knows what must be done."

Natchez put his hand on Colton's shoulder. "I will send one warrior to accompany you south to the river. Please be—"

Colton interrupted, "We will be grateful to clear our names, and this child will be raised properly. Emil is now my son!" Colton felt the impact of the words as he spoke them, as though they carried an armor that now protected him. "God has made it this way. I was not the father, but now I am. It was not the child's fault, so he shall be loved. God is good. He is with us every day. He will help us protect and raise up Emil."

"I ... mil ... E ... mil," Natchez said, trying to pronounce the name.

"Yes, brother." Colton nodded, smiling. "Emil."

"You are a great man, Colton, to take this child as your son." Natchez stepped forward and embraced Colton. With a small nod, Natchez turned on his heel and walked away.

Two days later, Colton and Wyola stood near the exit of the encampment, ready to depart. Thocmetony had wrapped the baby in a bundle of swaddling clothes and helped Wyola fit him into a papoose, so she could carry Emil on her back. Natchez, meanwhile, readied two ponies with what little provisions they could spare. Thocmetony embraced Wyola as young Angel stood by, watching and crying.

"Wyola," Thocmetony said, fighting tears. "God be with you, child."

Natchez stepped forward. "Colton, Wyola, Tinemaha will go with you." He gestured to a muscular Paiute man who looked to be about twenty years old, mounted on his horse near the two ponies. Tinemaha held a Paiute spear in his right hand and had a quiver of arrows with a bow strapped across his back.

"Thank you, brother," Colton said, his eyes moist from emotion.

He looked at Thocmetony, Angel and Wyola, who were all crying. Gripped with fear and uncertainty, but holding high courage, he swallowed back his tears, willing himself to remain strong. Deep down, he wondered if he would ever see Natchez and Thocmetony again.

21

A few days had passed, and the first early signs of fall had fully settled into the high, upper regions of the Sierra Nevada Mountain range. The days were growing shorter, and although it tended to still warm up through the early afternoons, the mornings and evenings had begun to become much colder. With the injuries haunting him, which Colton had suffered nearly a year earlier, it took him a little time each morning to work the cold out of his bones.

The first day of his journey with Wyola and the infant leaving Toi Ticutta had been difficult, to say the least. Colton was thinking a lot about all that had happened in these past four seasons of slow-moving time. Before all the events took place, their time together had always been reluctantly limited, apart from a few stolen moments in town and some rare moments at the Morgan outpost. In fact, the hours he had spent longing for Wyola were far more numerous than the time they had actually enjoyed each other alone. Thankfully, they were to do it now, since rediscovering each other through the multiple violent tragedies. Colton appreciated the sharing of a lot of time together over the past months in the encampment, watching Wyola's belly grow. However, that was no comparison to their togetherness in surviving so much death and haunting memories, jointly, within the past year gone by. Adding to that despair, in the form of stress and demonic thoughts of vengeance, was his constant anxiousness over the rape of his woman and his innocence in those murders. Colton wanted to revel in their new, unlimited time together, but it was hard to pause and feel joy, when survival and justice hung so precarious.

The first two days of their journey passed in near silence, as they tried to put as much distance as possible between themselves and the life they once knew. Colton's mind couldn't stop wandering, as he thought so hard about what was to come sooner than later, possibly, and the life, if any, they might share beyond that.

"People will come looking for you," he remembered Natchez saying as they bid farewell to each other and their Paiute friends. "I know you're innocent Colton, but they don't think so. They will shoot first and ask questions later. You know this," Natchez had said sternly just a few days ago, it seemed.

Colton appreciated the good and wise memories bestowed on him by his Indian friends, but some of the memories, even though righteous, haunted him as to what lay ahead.

Colton nodded to himself, knowing in the pit of his stomach what the truth was. He pictured JR, Colby, and the Morgan girls and wondered if they all would like to see him dead. He thought of the years he spent making such close friends and acquaintances of the Benton townsfolk, and the years he spent working diligently at the mine with Cyrus and Morgan. And the thought of all of that being gone, because of one judge's greed, was gnawing at him with fervor. Would his friends and family shoot first and ask questions later? He hoped it wasn't so, but deep down, Colton really didn't know what they thought of him. After all, he hadn't seen them since before the tragedy, the murder of Morgan at the mine and the discovery of Tahn-Se and Wanu by Natchez, Tavibo, and Wovoka, right where they had found him, caught up in the eddy, in the lower falls of Morgan Creek.

These dark thoughts brought him back very well to the first half of his life spent in chains. Back then, he was just a body, just a number, but also just a boy. His old master had even calculated exactly how much somebody like him was worth. The four or so years before the events of the past year, Colton was no longer just a slave. He was Colton. He was free. By written proclamation, he had the right to a good life, prosperity, and the pursuit of happiness. He had a name, a story, a personality, and a new heart, but most of all, that freedom. Freedom to make a life at all was everything. Life is not life without it, without freedom. His heart yearned for peace and freedom between all men.

However, since he was found barely alive and had recovered, Colton couldn't help but feel that there was, yet again, going to be a steep and heavy price placed over his head. *Dead or alive,* he thought, *that's how they want me. Is this time in my life worse than the early years of my life and those horrible whips, flogs, and chains?* It most certainly was. He was by no means free, not free at all. In fact, Colton could easily slip into being a prisoner of his own mind. He couldn't let that happen, to let the evil of this current life bring him to death. He had to defeat this demon's curse.

He thought of Cyrus, the only person who had ever understood him. He had been his cousin and best friend, his confidant, and his backup anytime he was threatened or in trouble. They had been each other's backups since they were children and then turned by white men into slaves. Cyrus was gone. Randall was gone. If the townspeople and citizens of Benton truly had come to believe Colton would kill his only friends, then he thought sadly, *they must all be far gone and lost in their minds as well.*

Colton certainly felt that way, like he was losing his mind, as he looked over at Wyola, who rode silently by his side. He realized in that instant, if he could just focus on her beautiful, yet stoic face, her strength, and what she had been through without him near her, then he should certainly man up and be as strong. Colton felt calm in her presence, as though she was a peaceful light in a world full of darkness. As long as Wyola was by his side, there would always be hope.

As he thought of these things, he found his mind relaxing. If he could just stay focused on Wyola, he would survive through the handing out of justice, for her sake. As far as the child concerned Colton, he kept asking himself over and over and over again: What child is this? What child is this?

Colton began to focus on their journey, daydreaming about their future and what it might look like down the road. *Is it the future I had always envisioned, even during those days spent toiling at the Morgan mine? Can we achieve those dreams through all of this? Can we still own land and a couple of cows and chickens, build a house, or buy a mule and maybe some nice horses too? Are these horses even our horses we are riding upon?* Again, he started to wander in his thoughts.

He looked back at Wyola and noticed her gazing straight ahead. *What is she thinking of? Is she imagining me spending my days working the land, maybe with a couple of friends, or my own son?* Everything would be peaceful, and he would be free at last. Wyola and Colton would invite their friends over for joyous dinners, where they'd laugh and sing into the early hours of the night. And they'd have more children, a house full of children. Colton always pictured having children with Wyola. Children were a true testimony to their love for one another. Now there was another life in this plan, Emil, a child he was forced by destiny to love like his own blood. Maybe they would give Emil brothers and sisters. Perhaps they would give him his own family. Colton wondered deep down, how he would feel about Emil if he had another real son of his own, not a bastard, which was how Colton feared the world would treat Emil. *Oh, what child is this?* He exhaled. What would this child think of him?

Such thoughts kept Colton awake, enduring hours of anxiety the past couple nights. These thoughts tormented him. However, he loved Wyola so much that he reasoned he had no choice but to unconditionally love this young one, a child not of his seed. These dark, racing thoughts would keep him awake, huddled around a small fire at night, drawing Wyola and Emil in to lie close to him and to the warmth, as if he hoped love really could wipe away all the darkness, they'd all endured so far and would continue facing in the future. *How much time being a father to him will it take for us to forget? How much time will it take for me to have real peace with this child?*

There was still so much to learn about the woman who rode next to him. Colton wanted to sit across from her for hours and ask her endless questions about her life. He wanted to know everything about her. *But is this the right time to focus on such questions?* When he did ask her things here and there, she always answered with enthusiasm and hope, even in this unbelievable time. *What gives her the strength to do that? How does she still know how to smile? Where does she glean her peace from through such tumultuous times?*

Sarah Winnemuccah, or Thocmetony, as she was known, was a deeply spiritual woman, a believer in Christ who steadfastly would sit for hours, days on end praying to the white man God in the heavens, teaching her tribe for years the truth, the Christ love, how they should know the love of this Son of Man who was also the Son of God, and make that love known to all on earth they had come in contact with. *Is this where Wyola gets her peace?* He had observed them, sitting for hours, praying together, reading the Book together, and sharing these things with the young children of the village as much as she would share and teach the elders of the tribe the same stories and messages. It had changed the Paiute deeply, and this was very pronounced and notable to Colton. Even though he thought he believed too, this inner demon of bitterness and resentment towards so many men haunted him. He had no peace. He was constantly tormented in the night by thoughts of the judge drooling over his girl, raping her, penetrating her and planting his evil seed inside of her. *How can she have defeated that evil seed in her heart? How does she move on with her life?* All Colton could think of, it seemed, was justice, but in the form of revenge. He was angry. And he was especially angry at God, although he didn't reveal this to Wyola, or anyone else. He put on a good face, especially in her presence, but this was his spiritual war going on inside of him. He yearned for distraction from these thoughts constantly.

"Wyola," he said on the third day, the wind whipping his face in a particularly biting kind of way. It had suddenly cooled down a lot. "Tell me about your parents. What was it like when you were a little girl?"

"My parents were my favorite people who ever lived," she said fondly, her voice soft as silk. The trace amount of Southern drawl added a remarkable cadence to her beautiful speech. "My mom was Choctaw Cherokee. Her name was Awinita, from Abbeville, South Carolina. And my dad lived across the Georgia border, in Elberton. He was an indentured servant for Judge Kensington living on his plantation there. He cooked and was an amazing horseman, who tended the judge's horses. During the war, my mom, my sister and I, came to live with our father at the Kensington plantation. When the war was lost, he brought us out West. As you know, my parents died while I was sleeping."

"Your parents," Colton said, "They were slaves for the judge?"

Wyola nodded. Colton felt the mingling of sadness and rage again inside of him. Even though he longed for distraction to pull him away from his dark and depressing thoughts of injustice served, he would easily draw back into them with just about every deep subject, as all seemed so close to evil, a mere few steps away. Every corner of his life was touched by this evil, and especially the past couple years by this malicious man. The judge's legacy of ruining lives had no bounds. His treachery remained unharnessed. There was a child pushed into Colton's life to remind him of this, every time the judge's name or likeness came up.

Wyola, suspecting Colton struggled with darkness like that, abruptly changed the subject. She loved Colton as if he already was her husband. They certainly planned to be married but hadn't had the opportunity yet.

"My father was from West Africa. I don't quite know where," she said. "He didn't like to talk about it. But, oh boy, did he know how to dance. I loved the way he danced." Wyola's face lit up as she thought of the memory. "He was a kind man, deep down, but I think the years of doing slave work had hardened him to the world. My father wasn't cut out for hard labor. He loved to talk and entertain. I think he would have made a fantastic politician, but the judge had him in the kitchen and corrals until he got sick." As she spoke, she looked down at a sleeping Emil, who was swaddled and wrapped in a sling across her body. "I hope there's some of my father in Emil."

"What about your mother?" Colton asked, eager to hear more of something brighter.

"She worked on the judge's plantation, too, once we had moved there to be with my dad just before the war started."

"Why didn't you all live together prior to that?" Colton asked, somewhat incredulous. He had never heard of Indians working on plantations or of black slaves married to Indians, but living apart. Back when he was a slave, all the slaves had been children of Africans. The only Indians that Colton knew were free or on reservations. After coming West, he saw many Paiutes working for the whites as paid workers and servants. *Well, I guess, as far as freedom goes, they are all slaves, if they're not really free.*

"She was forbidden by her father," Wyola reluctantly shared.

"It's ok, my Wyola. You can tell me anything, love. Do not be afraid," Colton assured her, smiling, now fully distracted from his dark thoughts to comfort her from hers.

Wyola was silent for a short time but then responded. "My mother and father fell in love before my father was sold as a slave. They had just married in Charlottesville and were going to start a new life of their own on the reservation, but the Fugitive Slave Act Law of 1850 came into effect, and my dad got caught up in it. A bounty hunter using false documents had captured him, claiming he was a slave, and then handed him over to Judge Kensington." Wyola sighed.

"I don't know exactly how my mother wound up in South Carolina before the war, as I wasn't born yet. But she was pregnant with me before they were forcefully separated. I had lived in the Choctaw range with my mom and sister since I was born, but when the war was coming, they rounded up the Choctaw to contain them, and my mom escaped with Lola and I to be with our father."

Little Emil started crying, and Wyola switched his position to make him comfortable again.

"The judge took us in because he needed more help, and we came free to him at no cost. Two for the price of one. He wasn't that bad of a boss until his side began losing a lot of men, plantations, and finally the war. Eventually his plantation was burned to the ground and his slaves freed. The judge claimed that my dad was an indentured servant and owed him money, so the North allowed him to keep my father as property during the war settlement times. The judge packed us all up in nine wagons to come out here and left Georgia behind, as he would put it, 'for the land of opportunity'."

Wyola pulled her scarf closer around her shoulders and continued. "My mother was deeply in love with my father and wanted to be with him at any cost, even if it meant our lives. She would rather die in his arms, all of us being together, than alone. My mom helped all the other slaves a lot, especially at the end, with all the confusion and murders happening, caused by all the rage at the loss of the war. She didn't like to talk about the past, but she loved to sing. When I was a small child, she sang songs about the birds and the coyotes. She sang about the spirit of all living things and how that spirit was alive in all of us. That we could feel it whenever we wanted. I think that helped her when times had gotten tough."

Colton fell in love with every syllable that fell from Wyola's mouth. She naturally spoke very eloquently and seemed to know when to pause. She was naturally brilliant, a highly intelligent and articulate storyteller. She had attended the white man schools for a few years, while on the plantation, as the judge wanted her to be his prized possession. So, in a way the captivity did play the key role in Wyola's life, a role diced up in fate of the evil times she had suffered on that plantation in the South East of the country. It was certainly ironic that this education endorsed by the judge allowed her wisdom of goodness, far greater than the judge ever expected or desired for any of his property of human subjects.

Colton enjoyed following her eyes as she stared off into the distance while she spoke, as if temporarily transported back into her mother's arms. He hesitated to ask his next question but felt an openness in Wyola, open to sharing her past and her story with him.

"Where are they now?" he asked. "I mean, where did you lay them to rest?"

Wyola cleared her throat and looked down once more at the sleeping baby as though he could hear her. "My mother and father are buried in Arizona, from what I understand. That is where the judge said we were, when I watched him bury them. He wouldn't mark the graves. He said I would never be back there to find it."

"The other immigrants had left us behind. Knowing the judge now, I'm not sure why he even buried them. It's not like him to show such compassion. Maybe he did it to harness me," she wondered.

"Oh, Wyola, I'm so sorry. We are together now. Why life is so tragic, I do not know, but I will do my best to bring you great joy. Hearing your story of suffering, somehow, comforts me from my evil thoughts of revenge," Colton said, now feeling like maybe he shouldn't have asked. He didn't want to upset Wyola or dredge up memories that might be too painful for her or worse, make her so sad to think about, yet he did want to know everything about her.

"If you ask me," she continued as though she couldn't hear him completely. "I think it was a broken heart my mom suffered from the most. You see …" Her voice trailed off slightly. She cleared her throat once more. "My mother was brought into the judge's quarters a year before. I always thought the judge did something to her, and now I know he did. I think the sadness and the worry was too much for her to take. My dad wanted to kill the judge for it, but the thought of her suffering somewhere alone, while he was dead or in jail, stopped him from doing it. And then we were forced to leave. I was too young to do anything about any of it. And then my parents were both murdered on the way West."

A shiver went down Colton's spine as he came to a sudden realization. He felt a lump in his throat as tears filled his eyes. "Do you think the judge could have something to do with it?"

Wyola just turned and looked at Colton. He understood that was an affirmation. Then she said the most stunning thing. "Colton, we must love our enemies. We must forgive, lest we be forgiven. Love is the only answer to all the suffering in this world, even if it means death." *Oh my God,* he thought to himself. He could never love such a man.

Colton's head filled with hatred of the judge, who had brought such severe and undeserved suffering and trauma to so many people. He thought of the dreadful nights Wyola, her parents, and the other slaves must have spent at the plantation and then on the journey West, how terrified they must have been constantly, with nobody to protect them.

Suddenly the biting cold that stung his bones didn't feel so bad. The host of friends he left behind in Benton did not weigh as heavily. Even the fear of a price on his head and him hanging in a noose seemed to dissipate.

Wyola was with him. He knew that this, ultimately, was all he needed to restart his life. *How can this beautiful young woman have kept all this so bottled up?* Colton thought he must find justice for this, her, her family, and himself. Now these thoughts expanded and grew tenfold.

"I'm glad we're together," Colton said quietly, looking into her eyes, which shone glossy with tears. "Wyola, I promise you, I will protect you and Emil, if it's the last thing I do. One day, there will be no more sufferin' for any of us. We're gettin' closer to that day by the mile. I swear to you. The judge will burn in hell for all of this," he concluded.

"Oh, Colton," she whispered back, taking one hand off the reins and stroking Emil's ivory face, which had a hint of pink, as he slept. "Colton, I do love you. You are a very good man. We cannot bring back the dead, but we can save you, and saving you saves me and this child," she proclaimed. *What does she mean, save me?*

They rode in silence until the sun started to drop behind the Sierras. It grew colder by the minute.

As they moved along the trail, Emil began to stir restlessly. Wyola situated the infant child to feed him from her breast as the horse continued forward. She pulled a deerskin coat tightly over both of them to protect Emil and her exposed skin from the wind. Being an excellent horsewoman, she could ride bareback with no hands and even run her horse in the same way, so she had no problem feeding Emil as she was riding. She had shared stories with Colton, how she had run upon her steed with bow and arrow, hunting for game, directing the horse with only her legs clasped around the girth of her pony. Those were the stories of old Colton loved to hear, and now he was reminded, watching her hold this child so gently and safely as they rode, she with no hands to direct her pony, yet it heeded her commands so faithfully.

"Let's find some shelter," Colton said, nodding toward a rocky hill off in the distance. He figured there would be a shelter of some sort in which they could turn in for the evening.

Colton spotted an overhanging rock outcropping that protruded horizontally like an eroded stone layer in one of the hills just up ahead. It was big enough to cover them comfortably without labor, and their fire could be set up just under the ledge, which made it feel intimate, almost cozy. *Actually, it's perfect*, he thought to himself. He drove his horse toward the location, pointing it out to Wyola as the baby slept. Colton carefully assisted his beloved partner down from her pony, careful not to wake Emil.

Wyola took over the shelter setup from there, while Colton secured the horses to some trees overhanging the ledge from above. He went to retrieve water from the stream they were traversing along before finding the ledge. Wyola went to feed Emil again and then arranged the few blankets and furs they had into a mock bed. Colton returned with water and started a fire.

Once the fire burned slowly, Wyola sat holding Emil and began to
hum, rocking him back and forth. Colton noticed the way the firelight
illuminated the left side of her body, making her light-brown skin glow
orange. The light reflected off her delicate collar bones with her chest
exposed, as she sat nestled between the fire and the furs spread out.

"Wyola," Colton said softly. She looked up at him, eyes wide open.
"You are the most beautiful woman I have ever seen in my life." Wyola
smiled widely, and her eyelids batted nervously as she blushed. Colton
felt as though he'd never spoken truer words before in his life.

22

Reese sat at the Carson City federal prison central quad area on the morning of October 3rd, 1871. It had been eleven months, three days, twelve hours, and thirteen minutes since the judge had double-crossed him. He remembered every detail, every single lie that had come out of the judge's chap-lipped mouth.

"And if you want yer share of the money, then you'll wait patiently in Carson City while I see to it yer monies are making a good investment," the judge had said back when Reese was behind bars in the Benton holding house.

I should've grabbed him by his red, fat neck and strangled the life and all his lies right out of him right then, Reese thought, fuming on the inside. He had been spending his time in Carson plotting various alternative endings to his last encounter with Judge Kensington. One of them involved Reese going straight to Benton and confessing every detail of the judge's plans. Another, in fact most of them, involved him blowing the judge's brains out before he could destroy someone else's life. Reese was taking zero responsibility himself. The narcissist that he was had no concept of reality by comparing himself with the other victims of the judge's evil doings.

Reese wasn't getting out of Carson anytime soon. The judge would not be coming back for him, and he certainly wasn't protecting his money. Reese was furious with himself for believing such an intrepid lie. *Over twenty years spent running from the law just to end up here,* he thought, *all for one harebrained plan that was half-baked and cockeyed to begin with. Am I no smarter than Rudy or the judge?* Reese thought of that piss-for-brains drunkard Rudy, drinking away his share of the profits while he sat wasting away in a cell without a dime to his name. And in his mind, accomplice or not, it was Rudy who killed the two main men murdered in the whole event. Ya, it might have been his bullets that killed Colton and Cyrus, and certainly his bullets struck them Injuns, but Injuns were Injuns, and war between whites and Injuns was a daily occurrence. It wasn't fair in his mind to be the only one paying any debts here, when all he might have done was shoot a couple warface Indians and some dirty rotten niggers.

Prison wasn't all that bad though. For one, Reese discovered he had quite a network. Apparently two decades of roaming the Wild West and meeting other petty criminals here and there meant Reese had plenty of friends, or friends of friends already in Carson. For another, he was still one of the tallest, biggest people around. He reckoned nobody would mess with him so long as they didn't want to be messed with in return. Finally and perhaps best of all was the fact that Reese didn't have to put up with any disgusted looks from the people around him. That was one reason he hated Benton, a town of upturned noses and prissy women who thought themselves too good for him. Reese had always despised the way the miners and the Benton townsfolk had treated niggers and immigrants better than him. It was nice to know that among the criminals he wasn't judged. He fit right in.

But am I really a criminal for such acts of shooting a nigger and a Paiute or two? his thoughts continued. Reese pondered this throughout his adult life. In his mind he had always done what was necessary to survive, to get ahead in a changing world where the rules of the game were unclear and continually changing. Regardless of that fact he did what he thought was good or what he knew was evil. The rules of the game always seemed to work against him anyway. The rules were made for other people and by those who benefited most from such statutes. The West was a free-for-all, in his opinion, and the line between good and bad, between thief and businessman was murky at best.

Reese thought of Randall and their work together at the mine. Randall was a powerful man who had earned the respect of his kin and townsfolk alike merely by working hard and remaining steadfastly honest. The judge was an equally powerful man who commanded respect based on intimidation, money, and power. Actually, as he thought about it, the judge didn't really demand respect. Folks were just downright scared of him. *Where do I fall in all of this? Why are people so afraid of the judge, yet allow him so much slack?* They certainly never allowed him any slack, or he would never have ended up here! *Am I a weaker mind than the judge, a weaker spirit? Hell no!!*

With those thoughts rattling in his brain, Reese knew his stay at Carson might be longer than he thought at first, but he knew it wouldn't be forever. He had never given up before, so why would he now? He remembered learning to steal at the age of five. His mother, Gladys, caught a horrible flu one winter back in his hometown of Oklahoma City. Reese's no-good father had gambled away most of their money and was usually too stinking drunk to take notice of his mother's failing health. To care for her, Reese would steal food and medicine from the local shop owners. He knew even at that age, that people saw what they wanted to see. He went in with a nickel or a quarter to buy something small but then returned home with a lot more.

"Where's yer mother, young man?" the beefy grocer with a thick mustache would say, looking down at the young Reese who was bigger and taller than all the kids his age in town.

"She's sick, sir, very sick," Reese then responded, taking care to widen his eyes, sometimes even crying when he needed to.

The shop owners would offer their condolences, occasionally giving Reese a sweet treat or an extra bun. By that time Reese had usually grabbed and concealed an extra expensive item and more. Pretty soon everybody began to know him as the poor boy with a sick mother and drunkard for a father. He played to that notion until his mother died several years later. Reese's father was long gone and had vanished at that point. As far as Reese knew he and the whole world were far better off if his father were dead. The hate in his heart hoped often that he was.

On the third day of his imprisonment, eleven months ago, Reese had already figured it was time to stop feeling sorry for himself and get to work. His work would begin by networking with his fellow imprisoned "colleagues." Breakfast was served at seven in the morning, and Reese decided to get his tray and sit near some other inmates who were already deep in conversation.

Due to his height Reese had never been able to make subtle entrances. As soon as he sat down three inmates turned and stared at him, taking a quick scan of his height as their eyes traveled from his feet to the top of his head.

"Well you're no shrimp, man. Who are you?" a man asked, who had been talking just before Reese had sat down. "I'm Leander Morton. This is Crazy Zac Anderson, and this here is Frank Clifford."

Leander Morton flashed Reese a mischievous smile that revealed three gold teeth. Leander had a boyish charm about him, and Reese figured that most women would probably find him handsome. He was about thirty years old, give or take, with big, blue eyes and shaggy brown hair. There was a long, red scar from the bottom of his nose to his chin, cutting across the right side of his mouth. Reese wondered what had happened. His nose was crooked as though it had been broken in the past. Leander's smirk made his otherwise slightly disheveled facial appearance more casual and inviting. Leander washed regularly. He looked sharp. He was a handsome, good-looking, clean criminal with a crooked, cut-up face, one would say.

"Reese Clybourne," Reese introduced himself, nodding and acknowledging first Leander and then the rest of the men. To Leander's right sat a wiry man with black hair, dark eyes, and no eyebrows. He looked at Reese with creepy, wide eyes, which did not seem to blink. Reese figured that must have been partly why he earned the name Crazy Zac Anderson. He just looked crazy. Across the table sat a slightly chubby, middle-aged man with a prominent lazy eye. He certainly didn't look like an average Carson City inmate.

"We, uh, we're just talkin' about why we're in this fix in the first place." Leander smiled. "But don't trust this son of a bitch," he said, taking a bite of sausage and pointing his fork at the man with a lazy eye. "Frank over here is in here because he was kissing his mother too much, the filthy animal."

Leander guffawed and finished chewing his sausage.

"Why are you here?" Reese asked, turning to Leander.

Reese figured he must be new too. Nobody had that kind of energy and zest if they'd been behind bars for long, unless they were insane. Maybe Leander was insane. Either way, Reese wanted to find out. Insanity was good for business in certain doses.

"I was convicted of robbin' a train last December. These guys were with me. They keep denying it, but they were there. The government also believed I killed two cavalrymen because I happened to be wearing one of 'em's gloves. Ha! General Canby wants my hide," he continued, "So, I figure I'm runnin' outta time. I gotta get outta here soon."

"That's funny," Reese said. "I'm in here cuz of a glove myself." He chuckled at the coincidence.

"What do you mean 'bout gettin' out of here?"

"I mean," Leander said, lowering his voice and narrowing his boyish blue eyes. "Me 'n these fools are working on a plan. Us and some others." Leander then continued, "They are planning on hangin' all of us, yuh see. We committed the first train robbery in the history of these here United States. Ya, we did, the Pacific Northwestern. Was quite the deal. Was in every newspaper across the country, it was now."

The other two nodded while Zac Anderson acknowledged sarcastically, "That part's true, but, hey, he didn't kill no one, ha."

Leander responded through his teeth, "Shut up, Zac. He didn't ask about that."

"A plan?" Reese said. "I want in."

"I'm sure ya do," Leander mocked, still smiling. "And why should we let you in?"

"I'm after Judge Kensington," Reese said, seeing a look of recognition strike Leander's face as he leaned back and nodded. "He's the whole reason I'm locked up here in this mess. Y'all saw it. It was in all the papers too. Lotsa people died."

"You was part of that doin? Wow, a lot of people did die from what we was readin' in here. Are they gonna hang you for that? Ya, of course they are." Leander put down his fork. "What am I saying? I mean, I hope you get freed up, but back to my question: why should we bring you along with us? Hell, you're big enough. You can just break these walls down here barehanded, like big ole Sampson did a thousand years ago," Leander offered as hilarity. "Ya, you can come with us, no problem! I was just kiddin' around with ya. Hope I threw you off."

"Ya, Leander's yer name, is it?" Reese questioned. "You're really funny. First of all, I don't have long hair, and Samson was over two thousand years ago. Secondly and much more importantly, I am comin' with ya, like it or not. I'll take two guards out to each one of yours, clearing a path for y'all," Reese threw back at him. "Soon as I get out, I'm goin' for Kensington to get the money he owes me!" Reese paused and looked around. "And then some. And trust me, boys. It's a lot."

The group talked more until the warden announced it was time to go back to their cells. Over time Reese got a pretty good understanding of Leander and his crew. They did not seem reckless like Rudy or sadistic like the judge. There was an understandable practicality to their plans, with just the right amount of gumption and sense of humor. Reese felt lighter than air. *What are the odds*, he thought, *day three and I feel like I'm already gonna be out of this sorry place?*

But then eleven months more passed Reese right by. In fact, quite some time passed by with little news from the others. Like an everyday ritual, Reese sat with Leander and his cronies at most meals, but the subject of escape somehow never came up again. Reese wondered briefly if he had imagined their initial interaction. Maybe it was all just talk. *I ain't no loon,* he thought to himself. He remained patient, mostly because there was nothing else to do, but also because he didn't want the other men to think he was too eager. That might spoil the plan. Over the course of time, he met some of Leander's other friends, including an ex-miner named William Russell, a horse thief named Thomas Ryan, and a weapons trader named Tilton Cockerell.

Just like the dinner routine, Reese was out in the courtyard the next day, lifting some bricks for exercise. He had been working on his physical fitness for several months. At his height, it was difficult to move quickly. But as his thoughts toward the judge became more vivid and violent, so too did his determination to stack the odds in his favor. *If I can kill him with my bare hands, then I won't need any weapon, and they won't have any evidence to convict me of murderin' a murderin' coward!*

As he lifted a brick, he noticed a squat man in the distance waving him down. It was Frank Clifford, the strange man with the lazy eye. Reese put down the brick and walked over. He noticed Leander, Zac Anderson, and several others standing with him.

"What's goin' on?" Reese asked, slightly breathless.

"I finally got the way outta here!" Frank said proudly, bouncing on the balls of his feet.

"Well, how's that?" Reese asked, keeping his cool, although he felt a huge sense of excitement and relief wash over him.

Leander shook his shaggy head and smiled. "He knows his way outta most anything. Except maybe his own mama." Leander paused while the others laughed. "But fer sure, he has gotten himself outta jail for free a few times."

"So, what's the plan?" Reese asked.

"All we gotta do is get to the roof." Frank tilted his chin toward the top of the building. "I can't do this one on my own though. There's a lot of firepower 'round these parts, as I'm sure you noticed."

"Ya, I've been trackin'. I can tell you every gun they got in here and where they are keepin' them. Go on. Go on," Reese said. "That's why I'm assuming we haven't discussed such a thing for eleven damn months." He wanted Frank to get to the point so he could judge the feasibility of the plan for himself. He was done following half-wits around with plans that didn't work and was tired of waiting. He was going to bust through the adobe walls any week now on his own, the way he had it figured, anyway.

"Like I was saying," Frank lowered his voice, "we gotta get to the roof of the storehouse. When one of us is sent in for the rice burlap and ice, we steal a saw from the shop. We can cut a hole in the ceiling to get to the roof. We is gonna do it without leavin' any debris around. From there, we can get to the high roof and have better access into Warden Denver's office quarters. Then two of us can break down into the armory and get to the Spencers, Colts, and Henrys."

"That's a bold plan," Reese said, taking it all in. This was going to involve a lot of demolition of the building structure, which would be hard to conceal. "That's a lot of demo this and demo that. How's that all gonna work?"

Leander nodded his head in casual agreement, but the others ignored their concerns.

"From the armory," Frank continued, "We will just shoot our way downstairs and out the main gate. We'll light the place on fire as a distraction. By that point, if there is anyone left shootin' at us, we'll just send 'em all to where they belong, six feet under, and make our way over to the Carson River."

Leander listened eagerly as though it were his first time hearing the plan.

"When is this happening?" Reese inquired.

"Let's get started next week," Frank said as the others nodded.

23

It had been nearly a year since Harriet lost her father. The weeks that followed after the budding young woman learned of her father's death had melted together like candies on a hot day. Half the time, she couldn't keep track of how much time had actually passed since JR raced into town with three bodies on his wagon, himself covered in charcoal and ash and looking as though he'd seen a hundred ghosts.

Learning that her father's burnt body laid strapped to the back of JR's wagon had caused her legs to lose feeling. At that moment, reality seemed to turn on its head. She screamed and then collapsed, feeling her body collide with the hard ground. She had wished, momentarily, that she could fall through the ground, to the other side of an earth where her father was still alive.

"No," she had screamed, forgetting her now older age and the female stoicism she had tried to emulate every day. She dissolved into wails as her mother bent down to help her up.

The months that followed were sleepless and tortured. Harriet had recurring vivid dreams of the day her father left and how before that last goodbye, Colton said he would be coming back into town. *Could I have stopped him from going to the mine? Could I have begged him to stay? Would that have even made a difference and allowed him to still be alive today? But how could I have known then?* No one knew back then.

Could Colby and JR have made it to the swell house before it burned, and her daddy, Colton, and Cyrus were killed? Will anyone ever know? It was now the past for her, a blur of historical recollection and wonder. It could not be changed, but only reconciled.

Before the court hearing, Harriet hadn't cared about what or how it happened. Her father was dead, and nothing anybody said would bring him back, her father with his kind and gentle heart, her father, the man whose integrity had been like glue, her father holding together his family and in fact the whole town. Harriet could not conceive of a future or even the town of Benton itself not including her father in it. His absence remained unfathomable and unresolved according to ninety percent of the Benton townsfolk.

Harriet knew, as did the whole town of Benton, that somebody actually frequenting the area was likely responsible for her father's death. She remembered standing, helpless, in the room as the men of the town discussed the evidence. Harriet felt sick to her stomach at all the men who stood before her. Not a single one, including the sheepish Colby and JR, seemed like men to her. They certainly weren't the type of man her father was. No, they were a far cry from that.

The judge's all-knowing smirk had burned itself into her memory, as did Reese's denying ways of his disgusting face. She knew that they didn't care that her father was dead. His death was of no consequence to them. She also knew by a spiritual instinct that the two men were guilty. She didn't know how, but she felt it in her gut and soul. The helplessness turned quickly to disgust and anger. In a tormented catch twenty-two, when she went to bed that dread filled night, her pillow grew stained with tears, and she vowed, she would not rest until she knew the truth about her father's last breaths. Even when Reese was whisked away to Carson City federal prison, she knew intuitively that there was far more to the story. Reese was only convicted for murdering Ardie Perseval, the mail courier, because they found his glove at the scene, but he was still unconvicted for her father's death and murder. *What of Colton? What of Cyrus?* She knew he had been there. *But how can I prove it?* Other people were involved for sure. Yet there was no proof of that either, at least not over the course of time, since the murders had taken place the year earlier. It was determined by the townsfolk that all the murders that day, six in all, presuming Colton was also dead, theoretically all had to have been committed by the same group. They had happened too close together geographically, within a thirteen-mile radius between the mine and the Benton Crossing junction, and were far too coincidental in their nature. Harriet knew, as did the whole town, because he was convicted of one murder, that Reese had to have been there. Reese had to know what was up. *But are they just going to hang him and be done with it? How will I ever learn who actually pulled the trigger if that happened? No*, she thought, *Reese has to remain alive. He has to tell the truth.*

Harriet had become the town activist of that fact, maturing her into a young woman quickly and out of her pampered ways real fast, over the course of nearly four full seasons since her daddy's death. She had grown so much and was determined to put the pieces together eventually in finding out these truths, hopefully sooner than later. The tragic events and their aftermath, as well as the tormenting talk in the town, had brought her out from being a child and transformed her to be a very intuitive woman.

But nothing has happened now for nearly a year. They received no more answers than they had on that first night. It was torture. Even when everybody else started to move on, Harriet's misery did not change, nor did her sister's anguish or her mother's deep sorrow, or the grief of those being part of this tightly knit network of relationships within the valley community.

One night in the early fall of 1871, Harriet's mother wrangled the down and depressed girls into leaving the house to go see JR and the others in the town. A message had been delivered to their ranch house that JR had an announcement to make. Harriet had risen from her bed, hair unbrushed and clothing unkempt.

"Dear girl," her mother said to her. Harriet hadn't seen life in her mom's eyes since the day they received the terrible news that had changed their lives forever. "We need to go into town. We need to go today."

"Mama, I can't. I was already protesting for months, and no one cares anymore," Harriet blurted out in a youthful depressed state. "I don't want to see anybody right now, especially down there," the fragile girl continued, running her hand through her messy hair. The thought of putting on her best dress sent her to the verge of tears.

"I need you to be strong," her mother said, a certain hoarseness in her voice. "For me, for Marcia, and most of all, for your father. We can all be strong now. I cannot pout and cry anymore," Barbara declared. "We must. We can and we should. Let's get ready."

Harriet nodded reluctantly and proceeded to go back to her room to get dressed.

The ride into Benton was silent, as Harriet had run out of things to say to her mother and Marcia. She wondered if she would ever be able to talk about the weather again or be excited to ride Magic anew, if for even one more time. She wasn't exactly enlivened now with these doubt-filled thoughts, sliding back into anger and distress. These two emotions ruled her most of the time, as they were constant and haunting.

It had been two weeks since she had last ridden the horse, and it still felt as though all the joy had been drained from the world, not knowing if it would ever come back. She didn't know if she would ever enjoy running in the wind on Magic's back again. Today they were going to take the old barn wagon. After all, the three of them had to pull each other out of the slog, but how? Maybe today would be the day they could start, toiling along the rutted trail on the old wagon.

The three Morgan women stopped in front of the Flowers' residence, where Penelope greeted them. She gave them each a hug, as they got off the wagon, but didn't ask how everybody was, and Harriet appreciated that. Penelope was an intuitive woman, the kind Harriet would strive to be, she thought. She didn't want to talk about how she was feeling, not to Penelope or anyone.

"Colby will be home soon with the others," Penelope said, holding Barbara's hand. "I expect we'll have quite a few people over this evening and I prepared all kinds of bites. Are you girls hungry? You should definitely eat. You have all gotten far too skinny under those garments you're wearin'."

Before they turned into the foyer, a carriage rolled up to the house, and five people stepped out. JR stepped down, wearing a collared shirt with a vest, top hat, and trousers. Harriet had never seen him in something so fancy, as he typically wore working britches or overalls, and a loose, white shirt. He helped Sarah Devine out of the carriage. She looked gorgeous, as usual. A purple bow held her beautiful curls together, and she wore a new purple dress. JR and Sarah were followed by Sheriff George Hightower, the big and tall gruff of an older man he was. He wore a bushy gray mustache matched to a pair of worn leather chaps and a cavalry uniform shirt he still revered and had saved from the war. He was followed by Martha Hightower, his wife, who reminded Harriet of a sweet old grandma.

Martha wore a casual navy-blue skirt as if to match her husband. Finally, Colby exited the wagon, wearing his typical work trousers and suspenders over a white shirt. Harriet wondered why JR and Sarah looked so made up. *Are they going somewhere?* Harriet looked down at her own wrinkled blue dress and quickly tried to fix her hair with her fingers, which was loosely tied together with a bow. She peeled back her shoulders and stood up straighter. Now she wished, she had snapped out of her depression, if at least for that day, and taken the time to iron her dress.

Sarah rushed toward Harriet and gave her a firm, full-body hug. "Oh, Harriet, how are you?"

Harriet wished she wouldn't ask, like Penelope, but she couldn't blame her. It was all, anybody could seem to think of saying.

"Hello, you two," Harriet responded, smiling. She felt more love and warmth radiate from JR and Sarah than she had felt in months.

"Why, hello to you, Harriet," JR said, smiling and tipping his hat. "Hello, Marcia!" It was such a stark contrast to see him like this, compared to his dirty, ash covered and disheveled appearance after he had come back from the mine that dreadful day, Harriet pondered.

Marcia said hello and looked down. Harriet's sister hadn't said much since their father's death, she was normally a quiet soul anyway. She had always been a very strong, young woman, but more in a tomboy kind of way compared to women like Sarah, Penelope, or even Harriet, who always wondered what was going on inside Marcia's head.

"Let's go inside," Sarah said. "JR has something he wants to share."

The group made their way inside the Flowers' residence to join a gathering of friends from the town who were already waiting in the living room. Penelope had prepared two loaves of fresh bread, an assortment of jams, and miniature lemon tarts. Penelope took a large kettle off the stove and began to prepare tea for the group as everybody sat at the large dining room table.

JR was normally a calm and collected man. Today, however, Harriet noticed him bouncing on the balls of his feet as he watched Penelope prepare the tea. He was certainly acting strange, and Harriet wondered what kind of news he was about to share.

"Thank you all for coming to this gathering." He looked at all the guests. "Penelope," he said, gesturing toward Mrs. Flowers. "Thank you, as always, for welcoming us into your home."

Penelope smiled and nodded as she was filling the teacups of their guests. Sarah moved closer to JR, and neither of them sat down as they were holding hands.

"Well, as you know, I just adore this beautiful young woman. Sarah is the most beautiful thing to happen to me, and well, the last year has been hard on all of us," JR said, looking directly at Harriet and Marcia. "By God's grace, I have asked Sarah to marry me, and she has accepted!"

Penelope let out an excited squeal. Martha Hightower inhaled deeply in surprise. Harriet was not expecting such news but felt her heart skip a beat. She watched her mother smile for the first time in the past ten months.

"Oh, sweetie," Barbara said, clasping her hands together. "Congratulations."

Sarah's porcelain skin turned into a light shade of pink, her green eyes emphasized by her purple dress. "Well, as you know, my family is coming out to Los Angeles for the Christmas holiday this season and will be staying through the winter. I will be leaving the day after tomorrow by stage to go be with them until the holidays. JR and I will be married right after Christmas. My parents will travel with me back to Benton for the wedding and then take the Transcontinental from Reno back home."

"Oh," Penelope said, rushing to embrace Sarah. "What's more beautiful than a Long Valley wedding!"

Harriet felt so much love in the room, she momentarily forgot that her father would not be at the wedding. She thought of JR's love for Sarah, causing her heart to skip another beat. She then thought of Henry and her adoration for the young man she hardly knew, nor had she seen him much since the tragedy. It seemed like years ago to her. Harriet stood up from her chair to hug Sarah, wishing again, she had ironed her dress to look more presentable.

Barbara looked around the gathering. "Where is Henry? Shouldn't he be here for his sister's engagement party?"

"Oh, he's down at the shop," Sarah answered. "He just had to wait for a delivery pickup and will join us here shortly."

"I should go get him," JR said and walked toward the door.

"Oh, let the boy be." Sheriff Hightower motioned for JR to come back into the room. "He's tendin' to your business while you've been out romancing." The room erupted into cheerful laughter.

Distracted by the talk of Henry, Harriet mused, "I am so happy for you both." She turned to JR. "Mr. Robert Morrison! But you'll still have to let Sarah come out and play, after yer all married n' all!" Everybody continued laughing.

"Harriet," Sarah said, beaming with excitement. "I would love for you to be my maid of honor." Then turning toward the other women, she added, "Marcia and Barbara, I would love it if you would be my bridesmaids, alongside Penelope." She took Barbara's hands into hers and squeezed them. "I just want all of you with me. You all have been so wonderful to me since I came out from Pennsylvania. I want my wedding to bring joy back into our lives between us."

Harriet could not stop smiling for the first time since her father's death. It was as if a load had been raised off of her. She would be Sarah's maid of honor, and the rest of her family would stand by as Sarah married the love of her life. Maybe she could even dance with Henry! Harriet wondered what Henry might say when he saw her dressed up. She thought of the wedding, of the flowers, and the cake. Suddenly she thought of her father not being there, and before she could stop herself, Harriet burst into tears. She felt so overwhelmed by the emotion in the room and the thoughts of the wedding that she didn't quite know why she was crying.

"Oh, Harriet," Sarah said as she hugged her and stroked her back.

"I ... I will miss you when you are gone," was all Harriet could think to say.

"What a tender heart," Marcia said, getting up to embrace Sarah and Harriet.

"No, it's Daddy," Harriet said, shaking her head and sobbing. "Sarah is leaving. So much time has gone by."

"Oh, honey," Barbara said. "She will be back."

"She's leaving. Daddy is gone, and no one has done anything!" Harriet cried, unsure who she was talking to or who was listening. "Feels so helpless. I ... I ... keep thinking about how Daddy won't be at my wedding." Harriet dissolved into tears. She felt guilty for crying but couldn't help herself.

"I will be there," Sarah said.

"Me too," Marcia added.

"We will all be there." Barbara got up and walked over to her daughter for a much-needed embrace. "This has hurt all of us, honey, even our friends and the people of this town. I think it's time now for me to be stronger, to lift you up, my little one, and get back to a normal life, so we can find the men who killed our Randall and the others. We can't do anything, feelin' grief and sorrow any longer. It's time for us to be the women Randall expected us to be! I know, you were really trying on your own, Harriet. I watched you use that attitude to protect your own heart from the pain and sorrow for many months, you literally grew up while I wallowed in misery. I should have been there for you, my daughter, and I am sorry I wasn't. We will do our protest now together, all of us, and we women will find the culprits and get to the bottom of our beloved Randall's murder, absolutely!" Barbara declared.

Harriet continued to sob and hiccup while her mother comforted her. She didn't want to get out of her depression, but she was laughing now through her tears because her lung spasmed. "It's OK mommy. I wouldn't have survived or grown up if I hadn't gone through all of this somewhat alone."

For the first time in so long, Harriet started to feel confidence coming back to her. Prior to the moment she found herself in now, she had felt so afraid to be normal again, as normal as she could be under these circumstances. She had wondered if everyone would simply forget about her father, but at least for now, she was no longer torn in her thoughts.

Marcia brought Harriet a glass of water to rinse the hiccups away. She smiled, hiccupped, plugged her nose and drank the water. She giggled and set down the glass. She, Marcia, and Sarah joined the embrace with Barbara. Within the hug, Harriet felt a strange mix of desolation, safety, and healing added by a bit of fear of her growing maturity. She pondered how growing wisdom and strength might change the anger and fear she had become so accustomed to. Harriet let the tears flow, more than they had in weeks. Before long, Marcia and

Barbara were crying too. As Harriet began to calm down, they were interrupted by the sound of the front door bursting open, slamming shut, breaking the silent love of their embrace.

The four women turned to see a very sweaty and breathless Henry Devine running into the living room, looking a bit disgruntled. He had a folded piece of paper in his hand.

"Henry," JR said in surprise as he quickly got up from his chair.

"What is going on, young man?" Sheriff Hightower asked, sensing the alarm in Henry's face.

"Sir," Henry answered, panting. Harriet figured he had sprinted the whole five hundred yards from JR's mercantile. "We just received a telegraph from Carson City. It's instructing us to pass it down the line immediately."

Sheriff Hightower stood up. "And? What's going on?"

"There's a breakout underway at the prison," Henry said, his eyes darting from the sheriff to JR, Harriet, and then back to the sheriff. He handed the paper to Sheriff Hightower.

Harriet peeled her head away from her mother's shoulder. She felt sick. "That's where Reese Clybourne is!"

24

Reese could hardly contain his excitement on the night of their planned escape. He had gone about his day as he normally would: breakfast, exercise, work in the rock quarry, and then dinner. However, every activity felt different, as he knew it would be his last day in Carson City federal prison. Trying to maintain a poker face was tough knowing what was up for the night.

Their plan had been running smoothly and on track over the previous weeks. Since the day they formalized the plan, Reese and the others had hardly spoken about it. Instead, they stayed up late at night, strategically removing the debris from the wall that supported the inside ceiling, which would lead the inmates to the roof of the prison. Just as Frank had instructed, they put the debris in their pockets, little by little. When they entered the work quarry for their daily work, each of them pulling a ball and chain that was attached to their ankle, they would empty their pockets when the guards weren't looking.

While working in the quarry as they were slaving away with sledgehammers and pickaxes, Reese would study the faces of the guards to observe how they moved, how they spoke. The captain of the guard, Volney Rollins, and another guard, F. M. Isaacs typically stood over them, stroking their double-barrel shotguns.

Occasionally, Volney would yell at them to hurry up and go faster. "Put your back into it," he clamored frequently.

They don't even see it coming, Reese was thinking, a couple of days before as he wiped the sweat off his brow. *Just wait!* This was going to be the last time another man would tell him what to do. Reese was done taking orders from anybody. It was time for him to live his life according to his own destiny, not society's choice made for him. It was about time to go and retrieve his gold from the judge and Rudy!

He was impressed with the way Leander and the others worked. For the first time in his life Reese felt like he and his co-conspirators were equal. He didn't have to worry about them like he did when the judge flew off the handle or when Rudy got too drunk and started shooting blindly, killing things. And concerning how he treated the workers up at the mine, well, that wouldn't have been tolerated here, so he was good to be an equal this time around.

That evening Reese grabbed his bowl and waited in line for the cook to serve him his grub while holding his ball and chain weight in his other hand, which twenty-four hours a day remained strapped to his ankle with an iron shackle. He walked toward his friends who were already sitting on the bench at the table. There was Crazy Zac Anderson without eyebrows, Frank Clifford, and Leander Morton. They were joined by Tilton Cockerell, William Russell, and another inmate whom Reese had never met, Maxwell Baker, a young, pale-skinned kid with strawberry-colored hair. He looked like a bookish kid, and Reese had no idea what he was doing in Carson, or if he was even old enough to be in the *Calaboose* or *Hoosegow*, as some people preferred to call a remote federal jailhouse. Regardless, this kid did not belong here either.

Reese noticed Volney Rollins talking to Warden Denver and some other prison guards. They spoke in the corner of the room, watching the inmates eat. *Do they know something is up?* Reese wondered. *Only one way to find out.*

After a while Warden Denver walked over to his assistant, Zimmerman, and Bob Dedmen, an inmate trustee, who worked for Warden Denver in his private quarters and was trusted by the guards. Dedman was vile, and as far as the prisoners were concerned, a traitor of sorts, a disgusting snitch and a rat.

All three of them left the dining room and walked toward the stairs leading to the warden's headquarters. Reese and the others did not speak. They ate slowly and silently. They all had discussed how this could be their last meal, and to eat up. It was gonna be any and all kinds of weather out in the wilderness, and being hungry through that first night free, well, they all determined that would not be fun.

Accordingly, the men ate up as much as they could. Reese figured that they, like him, were not that hungry because of the anticipation of what was to come. All the men ate normally, calmly, but took bigger bites, so as not to draw attention to themselves. That was of course, until he noticed Frank Clifford speed-shoveling with repetition a mountain of mashed potatoes into his already fat face and choking, then uncontrollably coughing the yellow mush all over Cockerell. "Come on now!" Cockerell exclaimed, but Reese literally stomped on his foot to shut him up, whispering in his ear, "Don't you be the one to screw this up, Tilton."

"Me?" Tilton glared at Frank, who merely smiled back and winked.

After twenty minutes had passed, Volney Rollins strode to the front of the dining hall to summon the prisoners back to their cells. Around the room dozens of prisoners began to rise. Everybody at Reese's table sat still. The time had come. Volney walked toward a heavy iron door that enclosed the dining hall. With a loud *clunk* he began to draw it back, swinging it open.

Reese felt the warmth of anticipation rise from his stomach to his face in a stinky burp. He looked at Leander, who gave him a nod and flashed his boyish, golden grin. Before the other prisoners finished standing up, Leander Morton jumped onto the table. This was it. Reese's heart thumped heavily in his chest.

"Now let's go!" Leander yelled. "Let's get the hell out of here!"

The prisoners let out a unified roar that echoed throughout the dining hall. Reese heard yelling and clanking coming from every direction. There was a loud *bang* as several prisoners pushed an empty table into the wall. Suddenly the result of two week's hard work unfolded before his eyes. The prisoners toward the front of the dining hall began to charge toward the iron door. Reese was in the center of the room, watching, as everything descended into chaos around him.

The dining hall became one big, raucous cacophony. Reese recognized a burly inmate, John Squire, who instead of scrambling out of the door directly charged toward Volney Rollins, who was standing there, braced for impact, clutching a baton. But Squire jumped on Volney, pinned him to the ground and hit him with a bottle, clearing the way through the iron door.

As a throng of prisoners began to run out the door, several others stopped to deliver final blows to Volney Rollins. *Now whose turn is it to be a smug bastard?* Reese thought. It looked easy. He snickered as Miles Cockerell hit Volney with a slingshot he had fabricated especially for the escape, striking him square across the brow and gashing him to the bone. With several swift kicks from prisoners on their way out the door, Volney lay in a crumpled heap. Finally another prisoner, Pat Hurley, dragged Volney's nearly lifeless body into an empty cell just past the iron door and slammed it shut as he cackled.

Reese waited until about half of the sixty prisoners had run through the iron door. Then he, Maxwell, Tilton Cockerell, and William Russell took a run for it, turning toward the stairwell leading to the roof. John Squire followed them. When they made it to the top floor, Reese, who was considerably taller than Maxwell and the others, pushed against the ceiling with all his might. After two weeks of removing boards and pieces of the ceiling, the whole roof began to cave in. Reese and Maxwell glued themselves to one of the sturdy walls and covered their heads to avoid the falling debris.

Once clear, Reese propelled himself onto the roof in one swift movement and proceeded to help Maxwell and the others through. Reese knew the plan like the back of his hand. He, Maxwell, Tilton, and William, would walk up on the roof toward the warden's headquarters, where the keys for the armory and gates were kept, and then meet up with Frank Clifford and Zac Anderson, who would try to get to the stairs leading to the warden's quarter from below. The method was to create as much chaos as possible.

The group bounced like cats across the roof, so as not to stand in any one place for too long, potentially causing collapse, or worse, getting shot through the roof from below. As they arrived above the warden's quarters, using a sledgehammer Tilton had brought along from a supply room, they busted through the roof in a combined effort. This was surprisingly easy due to subpar construction, allowing them to jump to the floor beneath them.

Loud screams ensued as they loudly and all together broke into the room. There they interrupted what appeared to be a very fancy and official-looking dinner. Reese saw a whirl of colorful fabric as ladies darted away from the table.

A man shouted, "It's the prisoners. They're on the roof!" The man pointed at them, and Leander gave him a confident, sarcastic grin.

Reese fixed his focus on Warden Denver, pushing back in his chair, attempting to rise up from the table now covered in a rush of falling debris as dust permeated the air from above. Lieutenant Governor Denver, wearing his full military garb, had an expression of complete shock and panic on his face as he moved. *What an imbecile*, Reese thought, remaining fixed and heading the warden's way. Denver didn't look all that impressive as Reese moved in close, towering over him. The dinner guests cowered in fear of what was happening.

Reese's mind flashed as he worked, generating reasoning for how he was good with what he was doing. *This guy, Warden Denver, is one day running a prison and changing his clothes, becoming Lieutenant Governor Denver the next, hosting a dinner and collecting money for re-election! What a phony! An evening certainly made to impose himself as "great and worthy" of these guests and their money!* Reese was thoroughly disgusted by the thoughts.

Being in his full military dress uniform, Lieutenant Denver naturally had his sword strapped to his waist to impress. The disgust felt by Reese suddenly turned to, *I'd love to run that sword right through you!* Reese pondered, without saying.

Just at that moment Frank Clifford and Zack Anderson charged toward the room, coming up from the stairs. Bob Dedmen, Lieutenant Denver's assistant, quickly picked up one of the dining chairs and tried to push the men back down the stairs, but to no avail. Once inside the room, Frank and Zack lunged at Lieutenant Denver. He attempted to draw his pistol, but Frank was faster and kicked it out of his hand. Denver reached for his sword, but with Reese right there grabbing his arm, young and quick Zack struck him instantly to the back of his head with a slingshot, causing Lieutenant Denver to fall down to his knees. William's second slingshot hit its target dead-on, creating instantly a gashing wound in his forehead. He went cross-eyed as Denver went all the way down to the floor sideways, landing unconscious.

In a swift move, Reese grabbed the keys from Denver's belt that would open up the armory. The ladies were screaming and started running down the stairs, followed by the prisoners. Denver was gravely wounded. *A governor, a warden, a lieutenant. None of it matters now!* Reese gallantly rejoiced within himself. *He is done!*

He blurted out, "Down for the count, are you, Warden?"

After they opened up the armory below the warden's quarters, they grabbed two Henry rifles, a double-barreled shotgun, several revolvers, and as much ammunition as they could carry. Reese was surprised with how well everything was going up to this point as the escapees ran into the prison courtyard. Chaos was everywhere. They had chosen the perfect day for their endeavor, since on Sundays the number of guards was reduced. A cold wind from the mountains was blowing when they reached the courtyard, and Reese was relieved that they would finally leave this dreadful place.

"Where are the others?" Reese riled as he looked around.

"There." Maxwell pointed toward a bush in the distance.

Reese could vaguely make out several figures crouched behind it. Behind the bush they joined Tilton, William, and Leander and distributed the weapons and ammunition among themselves.

"Be careful, boys," Leander Morton said. "I reckon half the guards are still inside, and the others are standing by on the other side of this courtyard. Things may get messy."

Tilton Cockerell laughed. "One more stop until we get to the horses. Let's get the hell out of here!"

Leander had grabbed one of the Henry rifles. Reese took a double-barrel shotgun and loaded the ammunition. He looked back at the jailhouse, where he could hear shouts and occasional shots coming from within. He noticed a fire starting at the southwest corner of the building. *Would you believe it?* he thought to himself, taking in the moment. *The first and biggest federal prison west of the Mississippi, and I just took it down together with the first-ever national train robbers in American history. What am I doin'?* Suddenly he snapped back into reality. *Who cares? This is great,* he thought to himself. *I'm alive again!!*

"On the count of three," Leander shouted, holding up his hand, with three fingers pointed toward the sky. "One ... two ... three!"

Reese and Leander charged forward followed by the others. They had to run with a half hop, as the balls and chains restricted their movements. Reese reached down and grabbed it with his huge hand. He turned and ran as fast as he possibly could while holding his shotgun steady under his armpit. They ran across the courtyard toward the corral in the distance. The ground was wet and muddy due to recent rain. Reese could still hear the tumult raging within the jailhouse. However as they ran across the courtyard, he could only hear the sound of their heavy breathing and boots hitting the ground.

Maybe we're in the clear, Reese thought. *Maybe we'll make it out without getting shot.*

As soon as the thought entered his head Reese heard a loud gunshot blast ringing out across the courtyard, followed by two more. The group of men skidded to a halt. Reese dropped his ball and chain while catching his gun. He raised and steadied the weapon and fired as fast as he could perform the lever action, discharging his two loads. Five guards were blocking their way to the corral. Leander returned fire, followed by Reese reloading and immediately firing, joining the others, altogether firing a barrage of lead at their opponents. Reese saw one guard fall to the ground and then another. *They didn't think we'd have weapons*, he realized.

Tilton Cockerell then charged straight into the gunfire, double-firing the two pistols he held in his hands. The three remaining guards fell to the ground. Reese looked around to see if any of his men had been hit. Tilton held a hand to his shoulder.

"Just a graze," he said, catching Reese's eye. "Bastards!"

"Come on," Leander said, waving them through the large cloud of gunsmoke he was standing in. The smoke swirled in the thick night air as they reached the barn next to the corral without any more surprises. Reese shot the lock on the door with his shotgun, and the men all ran inside. Each of them quickly grabbed the saddles, bridles, and other supplies, and ran toward the corral.

"Round 'em up, boys." Leander gestured to about a half-dozen horses standing in the enclosure. Reese had never in his life saddled a horse this fast. He looked over his shoulder and saw more escaped prisoners making their way toward the corral, since they had cleared the path.

"It's goin' to be hard to ride," Reese said, pointing toward the ball and chain still tied to his left ankle, "With these things on. These things are a real pain in the rear. Leander, how in the hell did you end up gettin' yours off?"

Leander flashed him a calm smile. "Well, brother, why didn't you just ask?" He reached into the pocket of his pants and held up a small key. Reese shook his head and snatched the key from Leander. He took off his shackle to see a swollen, bruised ankle below. "Now we're talkin'," he said as he briefly reached down to quickly massage his sore bones.

Tilton took the key after Reese and began passing it around to the others. "I never thought I'd be rid of that ball. Ha!"

The group quickly mounted the horses until they had all filed out of the corral.

"Let's head out," Leander said defiantly and spurred on his horse.

They heard a loud noise echo in the distance. Reese snapped his head around, expecting to receive more gunfire. Instead, he saw the prison fully engulfed in flames. The roof had completely caved in, and fire burst from the windows of the bottom floor. The scene was magnificent. Prisoners and guards alike ran from all doors of the building. Reese looked back, astounded at what they had done.

After they had put a considerable distance between themselves and the prison, the men stopped by the roadside to give the horses some rest. Reese sat down on a boulder and put on his boots. It felt amazing to have no more shackles. He walked over to his horse and grabbed another pair which were hanging from its neck, strung together by a string, and threw them to Tilton Cockerell.

"Put these on," he said and sat back down.

Tilton was rubbing his bruised ankles. "Never thought I'd be rid of that ball."

Other escaped convicts had joined them and gathered together, excited at their success, babbling profusely about all the events that had just taken place.

Maxwell looked at his barefoot feet and cried out, "Oh my feet!"

Reese snapped, "Geez, shut up! How are we supposed to hear anyone comin'? I'll get you some boots."

He looked around. "Looks like Frank and William didn't make it. Or Squire. Anyone seen Squire?"

"He was on foot," Leander responded. "I couldn't stop to get him. The warden shot Frank. I saw him run back inside, wounded."

"Let's go!" Reese called, wanting to get a head start on the mob. "We will head south. They'll be hot on our tail. Denver is hopefully dead, but I know word more than likely made it to Canby and General Batterman over in Virginia City."

Leander Morton agreed, "Cavalry and local militia, rangers and *vaqueros*, bounty hunters, we'll be chased by all of them, seeing this is federal jurisdiction, and they'll be spread all over, comin' for us from all directions. We gotta head south and quickly. We can't outrun the telegraph."

Reese said, "Let's head toward Leroy's, he owes me ten favors. It's narrow from Bridgeport south, and they will have to get to us in line, and Mono Lake is south a six-day ride. From there we can make Leroy's at the straight and get some supplies, clothes, grub."

With a swift kick he used his suddenly free ankles to spur his horse into action as the others followed. Ahead of them was a one-hundred-and-twenty-two miles ride, which would take nearly a week, to get to Leroy's. They were going to need to find a homestead and steal some food, which quickly became very evident to all of them.

25

Colton had lost track of the day. He couldn't tell if they had been traveling for five days or two weeks since leaving the reservation. He had been careful to travel in a non-linear path, in case they were being tracked on their way south. They never stayed in one place for more than a few hours, allowing Wyola to feed the baby and get a few hours of rest. Some nights they slept in abandoned mine shafts and caves, while other nights they found small outposts for wayward travelers and traders. They stayed outside and away from Walker, Gardnerville, and towns further south. Bodie and Bridgeport were far south for them, still, and a treacherous part of the journey, where it would be a challenge to conceal themselves.

The route was rough, and the nights grew colder and colder with each passing moon. Winter was a mere couple weeks away in the Great Basin and southwest, into the Eastern Sierra range. The freezing was on its pathway, working its way south, just behind them. With each passing day Colton slowly became more familiar with what to expect. He had grown used to the cold in his bones, the sleepless nights, and hunger pangs over the past year, bringing him more and more concern about Wyola and Emil. She was a strong woman and never complained, but he could tell she was getting very weary as time passed by, as fall and then winter were both approaching fast.

Colton was contemplating if they should skip the whole idea of justice and instead move straight away south, in haste, pushing toward Los Angeles to start a new life. They would need to live like outlaws, acquiring fake papers, and they would both have to change their names. He knew people that could do it, real professionals. But he knew they couldn't live like that forever, being on the run, always with the fear in his mind of himself being captured and turned in for a crime he had nothing to do with, and then actually committing a crime because of it. No, Colton wouldn't have any of it. He wanted justice. But life couldn't go on like this if he was ever going to have a future with his new family. Again he wondered if he needed justice, before he could truly be free. As time went on, he felt closer to Wyola.

Concerning this new son, his feelings were as they were. Each day was a testament to their love and resilience and a test for him regarding this child. As a result, their desire to be together kept growing constantly, sharing in the survival that consumed their days, but it was also a time for Colton to imagine the events leading to Emil's existence. From finding food and shelter in the wilderness to leading a transient, homeless life, and being capable of surviving and evading the people who were surely pursuing them, this was a tough time, which they would both remember in a very different, yet parallel, exact same kind of way.

One morning they awoke in a scratchy bed at one of those wayward roadside outposts, a small cabin near Virginia Lakes in the mountains. As Colton packed their belongings, Wyola fed Emil. Colton loved seeing them comfortable and hated to see them cold and hungry.

They had traveled upstream, alongside Virginia Creek, making it over Dundenburg Pass and the Conway Summit, passing through Dog Town, Willow Springs, and the Poor Farm without being noticed. These were places that were housing some very destitute vagrants and outlaws at all these creekside, outpost hangouts. They were filled with men who came to California for gold and silver, only to find pain, grief, and suffering. Gold was now mined by corporations in the Eastern

Sierras, with individuals being forced out of the process. People now had to work at the mines, and all a man could hope for was a miserable laboring job for a paycheck of nearly nothing. Poor Farm was born due to these realities. The destitute, with no morals left, preyed on travelers like Wyola and Colton, especially because of the color of their skin. Unfortunately for them, there was only one road in and one road out between the three shanty towns, and each one could potentially be a gauntlet of villains.

They had been in a rush since leaving Bridgeport the day before, scurrying to get through all three criminal roadside enclaves unscathed and as fast as possible, a real challenge with a wife and child. They had covered twenty miles the day and night before to get to Virginia Lakes, where they finished their night. Colton was still exhausted from the race through that gauntlet the day before, as was Wyola. But they had made it safely by two o'clock in the morning, made their bed, slept, and were now rising to do it again. She never said a word of complaint to Colton. She just did what was necessary each day to nurture, raise, and protect this child and to survive themselves. She was a very strong woman with no time for such a grievance as a complaint.

He suspected it was going to be harrowing from this point on to be heading south. *One day*, Colton thought, as he strapped on his boots early in the morning, *we'll live on our own farm in our own house. This evil will not defeat me!*

"I think it's time we move on," Colton said. "Shouldn't be too long of a ride today to get to the pass at Tioga."

Wyola finished getting dressed and smiled as she wrapped Emil snugly in fur and placed him into the papoose. "I'm ready." She grabbed her gun and her satchel, and with Emil on her back she went outside to her horse. It had been a cold night, and it would also be a cold day. The sun stayed hidden behind a layer of thick clouds, and a cold wind was blowing from the northeast.

Heading southeast along Virginia Creek, they followed the same road back they had come from late the night before, for about five miles. At the bottom of the canyon they rode south, on the main road leading to a bottleneck along Mono Lake, where the huge ancient lake pressed tightly against the toe of the Sierra Mountains. There was only one route through this geography going north or south, and it was the last single road into a town they would face. Further beyond this choke point the road opened up to forests and wilderness, where they would be safer.

The trail led to the south end of the lake, where the road just squeezed through a narrow isthmus of land. In the winter in heavy storms this area was impassable due to the high, steep terrain and heavy snowfall. Huge avalanches could break free and scour anything in their path, right into the lake.

Just past this point a gargantuan canyon, cutting through the Sierras, opened up. There was a trading post, a pig farm, and a cavalry outpost in the expanse. It was known as Leroy mining camp and had a population of sixteen, although the inhabitants were all descended from one family. Leroy and his wife tended a trading post, allowing travelers with no money to trade. The structure itself was made of timber log, halfway dug into the hillside for insulation and avalanche protection. The roof was covered in earth, small aspen, and grass, and the building was perched right at the intersection point of the route through the mountain pass west, over the Sierra range, named the Tioga Pass. That route converged with the north and south route Colton and Wyola were traveling. Because of the impending winter ahead there were many travelers this time of year, especially those who had to get through the mountain pass.

They had ridden for about nine hours when they reached the tiny outpost. Colton dismounted his horse and started walking toward the small hut to buy a replacement belly strap for his failing saddle which was worn out and needed a repair at the least. Here, they could barter for some provisions as well.

"You need anythin' while I'm in there?" he asked Wyola, who smiled, trusting he already knew what they needed but still made sure to seek her out.

She pulled her frock in tightly and hunkered down from the cold, remaining on her horse with the infant. "Be waitin' for you, honey. I don't want to wake up Emil," she said, lifting her hat while wrapping her scarf tight around her head and neck to protect her face from the cold.

Next to the trading post was a pen of pigs and a heavyset, toothless woman was outside, toting a shotgun slung over her shoulder by a makeshift rope strap. She was throwing corn husks at the pigs and calling them out of their shelter by funny names as if they were her kids. The bottom of her soiled dress was covered in pig manure, but she gave no care. Wyola stared in disbelief at the strange scene, pondering how hard it was for people building a life out here, including whites.

As she was waiting, she pulled the pocket watch out of her coat and opened it. She looked at the picture of her and Colton and touched his face softly with her finger. It broke her heart to think how his life had been destroyed by such evil and the uncertainty of them ever getting justice.

There was this recurring dream she kept having, where she was trying to push through a crowd of people to get to Colton, and each time she almost reached him the people would block her, holding her back. In her dream Colton kept looking for her, his eyes wide with fear as the judge placed a noose around his neck and then looked at her, laughing wickedly. She wanted to scream, but no sound escaped her throat. Then she would wake up, drenched in sweat. Wyola swore to herself she would do anything in her power to protect him, even if it meant they were going to have to spend the rest of their lives as fugitives.

Wyola was startled at the sudden sound of horses approaching the outpost. She quickly slipped the watch back into her coat and bundled herself up to hide her identity. As the horses passed her, peeking through a slit created by the wrap of her scarf, she instantly recognized one of the riders and her spine stiffened. It was none other than Reese Clyborne, accompanied by two other men. Reese shot her a quick look, passing by, as she pulled the skins tighter around her head and pulled up her frock coat collar.

Wyola noticed that Reese, under his heavy coat, was wearing a striped outfit that could only be a prison uniform. He was accosted by two other men, mounted on their horses, wearing the same soiled prison uniforms. One man wore a hat over his shaggy, brown hair and had a scar running down the right side of his mouth. The other was a young boy, no older than eighteen. He had strawberry-blonde hair, rosy cheeks and was completely barefoot, his feet appearing bloody and bruised. The men looked dirty, disheveled, and as if they hadn't slept in days.

Wyola couldn't believe her eyes. *What are the chances of Colton and Reese running into each other out in the middle of nowhere?* She acted like she was just trying to warm herself, pulling her skin tighter with one hand while reaching for her gun with the other hand, praying that Reese would not recognize her. She did everything she could to avert her gaze from the men. Reese had been over to the judge's ranch often enough to know what she looked like, but he had always ignored her and never talked to her since he didn't associate with the black folks, especially half breeds.

Reese and the man with the scar dismounted their horses and walked toward the outpost, while the young redhead stayed up on his horse, obviously not wanting to walk barefoot on the cold and stony ground. As fast as the men heard the sound of the door opening, Colton walked out of the building and Wyola's heart skipped a beat. He looked down at the ground as he was walking toward her with his scarf pulled up over his face and his hat tipped down, passing the other travelers.

Just when Wyola thought they were in the clear, Reese looked at them and yelled, "Hey, boy."

Colton continued walking.

"Boy!" he yelled louder this time.

Colton reached his horse next to Wyola and looked up at her. "You ok?" he whispered as he slowly got up on his horse, never facing Reese who kept staring at them.

"Just leave us be! We don't need no trouble!" Wyola said loudly while hiding, as if she were the Grim Reaper behind her frock skins over her head, barely squinting out. Her eyes narrowed as she, with the baby on her back, drew from under her hideskins a double-barrel shotgun, pointed and ready to fire at Reese.

Colton remained calm, never turning around to face the barking man. "I think the lady wants to go now," he said, his back facing Reese. He quickly drew two pistols in both hands, pointing them at the other two men as they started to move past Reese's left toward him.

"Well, if it ain't two lovebirds." Reese continued walking toward them, flashing a yellow grin.

Reese smiled, the same ear-to-ear grin he used to flash at Colton and Cyrus after a particularly rude remark. He looked quite pleased with himself, not deterred by his rugged appearance. His striped prison uniform was covered in dirt and yellow sweat stains under his coat. His buggy eyes were accompanied by giant purple bags below. Despite his considerable size Reese looked like he had shrunk.

"Leave it!" Wyola warned him as she raised her rifle and cocked her weapon while Colton mounted his pony.

With one arm Wyola kept the weapon trained on the men. Her command was stern and determined as she clicked her tongue and then spurred her horse, and without returning her weapon to its scabbard she began to trot away. Colton kept his head down and then turned and spurred his pony, running up close behind her, never facing Reese.

A moment of silence hung in the air for a split second before Reese finally turned away. "Let 'em go. We won't be too far behind them," he mumbled toward the other men as he spit on the ground. Reese gave one last evil grin toward Colton and Wyola's backsides as he watched them quickly ride away.

Reese opened the door to the outpost and entered, followed by Leander Morton and a limping and barefoot Maxwell Baker.

"What you boys need, Reese? Been a while," Leroy said, tending to some salvaged gear hanging from the wall in the back of his outpost, behind a counter.

"Been needin' some boots for the kid, some grub, and jerky. We need some clothes," Reese said, standing about three feet from the counter.

"How you gonna pay for all that now, Reese, bein' they just let ya outta prison and all?" Leroy asked.

"We have nothing," Reese said to Leroy, shrugging his shoulders. "But that doesn't mean you're not givin' us anything. What do you think, Leander?" Reese turned toward Leander who was standing next to him.

Maxwell interrupted, "I think he's gonna give me his boots. I can't take it no more, Reese. My feet are bloody stubs." He pulled a gun out of his belt, brandished it, and then cocked and steadied on Leroy.

Leander rubbed the scar on his face and laughed sarcastically. "Kid, put that away. Never disrespect a man in his own home. Ha! Leroy?" Leander pulled his stolen Henry Yellowboy out of the scabbard he was carrying and began to stroke it as the rifle pouch fell to the floor. "You should give him some boots. As Reese was sayin', we need some things. Now, we can take 'em nice, or we can just … take 'em!"

"Now settle down, gentlemen." The defiant tone had drained from Leroy's voice, and he sounded scared but bartering at the same time. "I know desperate times call for desperate measures. I'm sure me and Reese can figure something out! I'm one to always help an old friend in need, indeed!'

"I think I just saw a ghost," Reese replied as Leroy brought some boots and set them on the counter before Maxwell who greedily grabbed them and ran over, sitting on a stump to try them on.

Leroy brought a bottle of whiskey with some glasses and set them on the counter. "Well, every ghost deserves a drink! Which ghost did you see today, Reese?"

"That ghost just walked out of yer parlor, Leroy!" Reese said, emptying his glass in one gulp.

Leroy shook his head. "Well, I didn't see a ghost. Wait, yer not saying that's that Colton fellow who got blamed with you now, are you? For them killings down south a year ago?" He went to the back of the counter and shuffled through a stack of wanted posters until he pulled one out and slid it over to Reese. Leroy shook his head again, pointing at the poster. "That's not who was just in here. That black man's dead. No one's seen or heard from him in over a year."

Reese looked at the poster, then folded it up and put it in the pocket of his coat. "You don't say, Leroy?"

"Them's just some poor black folk moving south from Reno with a little kid on their back," Leroy suggested as he gathered the empty glasses together.

"What's it matter to you, Reese? We ain't got time," Leander said as he selfishly grabbed the supplies, getting ready to leave.

Maxwell walked around in his new boots and beamed. "They fit perfect! I'll take 'em!"

"Leroy, I'll be back with what I owe ya. Now we need some supplies, some food, some jerky, and some clothes. I'll be checking on who exactly that was just in here, when we get on outta here, so hurry it up."

"How are you gonna be back to pay me, Reese?" Leroy asked. "Everyone's gonna be out lookin' for you boys, all the way up until the day they catch ya."

Leander placed his hand on his weapon as he and Reese turned and stared at each other.

"Aaahh! Just take what ya need, and I'll be collecting from yer estate! Ha! Ha!" Leroy surrendered.

Reese smiled. "That's why I came here, Leroy. I knew you'd be the reasonable one I remember, the one always owin' me a favor. Hell, ten favors, Leroy."

Leroy nodded and turned back to tend to the gear he had been working on before the escapees' arrival. The men left the outpost with their arms full of supplies and bundled them up onto their horses. Maxwell felt like he was in heaven with his new boots, thinking to himself how funny it was that people never appreciated what they had until it was gone, himself included.

After the men arrived to join the other escaped convicts at a makeshift camp and had distributed the supplies among them, Reese, Leander, and Maxwell took off, riding ahead of the others.

Leander turned to Reese. "We never found yer boy, Reese."

Reese shrugged his shoulders and shook his head. "I'm thinking I did see a ghost. I don't know what I saw. The man I knew is dead. That, I know I saw!"

As Colton and Wyola continued riding, Colton felt undeniably calm given what had happened with Reese. *Of all the places in this world, what are the odds of running into Clybourne?* He couldn't help but feel heavy as he and Wyola were riding south toward Benton, the one place Colton was sure Reese wouldn't be headed.

They finished riding as the sun disappeared behind the mountains. Colton had become quite skilled at reading exhaustion on Wyola's face. She was resilient and tough, and he could not imagine a situation where she would demand to stop. However, Colton could see when her eyes became unfocused, and she would grow distracted. It usually happened in the late afternoon after she fed Emil.

Colton picked an even patch of ground away from the trail near Deadman Creek that was sheltered from the wind. As he cut branches for a shelter, Wyola began starting a fire, Emil still strapped to her back in the papoose. After he was almost done creating a makeshift home for them, Colton fetched some jerky and pine nuts he had gotten at Leroy's outpost. He handed some to Wyola and sat down next to her.

"No other woman in the world could or would do what you did," he said in awe. Colton had been thinking of the encounter with Reese all day. The way Wyola held a shotgun, her readiness to shoot, and her unflinching nerves were extremely impressive.

Wyola smiled as she bit into a piece of jerky. "My Indian friends would."

"I'm not talking about Indian ladies. I'm talking about beautiful women like you!" he said.

It was true. He had never met a woman so delicate, yet hiding such steely resolve and determination that was simply just in her bones. The other Paiute women were strong but stoic. Wyola radiated a casual warmth and even a sense of humor. She had an innocent tenderness about her. Even after the devastation put upon her by the judge and all the tragic loss in her life, she still was nothing but grace. On the surface, she was an easy woman to underestimate, but Colton knew better. She was incredibly strong, physically and mentally. She was the strongest woman he had ever known.

"Oh ya?" Wyola smiled. A rosiness flushed into her caramel skin as she donned a playful smile. She began to dig through the pockets of her coat and pulled out the long chain that held the pocket watch. "I love this picture of us in the watch. Remember that day so long ago it seems? With the photographer man?"

Colton remembered. "Yes, in Oroville."

Wyola nodded. "Well, look at it." She opened the pocket watch. Colton saw the two of them standing, looking into the camera. They were not smiling, but there was light in their eyes. "I'm keeping this with me 'til the day I die."

Colton was puzzled. "Then what do I get? I thought the watch was mine," he joked.

Wyola smiled as she bit her lip slightly. "Why, you have me, Colton, and everything I am 'til eternity. Including this child." She bit her lips again and looked up at him.

"I like the sound of that," Colton said and stroked her hair.

Wyola tossed her hair behind her shoulders. "We can continue tonight by you keeping me warm. Feels like some wind and snow tonight. Colton, you best be gettin' set for tonight and that warming you is gonna give me!"

Colton leaned in to kiss Wyola. "Not yet, Colton," she said firmly. "Get to the lean-to for the child."

"Ha, I'm told about you!" Colton said, rising to get back to the finishing touches for their makeshift home.

Wyola smirked. "What are you told?"

"Never you mind, little girl," Colton said, placing both hands on her shoulder as he returned to finishing the shelter.

That evening the wind was strong, and there was a little snow, just as Wyola predicted. The wind howled through the trees, blowing the snow in a thousand random directions, but their little makeshift home held up against the elements. As Colton got settled beneath the blankets next to the fire, Wyola sank in between the buffalo hide and glued her body to Colton with Emil sleeping next to them all bundled up in furs.

Colton wrapped one arm around Wyola's waist and the other around the back of her head to draw her close. She buried her face into his chest and began stroking his leg, causing any thoughts of Reese and the cold flurry around them to vanish. All that mattered was Wyola and every inch of her body. He would keep her warm all night. Wyola smiled and hoped she would never have that bad dream of being trapped, ever again, which was lurking in the darkness each time she closed her eyes.

26

JR could not believe the dissolution of law and order he had witnessed within a year's time. It felt as though all sense and belief had drained from the world. The initial shock of Morgan's death had slowly been replaced by anger and frustration. After all, how could one of the town's most beloved businessmen and employers get robbed, murdered, and have his mining property completely scorched? The Morgan mine was an enterprise benefitting the whole valley, and now it had been completely lost, without a man to run it. All the tragedy required a fitting and just explanation. Although Barbara had some of the men help her seal off the mine, she had no intention of becoming a sort of Randall replacement to benefit the town, and JR knew this deep in his soul. His town would never be the same until justice was served. According to the telegram just read, JR now knew that Reese, to avoid capture, would take the road less traveled, but he was probably coming their way. Sure, JR had fear in his bones the moment he heard Hightower's words, but he also knew he had to do what was right and lead men to find him. Was there an explanation to his nervousness and anticipation of the confrontation that could be before him?

Oh sure, there was an explanation all right, but everybody in Benton knew it wasn't the real story. There were so many missing pieces to the puzzle and too many holes; it simply wasn't adding up. Colton had been known by everyone to be a hardworking, respectful, and honest man, yet now he was a wanted fugitive. Judge Kensington had made sure Colton's wanted poster was being distributed widely after Reese had been arrested. The more he thought about it, the murkiness of finding the truth simply drove JR crazy. Such a foolhardy tale was a straight-up insult to his intelligence and a downright brutal assault on the kind Morgan ladies and also the valley, now without jobs and already showing signs of deterioration.

If you asked him, somebody had gotten away with murder and causing the depression of Long Valley, literally. Shortly after Reese had been carted off to the prison at Carson, JR had sworn to himself that he would not rest until the truth was brought to light, and now he realized that day might be within reach. But weeks had passed by and then months, and pretty soon JR did not know what else there was, if anything at all, he could do. *Is this what has become of the West, a place that is supposed to create economic opportunities and new beginnings? Has it become a place, where any fool can merely obey the laws they feel like obeying? A place where folks look the other way when a life is taken?* JR couldn't help but feel that everything he had worked so hard for his whole life, and his time since arriving in Benton, had been compromised and wasted.

The night when Henry Devine had stormed in to relay the news of the Federal Penitentiary breakout, JR and Sarah's engagement party was abruptly put to an end. JR, Barbara, Marcia, and Colby had run with JR and Sheriff Hightower back to the store to the telegraph machine. They left Sarah and Harriet behind, as Barbara did not want Harriet distressed any more than she already was.

The fact that somebody could break out of Carson City, which was rumored to be a fortress, was the last straw for JR. It seemed that in the ever-waging battle between good and evil, chaos and lawlessness had indeed triumphed in the end.

"All right, George, what are we working with here?" JR asked, his back thoughts and nervous heart now settling, being replaced by eagerness to get ahead of the situation. The last thing Morrison wanted was that things would not become any messier than they already were for his town. "Did the telegraph say anything more?"

The wrinkles in Sheriff Hightower's tanned face seemed to deepen as he spoke. "The whole place burned to the ground. Warden Lieutenant Governor Denver is alive, but severely injured, after being attacked by several prisoners. It is still uncertain if he will survive."

Marcia gasped. "How did they escape?"

"Still unclear," the sheriff answered, pouring over the telegraph. "Looks like the roof collapsed. The officials suspect the prisoners found a way to remove the material in the walls and ceiling to hollow them out."

"Do you think Reese led the escape?" Barbara asked in disgust. She, like JR, suspected that Reese had a hand in her husband's death, even though they didn't know the full story. She knew it in her heart.

"We do not know," Sheriff Hightower said. "But knowin' Reese like I do, and I'm sure him being more than likely the biggest, most intimidating man in there, I imagine he was one of the ringleaders, if not the ringleader."

"Any word from Judge Kensington?" Colby wanted answers as much as JR, especially after him having been there in person, with everything they had discovered that fateful day at the mine.

"We haven't sent word to him," the sheriff said, glancing first at Barbara and then back at Colby. "And I'm in no rush to do that, though he will probably know by now." He finished by scrunching his nose as though he had been exposed to a foul scent.

"He's busy with the mine anyway," Barbara said, folding her arms in front of her chest in dismay. "I've been in unfortunate negotiations with him, him wanting to get Randall's half of the mine and all. He keeps trying to pressure me into a deal that works best for him. I've closed up the shaft, it's under guard lock and key. The judge is fiddlin' around up there acting all innocent and caring, just waiting for a default on the deed. Well, my spirit is back alive and that will never happen! That man has no heart and no moral fortitude. He is truly a greedy monster. Meanwhile that mine lies in ruin. It's obvious what's happened there."

Suddenly Barbara started pacing the room back and forth as she fidgeted with the wedding ring still on her finger. The movement was so sudden and unlike her that even Marcia looked at her in surprise, as Barbara was moving about the room. Her brow was furrowed in deep thought as she continued to pace the small office. JR had never before seen Barbara look resolute like this. Even though the loss of her husband had shattered her entire world, she usually didn't show it physically, and vengeance just wasn't her nature.

After a few paces, she stopped and looked at the group, her hands on her hips. "Where do you think Reese is going? Where would he be headed?" She looked at the sheriff, as though expecting an answer. The thought of Reese's whereabouts clearly had rattled her. Being that JR had just considered the same exact thoughts, he already had figured out the answer. "Could be headed anywhere, I suppose, but my gut is telling me, if he was involved in Morgan's death, then he's coming this way for the stolen gold."

"I ... I don't know, Barbara," the sheriff said in surprise. We shouldn't speculate. We should be ready, however. I want you and the girls to head on home. It will be safest there, with your dogs and neighbors."

"That's a good question," JR wondered out loud. "And that's probably best, Barbara. If Reese is coming south and he was tied to the murders, he will be coming here to find the man we all suspect was involved, and that man lives past here, down in Chalfant as you know, so my guess is he is going to Chalfant and the judges' ranch".

"Either he's fleeing or he's comin' back for something," Barbara said with a visible shudder.

"His motives would say somethin' about what happened in the first place," Colby said, nodding deeply. "Maybe he has unfinished business with somebody in town. Maybe he just wants to get as far away from

Benton as possible and disappear for good. We just need to be sure there are plenty of men and guns available to protect our interests and head anything like that off, straight away."

"Reese doesn't seem like the kind to disappear," Barbara slowly said, looking at the floor.

"I concur, Barbara", Hightower responded, nodding his head.

Suddenly the door was opened and the Paiute, Mono Jim, entered the room. Jim was a close friend of Natchez and a Paiute delegate. He was tall, like most Paiutes. He wore a combined wardrobe of Paiute and white man clothes, on the mountain man side of attire.

"You received my message?" Sheriff Hightower asked.

"Yes." Jim nodded and took off his hat.

"Anyway," JR said, wanting to finish their conversation for Barbara's sake. "Jim, we were just talking about what to do next about this escaped convict situation we have here."

Jim turned to look at the sheriff. "George, we can find out where they're headed. There's gonna be some weather coming in, but we may be able to catch up with them if we head north tonight. I can and will find anyone coming this way from that direction, that shouldn't be."

Barbara still had her hands on her hips. "I want to know what you men are gonna do about Reese if he's in that group of convicts." She looked from JR to Sheriff Hightower.

"We will bring him here," the sheriff said uneasily. "Jim," he said, turning quickly to the new visitor. "What do you say?"

"I'm with you," Jim said. "My people still have many questions for Reese as well. We would like to join the effort. Lookout Mountain. I'll perch myself up there overnight, and by tomorrow night anyone coming this way, I'll see them."

JR felt more momentum in the previous five minutes than he had in months. Maybe it was good in a sense if Reese was one of the escapees, and that they were headed their way. Then they could potentially close this chapter in the town's history. He straightened out his hair with his hand and put on his hat.

"We will leave in an hour," he said. "Jim will be our guide. There's ten of us. General Canby and Batterman relayed, we should go west to Paradise and then move north, along the rim of the Sierras, if we want to pinch any outlaws between ourselves and his troops heading south. Let's pinch 'em off at Leroy's and the isthmus, if they haven't made it there already."

Turning to Mono Jim, JR said, "I agree. You head northeast, to Lookout. Anyone coming south will have to go between us. We will meet up there at Lookout by late evening if there are no passers by. Should anyone come between us, we will send up smoke, so keep a keen eye to the south and west as you watch the road from the north, watchin' for our distress smoke, and bring the men upon us."

Sheriff Hightower nodded. "If not past Lookout Mountain, then soon. They may well be there already. Some other possies are riding in from Mono Ville and as well from Bishop. Both sides of the state line are in search of these men. So long as you and your men can meet up with some other crew lookin' for these convicts, be patient. Don't forget. There's weather on the way." He looked outside the window of the mercantile. "I expect Barrington will be wiring in with their status as well," Sheriff Hightower injected.

The group began to don their coats to head back out into the cold. As the others filed out, Barbara grabbed JR's elbow. "JR," she said quietly, staring directly into his eyes as she pulled him to the side. "Shoot him if you have to. Don't you go and get killed on Sarah now."

Later that evening, JR and his fellow riders caught up to Mono Jim midway, close to Sherwin Dome. It was windy and cold, and some light rain had been falling for hours which might even turn to snow during the pre-dawn night. JR wondered if it would get any worse before it got better.

As the others settled their horses and set up camp for the night, he noticed Jim, standing stoically, looking out toward the mountains. JR walked up to him.

"Smell that?" Jim said, his gaze focused on the darkness in front of them. JR inhaled but did not smell anything. "Fire," Jim continued. "To the northwest of us, about two miles."

"What?" JR asked.

"There's a fire burning. About two or two and a half miles away. Over in Deadman's, behind White Wing Peak." Jim pointed into the distance.

JR nodded. He couldn't smell any smoke, but he had learned during all his years of being in business never to second-guess an Indian's sense of smell. Still, his men were cold and hungry, it was very late, and it was only getting wetter. "Well, let's get this fire goin', and we'll go check it out."

Jim took another look into the distance and up at the dark and heavy sky. "I don't think I'm gonna need to head up to Lookout Mountain. I think I'll stay here and ..." Jim suddenly shook his head. "They're not going anywhere," he said, changing the direction of his words mid-sentence based on his nasal analysis.

"How do you know that?"

"It's in the wind," Jim continued. "The wind speaks words one cannot hear."

"And you smell them?" JR asked, slightly befuddled. "How do you know they aren't leaving?"

They didn't have time for this, yet he had never known an Indian to speak what they did not believe wholeheartedly. He didn't quite understand how they seemed to know so much, not having had any education to speak of. Yet, when it came to the land, mountains, rivers, and even the animals, they were downright spooky regarding how much knowledge they possessed.

"Chicken, maybe some rabbit too." Jim drew in a deep breath through his nose.

"You can really smell all of that? That's amazing!" JR didn't know if he was being serious.

Jim finally turned toward JR, as if acknowledging him for the first time. "It's white men."

"And yer smell tells you this too?" JR asked.

"I can always smell white men." Jim smiled for the first time that evening, and then, after a pause, he added, "Food." He wrinkled his nose in slight disgust as he turned around and started to walk back toward the camp. JR, following closely behind, was shaking his head to himself.

The two men agreed that they should check out the situation by themselves, since most of the men who were part of the posse were spent and had already settled into their bedding under a canvas shelter, huddled around a large fire for the night. The arriving storm had only grown worse, and visibility in the darkness would be more challenging than usual.

JR and Jim mounted their horses and went out on a scout to see if they could pinpoint the location of the cooking. They rode in silence until Jim stopped his horse, lifting up his hand as if to signal to stop. JR followed suit and stopped his horse as well. Jim began to dismount and nodded at JR to do the same. He gestured toward a tree, and the two men silently tied up their horses before heading down a small trail toward a split between two large rocks. At the end of the path they reached a rise, coming out above a clearing in the rocks. JR and Jim heard faint voices in the distance and drew their guns. About one hundred feet below, they observed a roaring fire situated below a patch of red fir trees. Several makeshift lean-tos had been constructed and were spread out through the camp.

"It's Reese," JR whispered. "That tall one down there. We're gonna need backup. I have no idea how many there are." It was hard to make out the faces or how many there were due to the poor visibility, but there was no mistaking Reese's towering figure.

Jim held a finger to his lips. "Practice patience, my friend," he whispered. "They are not going anywhere right now. I need to hear what they're saying."

"You can hear them?" JR asked, unconvinced.

Jim swiftly scurried ahead of JR, turning quickly to motion for him to stay, as if commanding his dog. JR, for some reason, possibly fear, respected the request and stood by.

Jim scurried off into the darkness between the mountain sage and vegetation. The night was black as could be. Some time had passed, when suddenly Jim came back stealthily, emerging from the darkness and heading silently toward JR.

"Shh," Jim said, nodding. Moments later he spoke. "Reese was down there talking to another man."

"And what were they saying?" JR asked.

"Reese suggested they go to Morgan's ranch. The other man wanted to know if there is gold there. Reese said no, but there is a way to get to his gold from there. Now they've gone silent."

JR couldn't believe their luck in finding the escaped convicts on the first night of their search. Finally the answers they'd been looking for seemed to come into their reach, in order to swiftly restore a sense of justice in these parts of the mountains. But he also recalled advising the women to go home, and Reese was now planning to go to where they lived. The two men reached their horses and started mounting them. "Well, let's go to get the others," JR said.

"No," Jim responded, looking forward. "Half of our men have already gone to sleep. It is wet and dangerous, and very late. We will be fighting against the elements, and such conditions will not be on our side. We will come back at sunrise in the morning before they awake, and take them by surprise." Jim looked at JR in the near darkness as it started to rain. "Judging by this camp, they haven't run into any other people in days. They are confident. Their guard will be down."

JR wanted their mission to be over sooner rather than later, but he agreed. They quickly rode their way back to the posse of men, in a near downpour. Only Colby was still awake, tending to a dying fire. JR and Jim alerted him to their findings, letting him know about their plans.

For the four hours of night that remained until first light, JR hardly slept a minute. He remembered what Barbara had told him. *Shoot him if you have to.* JR had never killed anyone, never even hurt an animal. He didn't think such a thing was in his nature. However this past year had shown him just how dangerous the world could be when chaos had the upper hand. In mere hours, they would be riding into an encampment of outlaws who'd shoot first, not asking questions later. JR supposed this wasn't the time to hesitate on the trigger. But he also knew Barbara and the girls were heading into trouble. There was no way to get word to them of the words Jim had overheard.

At some point JR must have finally fallen asleep, for he awoke, being startled. It was still mostly dark and had stopped raining. He checked his pocket watch. It was five fifteen in the morning. He noticed Jim had already left on his horse, he obviously had gotten up some time before him. JR cleaned his weapons as the others trickled out from under their slickers. He let the other men know about their discovery and their plan to catch Reese and the other convicts by surprise in their camp upon sunrise.

The men were silent, as if going to battle, preparing their equipment and whispering to each other a hidden calculus. Sure, they were exhausted and tired from the few hours of sleep they had, but these men also all knew each other or at least their stories, left over from the Civil War. All of them were veterans. All had experienced plenty of sleepless all-nighters before having to survive a day of full-blown battle. An adrenaline rush came to a man in the hour of need, and most everyone knew this in those days. These were men of experience and courage, even after becoming farmers, miners, and mercantile owners. Muscle memory kicked in, and settlers became instant men of war, yet again in their life.

The men finally mounted their horses and began the two-mile ride northwest with JR leading the pack, way before the sun would be cresting the mountain peaks. The ground was covered by a light frost from the previous night's storm. They rode in silence until they reached the bottom of the hill.

"Leave the horses here," JR said, gesturing toward the tree they had used the night before, wondering why Jim wasn't there waiting for them, as he had assumed.

He began to climb up between the rocks to reach the clearing above the encampment. The plan was to split the group at the top and attack the encampment from two sides. By the time the men reached the top of the hill, the nascent of the sunrise made it easier to see, and although it was now past first light, the sky was still half way black and half way blue. The men looked eager, as if they were ready for anything that could be coming their way.

Just as the encampment became visible, JR could not help but feel that something was wrong. His gaze focused on the clearing below, where the ash of the fire was still smoldering. His heart sank. All signs of life were gone. The camp below had been abandoned before their arrival. Reese and the others were on the move.

Jim rode up abruptly. "I followed them out this morning. They are heading toward Sherwin Creek and definitely toward Morgan's ranch."

"Why didn't you wake me up?" JR cried out.

Jim shook his head. "Too many men would have died. I will track them until they get into a corner in Lake El Diablo. They cannot get out. This is wiser for us."

27

Harriet was spooked by the silence in her own home. Her mother had rushed them home quickly after learning of the Federal Penitentiary breakout. Harriet had been very quiet and not uttered a single word, becoming paranoid to an extent. She had never seen her mother so gallant and fearless, at least since her father had been killed. A week had passed since the escape, and the tide was beginning to turn in their household, for them to be ready to confront the man if he ended up coming their way. The moment Harriet was waiting for could be approaching, but she had fear in her heart to actually deal with it. She could visualize herself rallying around her mother's strength, but the child remained inside of her to a certain extent. She was still an adolescent, and the thought that real life could prove tragic, in the event of a confrontation, was very real.

It was early evening, and Harriet desperately wanted the day to end. She figured she would finish the chores, tending to the livestock and horses before calling it a night.

"I'm going to get to the animals," she called out to her mother and sister, neither of whom said a word. Harriet peeked her head around from the kitchen to the sitting room to make sure everybody was still alive. She studied Marcia heating up lead in a ladle in the fireplace while her mother worked casting shot from the hot lead in a hand carved soapstone. She remembered her dad had made it when she was a wee child. "Do you need my help, mother?" Harriet queried. No one answered as they were so focused in preparation. Marcia brought another batch of hot, melted lead, while her mother put the two halves of the soapstone together and grasped them tightly. Marcia then carefully poured the hot mixture inside a small hole into the stone. Barbara and Marcia moved on to packing powder into their pistols and pressing the cooled down shot into the cylinders of the Colt Navy revolvers. Harriet stood gazing at what her mother was doing. She stared at the guns until her vision blurred as she slowly muttered, "Mother, do you need my help? Marcia? I'm goin' out to the barn, gonna do the chores." Again no one answered or commented. The young lady soon became impatient with the ignorance of her existence and turned to walk out of the kitchen, shaking her head as she fixed her hair. *They sure are distracted by this.*

Harriet understood why her mother and sister were quiet. She knew they were beyond upset but also preparing for the worst. Still, though, she liked to imagine a day where everything would be normal again. She wondered if life would ever be close to what it used to be, what seemed such a long time ago. This was the same thought all the residents of Benton had, and as a fact, all the residents of the whole Eastern Sierras. Everyone was included, having witnessed all kinds of injustices on all sides.

Harriet trekked across the porch and the front yard area toward the corral, making her way into the adjacent barn. She heard her sister exiting the house, most likely to take care of pulling down the laundry. Harriet hummed to herself. At least she had the horses. Horses were incredibly intelligent animals. Sometimes she eerily felt as if they could read her mind. Magic always knew when she was feeling sad and put his head over her shoulder, so she could wrap her arms around his majestic neck and enjoy stroking his mane. Once inside the barn, Harriet grabbed a bucket and started to fill it from the oat bin.

She strode toward Magic's stall first. "That's because you're my favorite," she said, patting Magic's white nose and emptying the bucket into the trough in front of him. She continued to feed the other horses as Magic greedily munched on his oats.

As she passed by one of the other stalls to refill the grain bucket, she sensed something strange, like when one knew in their spirit something was off. Harriet paused in her tracks. She couldn't quite describe it, but she picked up on a certain presence in the barn. She pondered, *maybe I'm just being a scared child because of all that has transpired the past year, and especially today*. She moved forward, but her female intuition stopped her yet again. Someone was watching her. Suddenly, Harriet felt the hair in the back of her head stand on end. Her chest felt like it was going to pound itself right through her ribcage. With a shaky, outstretched hand, she gently nudged the stall door open as her heartbeat raced, backing up as she did it, straining her eyes to peep in.

"Uh, hello? Is somebody there? Who are you?" she asked, hoping it was nothing, and she was about to feel foolish. Yet her heart raced faster in fear. *Should I scream for help*? she wondered.

"Please don't scream," a shaky voice answered.

Harriet jumped back and shivered, as a jolt of fear ran through her body like a bolt of lightning. She instinctively steadied herself with her left arm on the gate to prevent herself from falling, and grasped the bucket of oats in her right as if to use it as a defensive weapon, raising it slightly and squeezing the pail handle ever more tightly, ready to swing and strike.

The voice continued, "I need your help! *Please.*" This time, the voice sounded soft, almost frightened. There was no threat or angry intonation Harriet could detect, and her heart began to cease its frenetic pounding. Feeling slightly more at ease, Harriet opened the door a bit more.

She saw a frame of a person diffused by the darkness, which appeared to be that of a non-threatening young man. The figure began to creep slowly forward, into the fading daylight that was illuminating the barn. When she got a better look, she could see it was a boy, not a man, as Harriet first thought. She judged by the way he looked that he couldn't be much older than herself. He had freckled skin and strawberry-blonde hair. The boy looked dirty, as though he had been traveling for days. *Have I met him before?* Harriet didn't think so. The boy timidly stayed in the stall, while she remained at the gate holding the pail as a defense.

"Why are you hiding there if you are not dangerous?" she asked.

"Because men are lookin' to kill me," he said, looking intensely into Harriet's eyes. "Was told to come here and ask for your mother to come out."

Men? What men? Harriet thought. *And what does this have to do with Mama?* The feeling of uneasiness returned, and she felt a shiver going down her spine.

"It's my friend," the boy continued. "He says he is innocent of all them charges thrown at him, and he would like to offer proof."

Harriet narrowed her eyes, all her senses suddenly alert. "You sayin' you know someone who knows who killed my daddy? What's your name?"

"I'm Maxwell," he said, still speaking with a soft voice. "I'm sayin' a man I met and traveled with says he was accused of killing yer daddy, and he wants to prove he didn't. Says he knows someone being after yer daddy's mine is how it all started, he did." Maxwell nodded as if to reassure her he was telling the truth.

A sudden realization started to dawn on Harriet, and she couldn't tell if she felt scared, curious, or a mix of both. "You … you was in prison with Reese," she concluded, wondering how a boy so young could be in prison.

Still, she thought, *how else would this boy know Reese?* She started putting the pieces together, which gave her more confidence as her nerves began to settle.

"I bet you got jail clothes under them britches. How do I know you are tellin' the truth? Where's Reese now?" Harriet stepped back, looking around as if Reese were about to step out from another stall.

"He's just yonder, over near the creek outlet and lake." Maxwell shrugged his shoulders before pausing and saying, "Yer very pretty." He looked her up and down, slightly smiling.

Suddenly something changed in his face. The innocence and boyishness had vanished. He was not a boy. He was a man, and an ex-convict at that.

"Marcia!" Harriet yelled at the top of her lungs, completely alarmed and unsure what to do herself. Her heart started pounding again, this time even harder, and she stepped back to increase the distance between Maxwell and herself, grasping the pail with both hands now readying to throw it at this person in defense and run. But she couldn't move to help herself. She froze.

"Wait!" Maxwell said urgently, holding his two palms out in front of him. "Why you yelling?"

"If he's innocent, then everyone should know." Harriet said louder, hoping someone could hear her distress. She suddenly didn't feel so scared of Maxwell anymore. If her life in the West had taught her one thing, it was that people liked to show their weapons if they had them, so now she raised the bucket, ready to swing and take the young prisoner's head off.

Maxwell continued pleading with her, slowly moving forward. "There's other men with him. It could get dangerous for you. Can I borrow some socks?"

"Marcia!" Harriet yelled again, this time louder. She took another step back. "Why should I give you socks?" She quickly glanced at the barn opening behind her, calculating her distance to it.

"Please, I'm innocent! I just need some socks now," Maxwell replied, looking desperate.

Outside, Marcia was pumping some water from the well into a pail, when she heard her younger sister bellow from within the barn. *Oh,*

Harriet, she thought, *must be needing some help with the horses.* She ignored her and walked with the water toward the house.

"Mama?" she called out to her mother inside the house, setting down the water. "Harriet's calling from the barn. I'm goin' to go see what the fuss is." She wiped her forehead with her hand and started walking toward the barn. As she passed the corner of the corral, she grasped a pitchfork and a shovel leaning against the rails, tools which might be needed in the barn to assist her sister.

Barbara had finished cleaning the weapons and was now engulfed in the mine's legal paperwork, when she heard her eldest daughter calling from outside. Distracted, she slowly got up and walked over to the screen door that led out to the porch.

"Yes, Marcia?" she called.

Suddenly a man jumped out from the shadows into the open, just about ten yards from her.

"Oh my God!" Barbara yelled, her hand reaching to her mouth in surprise.

"It's not like it seems." A filthy and stained Reese was approaching the porch.

Barbara turned on her heel and darted back inside of her home, where she grabbed a double-barrel shotgun and a couple shells she had just wadded from the table. Loading it swiftly, she ran back to the door and aimed it at Reese, who had stepped onto the porch into full view in the meantime.

"You have a lot of nerve comin' here after what you have done to my family!" Barbara spit as she felt anger rise inside of her, quickly turning into rage. She stood strong and did not waver, the gun clasped tightly with both her hands, one with a finger on the trigger.

Reese slowly lifted both hands to show her he was unarmed. "Barbara, wait. Before you shoot, I got somethin' to show ya. I did not shoot Randall. I'm here to make things right in this."

"You have three seconds," Barbara said, as she pulled the two hammers back on the old shotgun, aiming it right at Reese's head. "Marcia!" she called out, hoping her daughter was still within earshot.

Meanwhile, Harriet heard the door open in the barn as Marcia strode inside. She looked casual and unconcerned, shovel in one hand and pitchfork in the other. Marcia stopped as she suddenly saw the boy just a couple of feet from Harriet. Marcia shot Maxwell a confused and skeptical look, as though he were an unknown friend of Harriet's. Then she stiffened like a cat, ready to engage an opponent mouser.

"And you are?" she asked, her eyebrows raised.

"Just a kid needing some help," Maxwell replied with an innocent look on his face. "I could use a slice of bread, maybe two, and some of that water please. And oh um, like I asked from your pretty sister here, some socks. Do you have any socks?"

Before Marcia could answer, they heard their mother yelling from the house. Harriet and Marcia popped each other a fearful look and bolted out of the barn and back toward the house. "Stay there or we'll kill you," Harriet snapped at Maxwell as they left.

They ran across the yard as quickly as they could, bolting through the front door and into the house as Marcia grabbed her pistol from a holster hanging on the coat rack at the front door. They went through the sitting room, and Harriet nearly stumbled into a side table when she saw her mother in the kitchen, with her back turned and her shoulders arched, pointing a gun directly at Reese's head.

Marcia entered the scene and also pointed her gun at Reese, grasping the weapon tightly with both hands.

"Don't shoot him yet," Barbara said, staring directly at Reese who had his hands up, as she perceived her daughters behind her.

"What's he doin' here?" Marcia asked.

"He says he knows something 'bout yer father's murder. Says he didn't do it. Says he's gonna show us who did it and why. Says, although he was there, he had nothin' to do with it." Barbara said each word slowly through gritted teeth. Her mouth was twisted in disgust toward the man they had all once considered a reliable employee of their father. "I don't believe him. I say we are gonna hold him here 'til the men get back to Benton from searching for them."

"Shoot him where he stands, Mama," Harriet uncontrollably blurted out, as if by instinct.

"Now, the gun isn't necessary," Reese said, pouting his lip and motioning with his head toward Harriet because of her comment, as he raised his hands higher in a plea not to shoot.

"Who killed my daddy?" Harriet exploded, finally being close to getting the one answer she'd been looking for a whole year.

"Mama, I should go look for the other men," Marcia interrupted, looking toward the window.

Harriet stared at her sister, unsatisfied. Why was it that of all people, Marcia could not understand the seriousness of her plight? She wanted Reese to spit it out, the truth and all of it, right now, before the opportunity was gone.

"Are you crazy?" their mother said, turning her head slightly toward Marcia, without letting Reese out of her sight. "With all these criminals running loose, you stay in here with us!"

"Yes," Harriet said, feeling exonerated. "And there's another one in the barn. He was young and friendly, but I still don't trust him."

Reese's eyes darted from Marcia to Harriet and then to Barbara. "Well, I'm sorry to say there's a lot more than that. Let's see, we got Leander, Tilton, four others just right outside yer property, ma'am," Reese said, his voice a little condescending and matter-of-fact. His hands were still up high, but he had a more defiant demeanor about him now as he lowered them ever so slightly with caution, as if he alone could de-escalate the situation.

"Keep yer gun on him," Barbara directed Marcia, without taking her eyes off Reese. "Move yer ass over to the stove." Her shotgun was still raised as she motioned to the chair closest to Reese. "Bring that chair with ya."

"Now what are you doin'?" He picked up the chair and strode slowly toward the stove. Barbara got impatient and pointed closer with her gun, her face dead serious, now tilted down the sights of the gun barrel. Reese put down the chair slowly. "Now hold on. I'm moving."

Marcia walked behind. Suddenly she raised the butt of the pistol in both of her hands and quickly, and without any sign, struck Reese twice on the back of his skull as he was bending down, still holding on to the chair. Reese went down to the ground with a loud thud, half landing on the chair, crumbling it into pieces with his massive body weight. Barbara kept her shotgun trained on Reese, while Marcia quickly retrieved a lariat from the wall by the back door and motioned her mother to the Benjamin Thompson double stove. She slid out the bottom grease tray and pushed the heavy pan quickly across the floor and away from Reese. She tied both of Reese's hands tightly the way she would have roped and wrangled a calf. Marcia then cinched the giant's tightly wound wrists to the bottom leg of the iron artifact, wrapping the rope twice around the leg of the very heavy two-door, double wide oven. Barbara then set her gun down and helped Marcia to be sure there wasn't any way Reese could wrestle his way loose. Then Marcia wittingly wrangled his legs, tightly binding them with the same rope in a hogtie to the rear leg of the stove. There was no way he was moving an inch.

While they were working on him, Barbara muttered, "I am gonna tie you to this stove 'til we can get some help up here. If yer story is true, you won't be minding now!" Harriet watched as her mother and sister worked with surprising speed to tie Reese down, his body prone and wrapped around two sides of the large and heavy oven, two legs tied tightly to the left rear leg, and his hands stretched out, tied around the front right leg. He wasn't going anywhere. *Must be all the cattle wrangling skills*, Harriet thought to herself, almost amused. Reese started groaning.

Marcia looked up at Harriet. "What about the other men, Harriet?"

Harriet ran to the hat rack near the front door to grab a Henry lever action rifle. If there were more men outside, then she, too, needed to be well-armed. She crossed the room and grabbed a bandolier draped from the gun rack.

"Marcia," she said, stopping at the front door. "I'm gonna go look for them." Rifle in hand, Harriet bolted out the door.

Barbara was still busy with Reese and looked at Marcia. "Go with her. Check on the barn. Be careful!"

Marcia nodded and got up. It started pouring down rain, but Harriet didn't even notice as she was running past the corral and then entered the barn. She hesitated and took a moment to catch her breath. Then she called out in the direction of the stalls, "What's yer name? Hello? What's yer name?"

She heard some movement from a stall as the youth finally came out. He was skinny and not much taller than Harriet. "It's Max, Maxwell Baker," he said, flashing Harriet a half-smile. Harriet lowered her gun slightly but did not put it down. "They say I killed a man. Thing is, he was gonna kill me first. Nobody talks about that." Maxwell spoke as if giving a presentation to a teacher. "I threw a rock. It was a lucky shot." He shrugged his shoulders and held both hands out to the side. Then his eyes narrowed again, as if he were looking at Harriet for the first time. "Yer real pretty though. Come over here." He waved his hand and took a couple of steps toward her.

Harriet stood her ground, but she tried to hide the slight trembling of her fingers. "I'm not coming anywhere," she said sternly, lifting her chin while raising the rimfire rifle.

Maxwell moved forward quickly until he was just a few paces away. Harriet trained her gun on the young man ever so tightly, but the rifle was very heavy for a girl. It all happened in just a few, swift movements. Maxwell leaped at Harriet's legs, diving towards her feet and under the weapon. He tackled Harriet to the ground, knocking the rifle out of her hands. Harriet started to scream loudly.

"Calm down," he said. "I don't wanna hurt you. I just wanna kiss ya." He wrestled to control Harriet's arms outward as he tried to kiss her face. Luckily, they were about the same size.

Harriet, using her knees and feet, kicked and squirmed in an attempt to push him away from her with every ounce of strength she had left inside. Suddenly he froze, his face right in front of hers as he laid on top of her, and his eyes went wide, looking deeply into hers. Harriet was confused. It was as if the world had stopped. She looked at Maxwell's freckled face an inch away. His eyes were completely still, but then blood began to trickle from his mouth, and he collapsed to a relaxed state, slumping on top of her as his head dropped down to hers like a dead weight and hitting her forehead. The boy went instantly limp. Harriet squirmed, wriggled and shrugged, struggling to crawl out from under him. Then she saw Marcia standing above and behind Maxwell's now lifeless body by his feet, holding the pitchfork, which she had just shoved through his back.

Harriet screamed louder than she ever had in her life. The horses stirred at the sound of her wailing. Harriet, lying there in the dirt, alongside the dead body of a boy, buried her face in her hands which were shaking uncontrollably. Marcia stood motionless in front of her, looking incredulous as to what she had just done. Pitchfork still in her right hand, Marcia knelt down and wiped her forehead with the back of her left hand. Her dress was stained with dirt, blood, and sweat, her hair had escaped its tight braid. Harriet was in shock. Never in her life could she have imagined Marcia doing something like this. Nor had she ever imagined a boy dying in a violent way on top of her as he was trying to molest her. Marcia had saved her life and had killed a boy to do it. Harriet just lay there, her body completely frozen in shock.

"Harriet, I know you're scared, but we gotta get outta here," Marcia said softly and stretched out her hand towards her sister to raise her to her feet.

Harriet looked at Marcia's hand. She didn't know what she felt. She shuttered. She wanted to hide and cry. *What about mother?* Reese had said there were other men. *Are they lingering on the outside fence, ready to attack?* Harriet thought of her father. She began to snap out of her prostrated scare.

"Let's go," Marcia said and grabbed Harriet's hand, pulling her to her feet and wrapping her arms around her to lift her up.

Harriet nodded and wiped the tears from her eyes. They ran back toward the house as the horses were stirring about, errantly kicking all over Maxwell's lifeless body.

"Mama!" Marcia yelled, bursting through the door.

"I'm in here, Marcia," Barbara called, sounding like she was still in the kitchen.

Barbara's eldest daughter had been faster than Harriet and ran straight through the sitting room toward the kitchen. Reese had regained consciousness. With his arms stretched around and beyond his head from a rope the women had wrapped around the legs of the stove quite ingeniously and had tied to his ankles, Reese was literally in quite a fix, so he couldn't even move. He looked very agitated and uncomfortable, laying on his side with his front and face facing this iron beast. He wasn't going anywhere. Barbara stood next to him, towering over the man who usually towered over everyone else. She held her gun steady as he attempted to twist around to his backside and off his hip to see her face.

"You just gonna hold me here for three days 'til yer men show up?" Reese extrapolated with a twisted contorted body, trying his best to look up at her, wrenching in pain.

"Shut yer pie hole!" Barbara snapped.

"Mama," Marcia said, out of breath. "There's others. We have to—"

Suddenly the sound of heavy boots entered the kitchen. It was a bald man with unusually broad shoulders who had dirt all over his face. He had a gun in his right hand, pointed directly at Harriet's head whose neck was lodged in the grip of the man's left elbow. Harriet looked terrified and was fighting hard to escape his grip, trying to claw his arm with her hands and kick him with her feet, but to no avail. He bullied his way into the space, placing himself with the entry to his right, and Harriet between him and her mom. Barbara, holding the gun, was standing in the opposite corner of the kitchen, across from Reese on the floor tied to the stove.

Tilton drew his weapon with his free hand and trained it on Marcia. "I can shoot yer one daughter and snap yer other daughter's neck, all in one smooth move! How would you like that, Mrs. Morgan, is it?"

"Harriet," Marcia and Barbara screamed in unison.

Harriet tried her hardest to wiggle free of the large man who was almost a third taller than her. "Let … me … go!" she yelled, trying to stomp on the man's foot.

"About time, Tilton," Reese strained to get the words out of his chest, trying to lift his head as much as possible to do so.

"Don't you move, young lady!" Tilton replied while staring at Marcia, looking down his gun sights at point-blank range.

The women heard another set of footsteps, and a man with bright-blue eyes and shaggy hair walked into the center of the kitchen. A scar ran along the right side of his mouth. He somehow did not look as dirty as the others. He entered, aiming a Henry rifle directly on Barbara's face. It was Leander Morton, alive and well.

"Now untie him, and we'll just be on our way, ma'am," Leander said, with his eyes fixed dead center on Barbara's gaze.

Tilton, with his right arm holding his gun, as it wandered back and forth between the two sisters, squeezed Harriet tighter into the crux of his left forearm and pulled her to the front of him. This way he was challenging her mom to take the fact seriously that her child was looking as if she might pass out any second, and her other child could be shot in an instant.

"Do as he says!" a newcomer said, stepping into the room, with his gun now, too, trained on Barbara.

"There's a whole lot of men in town looking for you," Marcia gasped, while attempting to strategize a break from Tilton's gun sights.

"Marcia, shh, honey," Barbara whispered, looking indecisive, trapped, and panicked.

"We don't want no trouble, ma'am," Tilton said in a mock-polite tone. "Just gonna help ourselves to Reese here and a little food, and we'll be outta your hair. We got other business to attend to, you see, right, Leander?" Tilton turned and looked at the other man.

"Do as he says," Leander commanded, gun steady and aimed at Barbara's face.

Barbara continued to aim her shotgun at Reese, but she knew they were overpowered. Marcia anguished in her mind on what to do. She now saw her mother, yet again, back to being defeated, confused, and fear-stricken, like she was for the whole year. Barbara looked from Harriet to Marcia, Reese, and the other convicts. A few moments of silence fell over the room until Tilton instructed Marcia to cut Reese loose.

"Don't do anything stupid or your baby sister dies!" Leander threatened.

Marcia moved to the other side of the kitchen slowly, making her way to the pantry. She opened the door, pulled open an interior drawer and retrieved a long butcher knife made of heavy steel. She grabbed a fresh loaf of bread from the shelf and a bag of jerky, hanging on the door with a round of cheese.

"Here," she said curtly, throwing the bread, meat, and cheese on the kitchen table. She then moved to the stove and began to hack away at Reese's ties. Barbara had not moved and stood as if she was frozen.

Reese rose slowly, rubbing the back of his head, rotating his shoulders and wrists to relieve the pain from where Marcia had hit him and ever so professionally tied him. "You are quite a spunky little cheetah. No wonder Rudy favored you so much." Reese punched Marcia in the face, knocking her to the ground. Her mother yelled out to Marcia as Harriet screamed, but Tilton just choked the scream right out of her. Marcia was out cold on the floor.

The man called Leander grabbed the bread from the kitchen table and bit off a huge chunk from the top. He chewed loudly and said, "Ma'am, the gun. No need for anyone to die here tonight."

Barbara was still motionless. Should she shoot Reese for punching her daughter? Marcia came to, dizzying off the stars she was seeing from the punch to her face. She got to her hands and knees as blood poured from her nose. "Mama" she cried out. "Mama, let him have it!" She looked directly into her mother's face.

"He'll be the first one to die here today, Marcia," Barbara said coldly with her gaze fixed at Reese.

"No, Mama! Give it to them, now!" she said, practically shouting. "If you shoot him, you will die, too, Mama, and Harriet and I? Give him the guns, Mama, please. They win." Marcia yelled sternly as she retreated in her spirit, beaten and broken. They were done. The evil had won. "Give him the gun," she clamored once more.

Barbara lowered her arms until the rifle was by her side. She held it out with both hands shaking, as though it were an offering. Reese took the gun as Leander immediately released Harriet. Holding every ounce of fear deep inside of her, Harriet ran toward her sister, still kneeling on the floor, and fell into her arms.

The men took ten more minutes to rummage through the house, taking additional weapons as they went. At one point Leander asked the other men if they had seen Maxwell, to which the others shook their heads. As they traversed through the house, Harriet heard them muttering audibly.

"Here's what's goin' on next. Seeing your lady friend got us discovered!" Leander said, sounding frustrated.

"Mind yer own damn business. No one's gonna be around these parts for at least a day's ride. We'll leave before sunrise," Reese said.

"I don't know, Reese. You forgettin' who just saved your ass!" Leander huffed.

"Well, that lady's husband's old partner still owes me a big take. Even though he is dead and that crooked partner feels he is the one owed all of that, I know it's mine for the horse manure all of 'em put me through! The judge is gonna love it when I tell him I've seen a ghost." Reese continued muttering under his breath. "The women won't be a problem. We'll be gone by the time they get any notice down to Benton."

"Let's go, boys!" Tilton said as the men finally made their way back outside. "We got a lot to carry. Better to get a move on it now. Let's get goin' and see if we can't find young Maxwell." The men filled their arms with guns, food, and several coats and blankets. Struggling to carry everything, one by one, they left out the front door.

Silence permeated the kitchen. The Morgan women embraced one another for several moments. The three women were so tightly clutched to one another, they almost resembled a single unit. Barbara melted into hysterical anger, something both Marcia and Harriet had never seen before.

Through the window, they could see Maxwell's limp body being loaded onto a horse as the men finally rode away, leaving desperation in their wake.

28

The rain had turned to snow during the night, and the light wind twisted to a bone-chilling cold by the early morning. Daybreak's first light was slowly approaching. JR had been riding with his men for two days, nobody saying barely a word. He still couldn't believe that they had been within earshot of capturing Reese and nabbing the other convicts, and yet they were able to slip away, since the posse had decided to interrupt their pursuit due to the incoming storm.

Obviously JR was disappointed, but mostly in himself, that the wicked scoundrels had evaded capture yet another day. If they had stayed up all night, they could have cornered them at Crater Flats, they were so close. He wondered, *did the convicts know we were coming? Why else did they pick up camp in the second third of the night? It may have been simply a precautionary move by them to break camp in such weather. They can't be too far off now.* JR was confident that Mono Jim would get hot on their trail again very soon.

The posse was slowly nearing the Morgan ranch, trekking along Mineral Creek Road heading south. The men participating in the search had equally looked to Jim each day to lead the path for the group due to his impossibly elevated senses. JR wished he could be so tuned into the world around him. However the frustration of the previous days and past year continued to fritter away in his mind. He was easily distracted and lost in his thoughts that morning until he felt a strange sense of familiarity roll over him through the day-breaking chill. He felt it in his bones.

"This is where Ardie was murdered," he spoke out, just as the realization hit him.

The other men came to a halt as JR remembered his good friend, Ardie Perseval, who had been murdered in cold blood, just for doing his job to provide for his family. JR shuddered as the dawning morning seemed to get colder with every advancing minute. *Was Ardie the first to die in this crazy mess?* Inspired by the thoughts of such tragedy, he suddenly wrangled a renewed sense of purpose and revitalized anger, as he thought of his friends who had died that heinous day.

"You're right," Colby remarked sadly, trotting up to ride alongside JR and looking aside at him. "Which way forward from here?"

"Downriver," Jim said, who was riding just a hairsbreadth ahead of the two men. "We'll keep heading south following the way of the river. Two parties came through here, eight men."

"Our convicts?" JR questioned eagerly, hoping Jim's sensory awareness was spot-on. With Jim, he knew better than to keep asking ignorant, white man questions of a Paiute. Jim was an extremely valuable asset to any tracking mission. JR knew he could put his mind at ease with Jim leading the posse to their objective, capturing the vermin outlaws, even if they had missed their target two nights before.

His Paiute tracker guide nodded, and the other men followed suit. The party had ridden in silence since the early hours of the morning. Whenever someone became distracted or their mind wandered off to a thought, verbally expressed to the other men, Mono Jim would simply hold up his hand, and any erroneous, irrelevant banter would be halted immediately.

Pretty soon the darkness gave way to a heavy, gray morning sky with low-hanging, misting clouds. JR hoped that with the dawn would come a warmer, brighter day, but it didn't look like his wish was being granted. It appeared as if it would snow again soon, with the frigid crispiness lingering on another day.

"Woah!" Jim pronounced, stopping his horse. The rest of the men followed suit.

Jim looked at the ground. "Looks like two others covered their tracks behind 'em, between us and the convicts ahead of them. They're close behind, judging by this snowfall."

"What you see, Jim?" JR quizzed.

The men cautiously rode forward for several more minutes. The path next to the stream was turning into a road, covered by brush on both sides as they began riding up a steep box canyon, a road at about seven-thousand-five-hundred feet above sea level.

Vertically towering sheer rock and mountainous cliffs were adorning each side of the road as the men moved deeper into a basin. They were surrounded by twelve-thousand foot peaks and spires, rising three, some even four thousand feet over their heads. Rock tailings littered the pathway, as debris would continually fall from these steep mountainous cliffs, dislodged by rain and the forces of the wind over time.

Jim signaled for the men to hold their position once more, elevating his hand. Although he hadn't spoken, JR could see that Jim appeared quite serious. He silently withdrew his weapon from the holster and made eye contact with Colby, then nodded at him to do the same. Influenced decisively, the other men of the posse had drawn their weapons as well, slowly and steadily, though calmly.

Abruptly there was a crunching, snapping stir from the bushes behind the posse. Before all ten men of the group could fully turn around to face the source of the noise, JR saw two horses slowly emerge from the brush about fifteen yards behind them. He recognized the purple face and white beard of Judge Kensington, who was laughing as he revealed himself rancorously.

"Boom!" the judge yelled, looking maniacal, his white hair more tangled than usual and his eyes beaming wide. "Now settle down, gents." He tipped his hat as he trotted amongst and cut right down the center of the group of posse riders.

Rudy and the judge maneuvered toward the front of the line in order to address JR and Colby. Now realizing who it was, the men all lowered their guns and re-holstered them, shaking their heads.

"Nothin' to worry about men. It's just me and Rudy," the judge continued as he rode, pushing through the crowd in the narrow road, sounding jovial. "Just me 'n Rudy, offering our assistance to yer posse."

JR's heart was still racing. Just moments ago he had braced himself for the incoming attack of Reese and the other convicts. Instead, the judge and Rudy were standing before him, their horses looking frozen from the cold. Rudy was a sharp contrast to the judge's wired energy. He looked sullen and tired, and his eyes drooped below a shaggy leather hat. His shoulders slumped, like those of a beaten man or, more likely than not, an alcoholic off the wagon who had been running quite dry of liquor.

"Yer looking to get shot, Judge?" JR said angrily. "Awfully early for you to be out, isn't it? What are you doing up here so, so far from home?"

From JR's right, his horse tightened up against another pony. "Rudy been up all night?" Colby asked coldly as he assessed him and strode forward on his horse to clear Morrison's legs.

"So these were the tracks we've been observing," Jim said, resting his hands on the pommel of his saddle. "They apparently circled around, back behind us."

JR's heart sank. *Are we no closer to finding Reese?* He deliberated with himself to determine if the judge and Rudy were trying to distract them from finding the criminals. He kept scouring his weary brain and could find no other logical explanation for the judge's presence so far from his ranch in Chalfant other than he was more than likely involved somehow. Yet he was considering, why they would circle back behind him and his men, that remained a question.

"Let's get going. We are wasting time," JR alleged, as he turned his horse, focused off into the distance. They still had quite a way to go, and he did not want the judge distracting them from their mission, regardless if he was involved or not. *We aren't chasing the judge,* he reasoned, *and we have no time to pursue a 'maybe'. Me and my men need to remain focused on the task at hand, which are the escaped convicts from the prison outbreak. The posse was directly ordered by the military to do so at the command of Sheriff Hightower. The judge's involvement will make itself apparent, once Reese is recaptured,* he figured in the end. This frustrated JR, but he managed to work up a polite and professional tone. "We don't need or be wanting any of your help, Judge. Conflict of interest. Surely you can understand."

The judge pouted his lip, pretending as though he had been hurt by JR's words. "Hmm, ya don't say!" He flashed JR and the rest of his men with a wide grin.

The judge raised his hat, wiped his thin hair back, nodded at Rudy and returned his hat to his dome. The two rotated their horses around, spurring and charging right back down the middle through the splitting troop of riders. The two men continued at a gallop pace and rode off in the direction from which JR and his men had just come.

"That was quite ridiculous and quite suspicious, if you ask me," Mono Jim shouted over his shoulder back to the men.

Once clear, JR turned, looking back to his group of men. "How about those nerves, men? The gaul of him. Quite ignorant, I reckon. Nonetheless, compatriots." Moving onward, he added, "Remain vigilant, boys, there was something fishy about that encounter and likely proves to me what I have long believed but couldn't prove. I believe the judge is part of this whole mess the past year. So, if there were eight men upon eight horses, as Jim has noted for us this cheery morning, well, now there will be ten." The men all laughed, and the group moved on forward behind Mono Jim.

The posse rode for another thirty minutes. They were nearing the outskirts of Morgan ranch as they trotted along the west bank of what was now Crooked Creek. Then they crossed the water at the intersecting El Diablo creek, proceeding cautiously further up the steep canyon behind Mono Jim, who steadfastly signaled to the others that he was onto something.

When the weather was good, it was a magnificent sight to see the sun rise over the snow-kissed peaks, casting a soft glow across the lake. But on this steely gray day with low-hanging clouds, snow was beginning to fall once more. JR looked ahead at Jim, who sat up tall on his horse, looking alert as usual. The lack of sleep the night before and brisk morning of riding had clearly not weighed him down like the other men. His long black hair was braided firmly together behind his back and bounced up and down atop his cavalry frock, given to him by General Canby many years before. Many of the Paiute had half adapted to the white man's ways, living amongst them and proudly wearing their clothes. Jim exuded a quiet strength and razor-sharp alertness. It was as if he was plugged into some higher source or some strange connection to his surroundings. It seemed as if Jim was part of another world, one that JR could only get a glimpse of, as he watched his friend track down evil men. While JR was still mulling over these thoughts in his mind, Jim quickly halted his pony, flung his hand up to signal a slow stop and snapped his head around at JR with a serious look on his face.

"Can you hear that?" he whispered, nodding toward the trail that led to the ranch outpost. "I hear horses."

"The Morgan women?" JR knew the Morgan's had plenty of horses on their property.

"No, too many of them. Look!" With an urgent whisper, Jim pointed at the trail, about a hundred yards ahead to their right.

The other men looked too. Sure enough, there was a group of men, leading their horses out of the narrow path and toward the main road. One sat on his horse, but the others walked ahead and beside theirs, including a particularly tall man who couldn't be anybody but Reese. The fugitives had stopped to tie a considerable load to either side of their horses. JR spotted what looked like several guns, blankets and bags filled with what appeared to be food. He froze. *Should we wait in ambush and risk being seen, or should we charge straight ahead?* Before he could make the decision consciously, he felt his heels dig into the sides of his horse.

"Let's get 'em!" he yelled, charging toward the group of men.

He heard hooves follow behind as the other men began to race forward on their horses. As he galloped ahead, JR released his reins and pulled both of his weapons from his holster. He looked to his right, where Colby and James McLaughlin, another posse member, had caught up to him.

"Reese Clyborne is getting away," James yelled, jerking his head and spurring his horse toward him. Reese had caught sight of James, just as he had turned around from packing his horse. He moved a lot more quickly, once he saw the incoming posse. As he attempted to mount his horse, it got antsy and began resisting. Reese wrangled the spinning horse quickly, but it didn't calm and began pulling back in defiance while he pulled the reins. The posse raced very fast, getting closer and closer to Reese, trying to mount his pony. Colby raised his pistol and shot at Reese, just as he got onto the saddle.

Within the loud blast from his gun, Colby yelled, "He's hit!"

The bullet had hit Reese on the left side of his torso. The incoming gunfire completely spooked his pony at that point, causing it to rear up and leap quickly into a full gallop toward the road leading to the Morgan ranch. Reese frantically attempted to hold on as JR spurred on his horse and quickly raced after him down the trail.

At the same time, four to five other convicts had mounted their horses, and one at a time, it seemed, slowly began returning fire. JR could not make out their faces. In the rush of movement and gunfire and lead whizzing by, everything turned blurry. Both groups were rushing toward each other in an open clearing that was surrounded by trees, with the road on one side and the swampy marsh they called a lake on the other. If they met in the middle, there was sure to be a bloodbath. JR quickly dismounted his horse to duck from the gunfire and cautiously proceeded to follow Reese down the trail. Suddenly fire came from the direction Reese had gone, and JR took cover in the bushes by the side of the road.

Reese's voice yelled out from somewhere in the distance. "I'm hit, Morrison. I didn't kill Ardie or Morgan. You folks put away the wrong man."

JR yelled back, hiding in the bushes. "Oh ya? How so?"

Reese sounded much closer when he spoke again. JR could hear his own panicked breathing. "You guys need to be huntin' down that judge," Reese called, "And that Rudy Schaefer. They got the gold. They got Morgan's gold!"

JR heard someone rustling in the bushes and turned to his left to see James McLaughlin standing a few feet behind him. JR put a finger to his mouth as they quietly looked at each other. James stayed motionless while JR continued his conversation with Reese. He wondered why Reese was telling him all of this when he could just stay silent. *Why does he want to clear his name so badly?*

JR thought of the others involved in the situation. "And Colton?" he called out to Reese. "What of Colton and Cyrus?"

"That's right," Reese answered. "They stood to gain."

Gain? Gain what? JR thought.

"Well, that's mighty hard for me to believe. The judge, that's another story!" JR slowly moved closer in the direction where Reese's voice was coming from.

Reese went silent. For a moment, the only thing JR could still hear was the sound of his own heart thumping inside his chest. A few feet away James was trying to keep his horse quiet, slowly stroking its neck. JR was waiting for Reese to respond when he suddenly heard another, less audible voice squelch through the silence.

"Reese." The judge's voice was unmistakable. "Seems like you really got yerself stuck between a rock and a hard place."

JR tried to crane his head out of the brush to get a closer look, but he didn't want to risk being seen and getting shot. Just then, Jim and Colby quietly joined them by also taking cover in the brushes. JR put a finger to his mouth as they quietly looked at each other.

Reese responded, louder than the judge, "I saw Colton. Or I saw a ghost!" His voice got louder. "JR, they are here now!"

JR yelled back, "Oh, are they?" He shook his head, wondering if the judge and Rudy had been there the whole time, just watching everything from a distance. JR, Jim, and Colby looked at each other in silence while James was still struggling with his horse.

"Where's my gold, Judge?" the men overheard Reese say.

"Now what did ya go and do that for, Reese?" the judge said, sounding irritated.

Everything went quiet once more until JR heard the loud blast of a pistol, quickly followed by another shot. Suddenly gunfire erupted from behind them as two of the other escaped prisoners shot at them while trying to cross the clearing. Obviously they were looking to get other cover that would allow them a closer exit from this boxed up canyon they found themselves trapped in, like animals being hunted. These two outlaws were not part of the argument taking place between the posse, Reese and the judge, and as it appeared, they wanted no part of it.

JR turned around toward his men. "Stay here," he said to Colby. "You and Jim take these two. Keep defending the rear. Don't let them get around us and get to the exit of the canyon. I'm goin' for Reese."

Colby and Jim both nodded and moved back. JR quickly mounted his horse and rode along the edge of the brush, toward the trailhead where he believed he would find Reese. Suddenly the judge stepped out of the bushes to his left and with another loud shot fired directly at JR. He missed. JR fired back. More shots began to fill the air, but JR couldn't tell where they came from. He turned toward the brush as he suddenly felt a bullet hitting him. He went down, not being able to control his legs anymore. Everything went black for a second. He could hear, but he could not see anything. Searing pain shot up and down his body. He felt a hot trickle of blood starting to ooze at his backside.

"Wow!" he heard Rudy's voice say off in the distance. The sounds were warped as if Rudy's words came from a thousand miles away. JR wondered if his ears still worked. "That was scary! Hey, Judge, what did Reese mean? That he saw Colton? Colton's dead, isn't he? Man, I had a feelin' he got away!"

"He might just be sayin' that, Rudy. You don't know nothin'. Dirty rotten trader, Colton be, if you ask me," the judge said. JR heard him kick something heavy. "Reese be dead now, that's for sure."

Reese, JR thought, fighting to stay conscious while pretending to still be dead so the judge would not shoot him again. *Reese is dead.*

"Look, Judge," Rudy said. "I found this wanted poster in Reese's jacket. It's for Colton. This here's a federal warrant. How'd they get involved?"

"I don't know now, Rudy. But maybe cuz' Ardy delivered mail, a government responsibility. Just put it in yer pocket and let's get movin'," the judge hissed.

It was silent in the clearing, except for some breathing and the occasional shuffling of Rudy and the judge. JR did not hear any sounds of his men, the convicts, or the horses. *Where has everybody gone? Are they still hiding?* JR tried to slightly move his head to get a look around, but then decided against it. It was too painful. He felt paralyzed.

Suddenly JR heard the familiar cock of a pistol's hammer. Rudy's voice sounded closer and very determined.

"Gimme the key," Rudy demanded in a firm tone that JR had never heard from him before. "Gimme the key to the gold under yer house. I'm goin' to get my share and get outta here. Morrison knows. Everyone knows!"

The judge cackled as JR heard him coming closer. "Morrison knew. Yer really gonna pull a gun on me, Rudy? Why don't you settle down, boy?" The judge appeared to be calm. "Yer gonna get yer gold."

"No!" Rudy exclaimed, his voice cracking slightly. "You'll just shoot me like you just shot Reese. I don't trust anyone no more, especially you, Kensington. I already waited a year. I ain't waitin' no more."

"Now settle down, Rudy! If it will make ya feel better, I'll give ya the damn key."

JR heard a gun go off, but heard no yelling or bodies falling.

"You are going to regret that shot you just took," the judge said, removing what sounded like a ring of keys from his pocket.

"All of 'em!" Rudy yelled. "And yer guns."

"You don't think I wouldn't give ya the right key, Rudy? Ha! Yer probably right!" the judge snickered.

JR turned his throbbing head to the left, where he saw Rudy's feet walk over to a Henry rifle that was lying on the ground. Rudy picked up the gun and turned around to walk toward his nearby horse. Two shots rang out as Rudy screamed and dropped to the ground. JR could see his body, writhing in agony from the corner of his eye. With every ounce of strength left in him, JR was able to turn himself over, so that from under the brush he could observe the entire scene, using the support of his elbow. He saw the judge standing in the middle of the clearing, holding a Derringer he had just pulled out of his sleeve. He thought he saw Reese's body lying motionless about ten yards away. To his right, Rudy lay bloody and whimpering. He was still alive but looked to have sustained a serious wound to his scalp.

The judge had made his way over to the small clearing where JR was trying to conceal himself. Stepping over Rudy, who was writhing on the ground just to the other side of the bushes, the judge leaned over, peering over the bush and spotting JR laying on his back. The judge picked up the Henry rifle and checked it for ammo, then tossed it, where Rudy couldn't get to it. He turned around and looked at Rudy, shaking his head.

Rudy wondered, *why doesn't he execute me like he just did Reese?*

"Rudy!" the judge said sarcastically, "I've always pitied you, so today I'm going to let you live."

"Judge, why you doin this? I owe you money, don't I? You've never been a man to pass by even a silver dollar, Judge?"

"Well today, Rudy, that's why I'm gonna let you writhe there on the ground. Go, take care of these other scoundrels and come back and inspect your wounds, see if you'll survive or not, and then I kill ya, hahaha," the evil man snickered as he continued walking toward JR, who now sensed the judge's immediate presence.

"Kensington," JR said slowly, feeling each syllable send searing pain through his side. "Seems Reese had some things to say about ya." He groaned. The blood had completely soaked his shirt and he started to shiver, realizing the bullet that hit him in the back had completely passed through him.

"Ya, I was afraid y'all heard all that nonsense," the judge said, looking down at JR.

With great effort, JR reached with his right hand for his pistol and aimed it at the judge with trembling fingers. Then he unlatched a pair of shackles from his belt and threw them at the ground. They landed at the judge's feet. "Put these on ..." He panted, "Until we can all get to the bottom of it."

JR knew he must look pathetic, laughable even, to be making such a stand. In the judge's eyes, this would be JR's last stand. But it was all he could think to do. Maybe, just maybe, the judge could see how complicated the situation had become. "Now put that gun away, John Robert Morrison, will ya?" The judge laughed.

The judge looked down at the shackles and grinned widely. His flush face looked redder than usual as he holstered his pistol and put both hands on his hips. Then he crouched low to the ground, as if he wanted to inspect the shackles further. He looked at JR, who was trying to remove a neckerchief from his belt to stop the flow of blood.

The judge then looked around the clearing. Rudy had somehow crawled away. The judge, surprised at his unwillingness to just die, huffed, "Hmm, now where did that Rudy go?" He looked confused.

Suddenly gunfire was erupting behind them in the distance, far up the box canyon. Three, four, five, then ten blasts could be heard. JR knew it was the rest of his posse who had made contact with the other outlaws, and they were now fully engaged in a gunfight, a fight he would not be able to assist in.

JR looked aside under the bush to where Rudy had been writhing moments ago. The judge spoke the truth, Rudy was gone. JR labored to untie his neckerchief. He was fighting to survive with every morsel of strength that was left in him. He began to feel very drowsy and disoriented, as more and more blood was leaving his body. Cold chills were settling in. The purple neckerchief reminded him of Sarah's favorite dress. He thought of Sarah, and his heart swelled. *You will get through this. You are strong.* He couldn't tell if it was his own voice or Sarah's, that was urging, no, begging him to muscle through this. JR thought that James, Jim, Colby, and the others must be in a fight for their lives, too, as he heard more gunfire continuing up the canyon. *How did we get separated? We were just together. Where are they?* He hoped the others would be victorious and make their way back to find him, alone and dying, here with the judge. As more gunfire rang and echoed about the canyon, now farther away from him, he assumed the convicts were climbing higher and farther up this devil's canyon.

"Ouchie. That looks bad, John Robert," the judge said, his eyebrows raised as he pointed to JR's bleeding wound. He had been standing there quite some time. *Why hasn't he killed me yet,* he wondered. His voice sounded far away and fuzzy to JR. "I'm not putting on any shackles. Ha! Anyway…" The judge's eyes were bloodshot and wild. "I know you heard Reese yammering about Colton not being dead. We should both be out lookin' for him. My work's done here," he clamored.

The judge, crouching low to the ground, was just inches away from JR's face. He looked back at the shackles, reaching for them. JR wondered if the judge planned on tying him up. He looked up to the sky. *God, please,* he thought, *please deliver me from this evil. Please help me. Please let me live. Please don't take me from Sarah.* JR turned his gaze back at the judge, just in time to see him holding shackles in one hand and his Derringer in the other. The Derringer was aimed right at his head, and his stomach dropped. The judge pulled the trigger, but the bullet only grazed JR's left ear.

"No," was all he managed to moan. "No, please!"

"These little guns sure can be inaccurate," the judge said, talking to himself while inspecting the weapon. "And they really hurt to fire, I tell ya, John!"

The judge looked at JR one last time. He smiled. Then he fired again. It was loud, and then there was darkness, nothing but darkness.

29

Harriet felt helpless as she waited inside with her mother and sister. Reese and his convict cronies had left the Morgan home in the middle of the night. The women remained awake all night, too traumatized to even close their eyes for a few minutes. Harriet was deeply shaken by what had happened. There were no words to describe the feeling of being violated, not being able to defend herself. But mostly she was filled with anger, a smoldering rage, deeply planted inside her being. She wished she could have gotten one good shot into that Tilton before he grabbed her. Harriet's neck was sore and bruised from being nearly crushed by his elbow. She touched her neck gingerly as if to stroke the pain away.

The three women remained seated in the kitchen throughout the long night and well into the morning hours. They brewed pots of coffee without talking, except for peripheral comments. *Do you want another cup? Is that hot enough for you? Do you want some milk?* Harriet remained entrenched in her fear of Reese returning. In the early morning hours, they began to hear gunshots ringing through the air, not too far off in the distance, over near the marsh and again far up El Diablo Canyon. The snapping of bullets prompted Florence, who lived on the outskirts of the ranch's property, to make her way to the main house. She was a young woman in her early twenties, who lived with her mother in a small house on the edge of the Morgan ranch. She and her mother both helped on the ranch.

"What's goin' on?" Florence panted as she burst onto the back porch, a rifle hanging over her shoulder. She opened the door and came inside. "Is everybody ok?" She looked breathless and completely shaken.

Barbara invited her to sit down and poured her a cup of coffee, while she told her about everything that had happened the night before.

"They're back!" Marcia gasped when the first shot had rung out.

"No," Barbara croaked. "They're nearby, I reckon, but they aren't here." It sounded like the shots were fired over near the marsh and the last volley up Diablo Canyon, nearing the high country. "We are hearing echoes, honey." Barbara attempted to put the other women's minds at ease.

"I wonder if JR and the others have caught up with Reese and his thugs," Harriet said excitedly. She felt her strength return. *It must be Reese. Who else would they have run all the way up here into their house?* "Well sweetie, I'm sure it was the posse that cornered them, and a gun battle ensued. We need to pray for our men, that the Lord will protect and keep them safe, form a shield around them." Barbara got up to get more milk.

The gunfire would cease and then restart intermittently, but it certainly seemed to be moving further away from the ranch. The Morgan women mulled over the thought of riding out toward what they believed to be the source of the firepower. They agreed to wait until the gunshots ceased completely. Barbara did not want to endanger her girls any more than herself. Florence insisted on joining them, confident she could help. The heavy gunfire lasted only ten minutes or less. They kept hearing single shots being fired every couple of minutes for what felt like hours. They started to time the shots, agreeing to wait at least a half hour after the last one before heading out.

"Let's go," Barbara finally said.

The gunfire seemed to have ceased completely, and she pushed herself away from the kitchen table. Thank God Reese and the men hadn't found the armory of guns Randall and Barbara had hidden away in the barn. She rounded up as much armament as she could in a wheelbarrow and rolled it up to the house. She seemed to have recovered from the events of the previous hours, and once again she was the strong, logical mother Harriet knew. Her mother had always been a steadfast source of safety for her and Marcia, as well as the other less fortunate women and children living at the outpost. While he was alive, her father had been at the mine most of the time, working it, day in, day out, for most of Harriet's life. It was all she could remember.

The women prepared more ammunition over the next few hours, assembling the weapons. Once bundled up and armed, the women set out along an alternate side trail, leading from the ranch towards the marsh and beyond to the lake. A two-pony wagon driven by Florence, sitting alongside Harriet, trailed behind the horses. The path was covered by brush on both sides and was only wide enough for two horses to ride side by side or one wagon down the middle. Marcia and Barbara led the way, with Harriet and Florence bringing up the rear. They headed toward a clearing and a patch of trees that opened up to the marsh and lake which the Paiute had named Lake El Diablo.

As the women approached a crossing in the road ahead, Harriet was startled when her mother's horse suddenly stopped. "Look! Over here!" Barbara quickly dismounted her horse.

Harriet, Marcia, and Florence followed suit. "What is it?" Harriet asked, concerned.

"It's Reese," Barbara exclaimed.

Toward the end of the trail, near the center of a clearing, Reese's lifeless body was lying on the ground. He had been shot several times, and his entire prison uniform was drenched in blood.

Harriet shuddered as she arrived at the corpse. There were flies already gorging on its eyes. Reese's face was purple. He didn't look real. He looked as if he were made from wax, molded to look like Reese.

But it wasn't him anymore. Harriet stared down into his face, almost mesmerized by the strangeness of his body, lying dead and spread out, flat on his back before her. She was relieved to see that he could never harm anyone ever again, but at the same time she was fearful that the knowledge of what happened to her father had died with him.

Her sister's sudden and piercing scream snapped Harriet out of her thoughts. "Mama!" Marcia called out. Harriet could see her, waving her Spencer rifle up in the air. Harriet and Barbara ran toward her. "It's JR! Oh, Mama." Her whole body was shaking.

JR was lying slumped up against a small rock. His hand was still holding on to a purple neckerchief, and he had a bullet hole in the middle of his head. Harriet felt the support of her legs weaken under her body. Next thing she knew, she was on the ground, screaming.

"No," Harriet called as she sobbed uncontrollably and punched the ground.

Florence crouched down to comfort her. Wrapping both her arms around Harriet, she stroked her hair. "Shhhh, there now. Don't look."

Harriet cried, tears of anger and rage gushing from her eyes. "Sarah will be devastated. Who could do something like this? It's … it's not fair!" She looked up at her mother, almost expectantly, waiting for answers. Barbara and Marcia both wiped tears from their eyes. "JR is gone. Who did this? Reese?"

Harriet, suddenly feeling nauseous, thought she might throw up at the sight of JR. She couldn't look at him any longer. A huge hole brandished his forehead. She had witnessed the love JR and Sarah shared. How could Sarah go on living without him? The feelings of a hellbent, loveless, and murderous world draped over her spirit like a wolf in the dark of night, capturing its prey.

"Harriet, we have to go away from here," Barbara said firmly as she wiped away her tears with the back of her hand. "It may not be safe for us. We have to go now," she implored.

Harriet nodded and rose from the ground, trying to remember the strength she had felt around Reese and Tilton. As the nausea departed, she clenched her fists. *I will kill whoever did this*, she thought, *if they're not dead already.*

Marcia got JR's horse, and the women ventured further into the clearing as Harriet followed reluctantly behind. They walked toward the brush that separated El Diablo Creek from the road.

"I think I can hear horses over here, but I can't see anything," Marcia said sadly.

"Look!" Florence pointed at a body. "There's another one."

Harriet's stomach lurched. "I can't look. Who is it?"

"It's that man," Marcia said quietly. "Leander? He's definitely dead."

Harriet felt hatred well up inside of her. Maybe Leander was the one who killed JR. They continued walking through the trees, where they found a wounded horse lying next to another body.

"Who is it?" Florence asked.

"Jim," Barbara answered. "The Paiute guide." She shook her head and bent down toward Jim, who had fallen from his horse after being hit. His eyes were open, staring blankly at the sky. With two fingers, Barbara closed his eyelids. "God rest his soul," she prayed, requesting he would find comfort and peace with his Creator in heaven.

"We have to keep moving," Marcia said.

They walked farther into the brush, when they heard a groan. "Hello," Barbara called out and started walking faster in the direction of the moaning.

"Help," they all heard a familiar voice croak.

The four women hurried toward the voice to find two men slumped against a thick tree, discovering Colby sitting beside James. James had his arms around Colby's shoulders as though, at one point, Colby had tried to help him rise to his feet but failed. There was blood at Colby's hip, but he seemed coherent and alert. James had sustained a gunshot wound in his right leg, and his pants were stained with blood.

"Oh, Colby!" Barbara exclaimed, running toward him and falling to her knees beside the men.

"It was brutal," James said, panting, his face covered in dirt. "We got routed. Four escaped."

"Oh my God." Barbara was on the verge of tears again. "JR and Jim are dead. And two others."

Colby paused for a moment, as the news of JR's death seemed to hit him like a brick. He was visibly shaken and seemed to need some kind of blind reassurance to compose himself before speaking. The news of his good friend's death seemed to suck the life right out of him.

"Barbara, we gotta get to town quickly," he cried out, in more of a stress-filled moan than a request.

"We have a wagon," Marcia said. "Can you walk? We can help you. We should take Jim and JR with us. We can't just leave 'em here. God knows what the elements and animals will do."

Colby hobbled to the wagon, limping from what was a minor wound in his hip. Marcia and Barbara, the strongest and the tallest of the women, splinted James's leg with two branches and then helped him onto the wagon. He was unable to put any weight on his right leg and yelled out in pain every time he moved even an inch.

Once the two men were on the wagon, Barbara's face turned to stone. "I have some blankets in the wagon. We need to get JR and Jim on there, first. Let's get 'em wrapped up and take 'em with us."

Harriet whimpered, "I can't do it, Mama." Her body started to shake all over as she wiped away the tears that kept coming with her sleeve.

"You can, and you will," Barbara said sternly. "You and Marcia can try and lift Jim. Florence and I will move JR."

Harriet let out a small sob, and with a lot of effort, the women finally heaved the bodies onto the wagon.

The ride into Benton would take most of the day, and Harriet spent the first several hours crying, imagining all sorts of scenarios that might have produced such carnage. *When will it end?* she kept thinking. *First Father and now JR. Who is next? Mother? Marcia? What is left for us here?* Harriet imagined they would have to move, maybe back East where her mother's family lived.

It was nearly dark by the time they arrived on Main Street in Benton. The sun was long gone, and a full, bright moon shone overhead, casting vibrant hues into the wispy clouds above. The sky looked a blue-black hue, the thin white drawn out clouds appeared as angels of the night. As they entered the main road, Barbara urged the horses to go faster until they skidded to a halt outside of the Benton doctor's house. The nearest hospital was in Reno, and these men would need their wounds cleaned, stabilized, and sutured immediately. They would never make it to Reno, at least a nine or ten day ride away, without infection setting in.

Doc Swaggert, a baldheaded, squat-looking man, scrambled out the front door of his home, making his way to the porch. He appeared confused as to the commotion at such a late hour. Harriet looked at her mother who was beaten red and breathless.

"Well, hello, ladies. What brings you—"

"Doctor," Barbara screeched as she got off her horse, pointing to the wagon behind her. "Help these men. We must immediately alert Sheriff Hightower."

The doctor, taking note of Barbara's frantic state, said nothing and darted toward the back of the wagon.

"You two." She pointed to Marcia and Florence. "Help the doctor with the injured men. Harriet, you come with me."

Harriet gulped as her mother took off toward the mercantile. She heard the doctor yell out in alarm as she cast one look back at the wagon.

Minutes later they arrived, breathless, at the entrance of the mercantile. Barbara tugged furiously on the doors, but they wouldn't budge.

"They're locked, Mama," Harriet said.

"Doesn't matter," Barbara panted. "We have to get in there. Send the message." Suddenly Barbara pulled the sleeve of her dress down to cover her fist. She pulled her arm back and punched the glass window to the right of the door.

"Mama, what are you …" Harriet asked, trying to pull her mother away from the window, stepping onto the broken glass.

Barbara ignored her and carefully reached through the hole of the window to unlock the door. She let herself in and motioned for Harriet to follow her to the back, toward JR's office. Harriet felt her heart beating rapidly in her chest. When they reached the office, they found the door to be locked as well. With a forceful kick that made Harriet jump, Barbara easily smashed the thin, wooden door, before dashing to the telegraph machine on the desk with determination.

Harriet stood speechless, unsure of what to do or say. She thought she heard a noise coming from the front of the shop but figured she was imagining things. "Mama," she said hesitantly.

"Shh," her mother responded, typing furiously on the telegraph.

Suddenly they heard hurried footsteps rush into the office. It was Henry Devine, who looked sweaty and scared. He was holding a rifle pointed in the direction of the women, as though he expected to see a burglar in the office, ready to shoot. When he saw Barbara and Harriet, his expression changed to calm confusion as he carefully set the weapon down and wiped his brow with the scarf hanging around his neck.

"Barbara! Barbara Morgan!" he said, still out of breath, his bright-blue eyes wide.

Barbara, who was still typing furiously, did not look up. "I gotta get a wire immediately to Hightower."

Henry scratched his chin. "He went north to Aurora, to pursue seven of the escaped men from Carson City, you know, making their way that way, east. There were twenty-eight in all. Can you believe that?"

"I can," Barbara croaked. "It's frightful." She stopped typing and looked up at Henry, her blue eyes sparkling. "We need to alert him immediately. The army, too, and General Batterman." She took a deep breath as she continued, "JR is dead. As is Jim. Four or five have escaped." The words cascaded out of her mouth like a furious waterfall. "Oh my God, you should have heard it out there this morning, Henry. Reese Clybourne is dead!" Barbara shook her head in defeat.

Harriet watched the color leaving Henry's face at her mother's words. His face immediately froze and he didn't move, as though his brain was still trying to process what he had just heard. He looked from Barbara to Harriet as if he was seeing them for the first time.

"JR is dead?" he said shakily.

"I'm afraid so, Henry," Barbara said in a consoling voice, but Harriet noticed how drained and exhausted her mother sounded.

Henry looked between Harriet and Barbara again, still in disbelief. Harriet had never seen Henry look so young and vulnerable. He looked like a boy, terrified and confused, as tears leaked from his eyelids.

"No," he whispered, shaking his head. "No!"

"Where is Sarah?" Barbara asked.

"No. No, no, no. JR, no, you're lying!" he said, stepping back once more, his head shaking. His lip quivered as a river of tears then began to stream down his face. A deep insecurity had transfixed Henry's emotions.

"He's on the wagon outside," Barbara said solemnly. "I'm so sorry, Henry. Where is Sarah?"

Henry dissolved into his flowing tears and still shook his head in disbelief.

"She … left … on the stage … this morning … for Los Angeles. Oh my God." He took a deep breath and straightened up, as if attempting to regain his composure. He walked to the desk next to the broken door, opened up the drawer and pulled out a folder. "Barbara, here are the codes for Hightower, Canby, and Barrington. But they are looking for the others who made their way north. They can't come. What if they don't get it? What will we do?"

Barbara said nothing but continued typing furiously once more. Five more minutes passed in utter silence, except for the rapid clicking of the telegraph keys. Finally Barbara stood up and straightened her skirt. "Sent," she said.

"What do we do now?" Harriet asked.

"There's nothin' we can do," Barbara said. "We wait. I have to talk to Penelope and James's wife. You two don't have to come, if you don't want to." Barbara headed for the door.

Harriet didn't want to go. She didn't feel like she could handle watching more people she knew as they learned that their loved ones were injured or lifeless. There was nowhere for her to turn, except maybe to Henry, she questioned. Harriet did not want to sit any longer with her own sadness, but she also didn't want to experience more shock and more grief. She felt empty. Physically she was exhausted, but what was worse, mentally she was in agony. Henry was in no better condition.

"I'll make you some tea, if you want, or I can help you here," she offered to Henry. She did not want to be alone.

Here he was, the young and handsome man of her dreams, but she was incoherent, and those passions seemed lost forever. She felt so sad and confused as her mind was tormented. Henry, on the other hand, was in no mood to work. The morning had brought him even more confusion, sadness, and distress, in a mixed emotion of utter shock and heartbreak. Grief was soon to follow for all involved.

Henry paused for a moment in terror, as if he had a life-and-death decision to make. Harriet wondered if he was torn between growing into a man who would take care of business or remaining the child that he used to be and had left behind. Both being in that moment together, Harriet felt grateful for her mother, who had done so much for herself, Marcia, and the people of Benton.

Henry was glad she was there at the moment. If anyone should be with him under such anguish, it was Harriet. A few minutes had passed, when they both suddenly and mutually realized they were thrust into such a dire circumstance together, standing alone in a store with no owner. They were finding themselves quickly grateful that they were together now. After all she was up and down, all over the place. Henry had lost his mentor, dear father figure, employer, friend, and future brother-in-law. The two could carry each other through.

Harriet embraced Henry with a new found conscious appreciation for him. Henry manned up, realized the stake, and comforted Harriet to comprehend what her mom had faced in Reese, the outlaws, and the dead, with such resolve. Through Henry's heartwarming words and his strong embrace Harriet felt relief that she did not have to be the one in charge to handle breaking sad news to their friends, since she realized her mother was there to do that.

After all that had happened, for a moment, deep down in her heart Harriet did not want to be big or grown-up anymore. She thought of Henry, herself, JR and Sarah, her mom, and the others. Pondering such a tragedy, she wondered if she would find herself and Henry ever engaged or beyond that, even married. *Do I have a right to be?* After all, her dearest friend Sarah wouldn't be married now. *She will live alone in broken dreams, sadness, and deep grief.*

Her mind wandered. *Does Henry desire the same things?* The questions swirled about like a hurricane in her soul. She didn't want to see dead bodies or lose the people she loved, especially Henry, who was her dream. *Does he know how I feel about him?* She couldn't ask now. It would have to wait. *Why does this have to hurt so much?* she thought. *Do I have it within myself to be as strong as my mother one day? Can it be this day? It has to be this day,* Harriet determined.

After a while, she broke the long embrace. "It's ok," she interposed Henry, allowing him the grace with such permissive words to stay behind and process the way he was feeling, right there, right now, beside her.

Inspired to reflect a mature womanlike strength to Henry, internally surmising how much she had grown in spirit, she squeaked out, "Let's go have some tea now, and I'll help you sweep up the glass." She walked over to the stove in the corner of the mercantile, picked up the pot that was on the top and filled it with water. She placed it back on the stovetop, then turned and pulled the broom and dustpan from a hook on the wall nearby.

Henry, dazed and confused, sat in JR's chair, staring at the floor in front of him. Shortly after Harriet returned with some tea. She went to the front door, swept up the glass onto the pan and emptied it into the trash. She left the broom and pan near the door, walked over and sat on JR's desk next to Henry. He was still staring at the floor, sitting in the chair, not saying a word. Even through the silence Henry's presence comforted Harriet. She couldn't take her eyes off of his grief. She comforted him, rubbing his back as he sobbed. Before they knew it, an hour had passed as they were sitting together, calming each other's nerves and forming an eternal bond over this matter that would last a lifetime. How could it not?

Both were rising to form another embrace and then decided they should check on the status of the injured men. Harriet now felt stronger and more confident with Henry's closer relation through the disaster, even if it had only just happened that day over such a short time. She grew into the wisdom that it was time for her to comfort and inspire her mother and sister, making them proud. She felt that she had suddenly grown into a woman. She could always cry later when she was by herself, or Henry and she could cry together. *Who could have known a crisis such as this would create a bond between us, closer than I could have ever imagined or dreamed of?* she thought.

"Do you think Colby and James will make it?" Henry asked while carrying a lantern as Harriet wrapped her scarf tightly around her chest to ward off the cold. They walked quickly across the street, hand in hand, to Dr. Swaggert's house in the dark.

"I think so," Harriet said. "They seemed like they were hangin' on when we found them."

When they arrived at the doctor's house, they found Penelope, Barbara, and Marcia crowded around two tables in the front room of the residence. Each table was covered with what must have been a white cloth at some point. However both were completely crimson with fresh blood, which started dripping onto the wooden floor. James and Colby were lying atop either table with Doc Swaggert standing in the middle. Penelope's typically hardened face had melted in concern, and she was wearing her nightgown covered with a robe as she was stroking Colby's hand.

Colby was covered in a large bandage wrapped around his midsection and groin. He looked to be resting. Harriet wondered if he had been sedated and then noticed the glass of whiskey next to his right hand. James's face, on the other hand, was twisted in pain. There was a bloodied bandage wrapped around his leg, starting above the knee.

"We're gonna have to take yer leg, James," the doctor said. Marcia gasped. "The femur is completely shattered, your artery is shredded, and the tissue below the injury will be dying. You lost a lot of your blood. I have clamps cutting the circulation now. I would have to remove a foot of bone to hope to repair this, and the chance of saving it could cost you your life from infection, as gangrene is certain. The hospital is too far away to keep the tissues and bone below the fracture resilient to healing. It is the only way, James. I am sorry."

James bit his lip and grimaced. "Martha?" he shuddered, asking for his wife. "Where is Martha? You can't take my leg, Doc. You can't!"

"I can do my best to make a good life for you, James, but ya have to trust me in this." Doc Swaggert looked sternly at James as he wiped his hands with a wet towel.

James looked around the room, confused, as though he did not recognize any of the women's faces. "Heard talk today from Judge Kensington, you know," he said, addressing nobody in particular through the haze of his thoughts.

Harriet looked at Henry, who looked equally confused.

"Now, James, it's goin' to be ok," Doc Swaggert said, holding his shoulder, trying to calm him down.

James continued as though he hadn't heard a word, "Need to talk to the judge and that Rudy Schaefer. Need to find them. They know all about Reese. Reese claimed to see Colton and said Rudy shot Morgan, with the judge and himself present. They know a whole lot 'bout everythin'. Reese is dead."

"It's ok, James," Barbara said, stepping toward the table. "I got this. You just rest. Martha is on her way. She'll be here soon."

They were interrupted by a loud sob from Penelope. Her head was down as she buried her face in her hands. "Sarah's gonna die! Her JR! Right now, she's on her way to see her family. She won't hear about this for two weeks, soonest. How can we possibly deliver news like this over a wire? That would be so cruel and leave her in a disarray of anxiety and confusion."

Barbara shot Penelope a sympathetic but impatient look. This was too much emotion for one tiny doctor's office to handle. Penelope's cries must have woken up Colby, who started stirring. He attempted to sit up but grabbed the dressing around his stomach and hip, gasping again in pain. He slowly lowered himself back down to the table again, realizing he had to lie still to be in comfort.

"The judge," he said, his face looking ghost-white. Harriet wondered if he had heard James talking moments before. "It had to be the judge who shot Reese. JR was with James and Jim, chasin' him. We ran into the judge out there before the manure hit the fan. It had to be the judge! He was on his way to confront those men before us. How he beat us there, is questionable at best. He must have took the switchbacks. He knows exactly about all of the past year. Kensington has the answers. I'm sure of it!"

Barbara looked at the doctor, who was doing his best to console the two men. "Settle in, you boys. We'll get into that." Harriet couldn't tell if her mother believed what they were saying or if she was just trying to quiet them down.

"Now, you ladies ain't no vigilantes," James groaned.

Barbara stepped between the tables and put a hand on either one. "Now, listen to me," she said, looking at both men. Her tall, athletic frame looked impressive between the two injured men. Her long, blond hair was out of its normal bun fashion and was unkempt, yet somehow very beautiful. Her face was strained with exhaustion, but she looked stoic again, resilient and certain.

"Now is the time for justice. Yer gonna be a spell healin' now, James. I already notified the army and Hightower. There's no men left in this town. If they can come, Hightower should be here from Aurora in four days, the army in nine or ten."

Harriet heard Henry clear his throat.

"She meant no offense, Henry. We need you here." Marcia looked up at Henry and smiled.

Harriet quietly stepped out of the room. She needed a moment alone. *Rudy! Rudy Schaefer killed my father if what James said is true. And the judge, he was there too!* She let out a loud sob and leaned against the wall. Finally she had the answer she had been looking for over a year.

It was nearing midnight as General C. C. Batterman and General Edward Canby sat pouring over a table map next to a large stack of paperwork and many small military figurines. There was a fire crackling in the grate, which made the small room feel even cozier. The candle lights had almost burned down to their nubs, and visibility was growing dim. Two glasses of whiskey sat within arm's reach of the two men, who sat opposite one another at the rectangular wooden table of Batterman's Quarters in Virginia City.

They worked their way through whiskey in silence, as both were under immense pressure to bring order to the growing unrest out West. The politicians in Washington who were trying their darndest to demonstrate law and order in the Wild West, were not pleased with the Carson City federal prison breakout, and that was putting things lightly. In reality they were nervous due to the state of affairs that existed between the settlers, Indians, and military. What was more, Eastern investors had become increasingly reluctant to move their businesses out West with all the constant turmoil between the towns, settlers, military and the Indians. Generals Batterman and Canby were focusing on allocating enough men and resources to rebuild the Federal Penitentiary as soon as possible. It was bad enough that the prisoners had escaped, but the destroyed, ashen building lingered as a consistent reminder that chaos had beat out justice. They had no choice but to seize the upper hand, raze the structure and wreckage and start anew, if there was to be law and order protections from the federal government.

General Canby, a broad-shouldered, muscular man, was exhausted from his trip to Virginia City. He exchanged yawns with his counterpart, General Batterman, a polished man in his forties, whose hair was somehow still slick-backed and shiny, even given the late hour. Canby sighed and reached for his whiskey glass to down the rest of it when the door burst open and Batterman's assistant, John Clavis, breathlessly entered the room. Instinctively, Canby and Batterman stood up immediately.

"General," Clavis heaved, who was a boy of about eighteen and interested in joining the military. "Marked urgent." He held a piece of paper in his outstretched hand.

General Batterman took the letter from John and dismissed him with a nod. He opened it and quickly read over the content, rubbing his shaved chin with his right hand.

"Looks like they got a mess down in Long Valley with those inmates," he said, straightening his posture and giving Canby a serious look, his voice now void of exhaustion.

Canby sighed. "What's it say?"

"Looks like the town lost!" General Batterman continued, picking up the letter and reading it again, as if to make sure. "The men from the Benton posse are dead or dying. Three severely wounded. Four or five convicts moving south towards Round Valley. SOS." He shook his head.

General Canby straightened his collar. He had held out hope that JR and the posse would surely beat out the convicts. He looked at the map in front of him and then solemnly at the mountain of paperwork on the table. "Rebuilding Carson City can wait, General. We're going to have to send in support."

Batterman concurred, nodding, "You up for it, Canby? I know you need to get nor—"

Canby interrupted with confidence. "Sir, I'll leave straight away. Send a message back to Benton and Hightower as follows: 'The Second Regiment will arrive in four days.' We will call up a battalion from Fort Independence in Inyo County. They will head off anyone thinking of running south. Also, we will probably have some very angry folks thinking of being hero vigilantes. We must protect the town from falling prey to their own pain and detrimental anger over the murders, although I certainly cannot blame them," Canby continued without hesitation. He would see this thing through. He owed it to the people of Benton. Between the unrest on the reservation and the tragedy at the Morgan mine, the citizens of the region had had enough. It was time to bring in the military, bringing some law and order back to that town. To some extent both Canby and Batterman feared the vigilante and revenge model, as they knew it would be merely a signal of more death and destruction. They swore an oath to protect the American citizens, if even from themselves.

General Canby began organizing his paperwork, when there was a knock at the door again. He looked at Batterman, wondering if there was another update on the Benton situation.

"Ok then," he said.

"Yes, come in," Batterman said, looking confused.

John Clavis entered once more. "There's two men here to see you, Sir."

"Go on," Batterman said.

"A federal warrant, Sir."

"Send 'em in then." Batterman nodded at the assistant.

John motioned from behind Batterman, waving to the two men to enter the room. They wore thick coats and heavy gloves. One of the men had a long face with a thin, long nose. With reddish hair and light eyes, he looked rather Irish. The other man was tall and heavier. He had a thick neck, brown hair that was turning gray, and small, squinty eyes.

"How can I help you, Gentlemen? Federal matters?" Batterman asked.

The tall man spoke first. "Yes. I'm Bart Runion. This is Earl Perryman." He gestured, introducing the red-haired, Irish-looking man. "We are here on a federal warrant for one Colton Jaminson, regarding the theft of $40,000 U.S. Gold mint and the murder of mine owner Randall Morgan on federal leased mining claim 16643." Bart Runion spoke in a rush of sharp syllables, as though he had given that exact speech multiple times before.

"Yes," General Canby said and nodded. "Colton Jaminson. Been seeking him myself for some time now." It had been a while since he had heard Colton's name mentioned. He had thought that Colton was a lost cause ever since he escaped the Paiute reservation.

"We were at Numaga's encampment, and he was there. He's gone south. We are going that way into California in pursuit. Here's a copy of the warrant." Bart Runion took off his gloves, reached into his thick coat and pulled out a carefully folded piece of paper. He handed it to General Batterman.

"Well," Batterman said, after unfolding the document and quickly looking it over, "You two can ride alongside General Canby here. He happens to be heading that same way. It seems one of the other gents involved in this murder you find yourselves now mixed in, escaped from Nevada state prison in Carson, slingshot the Lieutenant Governor Denver, he did. Cracked his head wide open. Ya know, Denver was the acting warden at that prison?"

Bart Runion nodded as he looked at Earl, who had also taken off his gloves.

Canby added, "And we just got word. Seems they just killed all the men in a town south of here. Unfortunately for that town, the sheriff is over near Aurora guarding the Esmeralda toll at Sweetwater. We were just on our way to assist. It will help us greatly having you come along if you want. If yer looking for Colton, go to Benton, on to Chalfant, and we will turn toward the Owens and Round Valley. That's the last word on the coordinates of the convicts in a telegraph we just received. Those men be headin' south."

"You say these two men, Colton and the ex-convict, were in this together?" Earl Perryman grunted.

"That's what we think right now," Canby said and nodded.

"Them bastards!" Bart Runion added, shaking his head. "I want to put this to rest. I'll tell you what."

"Well, gentlemen, I hope you're ready for a cold ride. Let's get to it and restore law and order out there. Seems to be overdue." Batterman looked around the group of men and poured some whiskey for each of them.

30

As winter was approaching fast, it had become too cold for Colton and Wyola to camp outside. Colton had embarked them toward a warming hut, built as a lookout over the valley atop Bald Mountain, which was already covered in early snow. It was on their way south, a mediation point that he and Wyola could seek refuge in while winter passed, and there they could gather their strategy of redemption. After the near confrontation with the convicts at Leroy's outpost, he figured it would be best for him and Wyola to lay low for a while up there. Colton knew from what they had seen of Reese back there, that he and his gang were obviously looking for food and supplies. But he couldn't figure why he would be heading south, back toward the neck of the woods that had brought him such trouble, landing him in a federal prison. He knew it couldn't be good. *Can it be that Reese is seeking justice of his own, or is he seeking the gold that the townsfolk accuse me of stealing the night I was left for dead?* Colton knew now as well, who else was involved with that theft, the judge and Rudy, besides Reese, that was for sure.

After two days of particularly frozen nighttime weather they happened to find the isolated cabin on top of the lookout mountain, centered in the valley. Colton reckoned it would be safe for them to stay there two or three months, allowing winter to pass until the child grew stronger, and for Wyola to have some peace of mind to find her way toward any reconciliatory justice. He knew from his own experiences, settling himself in the West, cabins like these were littered throughout the Sierras and were typically only occupied during the spring and summertime months, and, more often than not, abandoned in the late fall and winter. They were at least a two-day ride away from any bigger settlements and had no strategy or plan, other than to keep to themselves in an isolated place to be protected from further mayhem. He wanted to find peace himself to raise his family, if only allowed two more months to live, and to come up with an undefeatable plan to get justice. The place overlooked the Glass Mountains, a range adjacent to the town of Benton, keeping them close enough to the justice they would seek, in due time.

The cabin was more spacious than anything they had experienced throughout their journey. There were two small cots, a stovetop, and even a makeshift table, which consisted of a repurposed telegraph cable wire spool, where they could sit and enjoy their meal. Wyola and Colton were remarkably adaptable. They felt gratitude toward every crackle of the fire and every piece of cooked meat they put into their mouths.

One morning Colton woke up early and did his best not to stir Wyola or Emil. He slung his rifle over his shoulder and donned his thick, heavy coat. They were out of good meat, and Colton wanted to see if he could catch some rabbits and squirrels before Wyola woke up. Maybe he would be blessed to hunt down a mule deer. The meat would last them for months when preserved properly. It also provided a task that Wyola loved, preparing stocks for winter, and the deerskin she would tan and sew into some new shoes and warm clothing for Emil. He looked at his family who were sound asleep, cuddled together on the small bed, looking peaceful. Colton smiled, hoping the two would get as much sleep as they needed before his return. His heart felt full as he stepped out into the cold, putting his hat on his head and departing into the woods. *Today I will get a deer*, he determined in his mind.

Colton first tried to hunt on foot, but he didn't have any luck at such a close proximity to the hut. He decided to come back to grab his horse, and he untied it quietly, trying not to wake Wyola and Emil. After putting some distance between himself and the cabin, he rode out for a deeper look into the woods.

Wyola stirred after she heard the front door open and close. She smiled and yawned, grateful to wake up in this little hut with her husband and child once more. *That Colton*, she thought, *what a man he is.* Emil woke up hungry, as usual. She unbuttoned her gown and held his small body to her breast as she hummed softly and covered him with the furs.

After she was done feeding him, she laid him to rest again for some more sleep and rekindled the fire, filled a kettle with water and set it on the small stove. Wyola thought she heard a horse stir outside and wondered if Colton was already back from his hunt. She smiled, excited to see what he would bring back for them. *That has been a very quick trip*, she mused.

The door opened with a forceful bang, but it wasn't Colton. A loud scream escaped Wyola's throat, as a short and very bloody man stumbled into the room. With one terrifying look at Wyola the man fell to the floor, facedown. Wyola quickly ran to the cot to protect Emil, who was bundled up behind some stacked furs to keep him out of sight. She grabbed her gun off the table and pointed it at the back of the stranger's head.

"Who are you? Who are you?" she shouted forcefully, her hands still shaking. She took a deep breath to calm herself down.

There was no response. She wondered if the man was dead. With the gun still gripped tightly in her palm, she reached her left hand down to check the man's bloodied neck for a pulse. She thought she felt something, but she was shaking too hard to tell for sure.

"Sir! Are you alive?" she yelled and shook the body.

With still no response, Wyola quickly poked her head outside the open door to make sure there was nobody else lingering outside the cabin. All she saw was the man's horse, untied and wandering about fifty feet away. She noted the man had left a blood trail leading to the cabin door before quickly closing it. As far as she could tell, she was alone with the strange man. Wyola walked toward his body and kicked it slightly with her foot, trying to wake him up.

"Ughhhhh," the man coughed as he rolled over, revealing a circumferencing wound to his forehead. "Help me. Please. Help me." His voice was low and lifeless. It sounded like every syllable caused him pain.

What is he doing here? What happened to him? she wondered.

Wyola's fear turned to sympathy. "You poor man." She walked over toward the pot of water on the stove. "I have warm water. What happened to you? Where did you come from, and why way up here?"

The man could barely let out groans of anguish. She poured a small tin of water, knelt by his side and held it to his lips. He swallowed a little and it seemed to help him, although most of it ran down his frontside.

The man still said nothing. Wyola tried to help him move. With her assistance he was able to slowly maneuver himself toward the side of the cabin, and Wyola grabbed a saddlebag and shoved it behind his back, so she could lean him up against a wall. With great difficulty and several groans from the man, Wyola hoisted him up slightly. As she placed her hands around his midsection, she felt a wound under his skin. It must have been a bullet. Again, she took a closer look at his face. There was something familiar about him. Then it suddenly dawned on her who was lying in front of her, it was that town drunkard Rudy, Rudy Schaefer.

"I know you," she said slowly. "You're the judge's man, Rudy." Wyola gulped, uncertain if she should be afraid.

She questioned again why he was alone, bleeding, and so far from town up in the mountains. His face looked sunburnt and badly bruised. The circumferencing wound appeared as though a weak gunshot had penetrated the skin of his left forehead, however not penetrating his skull, but instead passing around his head between the skin and bone all the way to the back of his head. Dried blood crusted the outside of his nose and mouth. There was brown stubble on his face, and he smelled of sickness and sweat. It almost made her gag, but she tried not to focus on the smell. He looked like he hadn't bathed in days. Rudy's eyes were yellow, sleepy, and unfocused. He barely looked at Wyola, and he seemed to be drifting in and out of consciousness.

"Cut it out. Please take it out," he groaned.

Wyola asked him, wiping her sweaty brow with the back of her hand, "Is the bullet still lodged in there?" She lifted his head, surveying the injury closely.

"Yes, it is," Rudy moaned but then screamed in agony, "Please, be careful!"

Wyola rushed to their saddlebags to retrieve emergency aid that could provide the man some relief. She opened it and pulled out a sharp razor, a small paring tool, a thick needle for sewing garments, thread, and some cotton to use as dressing. Rudy winced and groaned as she tended to his injury. The other bullet was lodged in his abdomen, just above his right hip, as she surveyed that injury. She grabbed a bottle of whiskey and poured the alcohol on his abdominal wound, expecting Rudy to scream, but he seemed to be passed out from either the pain or exhaustion. As she pulled the bullet out of his body with her bowie knife, he let out another painful gasp. His eyes opened wide for a moment. Then Wyola cleaned the wound with some more alcohol and began stitching it up the best she could. Rudy was out cold, again, unconscious. She heated her knife in the stove and then cauterized his wound, waking him. "Aaargh!! he screamed.

"I killed...," he panted, "I killed too many men."

"Shhh," Wyola said, seeing the man's face contort in pain. She got a cloth from a basin filled with water and rinsed it out, so she could clear the blood off his face and head and inspect the wound on his scalp. He continued to mumble under his breath, but it was barely audible. She warned Rudy, "I'm going to have to slice this one open to get to the lead. It's going to hurt. Please be still." Before a thought to pull away in self-defense could cause Rudy to take any action, she deeply sliced his forehead, and the bullet fell out. He went unconscious again. Wyola held his head and laid him to the floor. She thought, *there's nothing more I can do for this man. He's going to get an infection. He has lost a lot of blood. He will be lucky to make it.*

Wyola had compassion and empathy, even for her enemies. She was a pure heart and kind to all, as if it were her command. Even knowing he was the drunk friend of the judge, the man who was always stumbling and mumbling about, causing a raucous, she tended to his wounds as if there was hope even for a man like him.

At first, he didn't move or react in any way, apparently still out from the shock and pain he just endured at her hand. But then suddenly his eyes opened again, staring straight ahead as if he couldn't see. He focused and shot her another fearful look. "Oh God," he yelled, then looked away from Wyola, as though she was either some kind of monster or a heavenly creature. "Spare me! I'm gonna burn in hell for what I've done!"

"God can spare you," Wyola said slowly, trying to soothe Rudy, who was becoming more agitated. "Admit your sin to him and ask him into your heart. You can survive this in the everlasting. It's really the only hope we have when we die, you know."

Rudy's whimpers grew louder. He sounded terrified. "When I was a boy and my dad had died, there in front of his coffin, the preacher did say to me, he did say, there's grace upon grace upon grace! And Jesus said to the murderer, 'Today, you will be with me in paradise, in everlasting life.' I killed Morgan!" Rudy yelled. "I killed Ardie Perseval. I killed Indians, murdered 'em in cold blood. There's no grace for me. The judge shot me, as I deserve. He's following me, ya know."

As Rudy uttered those words, Wyola jumped back almost immediately. "The judge," she asked, uncertain if he meant what he said, "Is following you?"

Suddenly she heard noises coming from outside the cabin. *Thank God*, she thought, *Colton is back*. However, the voice that rang out was unmistakable, and it wasn't Colton.

"Rudy," called the sharp, nasal voice that Wyola had heard so many times before. An icy shiver made its way down her spine, and she literally froze in shock. It was the judge.

"Rudy Schaefer. Come on outta there now. What are you gonna do all holed up in there? You know." He laughed. "I'm just gonna come in to getchya!"

Wyola motioned for Rudy to stay silent. Grabbing her pistol from the nearby table, she moved silently to the window and peered out through a hole in the shirt they had hung earlier from the window as a makeshift curtain. She saw the judge standing about fifty feet away, behind a snow-covered pile of firewood.

"Come on now, Rudy!" the judge yelled, a wicked smile stretching across his face. "Come on out!" His hands were working the cylinder of his pistol as he packed black powder, a ball, and wadding into the device. "There sure is a lot of footsteps out here, and a horse you didn't have before," Kensington continued. "Where'd you find the energy to go an' rustle another man's horse, Rudy?" A brief pause ensued. The judge was going crazy. "You gonna ride two horses now Rudy? I don't think that would be possible in the condition I last saw you in."

"Better yet, who you got in there with ya, Rudy," the judge yelled as he checked his pistol and rifle for loads. He was very low on ammunition and maneuvered his way over to Rudy's horse, opened the saddlebags to find them empty. "Literally a poor, drunken bastard," he muttered to himself.

Wyola was terrified. There was no telling what the judge would do next. He looked more insane than she had ever seen him. His white hair was wiry, thin and tangled. His face was even redder than usual, and his eyes were wild and unfocused. Thinking on her feet, in one swift movement, Wyola broke the window with the butt of her pistol and fired a shot directly at the judge.

A horrible sound erupted from the judge's horse, as it wailed a groaning vocal sound before it dropped to the ground. She had barely missed him and hit the horse. The judge turned and looked at the horse, shook his head, and then looked back at the window. He was oddly calm.

Sighing deeply, the judge said, "Yer gonna make this hard on me now, aren't ya, Rudy?"

If the judge comes in firing, we will surely all be dead in an instant, Wyola thought. She called out the hole in the window, "He may not be the only one in here! Your child is here too!"

The judge rubbed his white beard with a thick, stubby hand. "Say it isn't so!" He turned to look back at his writhing horse, dying slowly on the ground. "What's with all the dead horses in my life? Geez," Distracted by what Wyola had screamed through the window, he frowned and pondered, *a son, huh. Just what I needed to hear, a bastard son. Oh boy!*

Wyola shuddered. *Has the judge completely lost his mind? Did he even hear me?*

"That's right, Judge ...your son! Remember when you raped me?!" she yelled even louder, emphasizing 'raped.'

Bam! Wyola stepped away from the window and pressed herself against the wall just in time, as a shot zipped through the broken window. The sound of the gunshots had woken Emil, who cried out. Rudy found enough energy, in his fear, to crawl back to the wall and lift himself to a leaning position. He slumped against the wall, whimpering and delirious. Wyola's heart started racing as she heard the judge coming toward the window. She felt trapped and panicked. *Colton,* she pleaded within her heart, *please, come back soon.* Emil started screaming at the top of his lungs.

"You'd be the only man in this world, who would shoot his own baby boy," Wyola yelled, trying to hide the panic in her voice.

"I ain't got no baby! Boy! And even if I did, it wasn't conceived by any rape done by me," the judge responded. "That's your fabrication, Wyola Everest!"

Wyola stayed glued to the wall near the window. She looked at the cot and realized just how far she was from Emil. Suddenly she saw the point of the judge's gun enter through the window. *No*, she thought in panic, looking toward the cot. The judge started firing wildly as shots erupted throughout the room. Wyola fired the last five shots in her gun toward the window, but to no avail. It all happened so fast. Wyola couldn't tell where the shots were hitting until she felt something heavy hit her chest forcefully. All the breath left her body as she hit the floor, next to Rudy. Wyola tried to scream, but there was no air left in her chest. Gasping, she tried to grasp at her breast.

Silence ensued. Through the pain, Wyola could feel the judge's presence in the room. He must have stuck his head through the broken window. She heard one final deafening shot and saw it hit the cot. *Not Emil*, she pleaded with God. *Please not Emil!*

"Rudy," the judge cooed. "Ruuuuuudy."

Silence. Wyola heard shuffling outside the cabin. She heard the judge fumbling with the locked door, which was bolted shut. Moments later, the judge's voice rang through the window once more.

"Got no more ammo left, you lucky bastards! I look forward to seein' you another day, Wyola. If ya happen to get through this, Rudy, I'll see ya in hell!"

Wyola heard heavy steps in the snow moving away as the judge wrangled, then mounted Rudy's horse and rode off with a loud "Hiya."

As the hooves swooshed through the deep snow and disappeared into the distance, Wyola cried out in pain. Her breath was back, but she could feel it getting weaker. With every ounce of strength she had left in her body, she began to drag herself toward the cot. The crying had stopped. *Is Emil dead?* Tears began to flow freely from her eyes. She had no idea how long it took for her to crawl to the cot. It felt like hours.

She didn't know whether Rudy was alive or dead behind her. She didn't care. Her time was running out and there was not enough for two.

When Wyola reached the cot, she could see movement below the furs. "Thank God," she sobbed, struggling to get Emil off the cot.

Wyola held him tightly to her breast, opening her dress for him to feed, if for only one last time. She covered Emil with fur as best as she could, while her belly grew warm from the blood leaking out of her chest wound. With every breath she took, there seemed to be less air she could take in as she gurgled on her own blood.

She fought to stay awake, but at the same time the idea of closing her eyes seemed peaceful and appealing. Her eyelids had the heaviness of lead as gravity begged them to close. Yet, somehow, she knew it wasn't time to go yet, and she had to hold on just a little longer.

Good things happened on his hunting venture, and Colton was excited as he was now riding back to the cabin with a fresh, dead deer draped over the shoulders of his horse in front of him. He hadn't had deer in months and could not believe God's provision. He had been chasing a rabbit, when he suddenly came across a fresh deer track in the snow, which he followed until he was close enough to get a good shot. He couldn't wait to see the look on Wyola's face, when she would see the deer.

As the cabin came into focus, he noticed something strange in the snow. Was that a horse? As he approached, a mass of brown fur and red blood became clearer. Colton saw an unfamiliar horse, certainly dead, crumpled outside the cabin near the pile of firewood.

Something was wrong. Colton's hair stood on end as he prompted his pony to speed toward the cabin. For some reason, he thought of the day Morgan died, when he had found Ardie's dead horse in the river. As he got to the cabin, Colton dismounted swiftly, dropping the deer in the snow, and drew out his gun quickly. He wasn't sure if he should stay silent or call for Wyola as he approached the front door.

It was locked. "Wyola!" Colton yelled. "Wyola!" He banged desperately against the door, trying to open the lock, but it wouldn't budge. Panicked, Colton ran toward the window on the side to get a better look inside. The window was broken, and shards of glass littered the snow at his feet. He poked his gun through the opening first, followed by his face. It was silent. To his right, he saw the body of a man slumped against the wall. *Is that ...*

"Rudy?" Colton exclaimed in shock. He looked toward the corner. The cot was in the shadow, and it was hard to see. With great difficulty Colton pulled himself through the window and over the sill. He winced as the broken glass first scraped and then cut his hands. "Wyola!"

His beautiful woman came into focus as he bounded toward the cot. She was on the ground with her back propped up against the cot, her face looking awfully pale. Her green dress had turned nearly dark brown from the chest down with her blood. It was clear she was shot. Emil was cradled in her arms. Colton looked from Wyola to Rudy, to Emil, trying to piece together what happened.

"It wasn't Rudy," Wyola whispered weakly. Her eyes remained closed, and her breath rattled in her throat. "It was ... the judge."

"Wyola, Wyola, oh my God," Colton screamed, his eyes filling with tears. He took Emil gingerly from Wyola's breast and set him on the bed, quickly examining him and covering him back up with the fur. Emil seemed to be unharmed, even though his belly and legs were full of blood.

"Where are you hurt?" he asked Wyola, trying to assess the extent of her injury. There was blood everywhere, even all over the floor, as she sat in it. It seemed as if she had lost half of all her blood.

"I'm dying, Colton. I feel it." Her whisper sounded like a song. She slowly opened her eyes. "Water ..."

"I'll be right back, baby," he fearfully stated.

Colton grabbed a canteen, hanging from a nail on the log wall. It was empty. He rushed out to his horse, took two canteens from the saddle, and ran back to the cabin. *Please, God,* he pleaded. *Please let her live. Let her live, God, please!* He wanted to scream but tried to be strong for her.

He cradled Wyola's neck in his hands and held the canteen to her lips. She sipped a little but then choked, coughing up blood.

"Colton," she said through a weakened voice. "Promise me you'll take care of this child. Promise me. None of this is his wrongdoing. Emil should live, Colton."

Colton couldn't hold back his tears any longer. His lips trembled as he stroked her head with his hand. "Rest, my love. Shhhh."

"And whoever ... humbles himself ... like this child," Wyola said, taking a weak breath, "Is the greatest ... in the kingdom of heaven." Wyola trembled in Colton's arms, struggled to speak, and then went silent once again.

"Wyola? I promise ... Wyola! Wyola, no," Colton yelled. He felt a weight leave her body as she went limp in his arms. He buried his face in her hair and heaved a giant sob. He knew she was gone and she was never coming back. *Why, God?* he thought, looking down into her peaceful, beautiful face.

Colton sat with Wyola for what felt like an eternity as he tried to come to terms with what his life would be like without her. He let his tears fall freely and sat in despair, still holding Wyola, and watched Emil sleeping on the cot. He thought about the judge and Wyola and the child.

Suddenly an unimaginable rage came over him. Colton stood up, roughly picking up the child from the cot. Emil was awake, silently looking at him and then starting to scream. Cradling the child in his arms, Colton blazed toward the outside world.

The snow was fluttering over his head as the sun sank in the sky. Colton ran through the snow, feeling completely numb to the biting cold around him, screaming at God in the heavens. About twenty feet from the door, he stopped and dropped onto his knees, holding Emil in his arms. He looked at the sky, wondering why the heavens above him would allow such a cruel thing to happen, for so long and to so many, taking everything he knew and loved from him. The flakes fell in chaotic spurts as he dropped the child into the snow in front of him.

Empowered by his rage, he drew out the long butcher knife he carried in his belt and held it up to the heavens. Then he turned the knife around and held the blade, aiming straight at the child's heart. Emil screamed in fear and focused on Colton, as the falling snowflakes kissed his tiny forehead. Colton's clasp tightened around the handle as he closed his eyes and lifted the knife again, to thrust it through the child's chest in one swift move. His hands started trembling as he held up the knife, struggling and crying. Finally, weeping loudly, he plunged downward, but at the last millisecond he turned to the side and thrust the knife into the deer that was lying next to the child in the snow over and over again, stabbing and stabbing, then letting go of the knife as he collapsed into the snow himself.

Then, just as quickly, something came over him. He picked up the child and held him as tight to his chest as he could, weeping and screaming and hugging him, which caused Emil to start to scream and wail again.

"I'm sorry," Colton sobbed. "I'm so sorry."

How can this child, born of evil and pain, live a normal life? How can I look at Emil and not think of the horrible things the judge has done to so many, including Wyola and myself? This child, because he raped my Wyola. This is NOT my child, this is the judge's child. "God, Oh God!" he yelled out in anguish to the sky. Yet in all his pain a realization overpowered him, stealing the anger from him. This child was innocent, and he would have to always cherish and love the part of Emil that was Wyola. He suddenly knew this, deep down in his heart, like God had literally reached down from heaven and pushed this peace into him. There was hope for him, there was hope for this child.

Colton drew the child close to his chest under his frock coat, rose up, and ran back toward the cabin. Emil continued to cry as though he knew what Colton had intended to do.

Colton was shaking as he fumbled to retrieve some goat milk from a snakeskin sack. He dipped two trembling fingers into the milk and put them into the child's small mouth. Colton could not bring himself to look at Wyola or Rudy. He covered both of their bodies. Feeling almost crazy inside, as if all had been lost, he pretended that he and Emil were alone in the cabin as he crawled into the cot with the child. He wanted peace and solitude. He pleaded for mercy and grace. He pleaded for instruction and clarity because his life was now cloaked in fog and anguish. Emil fell asleep almost instantly. Colton followed suit, desperate to clear his mind for even a moment.

He would bury Wyola in the morning and lay her to her final resting place.

31

It was the following day in the afternoon. Bart Runion and Earl Perryman were on the floor of the cabin after the gunfire subsided. A silhouette of a man stood before them, obstructed by the blowing snow and sunlight behind him. The baby wailed from the corner.

Bart heard Earl wince and inhale sharply. His hand had only been grazed by the bullet the stranger in the doorway had fired, and the injury seemed superficial but was strong enough for Earl to drop his gun. Bart craned his neck to get a better look at the figure before him. *Can this be Colton Jaminson?*

"Stop," Bart pleaded from his seated position on the floor as he raised his hands in full compliance. "We're here for ..." Earl looked to Bart, sitting next to him with subservient eyes, now captive to this stranger.

"I know why yer here," the deep, booming voice of the stranger responded, his guns still trained at the two men. "Yer here for the man who called for the warrant, Judge Kensington."

"What?" Bart interrupted. "Wouldn't he need a crony in the statehouse for a federal warrant? We have here a federal warrant for Colton Jaminson. It ain't from the judge!"

The stranger took his time before he started to speak. "The man who murdered my wife-to-be and so many others." As he walked away from the door, his face came into focus. He was tall with dark skin. He seemed strong, but there was a shadow about his face, something that made him look exhausted and miserable.

"The very man," he said slowly, with bitterness in his voice, "Who raped my girl, planted his seed, and bore that baby right over there?" After a short pause, he continued. "The same man, who tried to kill his own son, the very child I swore to raise to my girl before she died? That man?"

Earl looked at Bart, and the two exchanged confused looks. *Is what this man says true?*

"Why would you do that if he ain't yours?" Bart asked curiously, unable to help himself.

The man looked lost in thought. "Cuz Emil … cuz the baby … is Wyola's. And she asked."

"Pretty noble of you." Earl held a rag he had found on the ground over his slightly bleeding hand.

"Look," Colton said, "I'm not yer man. I can explain everything. I can take you to the judge. He was the one who stole the gold in that warrant. Tried to murder me and believed he did! Murdered Wyola and Rudy, probably all the others that year ago. He murdered my cousin, Cyrus, and Indians. That man? Rudy was here. I just buried him." The man looked off into the distance. "Not next to my wife. I buried her, too, but I didn't bury that coward next to her." The words fell from his mouth.

Earl nodded, unsure exactly what to make of the new development. "That was quite a mouthful, Colton Jaminson. Word has it you murdered Ardie Perseval, U.S. mail carrier. The reason we are here, and that's federal."

Bart added, "And the murder of Randall Morgan on a U.S. Mine claim. And for stealing $40,000 in U.S. Gold Mint right from that very mine. That's also federal."

Colton shook his head. He seemed tired and defeated, but there was also a strength and determination about him, as he still had his guns out, pointed at the two men.

"Is that so?" he said, his eyebrow raised. "Well, you can either take yer boots off and throw 'em over here with all yer guns and head on out this door ... or be shot. Which one is it? Because I'm tired and I'm leavin' with this child. Goin' to see the judge myself. This ends sooner than later. I'm done with hiding. And nobody is goin' to stop me. What's it gonna be?" Colton looked back and forth between Bart and Earl.

"Where'd this judge go?" Bart asked.

"I imagine he's on his way to the gold. It's the only thing outside of my word that ties him to the murder of Morgan. This child is a testament to his crimes against Wyola. Too many loose ends the judge can't tie up. I gotta finish him once and for all!"

"We ..." Earl said, taking it all in, looking at Bart, unsure of how to proceed.

"I'm sure if you dig hard enough," Colton interrupted, "You'll find he was part of all the murders that day. Yer mail carrier and a couple Indians. I heard from Numaga and Natchez that they were all murdered on the same day. The exact day, they plucked me dead from that same creek, they found our Indian friends murdered in."

"Who plucked ya?" Earl asked, thinking it would be quite an elaborate tale if Colton were lying.

"Natchez. Tavibo. Tsanomo. Anyway, are you goin' to give me your boots? What's it goin' to be? I would think that you two, being federal men of the constitution, would be inclined to investigate? Give me them boots now. Last chance!" he said, cocking his firearms. "Let's not wake the child now. Just take 'em off! Take the rounds out of the cylinders. Dump 'em on the floor, and put yer guns on the table!" Colton nodded at their feet, getting impatient.

"Our feet will freeze," Earl interjected. He looked at Bart, who just kept staring at Colton, not saying anything.

Finally Bart started to take off his boots and threw them toward Colton, one at a time. Earl followed suit. The two men rose to their feet, hands raised. There was nothing else they could do. It was uncertain what would happen next, but Colton seemed determined, and there was no telling what a determined man would do.

Colton raised his weapon and pointed to the door. "Let's go, guys. I was gonna gather our things and start at the judge's ranch. I'm just gonna send you guys out fer a spell. Looks like the sun's coming out!"

Bart was starting to get angry and yelled, "This is bullcrap! We'll help ya!"

Colton smirked and looked at Bart sarcastically. "Soon enough!"

With his gun trained at the two men, Colton waited as they got up reluctantly and headed toward the open door. Colton shot into the ground behind them, to force them to run out into the freezing cold. They kept hopping from one leg to the other outside, holding up their trousers to keep them from getting wet. It was almost comical. Colton added a few fresh logs to the crackling fire in the stove, grabbed his saddlebags containing all the provisions and carried them to his horse outside.

After he finished getting his horse ready, he walked back inside and got Emil. He hesitated for a short moment and then pulled Rudy's keys out of his pocket and left them next to Bart and Earl's guns on the table. He mounted his horse, with Emil on his back in his papoose, and Wyola's horse in tow. He stopped as he passed the freezing men, still hopping around in the snow.

"Count to one hundred. There's a fire in the stove so you can warm your feet back up. The keys you'll find in there, they were from Rudy. One of them might be the key to the gold." With that, Colton trotted away on his horse and disappeared into the distant trees, while the men hurried back to the hut.

32

Five days had passed since the incident at the hut, and Bart felt that they were no closer to finding Judge Kensington, as they were to being struck by lightning. After Colton had left them in the cabin, they decided to ride directly to the judge's house after getting their boots dry, which Colton had filled with snow and left outside. Boy, was Earl upset about that one! Regardless Bart pressed them forward as they needed to find the judge, Colton, or somebody else who could give them more answers.

Two days later they arrived at the judge's massive property to find the place completely ransacked. Drawers had been overturned with papers and trinkets strewn all over the floor. The judge's many workers and maids had evidently fled the property as well. There wasn't a soul lingering about, except for a couple of donkeys and pigs, running around in the fenced areas in the back, with chickens running amuck. Most of the ruins of the property were just random objects. However when Bart peered under the stairs leading up to the porch, he found a single golden coin. He prided himself on having a good eye. But why had it been laying there in plain sight? Obviously townsfolk had to have passed through at some point, looking for the judge or others at the ranch, for that matter. It had to be a recent error, he figured. That's what he enjoyed most about his job, detective work. Finding clues, clues that led to capture and justice.

"Look at this, Earl," he said, waving his partner over to where he had found it. He held up the coin to the sunlight as it glistened, a twenty-dollar U.S. Mint gold coin.

These be one of the coins! He pondered.

"Someone must have come for the gold," Earl said, taking the coin from Bart with vigor, in order to get a closer look. "It surely seems to match the stolen gold from Morgan's mine. I wonder who got here first."

"No doubt about that! The judge?" Bart asked. "Maybe he knew we were comin' and packed up everything."

"Why would he ransack his own property?" Earl wondered, stroking his chin as he peered around the disheveled house.

"To throw us off his trail? Or maybe someone else did, comin' after?" Bart guessed. He was at his wits end. Their journey through the Sierras had lasted much longer than he had originally anticipated. It seemed that just when they were nearing an answer, the mystery became more confusing.

"Coulda' been anyone, really. What about the Morgan women? Getting what was theirs in the first place? Or some of the angry townspeople? I mean, what of the killings at El Diablo? That has those townsfolk reeling. I'm hearin' they pinned the rest of 'em down in Round Valley. I'm pretty sure the judge's influence over his men has left him high and dry."

Earl shrugged and continued looking around the house.

"Let's hit the road. He can't be too far off now!" Bart declared.

It was nightfall, and they would leave at first light.

Early in the morning, just before sunrise, they departed Chalfant and headed up into the Long Valley to see if they might be able to pick up the judge's trail.

In the three days that followed, Bart and Earl's search party expanded. When their trail led them to the outskirts of the reservation, they crossed paths with Natchez, a Paiute Indian, who also wanted to see justice brought to light. Natchez insisted he come along. He was the legendary Peace Chief, an impressive rider, and a man who spoke with intensity in his eyes. He took along his grandchild, Angel Nellie, a small, energetic child of about eight.

"My people still want answers for our warriors' murders," he said, once Bart and Earl had explained who they were looking for. Natchez swore to them of Colton's innocence and told them of his and Wyola's stay at the reservation. He explained the rape by the judge and the discovery of Colton in the river, after they had found their own brothers the same day, just moments earlier.

As the three men watered their horses in the upper Owens River, they were also met up with General Edward Canby, whom they hadn't seen since Virginia City. He reported that most of the escaped convicts had either been killed or taken back into custody. He reiterated how three of them were hung in Round Valley by the townsfolk. Canby had also been discussing urgent local matters with Natchez and figured he would come along as well. Nobody had seen or heard from Colton. Bart wondered if he had disappeared into thin air.

On the fifth day Bart had nearly given up hope. He no longer cared about the federal warrant or the prize money. At that point he was simply holding out hope that justice, if such a thing even existed, could be served. He couldn't stand the thought of facing the Benton townspeople once more without results. After losing so many beloved friends and family, the people were devastated. He figured he would probably never be hired in that area again, being thought of as a bad memory, if they couldn't provide proof.

It was remarkably sunny and bright for a late November morning, and it had been warming up a bit. There was no wind and no snowfall as the search party rode along in silence. It would have been an otherwise pleasant ride, Bart thought, if it weren't for them roaming around seemingly aimlessly. He watched Natchez, with little Angel Nellie behind his back, leading the pack. The Long Valley was massive and sprawling. Mountains towered in every direction, covered in early season snow. Apart from the birds chirping in the trees and hooves crunching the ground, it was completely silent. Bart supposed that if the judge was in fact out there, the odds of running directly into him were dwindling.

They rode through a clearing, before entering a light wooded area. Suddenly an unexpected sound caused the party to look around. It was the unmistakable *hee-haw* from a donkey.

"What was that?" Canby asked.

"There." Natchez pointed off into the distance and to the right. "Up ahead."

A dozen yards up ahead, they spotted a furry, gray donkey sticking out from behind a tree. Bart looked around, skeptically, unsure why there was a lone donkey in the middle of the woods. Perhaps it had escaped from a nearby farm. Still, they were miles away from any outposts.

They continued forward until they could see the entire animal. "What on God's good earth is that?" Bart said out loud, unable to contain himself.

He had seen a lot in his life, but this was certainly a most peculiar scene. A short, plump figure sat backwards on top of a rather large donkey that stood motionless under a big oak tree. A rope was tied with one end to a thick tree branch above and the other end around the man's fat neck, creating a noose. He was perched precariously on top of the donkey, and it looked like any sudden movement could have sent him tumbling off straight into a hanging. His head was covered in a burlap sack. He must have heard the approaching party and tried to somehow make out what was going on around him through the fabric that covered his face. Even though it was cold he seemed to be sweating profusely in fear.

"Who did this?" Earl wondered, looking at the others who seemed equally perplexed. Natchez stopped and looked intensely at the person. "Judge! Judge Kensington!" he exclaimed and looked around the group at the other men. Somebody must have left the judge in the middle of the woods, on the verge of being hanged.

Little Angel Nellie said nothing. She was sitting behind Chief Natchez on his horse and looked up at him. He turned and nodded to her. She reached and grabbed a handful of grain from a saddlebag and threw some on the ground, right before the curious donkey, and watched, smiling. The donkey started to lean forward.

"No," the judge quivered as the donkey tried to move. "Woah! No!" His hands were tied behind his back, and he was stretching his neck and clenching his thighs together to avoid falling off.

Natchez looked at the judge, his eyes narrowing. "Tse'na'haha has looked upon you, white man. Justice is near done," he said sternly.

Just then the donkey slightly moved toward Nellie, eating the grains she had thrown to the ground. In a brief instant, the judge nearly fell off the donkey's backside but was able to keep himself on top of it, squeezing his legs together more tightly around the donkey's belly. The noose slightly tightened and Bart imagined how the judge must be sweating in fear, hearing small grunts and labored breathing coming from underneath the burlap sack around his head.

General Edward Canby approached the judge, mounted high upon his pony. Two of his mounted cavalry men rode to his right as Earl and Bart rode up to his left.

"If it isn't just who we're looking for. What are the odds of this, boys? What brings you into this here predicament, Your Honor?" General Canby drew his sword from his belt.

Canby moved forward to get a better look at the judge. He withdrew his sword, reached it out as if to poke the judge with it, right in his heart. The judge could certainly see this through the burlap bag over his head. "No, no," he gurgled.

Canby did poke him, right above his breast pocket, stabbing through two pieces of folded white paper sticking out, grabbing them and lifting them out with the tip of his weapon.

"Ouch, ugh", the judge murmured.

"What do we have here?" Bart asked, intrigued at what was unfolding in front of him.

General Canby sheathed his sword and then opened the papers and cleared his throat. "The letter reads as such:

> *I am guilty of the murders of mine owner Randall Morgan, federal courier rider Ardie Perseval, and two Paiute Indians the same day, and later that same night I shot Cyrus David. I also shot and killed my associates, Rudy Schaefer who actually shot Morgan, and Reese Clybourne, both of whom helped me shoot the Indians. I also killed many other men in my greedy pursuits and robbed them to get what I have. I stole Morgan's gold. There is $40,000 in U.S. Gold Mint hidden in a coyote hole out in the desert. The proof of matching gold mint coins is in my pockets.*
>
> *I, Judge Peter Howard Kensington, declare and plead guilty for my actions, and should be hanged. I plead for mercy to let God be the judge of me, in defense of the women whose lives I raped, pillaged, and murdered, as I sit upon this ass. The women of this valley hand me to you here and now. To Wyola or her child I leave my ranch.*

The general looked up at the other men in the posse and then to the judge. He read again, "The women of this valley hand me to you here and now. To Wyola or her child I leave my ranch. Signed, Judge Kensington."

"The proof is in the pockets?" Canby said, reaching into the pocket of the squirming judge.

"No. No," the judge sputtered again, trying to keep his balance as the mule stood under him and hee-hawed again, kicking its hooves, stretching his neck out for more food.

The general pulled out two gold coins. "Aha," he said, holding them in his palm, turning one over.

"Those match this?" Bart questioned as he reached in his own pocket, retrieving a coin.

In response Canby put one coin in his pocket and then tossed the other coin from the judge's pocket to Bart to compare.

With a large grin, Bart replied, "Seems here we found one exactly like it, Judge. Found it out at your ranch, under the house. Seems ya dropped one, Judge Kensington, or maybe your executioner did leave us a clue, knowin' you'd eventually be found here."

The donkey started moving forward again, and this time, the judge couldn't keep himself on top, fell off its back and began dangling, his toes just an inch above the ground. Swaying slightly, he steadied himself on his tiptoes to offset the pulling of the rope. He inhaled a shaking breath as the noose tightened around his neck.

Earl was shocked. A year of pain, suffering, and theft wrapped up like a Christmas present under a tree. "Should we cut him down before he dies or after?" he asked.

"No. No," Judge Kensington sputtered, tippy-toes now on the ground, neck completely outstretched and beginning to choke, while trying to maintain his balance with tiny, futile steps on his toes, however, to no avail.

A little distance away, on a hill overlooking the scene, Colton sat on his horse, observing as the men in the valley below were cutting down the near-lifeless body of the judge from the tree. He reached into his pocket and pulled out the watch Wyola had given to him. Emil was resting against his back in his papoose. Slowly he opened the watch, and a single tear fell on the picture inside as he looked at the beautiful face of Wyola.

Finally justice was served.

33

Bennington Cemetery, September 1945

Jacob walked up to Bennington Cemetery on this particularly beautiful California fall day. A strange mix of emotions washed over him as he reflected on the events of the past year. He was back from war, physically in one piece. Mentally, he wasn't sure. The war was over, so said the politicians. But Jacob knew a different kind of war was growing inside of him.

As he walked toward two particular gravestones, he clutched the locket that his grandfather had given him almost one year before, then put it in his pocket. Jacob tried to remember who he was back then as he had stood there trembling, with his grandfather's hand on his shoulder. It was time to say goodbye.

Jacob received the news that his grandfather had passed toward the end of his time in Normandy, before they had moved on to defeat the Germans and the war was won. His mother had written to him two months earlier from the day he read it.

> *Son, your grandfather passed away late last night. He*
> *went in peace. He lived a long life, full of blessings. He*

died so incredibly proud of you. His spirit lives on in you.
Be strong, and come home safe. We love you very much.

It was strange how the world seemed to stop. Jacob never knew a war zone could be so quiet, back on that day he read the note in France. His head exploded with all the questions he was never going to be able to ask his grandfather. Why hadn't he spent more time asking better questions? That evening, as he had stood on the edge of his ship, he resolved that if he couldn't explore his grandfather's life, he would at least explore his legacy. The thought of seeing his grandfather's grave, even just once, was enough to help Jacob hold on to the very end, to win the war.

He grieved that his grandfather was not alive to witness the end of the war or his homecoming. Yet as he paced through the sunny graveyard, he couldn't help but feel that he was not alone. He walked past rows of headstones until he reached the back of the cemetery, where two headstones stood side by side. One read *Colton Jaminson*, his great-grandfather. He remembered looking at it for the first time like it was yesterday, when his Grandfather Emil had shared this amazing story of great courage, perseverance, love, hope, and joy in the midst of so much sorrow...so much had changed since then. To the right, there was a new gravestone that read *Emil Jaminson*.

Jacob reached into his pocket and pulled out a folded newspaper. It was a copy of the *San Diego Union Tribune* from July 2, 1905. Jacob's mother had sent it to him, along with the news that his grandfather had passed. The headline read, *"July 1, 1905—Boiler Explosion Upon the USS Bennington Gunship PG4 Kills 66. Miraculously, Many Were Saved!"*

To the right of the main article was a photo of a young sailor who had been awarded a medal of honor due to his bravery that day. The name below the picture read, '*Emil Jaminson*'. Jacob smiled as tears filled his eyes. The resemblance between Jacob and Emil was uncanny.

He remembered what his mother wrote in the letter, *his spirit lives on in you.*

Jacob placed the folded newspaper on the grave before reaching into his pocket once more, to pull out two medals. One was Emil's medal of honor, given to him by his grandfather. The other was Jacob's own medal of honor, which he had been awarded for heroism in sacrificing his own safety by saving others. He inhaled deeply and let out a long, shaky breath.

Lastly, with that sigh of relief and peace, he pulled the beautiful silver watch from his pocket and opened it. There they were. The great cloud of witnesses who were watching him, in heaven next to Grandpa and Grandma.

"I never understood what you meant about legacy," Jacob whispered under his breath. "But I think I do now."

As the sun began to set in the sky, Jacob gazed across the rows of headstones, many of them fresh from the war, the grass not yet grown over many of the tombs. With a mix of sadness for those young men he fought beside and hope for his own future, Jacob turned and walked away from Emil and Colton's gravestones with joy and no need to wipe away tears from his eyes. His great-grandmother's and his great-grandfather's strength, as well his grandfather's heroism and their legacy would be told through his life, his attitude and his actions. He was amazed he even made it through this war and owed it all to this heritage in doing so.

Now he could walk tall and proud, not with a pride raised in self-glory, but with a pride rooted in the love his family held for each other. Perseverance and courage, sacrifice and honor, that's what he could stand tall for in pride. He knew now, he could be strong with solid integrity, with powerful love for mankind, strong compassion for others, and character. He lived with God's grace in his heart, thus, growing deeply grateful for God's protection and presence that he had witnessed personally himself so often. He didn't know what the future held. That was for certain. But he knew who held his future. He looked up toward the heavens and smiled. He was ready to live his legacy.

Hours later he was riding on a beach in Del Mar, California, atop a beautiful black steed of his own. He looked at the breathtaking sunset, a reminder that this day was done, tomorrow was never promised, and he would live in the hope he learned. He prodded his horse, and away he rode into the oceans edge and off into the sunset.

The End

SPECIAL THANKS

The Laws Railroad Museum and Historic Site, Bishop, Inyo County, California

The Eastern Sierra Museum, Independence, Inyo County, California

Central Sierra Historical Society, Shaver Lake, East Fresno County, California

Mono County Museum, Bridgeport, California

Bridgeport Inn, Bridgeport, California

Southern Mono Historical Society, Mammoth Lakes, Mono County, California

Lee Vining Chamber of Commerce, Lee Vining California

Bodie State Historic Park, Mono County Museum, Mono County, California

Benton Hot Springs, California

Laura Tennant-Dayton Museum and Historical Society of Dayton Valley, Nevada

Dayton Museum, Dayton, Nevada

Oregon-California Trails Association

Emigrant Trails West, Inc, (Historical Trail Society, non profit) Reno, Nevada

**Life Among The Paiutes - Their Wrongs and Claims -Sarah Winnemuccah Hopkins, Author

Sarah's (Tochmetony) autobiographical memoir and a history of the Paiute people during their first forty years of contact with European Americans-1883 (A must read)

Peter Sherayko, Author, Title: The Fringe Of Hollywood, The Art of Making A Western

Peter Sherayko, Author/Actor (texas Jack Vermillion, Title: Tombstone, The Guns and Gear

The Bishop Paiute Indian Tribe Center, Bishop California (Bishop Paiute Tribe)

Paiute Indian Tribe of Utah

San Francisco Chronicle - September 27th, 1871 - page 2

Stanislaus County Weekly News - September 29th - page 2

San Francisco Chronicle - October 6th, 1871 - page 2

San Francisco Examiner - October 10th, 1871 - page 3

San Francisco Examiner - October 24th, 1871 - page 1

San Francisco Chronicle - November 1st, 1871 - page 2

The Journal of the Senate, Second Session, of the Legislature of the State of Nevada, 1866, January 1st, 1866 - Carson City, Nevada

The USDA, NPS, USFS, Mammoth District (Inyo County) Lawson Reif

Jeremy Childs

Ryan Wotherspoon

Josh Childs

Henry Haggard

Clifford Mann

Steve Morrison

Mammoth Mountain Ski Area

USFS Minaret Station/Vista

Mammoth Snowmobile Adventures (Bald Mountain Hut)

AUTHORS NOTE

This story came to me over an extended period of time while embarking on my many adventures tooling around the mountains and valleys of the Sierra Nevada Mountains for a couple of decades on foot, on skis, carrying a fly rod or blasting away on my sno-machine with skis on the back.

The many true-life events and the peoples of the area inspired this twisting, fictional tale. Some character names I left as they were to grace them a portion and distinction, the attention they deserve and earned through their very tough lives settling the region.

There was no such thing as depression back then, people were too busy surviving. My desire is to bring them into the forefront thoughts of many who may be depressed today and who may read this story. I wish for the readers to ponder these ancient characters in wonder and awe of the time these Western American legends lived, survived and persevered through the harshest of times and conditions to settle the West and California.

In 2013 I was first inspired to write this story, namely out of a selfish desire. I was an actor at the time and wanted a better role for myself. God took that selfish desire and turned it on its head via His writing from my hands, walking me through that initial desire. It turned into something I couldn't ever have dreamed up on my own or imagined.

Early in the 90's I had found the area of this story by accident, following a devastating and heartbreaking event that took place in my youthful life. I wanted out of where I was. The pain was far greater than what I could bear, and I just had to escape and get away. I ended up in the region because of that fluke affair.

I had started skiing shortly before the devastating incident I speak of, albeit in Southern California, in the local mountains down that way. I fell in love with the sport. These circumstances happened while I was out of town, working near the place I found while skiing. Following that hurt-filled situation, I took an opportunity to travel to the area I had never been to in my life and instantly I fell in love with the place, awestruck by God's creative power.

Mountains, real mountains. Mountains I had no idea were in my state and much less only a six- hour drive from my Southern California coastal community home. I ran away from that home and moved into those mountains, and the skiing I had grown such a passion for took on a whole new experience.

The Sierra Nevada range is truly spectacular, rising 14,000 feet above sea level, so unlike that bunny of a hill I first learned to ski on. I couldn't stop looking at all the lines from top to bottom of those steep and exposed mountains. I wanted to hike and ski down every one of them, and that's what I did to lose the hurt and pain of a puppy love lost.

On those adventures I learned of the many historical, Old West legends and stories, and one of them in particular inspired this story: The Convict Lake Story. Ironically, Mt Morrison was the last ascent I made with an ice ax, cramp-ons and skis. Later, after I made the descent and barely made it out, I was truly exhausted, never thinking I would make it back to my vehicle which I could see in the distance. I learned on the way driving back south and home that the route was titled Death Coulier.

Previously I had already made the ascent and descent of twenty-three other Sierra Nevada peaks and as well Montana's Livingston and Stillwater Ranges, but this last one almost got me, on Mt Morrison.

Years early upon my first arrival in the region I had already heard of the Convict Lake story. The first time I ventured into that beautiful canyon, surrounded by peaks over twelve and pushing thirteen thousand feet, I saw the set of plaques on the north eastern edge of the lake, telling a story of multiple children who had perished ice skating the lake one fateful day. There was another set of historical landmarks touching on the story of how the lake had gotten its name. The place is amazing and one of the most beautiful places I have ever ventured to or fly-fished.

After returning back to San Diego coastal north county in the late nineties the many historical monuments and history of the region triggered a switch in me, and I began to conceptualize the ideas of what could have gone down in those valleys I had never seen. I continued my adventures up there, really digging into the mountaineering element, until that last ascent on Morrison where I almost died alone.

In the days of 1871 it held the name Mt El Diablo, or Devils Mountain, and I can agree with that. To ski Death Coulier was nearly impossible, and I should have done better research before attempting it alone.

Here is a tidbit on the Paiute legend of the name of the place, and why they named it the way they did. I pulled this from the Convict Lake Resort website and it reads as follows:

> The Indians are said to have called Convict Lake "Wit-Sa-Nap" bearing this legend. "The streams which flowed from the mountains were supposed to be filled with Pot-Sa-Wa-Gees, water babies, who lived in spirit, but were visible to the eye, having the face of an Indian child and the body of a fish. Hi-Na-Nu was a wise and good man, whose spirit the Indians reverenced,

and to whom they looked for guidance in earthly matters. However, he was endeavoring to capture the Pot-Sa-Wa-Gees as they traveled upstream. When the sources of the streams were reached the water became so shallow that the water babies were in great danger of being taken by their pursuer. They prayed to the Great Spirit for aid, and in answer he caused the waters to flow uphill to join the waters flowing down from the mountains, uniting in one, large, deep lake, wherein the little spirits found safety —Wit-Sa-Nap, the Convict Lake of to-day."

Sierra Club Bulletin Vol. IX, San Francisco, CA, 1915, Mrs. A.A. Forbes.

Three years later I got into acting by mistake, and that's a whole novel in and of itself, a story of how I went from being a master builder for thirty plus years and got back into the industry of entertainment I hadn't been in since the mid-eighties with my band Snakebyte. I will write that book someday, a testament of my life story, and what an adventure it has been.

Back to my selfish desire to craft myself an acting role and God's hand in it.

Well, I began to craft that role, but it blew up into so much more. I had never written anything, in fact, I rarely read. The most I read was the newspaper as a kid and typed a million texts to a girlfriend, drafted hundreds of thousands of emails and contracts, invoices, created templates, blah, blah blah…but never a screenplay.

It turned out I crafted by grace, of course, an amazing story that quickly became not about myself or an acting role any longer. The initial story about the Convict Lake event dwindled down to a very small piece of a much larger, fictional story of truth, mercy, grace, compassion, sacrifice and love, transcending generations, as a reflection of a single family's struggle to survive and to persevere through the hardships of persecution and prejudice, while having determined courage in the face of evil and darkness with unconditional love and forgiveness.

The screenplay took 2nd place, 1st Runner Up, for Most Ambitious Screenplay at the Palms Las Vegas Action on Film motion picture convention, hosted by a great man, Del Weston, who unfortunately passed away this past year. "Scene 49" from the same screenplay, which we extracted from that original script and retitled as "Reconveyance" was shot in Nashville by Ryan Wotherspoon and Jeremy Childs, receiving the Best Western award at the same Palms Las Vegas event.

I am the owner of Snakebyte Productions and Entertainment Group, LLC, which was born out of that screenplay.

In early 2014 I met a young group of filmmakers out of Cal State Long Beach who had casted me for a lead role in an award-winning short film, titled "Peace of Mind". We went on with that Short and were chosen Top 200 in the internationally acclaimed Project Greenlight, founded by Ben Affleck and Matt Damon, *(40.000+ submissions were in that project)*.

Later in 2014 I thought I would raise the money on Kickstarter to make my film. That was a joke and a far-fetched dream, which I realized very quickly. Instead I started my company, forming an LLC to raise $50.000 on the Kickstarter and Megafounder platforms. The kids from CSLB, my wife and I all went up to the Sierras and shot the opening scene to the screenplay, and hence the cover of this book.

Since that time we have established a nationally recognized, diversely solid motion picture production company, however, a friend had suggested years ago, in the beginning of this adventure, that I should convert that screenplay and publish a novel.

In my busy schedule building a production company, with gear and vehicles and a beautiful studio, I scrapped out the time over a couple of years and did just that, and here we are today, you are reading my first novel.

What is my endgame, you might ask. I will strive to get this story told on the big screen, meanwhile continue to strive forward, growing this company to a point that may allow it someday.

I would be eternally grateful to you, the reader, to please pass on the word about this story, because I truly do believe in my heart and soul, this was all God's doing to advance some form of good over evil, no matter how small it may appear, that was the purpose.

As the writer and creator of this story, my goal, while crafting the original screenplay, was of course to make it the best I could make it, creating multiple plots driving the story and characters, yet they all come together perfectly in the end.

But I had no idea, while I was writing, of the multiple controversial subjects buried within that effort. It wasn't until at least a couple years later, around 2016 or so, my wife pointed out the Right to Life issue buried in the story, totally unintended. I needed a baby, and I needed an interesting story around the baby and came up with this.

Then a year after that I realized how the racism in the story played out, and then the clencher for me was the OJ glove thing and the fact that Colton Jaminson, my hero, doesn't shoot or kill anyone. He became the hero because of how he managed his feelings for the child, especially after losing Wyola, the love of his life. He had to have fought some serious demons within himself to even love that child and make him who he came out to be, as described in Chapter two.

I hope you will enjoy this story and share it with your friends.

ACKNOWLEDGEMENTS OF LOVE AND GRATEFULNESS

I would like to acknowledge those who rescued me, encouraged and loved me in my deepest sorrows, wrangling me back to a place of hope, joy, peace and the greatest of all, Love.

My first acknowledgement goes to my God whose Holy Spirit lives forever in me, and especially to my Lord and Savior Jesus Christ, who continuously pursues me without ceasing my whole life. You rescued me from the pit and wrote this story through my hand. I am continuously humbled by Your grace, each and every day, grace upon grace upon grace; and You purposed this adventurous story through me and these hands. I am so grateful. I love You with all my existence.

To my mentor and brother in my faith, George, I love you man... You were the key that opened my life to a whole new understanding of what is real and truth. Thank you for mending the fractures of my life through my serving in that most unfractured place.

To my mentor and father after mine had passed, PD, I will never forget my first day and what you said to me at my home that forever changed my life. It took years to grow in understanding those words of truth, but they are forever ingrained in my soul till I leave this place. Love and miss you so much, my brother. An inspiration!

To Aaron, you are a maestro leader, who has encouraged me and strengthened me through your direction. I love you so much, young man.

To Chris W. We are so much alike and yet so very different. You hearten to encourage, embolden and motivate my week, every week, my friend. I love you so much and thank you for your heart of love.

To my family of fourteen years at Las Flores. No words can articulate how much I love and need you, and will never leave you in spirit.

To my dearest friends who stood by me when no one else did, Barry N. and Michael C. I pray for you every single day. Forgive me if I disappointed you.

To the bestest friend of my youth. I pray you will be in heaven with me. I sit with you from time to time at D Street. I will love you always. May grace and mercy have led you to that joyous place.

To my dad, Richard…I really miss you and long for your love every day of my life. I am you, and you are in me. I will see you in the heavenly place.

To my mom who supported me through the hardest times, I love you Sigrid. <3

To my sisters, I miss and love you both much. Forgive me for any disappointments I may have brought to you through your years. My fondest memories of you and I together are of us playing cowboys and indians for many days over time throughout our childhood. <3

To my cousin Johnny… I love you, man. God bless you and your wife, forever!

To Elvira and Sherri, Thank you for you, your perseverance, determined love and devotion to the children and your grace beyond graciousness. I am indebted to you forever.

To Dan M. for all you allowed in me in some really tough times. Your integrity throughout the tailoring of my son will be with me throughout all my days. Thank you, Dan, for you!!

To Chowie, who is a dearest friend and dearest antagonist!

To all my youthful friends in Encinitas, CA. I miss all of you so much. FB has been a dream for me to reconnect. I cannot wait to see all of you again someday, if not here, then let's meet up for sure up there!

To Wally, Andy, Jonny.....always will wish you the best this life has! Man, that was fun, a key to who I am today. I love you, guys. See you soon, here or there!

To all those who steadfastly stood by and supported this story, believed in it and hoped alongside me, to get this thing to the big screen someday. Thank you...I love and cherish you all.

To David G, Jason C, and Edna L. I love you guys so much. Your sacrifice for this story was from your hearts, and I will never forget.

To Kevin J, Snakebyte Productions wouldn't be what it is without you and your dedicated service.

To Jeremy C, Josh C, Ryan W, and Henry H, Jon Peterson - Words cannot express the appreciation I have for your early passion for this story, the reels, and what you guys did in support of it. God bless you guys. Holly and I both hope to see you all very soon!!

Thank you especially to Peter and Susan S. I wouldn't be who I am without your love and inspiration...it was contagious... Your love for the West drove me to make this story as accurate as I could make it!! Your grade will be my everything, and I'm so much looking forward to it!

To everyone I ever met in my life - I truly appreciate every moment and each and every recollected memory that comes from time to time. So much of my life is written into this story, and it lives in me through all of you, God Bless You All!!!

The Bishop Paiute Indian Tribe Center, Bishop California

Paiute Indian Tribe of Utah

Thank you, Mammoth Mountain, Steve Morrison, Clifford Mann and the whole Sierra range, Long Valley Caldera and Owens Valley... I love you oh so much... and NW Montana Too, what would we do without you too!!!

USDA/USFS Mammoth Lakes District, Inyo County, and special thanks to Lawson Reif.

Thanks to you, Gabrielle. You were the key ingredient to start this journey from a screenplay and turning it into a novel. Amazing what you did in that endeavor. I am so grateful to have met you.

And last, *but* certainly least, thank you, Lilly, for pooping in my suitcase and burying it under the socks!!... I won't miss you when you die!!!...haha...just kidding, love you Lilly Putz!!